The shining splendor of our Zebra Lovegram logo on the cover of this book reflects the glittering excellence of the story inside. Look for the Zebra Lovegram whenever you buy a historical romance. It's a trademark that guarantees the very best in quality and reading entertainment.

LAWMAN'S TEMPTATION

"Lady," Tanner drawled, "the only trouble you're likely to find is if you tease me any further."

"Marshal, am I teasing you?" Elizabeth asked with exaggerated innocence.

"I promised myself I was going to warm your backside for running away this morning."

Not the slightest bit disturbed, she smiled. "Do you always keep your promises, Marshal?" she asked as she reached beneath his leather vest for the buttons of his shirt.

"Eventually." His breathing was labored and shallow by the time she opened the last button.

Elizabeth parted his shirt, holding the material away from his skin. Her gaze was warm with pleasure as she surveyed what she'd uncovered.

"Right now," he drawled, "I have in mind other places to warm. . . ."

PASSIONATE NIGHTS FROM ZEBRA BOOKS

ANGEL'S CARESS   (2675, $4.50)
by Deanna James

Ellie Crain was a young, inexperienced and beautiful Southern belle. Cash Gillard was the battle-weary Yankee corporal who turned her into a woman filled with hungry passion. He planned to love and leave her; she vowed to keep him forever with her *Angel's Caress*.

COMMANCHE BRIDE   (2549, $3.95)
by Emma Merritt

Beautiful Dr. Zoe Randolph headed to Mexico to halt a cholera epidemic. She never dreamed her caravan would be attacked by a band of savages. Later, she refused to believe that she could love and desire her captor, the handsome half-breed Matt Chandler. Captor and slave find unending love and tender passion in the rugged Commanche hills.

CAPTIVE ANGEL   (2524, $4.50)
by Deanna James

When handsome Hunter Gillard left the routine existence of his South Carolina plantation for endless adventures on the high seas, beautiful and indulged Caroline Gillard learned to manage her home and business affairs in her husband's sudden absence. Caroline resolved not to crumble and vowed to make Hunter beg to be taken back. He was determined to make her once again his unquestioning and forgiving wife.

SWEET, WILD LOVE   (2834, $3.95)
by Emma Merritt

Chicago lawyer Eleanor Hunt was determined to earn the respect of the Kansas cowboys who openly leered at her as she was working to try a cattle-rustling case. The worse offender was Bradley Smith—even though he worked for Eleanor's father! She was determined not to mistake passion for love; he was determined to break through her icy exterior and possess the passion woman who lurked beneath her.

Available wherever paperbacks are sold, or order direct from the Publisher. Send cover price plus 50¢ per copy for mailing and handling to Zebra Books, Dept. 3336, 475 Park Avenue South, New York, N.Y. 10016. Residents of New York, New Jersey and Pennsylvania must include sales tax. DO NOT SEND CASH.

PATRICIA PELLICANE

DESPERADO PASSION

ZEBRA BOOKS
KENSINGTON PUBLISHING CORP.

To Andrew and Karen, so special, so loved.

ZEBRA BOOKS

are published by

Kensington Publishing Corp.
475 Park Avenue South
New York, NY 10016

Copyright © 1991 by Patricia Pellicane

All rights reserved. No part of this book may be reproduced
in any form or by any means without the prior written con-
sent of the Publisher, excepting brief quotes used in reviews.

First printing: March, 1991

Printed in the United States of America

Prologue

Low-hanging clouds obliterated stars that could light up the desert, making it almost as bright as day. The air was heavy, hot and thick with the feel of coming rain. A mask covered the lower part of a stern, determined face. The rider waited, strong, steady hands controlling the horse that pranced nervously.

The stage was late, a usual occurrence, for the line had yet to establish a station between Steward and Willowbrook and the animals would have long since grown tired. The stage didn't often travel at night; the dangers to be encountered on long stretches of empty desert multiplied drastically after dark. That it was traveling on this night was meant to be a secret, for it held a prize whose loss might bring about the destruction of one certain man.

Somebody would be riding shotgun, but that mattered little. The moment a shot was fired and the call was given to stop, guns were instantly thrown down. The men couldn't be blamed, after all. Who was brave enough to draw on a pistol already aimed at his heart?

After six robberies, there had yet to be an injury. That

is, if you didn't count blows to pride and the very real emptying of one particular man's pockets.

The horse stirred and gave a whinnying sound as the distant rattle of wheels echoed over the silent desert floor. It was very late, but the stage was coming. For a time, the rider had thought those in charge might have changed their minds and scheduled it for daylight hours.

The ambusher expected no trouble, and yet his heart pounded so, the beating could almost be heard. It was always like this: hands trembled ever so slightly, palms grew moist with nervous sweat, breathing accelerated to near gasping proportions.

The stage was coming faster now. The driver knew they weren't far from their destination. No doubt because they traveled at night, he expected to make Willowbrook unscathed.

A smile curved the firm mouth beneath the mask. All are doomed to suffer some degree of disappointment.

A minute or so more.

Two large lanterns lit up the area immediately preceding the racing stage. The rider moved partially from the protection of a huge rock, pulled the gun free of its holster, and fired into the sky.

Curses filled the night as the horses were abruptly brought to a stop. For a moment only the echo of the gunshot and the strained breathing of the horses could be heard.

"Throw down your guns." The whispery sounds came from out of the darkness.

Three dull thuds followed, as heavy guns hit the dirt road.

"Now the box."

Neither the driver nor the man who rode at his side thought to deny the existence of the box. They had no idea what it contained, and if they had they wouldn't have cared. Nothing in it belonged to them. Nothing in it was worth dying over.

A heavier thud sounded as the order was quickly obeyed. From the light cast by the two lanterns a large metal box could be seen lying on its side, perhaps three feet from the stage.

The rider smiled and nodded with satisfaction, although neither gesture could be seen in the dark. "Tell Stacey to try again," the disguised voice instructed.

The words were barely uttered before the driver snapped his whip over the backs of the animals and yelled for the lazy bastards to get him the hell out of there.

Chapter One

Tanner Maddox, one of Nevada's most outstanding lawmen, brought his horse to a stop before the sheriff's office in Willowbrook, a small town in the southern part of the state. He was exhausted, having managed, as usual, little sleep while traveling the distance from Virginia City. His weariness showed clearly in the slump of brawny shoulders and the stiff, unusually awkward movements he made when dismounting. It showed too in the deep lines of fatigue around his mouth and in eyes that were bloodshot from days of squinting against an unrelenting sun.

An old man sat dozing some twenty feet from where Tanner had stopped. His chair was tipped back, and it leaned against the wall of the building at a precarious angle. Jason Barlow, the town drunk, didn't speak much, but it was a well-known fact that he knew just about everything that happened in the town. From beneath the brim of his hat, sharp eyes took in the travel-weary, tall man. A slight breeze fluttered the stranger's long tan coat, and a marshal's badge glittered in the sun. Jason felt a sudden lurching of his heart as fear's sickly fingers slid down his spine, but he instantly squashed the sensation. This marshal wasn't after him, he silently insisted. No, he couldn't be arrested for the thoughts and plans still in his mind.

Tanner's spurs jingled as his booted feet stepped upon the uneven wooden sidewalk that ran the entire length of the town on both sides of the street. He slapped his hat against his legs, allowing a cloud of dust to bellow out and about his person as he headed toward the open door of the sheriff's office. His eyes were on the tiny woman who stood directly in his path. He barely noticed her long gray dress or the straw hat that covered her hair. It wasn't her diminutive size that had caught his attention. Nothing about her had until he'd heard her speak. Then her husky voice had crashed with dizzying precision into the pit of his stomach and had stopped him in his tracks.

"Thank you, Dave," she was saying. "I appreciate your help."

Tanner's brow creased in a puzzled frown as his body helplessly reacted to the sound. He shook his head, denying as nonsensical the force that spread throughout his body. Jesus, he was more tired than he had imagined if the mere sound of this woman's voice could bring a tightness to his stomach, a stirring to his loins. Tanner almost laughed aloud at the sensations that gripped him. He hadn't even seen her face. She was probably some dried up old crow, weathered and wrinkled, like too many of the women who lived their lives beneath Nevada's brutal sun.

The truth of the matter was he'd been too damn long without a woman. No sooner had he finished his last assignment than the governor had sent him three hundred miles east to this small sleepy town. He'd barely had time to catch a nap and pack a clean shirt before he'd left Virginia City.

Elizabeth Garner felt a presence behind her. A natural, sweet smile was already forming by the time she turned to face the largest man she'd ever seen in her life. He stood a good head taller than most and dwarfed her petite form.

Her chocolate eyes widened in surprise as they took in his rugged good looks. He wasn't what you'd call handsome. His features were large and craggy, his skin weather-beaten. His jaw was square, his mouth too wide, his cheeks unshaven, and his mustache and dark hair were in dire need of a trimming. But his eyes. Elizabeth almost gasped at the crystal clear blue that shone out of a face tanned as dark as any Indian's.

She tore her gaze from his eyes to his dust-covered coat. Rolled from wrist to elbows, the sleeves exposed thickly muscled, brown forearms. Tied around his throat was a blue scarf. His shirt, of nearly the same shade, was partly open, displaying an indecent amount of dark curling chest hair. Elizabeth swallowed, her brow creased with confusion. Though the sight of this man had caused her mouth to go dry, she denied the odd flicker of sensation that suddenly fluttered to life in her chest and turned quickly away. With some effort, she managed to focus her attention on the sheriff, who had followed her to the door. "You won't forget Friday, will

11

you, Dave?" she asked sweetly though aware that her face had reddened for no apparent reason.

"I won't forget, Elizabeth."

She smiled at him, then directed a short nod toward the silent man who stood to her right. Turning, she walked down the sidewalk, never realizing she'd left behind her a man close to being thunderstruck. With a clearly dazed look in his eyes, Tanner stared after her.

"Who the hell is she?" he heard himself ask, in an oddly shaken voice, as his gaze held on her slender back. A moment later it lowered to focus on her gently swaying skirt.

"Who the hell are you?" Dave Jessup asked, feeling a sudden wave of protectiveness as he faced the dark giant who blocked his doorway and dared to stare at Elizabeth in so hungry a fashion.

Tanner tore his attention from the pretty woman and faced the glaring, young sheriff. He grinned as he reached into his shirt pocket and pulled out a neatly folded white paper. "Maddox," he said as he handed the paper to the sheriff, his gaze once again focusing on the woman he'd just encountered. "Marshal Tanner Maddox." He nodded in the general direction of the departing woman and asked, "How the hell do you get any work done around here?"

Dave Jessup grinned as he watched the marshal's dazed expression. He moved back into his office, holding the door in silent invitation for Maddox to enter. Dave knew most of the men in town reacted in much the same way Maddox had to the town's most recent arrival. If it weren't for the fact that he loved his bride of almost ten months, almost to desperation, he might have found himself joining the throng of panting admirers. "I manage."

"How?"

Dave grinned as he settled himself behind his desk. "I'm married."

"But not dead," Tanner said. Damn! He'd never felt anything this powerful in his life. He only hoped that fetching woman wouldn't give him too hard a time. In his arrogance, rightly deserved since he'd never had to do more than make his wishes known in order to bed a woman, he never imagined he wouldn't be able to convince her to see things his way.

Dave laughed. "No, not dead. In love with my wife. Sally and Elizabeth Garner are friends."

Tanner nodded as he digested the information. Her name was Elizabeth Garner. And she was the most beautiful woman he'd ever seen. Lord, even with all the women he'd known, he'd never imagined one existed with that kind of sweet, madonnalike beauty. He sat and, suddenly stiff, leaned forward. "She's not married, is she?" Tanner asked, wondering at the sudden fear that gripped his chest. He'd been hopelessly bedazzled by smooth honey skin and the wisps of jet black hair that escaped her bonnet. Her eyes were the most spectacular shade of rich chocolate brown. And her lips, sweetly pink and devoid of artificial coloring, had made his head swim at the thought of touching them with his own. He hadn't thought, till now, to look at her hand.

"Nope. She's a widow lady. Owns a boardinghouse." Dave gave a short nod toward the opposite end of town.

"Boardinghouse, huh?" Tanner repeated almost to himself, knowing he wouldn't be staying above the saloon during this visit. He accepted a glass from the bottle of whiskey Jessup had taken from his lower drawer. It went far toward washing away the dust of the trail. A moment later he got down to business. "You got anything new on those robberies?"

"There was another one last night," Dave stated wearily, knowing of course that the marshal spoke of the trouble that had been plaguing the stagecoach line these last six months.

"Again?" Blue eyes quickly met gray across the desk.

At the sheriff's nod, Tanner continued, "What happened?"

"Same thing as before. The stage was stopped, the box thrown down. Then the stage took off. When I went to find it this morning, everything else was left untouched." He shrugged. "Except Mr. Stacey's packet. Claims over thirty thousand is missing this time."

Tanner whistled between closed teeth. "Any idea why they're taking only Stacey's money?"

"None."

"Anybody see the gunman? Any witnesses?"

Dave shook his head. "It was dark. Seems to be the same man though. Whoever he is, he's small. No identifying marks that we know of since everything to his fingertips is covered. But he speaks with a deep voice." His lips thinned into a tight line of disgust. "Beyond that we don't know a thing."

"Who the hell is this Stacey?" Tanner asked. Having done his homework he knew well enough who the man

14

was, but it never hurt to ask questions. He just might find out something he didn't already know.

"The richest man in these parts." At the inquisitive lift of Tanner's black brows, Dave continued, "Among other things, including the bank and most of the buildings in town, Mr. Stacey owns a silver mine up near Eureka."

Tanner nodded. This information was common knowledge. He'd have to dig deeper into the man's background to find out what he wanted. Someone had set out to get Stacey, and not simply because he was rich. What Tanner wanted to know was why. If he knew that, it wouldn't be long before he knew who. "I take it he's pretty upset."

Dave shook his head. "Not so as you'd notice. He's rich enough to afford the loss." Dave's shrug bespoke his apparent unconcern. "He's more annoyed than upset."

Tanner smiled and wondered how rich he'd have to be before he'd merely grow annoyed when robbed?

"Promised to hire a couple of guns to ride the next shipment."

Tanner shook his head, his lips thinning until they were almost hidden beneath his mustache, as he contemplated the results should guns be brought in. "There's been no killings so far. Hired guns always bring trouble."

Dave nodded in agreement. "No law against a man protecting his property, though. Ain't much any of us can do to stop him."

Tanner grunted knowing the sheriff was right. Robbery was one thing, hiring guns another matter entirely. He didn't want to see anyone end up dead. And he'd

15

never come across a case where hired guns did anything but kill. "I think I'll have a talk with this Stacey. Maybe you could point out his place."

"If you came in from Virginia City, you must have passed it just before you came into town."

"That white mansion on the hill?"

"The one and only," Dave returned, unable to hide the flicker of distaste in his eyes.

"I take it this Stacey ain't one of the most liked folks in these parts?"

Dave shrugged and poured himself another drink. "Last week his bank foreclosed on Jamie Harrison's place. Put the family out with little more than the clothes on their backs, and because I'm the sheriff, I had to help him do it." Dave shook his head with disgust. "That kind of thing sticks in my craw."

Tanner watched the man across from him down his second drink as if to wash a bad taste from his mouth. Tanner narrowed his eyes in thought. It wouldn't be the first time a lawman went bad. He didn't have any real cause to suspect the sheriff, but it was his policy to suspect everyone until he found the culprit. "Do most folks around here feel like you?"

"Probably. If you're askin' if the man has enemies, I guess you'd be better off askin' if he has any friends."

"Does he?"

"He's courtin' Elizabeth Garner."

Tanner's blue eyes widened and then narrowed, hardening into cold chips of ice at the news. For some reason he hadn't suspected that woman would be swayed by a man's wallet. Fool that he was, he reflected. Damned ri-

16

diculous on his part. He didn't even know her. But he sure as hell was going to — and know her well before this job was over.

"Is she the only one in town who takes to the man?"

"There are a few others." Dave shrugged. "Mostly men who work for him. Still, a man as rich as Stacey is bound to have a lot of enemies."

"Yeah, but which one hates him enough to try to ruin him?"

Elizabeth laughed as she lunged for the ball. She caught it off balance, but she managed to swing around, gain her footing, and send it crashing back to one of the widely spaced children facing her, and all with amazing speed. "Better," she shouted. "Much better."

Tanner came around the corner of her house and stood for a moment, watching her catch and throw. She wasn't much bigger than the boys and girls who cried out for the next chance to catch her throw. At a glance, one might think her a child at play, but not Tanner. His sharp eyes immediately detected her among the small group of children. No matter that she wasn't the tallest, Tanner would never have mistaken that form. Even from the back it proclaimed her all woman.

Her hair, black as a raven's wing, was slipping free of its knot and fell in long strands almost to her hips. Tanner felt a wave of incredible need rush over him as his fingers itched to mesh with that dark shining mass of curls.

"Ma'am," he said as he moved to her side, dipped his

17

head, and touched the brim of his hat with his fingers.

Elizabeth gasped with surprise to find the stranger she'd seen at Dave's office standing in her back yard. The fact that he stood far too close did not escape her notice. Brown eyes collided with blue, and for a moment were unable to pull away. What was wrong with her? Why should this man have so startling an effect on her? Why did the sight of him, standing so close, make her heart thunder with . . . with what? Fear?

Elizabeth was about to move aside, allowing each of them more room when the ball she had just thrown was returned. It hit hard against her temple. An instant later she uttered a soft, low sound of surprise and then knew only blackness as she fell into Tanner's startled arms.

Tanner cursed as she suddenly collapsed against him. Two little girls screamed, and three of the four boys slowly came to stand by the fallen lady. "Is she all right?" one of them asked.

"She'll be fine," Tanner responded. Already kneeling at her side, he felt for a pulse at her throat. "You folks best run along home now. I'll help Miss Garner inside."

Tanner wanted for the lot of them to leave before he dared to lift her in his arms. He didn't care much what people said about him, but he wanted to bring no scandal upon this lady. Alone with her, he was tempted to take her inside and find her bedroom. His mind swam with delicious thoughts of loosening her clothing once he laid her on the bed, but no. He dared not be so bold. He wanted to get to know this woman, in the most basic sense, but doing what he had in mind wouldn't help him to gain her trust. In truth, if she was the lady she appeared to be, she'd only despise him for his daring.

Tanner gathered her unconscious form into his arms as he came to his feet. Lord, she weighed little more than a feather. How could anyone as round and full figured as she was weigh so little?

Tanner forced himself to head for the rocking chairs that sat empty upon the back porch. He settled himself in one and shifted her in his arms so he might better study her face.

She was a bit pale, but her breathing was regular and even. Tanner knew she'd soon awaken, probably with the most awful headache.

Elizabeth moaned. Her eyes fluttered open and then closed almost immediately. The pain was enormous. What in the world had happened to cause such discomfort? She dared to open her eyes again and then sighed with relief. She was dreaming. No doubt the pain was only part of the dream. What she couldn't understand was why she should dream of the silent, strangely attractive stranger she'd noticed outside Dave's office.

She felt movement beneath her. A moment later she realized she wasn't lying in her bed. Elizabeth gasped. She hadn't been sleeping at all. This was no dream. There was a man holding her. Good gracious, she was on his lap!

She struggled against a wave of dizziness in order to get up, but the man's arms firmly held her in a reclining position.

"Easy, love," he said as he felt her stir. "You took a blow to your head. Just stay still for a bit."

"I most certainly will not! Release me this instant."

Tanner loosened his hold on her and watched as she struggled into a sitting position. Lord, the things her bottom was doing to him. He only prayed she was dizzy enough not to notice.

Elizabeth tried to stand, but the moment her feet touched the ground, she moaned and swayed. A second later, with a groan, she plopped back onto his lap, not realizing she had done so as she clutched at her aching head. "What happened?"

"You got hit by a ball."

"Thanks to you," she muttered ungraciously as she remembered the last few moments before she was struck.

Tanner grinned. So the lady's disposition didn't quite match her lovely face. His eyes followed the graceful slender curve of her back as he realized this discovery only seemed to add to her appeal. He liked his women sassy and feisty. And this one, although she didn't know it yet, was his.

Elizabeth seemed not to notice she was sitting on his lap. In truth she was aware only of the throbbing pain in her head. Tanner smiled and almost sighed with pleasure, perfectly content for the time being for her to remain where she was. "I do apologize, ma'am."

"Where are they?"

"The children? I sent them home."

Elizabeth managed, but not without some effort, to glance behind her. "Did you. . . ?"

"I waited for them to leave before I picked you up. Don't worry."

"I'm not in the least worried."

"Then why'd you ask?"

Elizabeth sighed, unwilling and unable to continue this argument. They both knew she was worried about her reputation. There was no sense in denying it. "Exactly what is it you want here, Mr. . . .?"

"Maddox. Tanner Maddox," he offered, unable to suppress his grin, for he'd never before had a conversation with a beautiful woman who was perched upon his lap. Well, actually he might have had one or two, but those women had not been as lovely and the conversation had been on other matters entirely. "And what I want is a room." Her silence prodded him to go on. "You do rent rooms, don't you?"

"Not to strangers." Especially not to strangers who look like you, she added silently.

"Dave Jessup sent me over."

"Mr. Maddox, I'm an unmarried lady. It's most unseemly for a single gentleman to rent one of my rooms."

"You mean you don't rent them to men?"

She didn't answer. Now what was she supposed to do? Dave had sent him. What excuse could she give to refuse him a room? If she could only think . . . If this pain and dizziness would go away just for a minute . . .

"I guess Dave was wrong about you owning a boardinghouse."

"He was not wrong." Elizabeth sighed tiredly. "I rent to men as well as women. Mr. Barlow and Miss Dunlap are currently in residence." She carefully came to her feet, fighting the need to moan and fall back against him. "I'll show you . . ." she began just as the fight was taken from her. A soft sound escaped her lips and she swayed.

"I'd better send for the doctor," Tanner said, instantly at her side, his arm wrapped around her shoulders.

"No. I'll be fine. Thank you." Elizabeth lowered her head, her gaze now on ground that refused, despite her silent insistence, to stop swaying. "You can let me go now."

Tanner again did her bidding and then cursed as she took one wobbly step. The next would have landed her flat on her face had he not instantly scooped her into his arms. "Don't argue with me. I'm sending someone for the doctor." He kicked her back door open. "Tell me which room is yours."

Elizabeth muttered directions, too weak and dizzy to offer further argument. She heard a sharp scream and then Tanner's deep voice, strangled with amusement if she wasn't mistaken. "The lady's been hurt. Go for the doctor." She was almost asleep by the time she felt the softness of a bed beneath her. Her eyes were closed as she whispered, "You've probably terrified poor Miss Dunlap."

"Probably," Tanner agreed with a chuckle. "Rest now. I promise I'll explain it all to Miss Dunlap later."

Elizabeth felt gentle fingers at her throat, but hadn't the strength to remark on the unwanted attention. She did feel more comfortable with her bodice opened a bit. Idly she wondered exactly how far he had unbuttoned her dress, and for perhaps the first time in her life, she didn't care.

Tanner awakened the next day to the soft sounds of

feminine laughter and the heavenly scent of baking bread. He'd slept longer than usual, no doubt due to the luxury of a comfortable bed and the fact that he'd barely slept at all since leaving Virginia City.

Tanner eyed the pretty room he'd taken the previous night. Taken in fact because Miss Garner's room was next to it. A grin broke across his firm mouth when he noticed the frilly curtains fluttering in the early morning breeze. He couldn't remember the last time he'd slept in a room so obviously decorated by a woman. Not since he was a kid, he supposed. Suddenly, and for the first time since leaving his childhood home to go off to school and then to become an officer of the law, Tanner felt a real emptiness. But he couldn't understand why.

He enjoyed his life. Wouldn't trade the work he'd chosen for a dozen houses and a thousand ruffled windows. Now what the hell had brought that to mind? Who had said anything about trading?

Tanner didn't have to think long to discover the cause of that foolish thought. Elizabeth Garner was enough woman to lead many a man astray. Still, no matter how appealing, she'd never gain that kind of power over him. He was too old, too set in his ways to change. He liked his life just as it was. He didn't long for family, roots, and home. He enjoyed his freedom, always had. He'd never be fool enough to give up the ability to take off and ride where and when he pleased. A wry smile twisted his lips. No woman, not even the beautiful Elizabeth Garner, was ever going to change that.

Tanner made quick use of the water and towels he found on the small dry sink in his room. He then changed into a clean shirt and pulled on trousers, boots, and gunbelt. From his saddlebags he took mirror, soap, and razor and prepared to make himself a bit more presentable. He might not want to settle down, but he definitely did want the lovely Elizabeth. Damn, he'd have to be dead not to. Arrogantly he wondered how long it would take before she succumbed to his charm and joined him in bed.

Elizabeth was laughing at something Miss Dunlap had said when she realized her most recent boarder was standing in the kitchen. Her laughter came to an abrupt stop.

Tanner cursed the ache that suddenly twisted at his chest as her lively eyes sobered. "I'm sorry if I awakened you, Mr. Maddox."

"Should you be out of bed?" he asked gruffly, ridiculously annoyed that she had stopped laughing simply because he had entered the room. "Didn't the doctor say you needed at least one day of bed rest?"

"He did, but I'm fine. No more dizziness. I suspect the injury wasn't as serious as he imagined."

"Still, you should—"

Elizabeth interrupted him. "Are you hungry, Mr. Maddox?"

Tanner nodded, knowing from the determined set of her chin there was no sense pressing his argument. The woman was out of bed, after all. It would take some powerful arguing to convince her to go back. "I guess I could eat some of that bread you've got baking."

Elizabeth laughed, the sound soft and pleasurable. She nodded toward the large kitchen table. "Sit. I'll get you something directly."

She formally introduced him to the pale Miss Dunlap, even though he had made her acquaintance the night before during the doctor's visit. Gloria Dunlap made the appropriate response, then glanced at the watch pinned to her thin bodice, gathered up her papers, and was off to meet her students. A blond aging spinster, she taught school in Willowbrook.

Tanner leaned back comfortably in his chair and watched his landlady work over the stove. Moments later Elizabeth brought a plate piled high with bacon, eggs, and thick slices of hot bread to the table. Marmalade and fresh butter were set beside it while a huge pot of coffee rested at the back of the stove for refills.

Elizabeth took a break from her morning chores to sit opposite him and sip a cup of the brew. "Have you business in town Mr. Maddox, or are you simply passing through?"

"Business," he said, as he swallowed a mouthful of fluffy eggs and washed it down with deliciously rich, black coffee. "I guess you've heard about the trouble with the stagecoach line."

"I have," she said. Her brows raised in inquiry, head tipped to the side, she waited for him to go on.

Tanner shot her a smile. "I'm the marshal in these parts."

Elizabeth's eyes widened with surprise. She sank further into the straight-backed chair and almost moaned. What abominable luck to have the man living under her roof! How was she to go about her business with him there? "I was under the impression a marshal wore a

25

badge."

Tanner parted his open vest to show her the badge pinned to his shirt.

"You'll be staying a while then," she said, less a question than a statement of fact.

Tanner shrugged, trying to ignore the obvious — this lady wasn't overly thrilled to hear his intent was to remain. He couldn't stop the hardening of his voice. "For as long as it takes to bring the man in."

Elizabeth's lips suddenly quivered as if she fought some secret battle against laughter. There wasn't a doubt in her mind that the end was near. This man's eyes revealed his intelligence. He wouldn't be easy to fool; yet she couldn't stop the smile that came to her lips. Was he smart enough to look right under his nose?

"You're laughing. Why?" he asked, his eyes more intent as they were drawn to a mouth that promised to be lusciously sweet.

"Am I?"

"I have the feeling you think I can't do it."

"Can you?"

"I wouldn't bet against me, not if I were you." It was obvious this woman didn't know of his reputation. Not a man to brag, Tanner could have told her he'd never yet failed to get his man.

Elizabeth shrugged. "Folks around here might not take too kindly to your stopping him. Your outlaw is becoming something of a legend. A Robin Hood, of sorts."

"He gives the money to the poor?" Tanner asked, in his voice a mixture of amazement and dread. Damn, this was just what he needed. A thief who'd become a martyr when caught. And guess who'd be labeled a bastard for simply doing his job? Tanner muttered a low, angry curse.

"You seem upset. Does it bother you to find out he doesn't keep the money for himself?"

Tanner shot her a look of disgust. He didn't need this aggravation. "The trouble is, it bothers most people — or it will when I find him." He gave her a long, searching look, wondering exactly what she knew about this business. "Jamie Harrison wouldn't have been the last to receive help, would he?"

Elizabeth shrugged and sipped her coffee. "I couldn't say. As far as I know the Harrisons left these parts last week."

"After your friend kicked them off their place," he reminded her.

Elizabeth looked into her half-filled cup and replied defensively. "He wasn't at all happy about that. It was business. Mr. Stacey has to protect his investors' money."

Tanner nodded. "How come you don't seem too upset over the robberies? It is, after all, your friend's money that's taken."

"Luckily, Mr. Stacey is rich enough so these robberies are proving to be merely an inconvenience."

"Is that why you like him? Because he's rich?"

"Mr. Stacey is very nice. I'm sure my feelings for him have nothing to do with your investigation, Marshal." Elizabeth had a time keeping her expression under control.

"Anything that relates to Mr. Stacey might help this investigation, Miss Garner."

"How?"

He gave her a hard, cold look. "Someone hates him enough to want to see him ruined."

Elizabeth sat up straight, and her eyes widened as tendrils of fear slid down her back. She repressed the shiver that threatened. This man was no one's fool. She'd have to be careful. Very careful indeed. Her voice shook as she spoke, convincing Tanner he'd upset her unnecessarily. "Well, it's ridiculous to point the finger at me. The man has asked me to marry him. Why would I consider marrying him if I was planning his ruin?"

Tanner shook his head, his eyes softening at her look of fear. "I'm not pointing a finger, ma'am. I'm simply stating a fact. Anything you know about the man might prove important." He gave her a long, searching look. "Are you planning to marry him?" He forced the words from a throat strangely tight.

"I'm considering it."

He couldn't help himself. He had to know. "Because you care for the man, or because of his wealth?"

Elizabeth's cheeks darkened with obvious anger. "I don't think that's any of your business."

"I told you, everything about the man is my business," Tanner snapped, annoyed at his inability to keep his anger under control.

Elizabeth smiled, trying to lighten the moment. "I believe it's said that it's as easy to love a rich man as one that's poor."

"So you love him," Tanner remarked almost to himself as a sickening feeling hit his stomach.

Elizabeth neither denied nor agreed with his statement. She came to her feet and began to clear the table. "As I've already said, Mr. Stacey is a very nice man."

Tanner's eyes narrowed in puzzlement. Why was it her words didn't ring true? Could it be the sudden harshness he detected in her voice was only his imagination? Why, then, didn't she simply come out with it. Did she love him or not? How difficult was that to answer?

Tanner pushed back his chair and muttered sharply, "I've got things that need doing. Thanks for breakfast."

Elizabeth smiled as she turned from the sink, her eyes holding an almost wicked gleam. "You're very welcome, Marshal."

Tanner pushed aside the odd sensation that she was again laughing at him. No doubt his first impression of her temperament had been colored by her injury. Obviously she was simply an extremely cheerful person.

Chapter Two

Tanner stepped into the cool, dim interior of the two-story, brick building, his boots tapping loudly upon smooth marble floors. Expensive paintings dotted the mahogany-paneled walls, and the air of elegance was oddly out of place in the small, rough, western town; as was the quiet, almost subdued efficiency of the place.

Elizabeth might have excused Stacey's actions by proclaiming him merely the protector of his investors' money, but Tanner knew well enough, even before he had left Virginia City, that most of the money in this bank belonged to the man himself. Tanner had no doubt, despite the opinions of others, that the recent losses were more than simply annoying to Stacey. No one could afford to keep on losing that kind of money.

When Belle arrived he'd know exactly how much damage these robberies had caused. A smile touched Tanner's firm mouth as he thought of the woman he hadn't seen in more than a year.

Belle Mason worked for the Wells Fargo Company. She knew more about banks and their bookkeeping systems than anyone alive. Over the years her path had often crossed Tanner's, and a relationship of sorts had developed between them. From the first they had been sexually attracted to one another, but each had known, even back then, that what was sought in the other could have no permanence. Their moments together were rare but necessary outlets because of the nature of their work. Danger, a powerful aphrodisiac, had brought them together. To their mutual satisfaction, each had taken what was needed from the other, having no regrets when they went on alone to further assignments.

Over the ensuing years had come a measure of maturity. Perhaps they'd grown accustomed to the danger at hand, or had merely become confident that they could win out against the lawless. Whatever the reason, their relationship had evolved into a quiet fondness that no longer needed physical release. They were truly friends, a rare and precious situation between a man and a woman.

Tanner grinned, knowing the shock this town would suffer once Belle arrived. The woman could curse fluently in three languages and never hesitated to do so at the least provocation. She could outdrink and outshoot anyone he knew. And to top it all off, she smoked cigars and wore the most outrageous hats ever created. Yes, this town would definitely stand up and take notice once she arrived.

Tanner stopped at the first desk and waited for the bespectacled young man to look up from his papers. "Can I help you?" he asked after Tanner finally cleared his throat impatiently.

At seeing the bank employee's face at last, Tanner realized he was little more than a boy, and was decidedly feminine in appearance. His features were fine, his pale cheeks held no telltale shadow of a beard. Tanner shrugged aside a moment's distaste. The boy was young. No doubt he would soon grow to manhood. Some were simply later than others in achieving maturity. Besides, it wasn't his concern if Stacey hired children out of the nursery. All he wanted was to find out who was behind these robberies. "I'd like to see Mr. Stacey. They told me, at his home, I'd find him here."

"Do you have an appointment?"

"I'm afraid I don't."

A feminine flutter of a hand caused Tanner's eyes to narrow speculatively. "I'm sorry." The voice was noticeably higher than one would expect in a lad of at least sixteen years. "If you'd like I could make one for you. Mr. Stacey doesn't see anyone except by appointment."

"Sonny, you're not near bein' sorry, but you're gonna' be if you don't tell Stacey that Marshal Maddox is here to see him."

The boy ignored Tanner's more than obvious threat and turned to the huge book that lay upon his desk. With pen in hand, he examined it. "Let's see. I can put you in for—"

He never finished the sentence. In truth he forgot what he had been about to say since all his attention was suddenly focused on his very real need to breathe. That he was obviously unable to do so was directly attributable to the fact that Tanner had yanked him to his feet and now held him by the collar, hanging over his desk. "Maybe you didn't hear me. I said tell Stacey that Marshal Maddox is here to see him."

"Is there a problem?" The sharp voice came from Tanner's right.

Tanner relaxed his hold on the boy and sent him crashing back to his chair. He could hear the youth gasping for breath, but ignored the sounds as he turned to a tall meticulously groomed gentleman flanked by two muscle-bound brutes. Tanner leaned his hip on the corner of the desk, folded his arms over his chest, and silently watched as all three approached.

"This . . . this . . . *man* wants to see you, sir."

Tanner grinned, unable to remember when the word "man" had sounded more like a curse. His eyes narrowed dangerously as the bodyguards stroked the handles of the guns strapped to their thighs. "Easy," he said, the word a husky threat. "You boys best be knowin' what you're doin' before you draw on a U.S. Marshal." Tanner almost sighed aloud as he watched the men relax their stances and allow their arms to hang loosely at their sides. He had no fear of being outdrawn. He knew he could handle himself against these two. But this wasn't the place for a gunfight. Any one of the dozen patrons of the bank could be injured if he allowed the moment to get out of hand. Tanner nodded to the man between the two thugs. "You Stacey?"

"I am," came the terse reply.

"I'd suggest, in the future, you make yourself more accessible to the public." He shot a glance at the boy still struggling to regain his normal breathing. "This boy here could have gotten hurt if I wasn't a patient man."

A sputtering sound came from behind the desk. Whatever the lad was about to say was instantly brought to an end by a quick, hard look from his boss. Cold blue-gray eyes lifted to Tanner's amused gaze. "Yes." Stacey nodded. "You will forgive my employee, Marshal. I'm afraid Brian is a bit overprotective of my time. He realizes how valuable it is."

Tanner felt an instant dislike for the man with the cold gray eyes and colder handshake. He watched, his expression revealing amusement and scorn as Stacey deliberately wiped his released hand on a frilly handkerchief taken from his coat pocket.

What the hell did Elizabeth see in him besides his money? He was nothing much to look at. Tall but thin to the point of being skinny. His nose was long, his nostrils pinched as if he continuously smelled a particularly unpleasant odor, and his complexion was pale, almost gray. As for his mouth, it was a tight line. Tanner's own mouth turned down into a grimace as he imagined the lovely warm Elizabeth in Stacey's cold embrace. This man wouldn't dirty himself with sexual sweat. Not a hair would be put out of place during one of his romantic encounters. If he kissed at all, he'd do it with his mouth closed.

The picture of Stacey and Elizabeth didn't sit well

with Tanner. Actually the picture of Elizabeth in any man's arms but his own was enough to cause his temper to rise. He felt no little amazement at realizing this. Damn, but he couldn't remember a time when a woman had so completely absorbed his interest. But this wasn't the time to think of her. Firmly he forced his thoughts back to the business at hand.

As a rule Tanner didn't throw his weight around. He had confidence in his abilities and saw no need to assume a superior role because he was the law. He was a marshal and cared little who liked it or didn't; yet he now found himself unable to stop the threat that tumbled from his mouth at Stacey's sneer of distaste. "I wouldn't want to bring him in for obstructing an investigation." He nodded over his shoulder in the direction of the boy. "The next time I come to see you, I expect—"

"Of course. Of course," Stacey hastily interrupted as he moved toward the large door just off the bank's lobby. "Please come into my office. We can talk there in private."

Tanner nodded and followed him into a large room. If he thought the bank's lobby bespoke opulence, it was nothing compared to the owner's private office. The room was huge, its highly polished floors dotted with expensive Oriental rugs. Three walls were covered from ceiling to floor with shelves holding small, beautiful pieces of art and, Tanner was sure, an occasional leather-bound first edition. A black marble fireplace occupied most of the fourth wall. Stacey definitely enjoyed his creature comforts, Tanner mused. One could only imagine the luxury of his home.

"Please sit down, Marshal," Stacey suggested as he moved behind a huge mahogany desk and settled himself in a deep red, leather chair. "May I get you something to drink?"

"Thank you, no," Tanner responded as he sat facing the desk. A quick look toward the door assured him that they were not alone. "I thought you said we could talk in private?"

"I'm never without my men."

Tanner grinned. "That must prove interesting at times."

Stacey ignored the jeer and asked, "Now, how can I help you?"

"Actually, I thought I was helping you. Seems to me someone's out to get you, Stacey. Any idea why?"

Stacey shook his head. "I'm afraid I don't."

"No enemies?"

Stacey smiled, and his heavily lidded eyes widened with mirth, sending a shiver of disgust down Tanner's back. God, the man looked like a lizard. "You have to understand, Marshal. A man doesn't reach my position without ruffling a few feathers."

A smile tugged at Tanner's mouth upon hearing this understatement. "I'd say someone hates you enough to try to ruin you. Someone with ruffled feathers hardly qualifies."

Stacey shrugged a bony shoulder. "The wording hardly matters, does it? The point is I know of no one who could be behind these robberies."

"Are the shipments kept confidential?"

"Of course."

"Who knows about them besides you?"

"My man in Eureka."

Tanner nodded, knowing the man was being checked out by the Wells Fargo Company people. "No one else?"

"No one."

"Not even those two?" he nodded toward the two men still standing inside the door.

Stacey shook his head and repeated, "No one. What are you going to do?"

"I'm going to find him, Stacey. And when I do, I'm going to send him to prison." Tanner waited a moment before he went on. "More to the point, what are you going to do?"

"What do you mean?"

"I mean there's talk about you hiring guns."

"There's no law against it, is there?"

"No one's been hurt so far. I wouldn't want to see innocent people killed by a trigger-happy killer."

"That won't happen."

"Something impossible for you to guarantee, once they're hired."

"They'd only be protecting my money. You people can't do it."

"We'll do it."

"When? When there's nothing left?"

Tanner stepped into the dusty road, his head lowered,

his eyes on the ground before him as he mulled over the interview with Stacey. The man was lying. He might not know who was behind these robberies, but he suspected someone. At the very least he was hiding something. A puzzled frown creased Tanner's forehead. If Stacey knew, why was he keeping the man's identity secret? Could it be his intent was to handle the problem himself? Tanner shook his head. No, not himself. He might order one of his guards to do his dirty work, but he wouldn't do it himself. The man didn't have the guts of a jackrabbit. There was no way he'd face down a gunman.

Tanner decided it was time he found out more about the mysterious Mr. Stacey. He was heading for the telegraph office when he spied Elizabeth coming from the general store, her arms laden with packages.

"You shouldn't be carrying these," he said as he fell into step beside her.

She blew a stray curl from her forehead with a puff of breath and raised her gaze to his merry blue eyes. Her heart seemed to stumble before it remembered to continue beating, and when it did remember, it was decidedly louder than usual. Lord, but this man was handsome. She hadn't thought so at first, but he was. Especially when his eyes twinkled and white teeth flashed beneath his mustache. Idly she wondered how that mustache would feel against her skin. An instant later she almost stumbled with shock at the thought. Good gracious, what in the world was she thinking? Instantly she forced the wayward supposition from her mind. It was the wrong time. The wrong place. The

38

wrong man. No sense getting herself in a state over something that could never be. "I wouldn't be if I could find a gentleman to help," she said.

"Now why didn't I think of that?" Tanner grinned down at her. His mustache twitched with his amusement. He looked quickly around them and then sighed as he shook his head, feigning disappointment. "Trouble is, I don't think there's a gentleman in these parts."

Elizabeth laughed. "I'd settle for a strong back then."

"Oh, if it's a strong back you need, I can help you there," Tanner said as he reached for the packages. There were four in all, and it took some doing on both their parts not to let one slip from his grasp. During the process of removing them from her arms, his fingers accidentally grazed her breasts. Elizabeth knew the light brush was an accident, still she couldn't hold back her soft gasp of surprise. She moved quickly away, creating space between them. Tanner instantly realized what he had inadvertently touched. What he didn't know was that his eyes darkened to a midnight blue, nor did he sense the devastating effect his touch had had on her. "I'm sorry," he said, though he'd never in his life meant it less. His hands tingled to know more of her. His body ached to lean closer. His mind screamed that he should throw the packages aside and do just that. "I didn't mean to—"

"I know," she said quickly, interrupting him as she waved his apology aside with an unsteady movement of her hand. "Thank you." Elizabeth sighed, anxious to change the subject and aware of the shaky sound of her voice. "They were quite heavy."

"I met your beau this morning," Tanner finally said, after searching his brain to find something that would ease the strain between them as they began to walk toward her house.

"My . . ." Elizabeth raised eyes filled with confusion. "Oh, you mean Mr. Stacey." She shrugged a slender shoulder. "I wouldn't exactly call him my beau."

"Wouldn't you? You told me yourself he asked you to marry him."

Elizabeth smiled and shrugged again. "So?"

"And you said you're considering it."

Elizabeth laughed, her eyes twinkling with merriment. "Ah yes, I remember now. This morning, wasn't it?"

"Are you teasing me?" he asked while shooting her a sharp look.

Laughter sparkled in her warm eyes. "And if I was, would you cart me off to jail?"

Tanner sighed and asked again in a voice that held a bit more authority. "Is he or isn't he your beau?"

"Why?"

"Because I want to know."

"Why?" Elizabeth asked as she ran up the three steps to her front door. She stepped inside, holding the door for him. "Has it something to do with your investigation?" she asked, her hands busy removing the large pin that held her straw hat in place.

"All right. We'll try it this way. Are you seeing anyone else?"

40

"No." The corners of her mouth twitched in amusement.

"Why?"

"No one else has asked to see me," she said simply.

"You mean you might be interested in another man, if you were asked?"

"That would depend on the man, I would say." Elizabeth remarked as she took the packages from his arms and brought them into her kitchen.

Tanner followed her through the parlor and stopped at the doorway. "But I thought you were taken with him."

"Who? Mr. Stacey?" Elizabeth smiled again. "He is very nice."

"Reminds me of a lizard," Tanner grumbled with no little measure of disgust.

Bubbling laughter came from Elizabeth's throat. "That isn't very nice. If you didn't have a hand in making him, you've no right to criticize God's work."

"God, eh?" Tanner leaned against the kitchen wall, his arms folded across his chest, and watched as she put the things away. "It couldn't be his parents were simply ugly as sin?"

"Mr. Stacey isn't the least bit ugly," she said defensively. "His manner might be overly refined, something not often seen this far west, but his features are good."

"Good for what?"

Elizabeth laughed and shook her head as she pumped water into a large coffee pot. "Shame on you, Marshal."

Elizabeth was nervous. Her hands trembled slightly as she measured coffee into the pot. Drat! Why did he

41

have to stand there like that? Why did he stare at her? Didn't he realize his blue eyes were bound to shake a woman?

She patted her jet black hair self-consciously as she turned to face him. "Are you hungry? Would you like something to eat?"

Tanner was almost tempted to tell her what he was hungry for. Instead he shrugged and sat down at the table. "What I'd like is to ask a favor."

Elizabeth tipped her head to one side as she waited for him to go on. The tiniest of smiles touched her wide mouth. She couldn't have known how fetching that made her look. Tanner had a time of it remembering what he had been about to say.

"A woman is coming in on the stage, probably today. She's going to need a place to stay."

"Oh." Elizabeth's eyes clouded with disappointment. An instant later she recognized the smug look in his eyes and realized that her disappointment had been obvious.

Tanner gave her a slow, lazy grin. He stretched his legs out before him and leaned comfortably back in the chair. "It's not like that. She's an associate."

"Of course," Elizabeth remarked, suddenly the prim and proper landlady. "It's also none of my business."

"You could make it your business," he said, his voice low, his hunger clear in the long, searching look that moved slowly from her toes to her hair.

Elizabeth let out a small gasp and took a step back. In her eyes was a look of pure terror. She didn't want this. Not now! She had a mission to accomplish. She had a

42

pledge to honor. There was no place in her life for a man. Especially not this man.

"I have a room free," she struggled to keep her voice steady, her breathing even. "You can bring her here, when she gets in."

The stagecoach rumbled into town amid a cloud of swirling dust. The driver strained at the reins for control while, forgetting himself for a moment, he roundly cursed beasts who did not want to slow down.

The ladies who stood nearby pretended not to hear. The men simply shrugged, knowing the man couldn't be held accountable after the exhausting hours he'd spent at the reins.

The stage at last rolled to a stop. The dust hadn't settled before a tall, handsome woman with a mass of strawberry blond hair swung the door open and jumped unassisted to the ground. She shook the wrinkles from her forest green traveling dress and adjusted the most outrageously decorated hat. "Damn, I thought we'd never get here," she said to no one in particular, while rubbing her bruised bottom.

"Far as I can remember," said a low voice, "you got enough cushioning there to make it around the world and back."

Belle Mason turned toward the man who spoke, and a great smile flashed even white teeth as she flung herself into Marshal Maddox's arms. "Tanner you ugly, old bastard. When are you going to quit marshaling and

43

make room for some young blood?"

Tanner flung his head back and roared with laughter. "The day I dance at your wedding."

Belle shot him a look of annoyance. Why the hell did the man forever bring up her unmarried status? Who was he to talk anyway? Besides, it wasn't as if she'd never gotten a proposal. There was nothing wrong with remaining as she was. What was so great about being married and living under some man's thumb?

"What the hell are you doing rubbing your ass in public?" he teased.

She disengaged herself from his arms. "I didn't know anyone was standing behind me."

"You should have." His eyes grew serious and narrowed in thought. "You're not losing it, are you Belle?"

Belle shot her longtime friend a scathing look of pure disgust and boasted, "I'm better than you'll ever be."

Tanner looked her in the eye for a long moment before nodding. "I've got us a place to stay."

"Good. I need a bath and something to wash this godforsaken dust from my throat."

They waited for a minute before the luggage was unstrapped from the back of the coach. Tanner, with one large suitcase in hand, swung an arm over her shoulders as he led her toward Elizabeth's boardinghouse. "Watch your manners, will you, Belle? The woman that owns this house is a lady."

Belle stopped short. Her blue eyes filled with delight as they searched his face. "Lord! Are you telling me you've finally taken the fall? After all these years?"

Tanner's expression darkened dangerously. Anyone but Belle might have felt more than a twinge of fear at his obvious anger, but she had known this man too long to worry about his rages. She merely grinned at his fierce look.

"What the hell are you talking about?" he demanded.

"Damn!" Belle laughed aloud. "This is good. I've waited a long time to see some woman get under your skin."

"You're out of your mind. Nobody's under anyone's skin. I've only known her for two days."

Belle laughed again, knowing he had just admitted more than he realized. "Sometimes it doesn't even take that long," she said knowingly. "Sometimes it only takes a minute. Sometimes you know in a look."

Tanner said nothing, his thoughts going back to the moment he'd first seen Elizabeth. It wasn't true, of course. Granted, he'd been stunned by her exquisite beauty. Who wouldn't be? But he didn't feel anything for her. Besides, he'd taken that road before. He was too old to fall in love again. All he wanted was what any normal, healthy male would want, and that was to spend some time in her bed.

"I like your friend," Elizabeth said as she stepped on to the darkened porch and saw Tanner leaning against one of the posts that supported its roof.

"Is she sleeping?"

"I think so. She was exhausted."

Elizabeth saw his shoulders shake and listened to the low sound of his laughter. "I should compliment you on your control. I have to say that that was the worst yet."

Elizabeth grinned. "I can't remember when I've ever seen anything half so fascinating."

"And the grapes?"

"Mmmm, purple grapes on a green hat, topped off with the largest bluebird in existence." Elizabeth bit her lip in an effort to hold back the laughter that threatened. "It was unusual."

"I thought your eyes were going to fall out of your head when she lit that cigar after dinner."

Elizabeth grinned as she moved to one of the rocking chairs and sat. "Yes, well, I must admit I was a bit surprised."

"You covered it well, by offering her a dish for her ashes." Tanner watched her rock, her gaze upon the deserted road. "You didn't have to allow it, you know."

"Oh, I'd never do anything to make a guest feel uncomfortable."

Tanner wondered what she'd do if she knew how uncomfortable she made him? "Are you always so considerate of people and their feelings?"

"I try to be."

"Do you receive the same consideration in return?"

Elizabeth smiled as she looked up at his shadowed expression. "We usually reap what we sow, Marshal."

"Where's your beau tonight?"

Elizabeth grinned. "If you mean Mr. Stacey, I don't see him but once a week."

46

"Why? If you were mine, I'd . . ."

Elizabeth stiffened. She didn't dare ask what he was going to say. She didn't want to know. He took a step forward. Hurriedly she came to her feet and moved back. Her mind raced for something to say, knowing the longer the silence between them, the greater the chance he'd come to her. She couldn't allow that to happen. "Mr. Stacey is involved with business most evenings. By the time he's finished, it's too late to go visiting."

"And you're satisfied with this relationship?"

"I'm not lonely, if that's what you mean. I have many things that occupy my time."

"What kinds of things?"

Elizabeth laughed. "Are you always so inquisitive?"

Tanner shrugged. "Habit. I'm sorry if I was out of line."

"You weren't." Elizabeth sighed as she watched a lone rider pass her house, heading for the cheerful sounds of music and laughter coming from the other end of town. "You might want to make yourself scarce tomorrow night, Marshal. I'm having a party for my friend Sally. A surprise party. She's having a baby."

"And I'm not allowed to come?"

Elizabeth gave him a small smile at hearing the disappointment in his voice. "It's not that you're not allowed. There will only be women there."

"You might not believe this, Miss Garner, but I like women."

Elizabeth grinned, knowing he was teasing her. "I never doubted it for a moment." She bit her lip in an effort to suppress her laughter. "I suspect you'd cause quite a commotion, not to mention a few jealous husbands, if you came."

"What kind of commotion?"

"Well for one thing the ladies would be all aflutter to find you there. You must know you're an exceedingly handsome man," she said honestly and then nodded as she imagined Mabel and Harriet in his company. Lord, they would have a time keeping their hands to themselves. No doubt the marshal would enjoy that. She frowned slightly at the imagined scenario. "Yes, I believe that would cause a bit of a stir. And then, of course, they wouldn't be able to talk as freely with a man present."

"What kind of things would they say that a man cannot hear?"

Elizabeth grinned, her eyes wide with amusement that he should dare ask such a question and, worse yet, expect an answer. "Would you like a glass of lemonade?"

"I suppose you're going to ignore my question?"

"Coffee perhaps? I made a cake today and iced it with sugar."

Tanner laughed. "You know, I don't think I like the idea that you're not the least bit afraid of the law, Miss Garner."

"The law is there to protect the innocent, is it not? What, then, have I to fear?"

Tanner gave a reluctant nod. "It's not your lack of fear. It's your lack of respect."

He watched her walk toward the door. Her eyes held a

devilish gleam. "I'll heat up the coffee."

Tanner watched as she moved out of sight. It was a moment before he realized she had never denied his accusation.

Chapter Three

The soft tinkling sounds of feminine laughter drifted sweetly over the hundred yards or more that separated the house from the barn. The windows were open. Lanterns burned in both the parlor and kitchen. He stood in the shadows and watched for her, never realizing how much he needed to see her until he sighed with pleasure as she moved by a window. She carried a glass; a gentle smile curved her lips as she listened to one of the women talk. Tanner made a low aching sound as an almost crippling sense of loneliness suddenly hit him like a physical blow.

Tanner purposely shook away the spell she wove. His mouth drew down into a grimace. Damn it to hell! What was he allowing this woman to do to him? How could he, after only knowing her three days, feel lost and at loose ends when not in her company? It was ridiculous! Impossible! She couldn't have gained such power over him. What then was he doing here, waiting in the shadows of the barn like a lovesick adolescent? There were women aplenty at

Lucy's. And any one of them would have been happy to ease the ache between his legs; an ache that seemed only to grow in strength since he'd first caught sight of Elizabeth. Why the hell wasn't he now positioned between a pair of willing white thighs?

Tanner groaned at the thought, knowing he'd find a measure of physical release with a woman, but he was aware that that wouldn't be enough, not near enough. He needed more. He needed to touch Elizabeth, kiss her, breathe her in. Only this one particular woman would satisfy him.

He cursed, a low ragged sound of torment, knowing he wanted her as he'd never wanted another. He cursed again. He had to get her out of his mind. He couldn't live like this. It had been only three days, but each day he was growing more useless in his work. He couldn't concentrate on anything but the imagined taste of her mouth, the touch of her skin, the sweet woman-scent of her. If he didn't take her and be done with this longing, he'd never find the culprit behind these robberies. God, Belle would just about laugh herself to death if she knew how helpless he felt.

Elizabeth leaned her back against the wall in the parlor and sipped her wine as she listened to the unusually outrageous comments of her friends. As each hour passed, they got decidedly worse, led on by an outspoken and particularly rowdy Belle. No doubt the lateness of the hour and the liberal amount of sherry imbibed played a part, but she'd never known any of them to be quite so bold.

Her cheeks darkened at yet another bawdy comment. Elizabeth knew her guests would speak more gently if they knew that the Widow Garner had, in fact, never been wed, for remarks on subjects such as the physical intimacies of married couples or the male anatomy were never hinted at in an unmarried lady's presence.

Elizabeth had assumed the guise of widow when she'd realized the danger of traveling alone. A lone lady in mourning was catered to rather than leered at by her fellow travelers. Also, once settled, she knew her every action would not be scrutinized by ever-watchful eyes as would have been the case had she been a miss.

She thanked God that Tanner had gone along with her suggestion and kept his distance. There was no telling what these ladies would do or say in their present conditions. Especially in the company of a man who could turn any lady's head when cold sober.

Idly Elizabeth wondered what he was about. She shook her head, calling herself every kind of fool. He knew no one in town. There was nowhere he could have gone but Lucy's. No doubt he was right now . . . Elizabeth shook her head again, denying that the thought of his being with another woman bothered her. It didn't matter where the man was. It didn't matter what he was doing. What he did was certainly none of her concern. And, if she wanted to continue the work she had started, she had better remember that.

It mattered little that she was attracted to him. She didn't care that his blue gaze could cause her to shake with the need to touch him, that his white smile could melt her heart, that his very presence could cause her stomach to do somersaults. She was strong. She could and would fight the attraction. The man was dangerous. More dangerous than anything she'd ever encountered.

Elizabeth breathed a sigh of relief for the gathering was breaking up at last. She gathered the ladies' wraps and gave them out as the entire group headed for the front door.

Within moments the night air was filled with cries of laughter and general merriment as the women managed in their mild state of inebriation to climb into their buggies and call out cheerful good nights.

Tanner walked to the front of the house just as the last two had stepped outside. One of them exclaimed in a loud drawl he imagined was meant to be seductive but which came out as a drunken slur, "Well, hello." Her voice deepened with undisguised interest as he moved into the light coming from the open door. "Are you the infamous Marshal Maddox we've heard so much about?" she asked shamelessly, knowing quite well who he was.

Tanner grinned as she and the woman with her came down the steps and sauntered up to him, positioning themselves on either side of his tall frame. The blonde, just a pound or so short of being fat, grinned up at him. "Why didn't you come to the party? It would have been ever so much more fun."

Elizabeth stood upon the porch and scowled with unreasonable anger as the two women grasped Tanner's arms. "Mabel," Elizabeth said, careful to keep admonishment from her voice as she moved down the steps, "Joe will be getting worried."

"Oh, pooh." Mabel pouted, assuming what she no doubt thought was an adorable expression. In truth, it merely made her chubby cheeks appear more so. "Joe is always worried."

"Joe's her husband," the woman on his right offered by way of explanation.

"And what's your husband's name?" Tanner asked, his head dipping low, his deep voice sending chills down Elizabeth's spine. She could only imagine what it was doing to the two who held on to him.

Elizabeth scowled again as she watched him flirt, knowing these women wouldn't stop talking about him for days, weeks, maybe years.

"Mine?" the woman asked, then followed her question with a shrill, piercing laugh. "I've been a widow for years."

"You'll have to excuse my friends, Marshal," Elizabeth said, coming to his rescue whether he liked it or not. "They don't often get out. I'm afraid they've enjoyed one glass of sherry too much."

"Oh, Lizzy, you old stick-in-the-mud," said the

54

taller and thinner of the two. "A glass of sherry, actually a whole bottle, wouldn't do you any harm."

"Thank you, Harriet. I'll take your suggestion under consideration," Elizabeth said in her most prim manner. "Now, if you'll let go of Marshal Maddox's arm, he can come inside. I think we've kept him from his bed long enough."

Tanner was biting his lips to keep from laughing. If he didn't know better he might have believed her jealous. She sure as hell was acting like she suffered from the ailment. Why, the look she was shooting at her friends was enough to sober them on the spot. He bit the inside of his lip to force back his grin. For the first time in days, Tanner could honestly say he was enjoying himself.

"I could always . . ." Harriet began a low whispery suggestion. From the look in her eyes, the pretty pout of her mouth, and the way her body was curving into his, Elizabeth had no doubt what was on her mind.

"I'm sure you could, Harriet," she said abruptly. "Perhaps another time. For now, Joe is sure to be concerned. You promised to have Mabel back at a reasonable hour."

Harriet mumbled something that set Tanner's shoulders to shaking with mirth. Elizabeth could only give thanks that she'd missed it.

"Maybe we could talk again, Marshal," Harriet said as she reluctantly released his arm. She then guided her stumbling friend toward the last waiting buggy.

"I'm sure we will, ma'am," Tanner said as he tipped his hat after helping both of the wobbly women gain their seats.

Harriet Trapper snapped the reins against the horse's back and waved goodbye as the buggy suddenly lurched forward. It then sped down the desolate street toward their homes at the other end of town.

"They're not going far, are they?"

"Not far enough," Elizabeth grumbled as she turned to go in.

"Perhaps I should follow them. To make sure they get home all right."

"Why not?" she said abruptly. "I'm sure they'd love the company."

Tanner's eyes widened at the sound of her voice. "Are you upset with me?"

"Me?" she asked, stopping on the bottom step of the porch. She turned and faced him, her eyes slits of black fury. "Upset? Whatever for?"

"Well, you're sure acting mighty strange."

"Am I? Perhaps I'm just not accustomed to such a disgusting display."

Tanner chuckled and gave a boyish shake of his head. "Oh, it wasn't so bad. I'm sure they didn't mean anything by it." He shrugged a broad shoulder. "They were just having a little fun."

"I wasn't talking about them. I was talking about you."

Tanner blinked in surprise. "Me! What did I do?"

"You led them on."

Tanner almost grabbed her then. She *had* been jealous. His heart pounded with delight as he fought to keep a smile at bay. His words were low, taunting, and silky smooth. "Now, how do you suppose I did that?"

Elizabeth had no idea what had come over her, but again she suddenly seemed to lose all control as she pictured his obvious enjoyment when the two women leaned in to him. Words tumbled forth of their own volition. "Tell me you didn't enjoy their attentions. Tell me your tongue wasn't practically hanging out of your mouth while you stared down Harriet's dress."

There was a moment of stunned silence, and then Elizabeth gasped, realizing what she'd just said. How could she have voiced such an accusation? Lord, she sounded like a jealous shrew. And she had no right to be so possessive. She couldn't believe this was happening. Worse, she couldn't think of a way to still her wayward tongue.

Tanner kept his features even, not daring to show a flicker of the happiness that suddenly filled him. She was furious. That had to mean she cared a hell of a lot more than she showed. He studied her look of confusion and knew she cared more than she even realized.

"Her dress?" he asked calmly. "What are you talking about?"

"Nothing," Elizabeth said, her voice low and stiff.

She wished she had never spoken those ridiculous words.

"Tell me," he insisted.

At his insistence, her anger came back in full force. What difference did it make now? She'd damned herself already; she might as well go on. "I saw you looking."

Tanner felt a slight annoyance. He didn't take to being accused falsely, no matter the provocation. "You didn't see a damned thing and you know it. It was too dark."

"Uh-huh! So you admit you were looking," Elizabeth snapped, a note of triumph in her voice.

Tanner's eyes narrowed with a clear threat. Had Elizabeth not lost the last of her control, she might have noticed, might have turned on her heel and run for the safety of her room. "The only thing I'll admit is those glasses you wear to read might be put to better use if you wore them all the time." He moved a fraction closer. His warm clean breath hit her in the face as he spoke. "If it was my intent to look down a woman's dress it sure as hell wouldn't be Harriet whatever-her-name's. It would be yours."

Elizabeth gasped, suddenly aware of the hungry look in his eyes. She attempted to move back, but forgot she was standing on the steps. She stumbled, almost falling backward, and then gasped again as Tanner's arms came around her and drew her body to his.

"Don't," she whispered, almost desperate for him

not to touch her. She felt so stiff, she wondered if she might break as he pressed her against him.

"Don't what?" he asked as his mouth hovered inches above her own, his legs almost failing him as lust exploded in him. His body had never felt more alive, more filled with need.

"Don't touch me." It was a thin, whispery response.

But it came too late. There was no way he could stop the descent of his mouth. "Aw honey, you can't ask that. Ask me anything, anything else," he groaned as the feel of her softness penetrated his senses and his mouth covered the sweet lips that had mesmerized him from the start.

His kiss was gentle. A feathery touch, an exquisite sampling of taste, of feel. A coaxing that promised limitless pleasure.

After experiencing the steel grasp of his arms, Elizabeth hadn't expected a tender assault. And it was that very tenderness that was her undoing.

She couldn't seem to keep her mind clear. She knew she wanted to push him away. To shake her head and free it of the fog that was seeping over her.

Elizabeth sighed as she allowed herself the tantalizing sweet pleasure, and she leaned closer to him. She forgot to fight him. This felt so good, so sweet, so right.

His arms tightened around her, drawing her closer as he deepened the kiss. He angled his head so his tongue might better sample the texture of lips as smooth as silk.

Elizabeth put her hands on his shoulders and tried to break his hold. Her whole body stiffened. What was he doing? Licking her? Good Lord! What could he possibly mean by kissing her in such an outrageous fashion?

"Open your mouth," he murmured against her warm flesh.

"No," she said, unknowingly giving him the entrance he needed to the sweet dark honey of her mouth.

She gasped at his audacity and tried to pull away. This was awful! Whoever heard of such goings-on? People didn't kiss like this! But Tanner ignored her struggles, apparently determined she'd stay and endure.

Elizabeth sighed, knowing she hadn't the strength to break his hold. She'd stay put for the time being. She could stand anything for a time. Actually, it wasn't as bad as she had first thought. The way his tongue had slid into her mouth had shocked her more than brought on disgust. Oddly enough his tongue was causing some unusual happenings deep within her. She felt an ache begin to grow. Not an uncomfortable ache, just a pressure of sorts.

Tanner, reluctant to leave her mouth after finally gaining entrance, breathed against her lips. Elizabeth was immediately filled with his scent and taste. And then the most unusual thing happened. She felt an instant weakening in her knees and moaned as she slumped heavily against him. Suddenly the hands that had tried to hold him away moved to his neck and brought him closer. She hungered for more. Her body felt wildly alive. Her heart pounding against the wall of her chest, she heard his low groan and sighed with delight as he held her closer yet.

His mouth was sucking at her, seeming to take everything she could give. And that wasn't enough. His tongue drove deep, imitating the movement of his hips against her belly. Then his hands moved to her rounded backside and lifted her so their hips and mouths were almost even.

Elizabeth swayed drunkenly, her senses alive and yearning to discover more of this delight. She felt new textures as his tongue moved over her teeth, the roof of her mouth, her own tongue. Rough and smooth, but most of all sweet. She breathed his scent and realized she'd never known a man could smell so wonderful. She tasted his mouth, clean with a trace of whiskey, and knew nothing would ever taste as good again.

His hair was soft beneath her finger. His beard scratched her skin. She loved it. And best of all his mustache teased and tormented her flesh until she thought she might scream with the pleasure.

"You were jealous," he gasped as he tore his mouth from hers. "Why?"

"Certainly not," she moaned. Chills raced up her spine when his mouth brushed along the sensitive column of her slender neck.

"You were. Why?"

"I don't know," she admitted, then released a low helpless moan as his mouth slid to her ear and his teeth gently worried the lobe.

Tanner heard that soft moan and asked thickly, "Do you like this?"

"No," she whimpered, though her actions denied her words.

Tanner chuckled as he felt her body grow softer against his. Lord, she was practically melting in his arms. If she didn't like it, she sure as hell put on a good act.

Without his lips on hers, Elizabeth's senses began to clear. Her hands came to his shoulders and she pushed against them in an effort to free herself. But even she realized the effort was less than determined as she declared, "This shouldn't be happening. I'm afraid I'll have to ask you to leave my house."

Tanner only chuckled as he nuzzled the pulse point in her throat. "That afraid, are you?"

"Of what?"

"Me, you, this thing that's happening between us."

Elizabeth managed to put some distance between them at last. She almost sighed her relief, but forced her voice to grow hard with determination. "There's nothing happening between us, Marshal," she said as she gained some control over herself at last. She sped up the last two steps to her porch, only to find he'd followed her.

"Isn't there?" he asked, his chest against her back, his arms encircling her waist. "Then why do you want me to leave?"

Elizabeth broke his hold, spun around, and glared up at him. He was so close she had to tip her head back to see his face. "How can you stand there after these last few minutes and ask such a question?"

"Are you going to tell me you didn't like it?"

"I most certainly did not," she lied.

"And I suppose I only imagined that you responded? It wasn't you who went all soft and warm in my arms? Your arms didn't slide around my neck and hold me while you kissed me into near madness?"

Elizabeth's cheeks burned red. "You are a beast."

"Maybe," he conceded with a nod. "But at least I'm not a cowardly liar."

"And you're saying I am?"

"I'm saying, you can't run away from this."

Elizabeth felt as though she were fighting for her life, and in a way she was. She couldn't let this man into her life. She couldn't allow this to happen. Her hands balled into fists as she faced him, sneering. "Get it into your head, Marshal, there is nothing to run away from."

"I suppose your heart is not pounding, like mine," he said as he reached out and boldly covered her breast with his palm.

Elizabeth's knees trembled, and she almost fell against him. A groan began deep in her throat, but somehow she found the strength to shove his hand away. She was gasping for breath. "If my heart is pounding, it's from anger at your unbelievable daring."

"And, of course, you don't want me to kiss you again?"

"I most certainly do not."

"Maybe not, but you like it right nice when I kiss you," he said as he abruptly pulled her against him again. Elizabeth raised a hand to slap his face, but even though his gaze clung to hers, he guessed her intent. He instantly grasped both her hands and forced them behind her, to be held firmly but gently by one of his. She turned her face away. It couldn't happen again. She mustn't ever give in to this temptation again. Deny it she might, but she knew she went wild when he held her, kissed her, touched her.

She couldn't avoid him. His mouth merely followed every twist and turn of her head. A moment later he lost patience and, with his free hand, grabbed her head, burying his fingers in silky black hair, pulling the pins free until tresses tumbled down her back almost to her hips.

Elizabeth screamed her outrage, but the sound was muffled and absorbed by his mouth. He moaned with pleasure as she moved against him, in an effort to be free. "Stop," she said, but it came out as a weak imitation of her usual voice and even she recognized that. She swore she didn't want this. Please, she silently begged as she strained against the need building in her. But he wouldn't relent. He was determined to prove her wrong. To prove she wanted him as much as he wanted her.

His mouth was wild in its need, ferocious in its hunger. There was no tenderness now. He gave no quarter, but demanded complete surrender. He wouldn't be satisfied until she acknowledged her need for him. Elizabeth suddenly knew the hopelessness of denial. With a moan that bordered on despair, she was drawn into the depths of an almost violent passion.

Hands touched only to move on and return, unsatisfied, to touch again. Heads twisted, slanted, as lips tried to find succor. He wrapped her hair around his fist and brought it to his face, breathing in its scent with a groan of agonizing pleasure. Mouths opened wide, and tongues fought a duel that drove their passion out of control. Tanner cursed the fact that they had no real privacy. Yes, he could kiss her here undetected in the shadows near her door, but he couldn't do much more. Why hadn't he waited till they were inside before starting this? A few steps down the hall would have brought them to her bedroom. Now he wondered if he had the strength to wait until they got inside.

Elizabeth whimpered her loss as his mouth left hers to taste and discover the sweetness of her throat.

"God." His voice trembled as he returned his mouth to hers. "It's worse than I thought."

He wasn't holding her close enough. He had to touch her, feel the softness of her skin. His fingers disposed of the buttons of her bodice, and he sighed with delight as they moved over the lacy thing she wore underneath.

She was melting; fire burned throughout her body. Heat, unlike any she'd ever known, spread through her veins. And the only thing that helped was the touch of his mouth on hers. Only it wasn't helping. She was growing hotter, more hungry, eager to experience more of this pleasure.

Elizabeth sucked in a small glad cry as she felt the heat of his mouth graze her shoulders and slide to the tops of her breasts. Her bodice lay open. She blinked with surprise, unable to imagine how that had happened without her noticing.

Tanner hissed as he drew breath between clenched teeth when his hand gently brushed against her breast. His fingers grazed over it, his thumb moving over the tip, massaging until it hardened.

Elizabeth closed her eyes to the pleasure and gasped, a low aching sound. Her head fell back, her hips pressed snugly to his. She moaned softly and lifted her face to his, lips parted to better enable her to breathe.

Tanner had no choice but to lower his mouth to hers for another devastating kiss. "You're right," he choked out as he struggled to control his breathing, his lips leaving hers and burying themselves in the sweetly delicate spot where her shoulder met her neck. "I've never known a woman who hated kissing more."

"Oh, I'm sorry." The soft voice came from just inside the door. "I was worried when Elizabeth didn't come back."

Tanner's head snapped up, and he shot his partner a hard look of fury.

Belle whispered a quick good night and disappeared inside. A moment later Tanner heard her bedroom door close.

Knowing their passionate moment was gone, he gave a long weary sigh as Elizabeth stiffened in his arms. He rested his forehead against hers and smiled at her stunned expression, knowing she was baffled by the wildness that had come to life between them. His fingers quickly redid the buttons of her bodice. Her eyes had begun to clear of the fog of desire, and she watched in silence as he smiled tenderly and tucked a lock of jet black hair behind her ear. "Good night, Elizabeth . . . love," he said, so softly Elizabeth wasn't sure she'd heard him correctly. He planted a quick kiss on bruised lips and stood aside.

On trembling legs she turned from him and walked stiffly into the house. She closed the door behind her with the greatest of care, as if the slightest sound would surely cause her to shatter into a million pieces, and went straight to her room. In her dazed state, she forgot to extinguish the lights that blazed in the kitchen and parlor.

Tanner's heart had never felt so light as he went about that chore himself. She wasn't thinking clearly, and he knew it was because of his kisses. God, he couldn't wait to hold her in his arms and kiss her again. He'd never known a woman to surpass her passion. Oddly enough she had seemed an innocent. Tanner brushed the thought aside. She was a widow. Of course she wasn't an innocent. But he could have sworn she hadn't known what he was about when he'd kissed her. Tanner shrugged. Perhaps her late husband was less passionate than some. A grin teased his mouth, and his eyes narrowed with remembered pleasure. No matter. He was more than willing to show the Widow Garner exactly what she'd been missing.

A wide grin spread across his mouth and he sighed with relief, knowing the solution to his problem was close at hand. Once he had her, he could put all thoughts of her aside and get on with the business that had brought him to Willowbrook. If Belle hadn't interrupted them, he would be sharing Elizabeth's bed right now. Tanner gave a low confident laugh as he closed the door to his room. It didn't matter, this delay. He'd have her and soon be back to normal again.

Elizabeth dressed in a plain, white cotton gown, but never went near the bed. After almost an hour of pacing, she sat in the small armchair in her room, thinking of the disaster that had befallen her. This couldn't be happening. She wouldn't allow it to happen. She wasn't the kind of woman to bed a man and think nothing of it. And she couldn't bed him while she had business to see to. Lord, what was she to do? The question haunted her long into the night. An hour before dawn Elizabeth got up from her chair, dressed again, and went into the kitchen to start the fire for breakfast, still no closer to understanding her reaction to the marshal or what she was going to do about it.

She was bent over the stove, adding to the fire, when she felt a presence behind her. He hadn't touched her, nor had he made a sound, but she knew he was there, no doubt enjoying her present position. "I'd appreciate it, Marshal, if you'd choose to leer at another."

Tanner chuckled as he leaned his hip against the table. "How do you know I'm leering? You haven't turned around."

Elizabeth sighed as she straightened. She walked to the sink and began to pump water into the coffee pot. How had she known he was there in the first place? She shrugged. She just had. "This isn't going to work."

"Go for a ride with me tonight."

"I'm having a headache tonight," she said as if she planned some special event.

"Are you?" he asked, while a grin curved his mouth into a devastating smile, a smile she missed since she refused to look his way. "Perhaps I could ease your pain."

Elizabeth let out a short humorless laugh. "Unlikely, since you are the cause of it."

"I've been known to bring a fair amount of comfort now and then," Tanner said with insufferable arrogance, suddenly close behind her.

Elizabeth quickly moved away, knowing she couldn't allow his touch. There was just no telling what she might do if he touched her. She didn't trust him, and she trusted herself even less. She spun around and faced him. "Oh? And are you a man of medicine as well as the law?"

Tanner shrugged and smiled smugly. "I know certain cures well enough."

"No doubt," she snapped, unreasonably angry now. Actually, the more cheerful he seemed the angrier she felt. "I believe I'll forgo your ministrations this time."

"Do you have these headaches often?"

"Only when necessary."

"I see." Tanner's finger rubbed against his mustache as he gave her answer some thought. Elizabeth couldn't help but remember how those silky hairs had felt against her skin. She closed her eyes willing away the memory. "You're afraid to be alone with me."

Elizabeth laughed, a short, almost pained sound. "Afraid? Hardly. Terrified is closer to the truth."

"Why?"

There was no way she could tell him the truth. It was ridiculous to have imagined last night that she could. He was a man sworn to uphold the law. He'd neither understand nor care about her reasonings. Finally she sighed and gave him an answer she knew he'd believe. "I don't know myself when you touch me."

"Is that so bad?"

Elizabeth smiled. It was worse than bad. It could very well prove to be disastrous. "Marshal, when you finish your assignment, you'll move on to the next. Why would you want to be bothered with me? Nothing can come of it."

"We could be friends."

Elizabeth did not realize her smile was almost sad. "Thank you, I have enough friends."

"Is it Stacey? Do you love him?"

"Yes," Elizabeth grasped at the first thing that could possibly save her from the man. "Of course I love him. I'm going to marry him."

Chapter Four

The glow of more than a dozen candles cast the room into soft shadows and added color to Elizabeth's already overheated cheeks. Her demure smile felt frozen into place as she watched the man at the far end of the gleaming dining-room table dab at his thin lips with a snowy linen napkin.

Stacey's hand reached out for hers as he came to his feet and moved to her side. "Would you enjoy a sherry, my dear?"

What she'd really enjoy were two fingers of her father's best Kentucky bourbon. She definitely needed something stronger than sherry to bear this man's company. Elizabeth hid her smile behind her napkin as she imagined asking for the brew. That would shock Stacey out of his stiff, elegant breeches, she had no doubt.

Odd, but she couldn't put a name to her emotions. Something was bothering her . . . but what? That she hated this man was obvious. Obvious, she prayed, only to herself. But it wasn't hatred that inspired these oddly reckless and restless feelings. She had been seeing Stacey for months and had never suffered from these unsettling emotions before. Elizabeth smiled and nodded her agreement, as she knew he expected. "Shall we withdraw then to the parlor? We can have our coffee there, as well."

"Why not the library, Jonathan? It's more comfortable there."

Jonathan gave her a knowing look. As always, his high-pitched laughter grated on her nerves, for some reason more so tonight. "Would you have another motive besides comfort for preferring the library over the parlor?"

Elizabeth forced her lips into a smile, even as her heart thundered wildly in her breast and fearful chills raced down her back. She could only pray her expression matched the innocence in her voice. "What do you mean?"

"You're becoming quite good at our weekly sessions. I envision a day when you'll soon give me some real competition."

Elizabeth silently cursed her inability to keep the flush from creeping up her neck to set her cheeks aflame. She prayed he'd take the sudden coloring as a reaction to his compliment, rather than guilt. Get a hold of yourself before you ruin everything, she silently scolded. He's only teasing. He knows nothing of your plans. As she read the humor in his gaze, she forced a laugh, only realizing as it came out that she had been holding her breath. "Surely you can't expect me to improve without practice."

"Then I shall give you all the practice you need,"

73

Jonathan said as he guided her toward the library and the chess board that awaited them there.

Elizabeth felt a shiver of disgust and cursed her body's reaction to his touch. With every visit, it was getting harder to hide her revulsion for this man. His overly refined manners, although unappealing, she had once taken in stride. But of late, she couldn't help but notice that those manners, the occasional lifting of a brow, and certain other gestures were distinctly feminine.

With his white hand resting casually upon her lower back, Elizabeth involuntarily shivered. "Are you chilled, my dear?"

Chilled? Was he out of his mind? She could hardly breathe due to the stifling heat. Did he never part those velvet drapes or open a window? "No, I'm fine," she murmured as she entered the dark room and sat in her usual place.

"It is a bit damp in here. I wouldn't want you to become ill."

"I'm fine, really," she said, refusing to seek his pity lest he add to her discomfort. Still, she knew what would come next. What always came next, no matter the season.

"Nevertheless, I think it would be wise to start a small fire." He shot her a quick smile. "We can't be too careful, can we?"

Elizabeth almost moaned aloud as she watched him set a match to a perfectly laid fire. Already she couldn't wait to get home and rip her high-bodiced, long-sleeved dress from her sweating body; yet he was going to compound the heat a hundredfold with a fire.

Obviously the man had acclimated himself to this heat, whereas she had not. Still, the blistering summer days had not affected her as did the pressing, suffocating heat of this house.

The place was huge, and no doubt able to hold five dwellings such as hers on the first floor alone. Had it been decorated with a lighter hand, it might have been a true showplace, with its marble floors and cathedral ceilings. As it was, it simply looked cluttered. Every corner of every room was filled to overflowing with tables of varying sizes. Many were inlaid with mother of pearl, marble, slate, or glass; but all were covered with figures of jade or porcelain, Chinese vases, precious bowls, and delicate crystal. Each article was in itself a masterpiece, an exquisite work of art, but when they were amassed, one was hard put to discern the beauty of any one piece. Combine so many delicate pieces with an overabundance of potpourri, plants, and ferns, plus the heavy red velvet window drapings, and it was a wonder Elizabeth didn't have an attack of claustrophobia.

She had been in many lovely homes, from Washington to New Orleans. Never in her life had she seen anything to equal this crass show of extravagance.

Stacey proclaimed himself a collector, but he lacked exquisite taste. In truth less than half of what he displayed would have been too much. It was obvious to Elizabeth that the man needed to boast of his worth, but his decorating style barely offered a person room to walk. She hid her grin. The atmosphere was as stifling as the temperature.

They sat opposite one another on matching, thickly cushioned leather chairs, an ivory chess set positioned between them. Elizabeth was thankful that little conversation was necessary as they pondered their moves. She sipped her sherry as she watched his long white fingers move his king into a threatening position. "Check," he said, his blue-gray eyes taking on a decidedly victorious gleam.

Elizabeth smiled and purposely fluttered her eyelashes in what she hoped portrayed her helplessness. "I'm beginning to believe I'll never be a match for you, Jonathan."

"Nonsense, my dear," Stacey returned as he waved aside her disclaimer. "I see your improvement at every sitting. If you keep up this progress, our skills will soon be equal."

Elizabeth merely smiled as she imagined his shock should he come to know that she could easily best his amateur playing in no more than three moves. From as far back as she could remember, she and her father had played. How many nights had she spent in the security of her family's home, practicing her skill on any who dared to think she was but a woman and therefore no contest?

Elizabeth leaned back in the chair as happy memories of that time came to mind. Then she sighed, knowing those precious moments were not fully appreciated until it was too late. If only . . . But no. She wouldn't think on what might have been. She was here because of this man. The day wasn't far off when she'd see him ruined and know her revenge was complete.

"I can see you're tired. Perhaps we should make an early night of it."

She only smiled her agreement. As far as she was concerned, she couldn't get out of this man's company soon enough. "I'm sorry." She brought two fingers to her temple. "It's just that I have a slight headache." And no wonder, she mused in silence. It was nothing short of a miracle that she was able to breathe in such heat.

Stacey came to his feet. "You should have mentioned your headache sooner. I wouldn't have kept you so late."

"It's nothing really," she protested. At least it will be nothing once I get out of here, she silently added. "I'm sure it will be gone by morning."

"You're working too hard. A lady like you has no business catering to the riffraff you take in. You should have servants of your own, not be soiling your hands working for others."

Elizabeth raised a hand in the hope of forestalling their usual argument. "We've been over this before, Jonathan. Unless I'm willing to starve, I've little choice in the matter."

"You could marry me."

"It's too soon. I'm still in mourning." Elizabeth's eyes never wavered. She was getting so good at telling the lie she almost believed it herself.

"Of course, of course, my dear. I quite understand. We'll speak of this at a later date." He was walking from the room as he suggested, "Why don't you warm yourself before the fire while I get your wrap and send for the carriage?"

Elizabeth watched the door close behind him and waited for his footsteps to recede before she made a dash for the massive mahogany desk. Like everything else in the room, it was littered with objects. Idly she wondered how Stacey was able to work with all that clutter.

Amid the papers, pens, and figurines sat his leather-bound appointment book, opened to the day's date. Elizabeth scanned the page and grinned at the last entry. Eleven o'clock was printed in black lettering and twice underlined. Considering the bold stroke of hand, the hour obviously held some importance. Now what could be happening tonight and at such an hour? Certainly it was too late for a business meeting. Perhaps it isn't business, she mused. Perhaps he is planning to entertain yet another guest. Elizabeth almost laughed aloud at that thought. Perhaps, but she doubted it. No, more likely another shipment was due in at that hour. The man was shrewd. No one would suspect another to follow so closely behind his last loss. No doubt he was counting on just that kind of thinking. Elizabeth shrugged. In any case someone would be there, waiting to find out. Perhaps Stacey's losses were becoming more than the mere inconvenience he'd first proclaimed. Elizabeth could only pray it was so.

She was standing before the fire long before she heard his approaching footsteps. A grin curved her lips. Since Stacey was some inches shorter than he'd readily admit, the raised heels he always wore struck the flooring and always alerted her to his coming. No doubt his movements could be heard throughout the house.

Jonathan leaped from the carriage. With his hands at Elizabeth's waist, he swung her to the ground amid a swirl of lacy white petticoats.

From the darkened corner of the porch, Tanner cursed the moonless night, positive he could have glimpsed a stocking-clad ankle and more had the moon and stars not been overcast. He watched now, as the two stood caught in the soft beam of light that shone from the parlor window and spoke in low tones. He couldn't catch what they were saying, but he wouldn't have felt the least prick of conscience had he been able to hear all.

In parting, Jonathan gave Elizabeth a light peck on the cheek. Tanner wondered why that gesture caused his hands to tighten into fists. God, you'd think he cared about the woman, what with the way he was acting lately. He almost laughed aloud at the thought. He was thirty-six years old, and though he'd lived most of his life alone, he'd never suffered for female companionship. He'd had his share. More than his share, if the truth be told. He was a goddamned fool to think of this woman as more than just a body to warm his bed. Damn! He didn't need complications at this late date. No, he didn't care who kissed her as long as he got his share.

A moment later Jonathan climbed into the carriage, and the closing of the door signaled the driver to get under way. Elizabeth watched the swaying vehicle until it was swallowed up by the night.

A low, surprisingly wicked chuckle escaped her as she suddenly spun about, clutched her full skirt with one hand, and bounded up the steps to her front door. She let out a tiny squeak of alarm as a match flared to life to her far right, then jumped back. The hand that had held her skirts was now pressed against a pounding heart as she fought the need to scream.

Elizabeth heaved a sigh of relief, her fear instantly put to rest, as the match illuminated Tanner Maddox sitting in a chair, lighting one of the cigarettes he rolled. She scowled at the man, her body stiffening with annoyance, and without thinking moved in his direction. "Have you nothing better to do with your evenings, Mr. Maddox, than sit in the dark and monitor your landlady's comings and goings?"

Tanner grinned. The dark night had not disguised the momentary fright he'd given her. He couldn't rightly blame her if she chose to bestow upon him the sharpness of her tongue. The thing was, he kept thinking of better uses for that intriguing organ. He again felt a stirring in his loins, not an uncommon happening when he was in her company. He wasn't a patient man. He wouldn't wait for long. He was going to have her, and a hell of a lot sooner than she expected. "Is that what I'm doing?"

"Aren't you?"

"Actually, I was just enjoying a cigarette before turning in." Elizabeth wasn't happy to realize her eyes were growing accustomed to the darkness, for it enabled her to see the wicked grin that flashed even white teeth. She cursed the ridiculous effect it had on her ability to breathe, then held on to the back of a chair when she felt shaky. "Care to join me?"

Elizabeth wasn't absolutely certain of what he was asking. Had he dared to ask her straight out to join him in his bed, or was he merely suggesting they share a smoke? Surely she wasn't mistaken. There was some hidden meaning behind those seemingly innocent words; yet she couldn't fathom even this man being so bold. Determined to ignore the suspicion that refused to subside, she chose to answer the question with, "I'm sorry. I don't smoke."

Tanner did a sorry job of hiding his laughter. He took a long drag and sighed with apparent pleasure. "You don't know what you're missing."

Had she been able to see no more than a vague outline of his form, she'd have easily detected the sly humor in his voice. It raised her hackles. She now knew he hadn't been talking about cigarettes. Instead of offering him a stiff good night, she found herself blurting out, "Shouldn't you be out doing what the citizens of this state pay you for?"

"You mean finding the fella behind the robberies?"

"Exactly."

He shrugged and took another drag on his cigarette. "Where would you suggest I start?"

"How about Pennsylvania?"

Tanner chuckled at her snide comment. "A bit far, don't you think? I don't imagine the man rides more than halfway across this country each time he takes a notion to rob a stage."

Elizabeth shrugged. "Who can say? You might find a clue there. Being the conscientious man you are, I'm sure you wouldn't want to miss anything."

Tanner grinned. "And you believe me to be conscientious. I wonder why?"

Elizabeth wondered at the thought herself. In the shadows of the porch, he looked thoroughly dangerous. He hadn't shaved, and the dark growth on his cheeks and chin only added to the already disreputable impression he made. Still, something about him spoke of determination, of honesty, of honor. There was a clearness to his eyes, a certain lazy confidence in his stance. She scowled at her thoughts. That was her imagination, of course. For some ridiculous reason she was ready to grant him qualities she couldn't know he possessed. She shook away these thoughts and concentrated on answering his question. "You stroke me as a man who wouldn't give up on a cause."

"Depends on the cause, don't you think?"

"What are you hinting at?" she asked as she took a step back, not liking the way his voice had suddenly dropped to a sinister, husky drawl.

"You wouldn't be afraid of me, would you, ma'am?"

"Of course not." Elizabeth returned as she shot him a condescending glare. "I merely commented that you can find something more interesting to do with your time than sit here in the dark."

Tanner came to his feet and flicked his cigarette into the yard. The tip glowed red as the butt arced through the air to land on the sparse grass that constituted Elizabeth's front yard. He came toward her then, his movements little more than a swagger, and smiled at the look of trepidation that suddenly came into her eyes. Elizabeth had no choice but to back up. His voice, low and seductive, was sending chills down her spine. "Now that you mention it, I can think of one or two things."

"Good," she said, refusing to recognize the meaning behind his words, and then she almost groaned as she realized the word had come out as a mortifying squeak. He was close. Too close. Elizabeth's heart pounded as she once again stepped back, only to have him follow her until her back was pressed against the door. She had to think of something. She couldn't just stand there inches from the man, breathing in his scent, feeling the heat of his body surround her, and say nothing. In a moment he'd kiss her, and she knew from past experience she hadn't the strength, or perhaps the will, to stop him. "Don't let me keep you if you're ready to retire for the night," she said. Then she almost groaned as a smile curved his lips. What in the world was the matter with her? She knew well enough what he had on his mind. How could she be so foolish as to bring up the very subject she wished to avoid?

"Funny you should mention it, but that was exactly what I had in mind." He let out a low delicious chuckle at seeing her pained expression. "You know it gets mighty cold at night," he remarked. "I was thinkin' —"

"I'll get you more blankets," she quickly retorted.

"Actually I was thinking of something better than blankets to keep me warm."

Elizabeth stiffened as she watched his head lower. "Don't," she said, her voice holding a sharper desperate edge.

"You don't love him," Tanner growled, as his warm breath slid over her cheek and down the side of her face. She shivered as his mustache brushed against her temple.

"Stop this," she said on a shaky indrawn breath.

His mouth lowered to her cheek and ear. "You don't love him, and he doesn't love you."

"You don't know that."

"Don't I?" He gave a low, knee-weakening chuckle. "No man . . . no real man," he amended, "would say good night with a tiny peck on the cheek."

Jonathan respects me. He knows I'm still in mourning."

Tanner drew back and watched her through eyes narrowed into slits. "Bull! He's not man enough for you."

"And I suppose you think you are?" she asked, her

fear of what his proximity was doing to her senses receding as anger began to take its place.

"Damn right, I am," he stated arrogantly. "I'd know how to kiss a woman like you."

"Like me? What do you mean, 'like me'?"

Tanner's voice softened; his eyes glittered with some unnamed need. He nodded his head and said simply, "You're different."

Elizabeth was dying to know what he meant by that; yet she was terrified of asking. "I'm in mourning," she finally managed, hoping it would make a difference to him. "Have you no decency?"

"You're wearing gray. How long has it been?"

She couldn't remember the lies she'd told. Not with him standing so close. Elizabeth silently cursed him for the confusion he'd wrought in her. "I can't imagine how that is any of your concern."

Tanner grinned. "Can't you? How long has it been since a man held you in his arms and loved you?"

Elizabeth's beautiful lips twisted into a scowl. "You make me sick."

"Like hell," he said as he closed the distance between them. Elizabeth gasped and knew a moment's panic. She'd never found herself in so dangerous a position, and yet, though obviously threatened, she could not maintain the fear. The hard strength of him pressing against her brought a soft sound from her lips and caused her knees to grow weak. She bit her lips and tried to turn from his gaze, but he cupped her jaw and forced her eyes to meet his. "I make you nervous. Maybe even a little scared. But one thing's for sure, I make you hot and hungry." He smiled almost gently as his knuckles ran over her cheek. "I can see it in your eyes. I can feel it in your body."

"Lord, but you are ridiculous," she said on a shallow breath. Her lungs were clamoring for air, but Elizabeth dared not breathe deeply lest her chest brush against his. "You should hear yourself. Why, it's laughable."

"Odd, but I didn't hear you laugh the last time I kissed you." His smile was wicked. "If I'm not mistaken, you even kissed me back."

Elizabeth suppressed a shudder as she fought against the silky smoothness of his voice. She'd never admit to that momentary loss of control. The man's arrogance was not to be borne. Certainly it needed no further boost from her. "I most certainly did not kiss you back," she denied coolly. "I merely accepted your kiss because you took me by surprise."

"Liar. If Belle hadn't interrupted us, we would have ended up in your bed, and you know it."

"My God, you are the most outrageously arrogant man I've ever had the misfortune to meet. How dare you come here and force your attentions on a lone, defenseless woman?"

"Defenseless?" Tanner laughed, his teeth flashing white against two days' growth of beard. Then his eyes hardened, and Elizabeth felt a chill race down her back. "Lady, you're about as defenseless as a mountain lion." His mouth tightened with anger. "And, for your information, I didn't force anything on you. After one kiss, you were all over me. Your mouth was hot and wet and wide open, begging for my tongue just like your body was begging for my—"

The sudden, sharp sound of a slap split the quiet night like a gunshot.

For a second, Elizabeth couldn't imagine what had caused the sound. A moment later she stared in surprise at her tingling palm. It was only then that she realized what she'd done. "Oh, no," she gasped, clearly aghast at the act. "I'm sorry. I didn't mean . . ."

The rest of her words were lost in the anger of his mouth. Without thinking, he'd taken her up against him and crushed her to the length of him. His lips were hard, almost brutal, as his tongue demanded entrance to her mouth. She tried to pull away, but his fingers threaded roughly through her hair, causing the pins to loosen, while he held her mouth with his. It wasn't until Tanner heard her soft moan that he realized he'd used excessive strength.

Elizabeth felt none of the pain she might have known at this less-than-gentle handling. Her mind was besieged with terror. Terror of her own response. She couldn't let this happen again. What he'd said was true. She had wanted . . . wanted . . . She didn't know what exactly it was that she'd wanted, but it definitely involved more of these kisses. She had to stop him now, before he again robbed her of thought. She had brought this sudden lapse of control upon herself with that slap. What she didn't know was how she was going to get herself out of an untenable position. She was no match for his strength, and she couldn't call out for help. She'd be mortified if anyone saw the situation she was in.

Tanner cursed and pulled his head back. Her eyes were wide, filled with fear. He couldn't know that the fear was directed at herself rather than him. "Don't look at me like that," he groaned as he eased his hold on her. Then his mouth gently touched bruised lips. The rough, exciting texture of his beard almost caused another moan to escape from her lips. "I won't hurt you. God, I'd never hurt you."

"Let me go," she said, breathless now, her eyes wide, her body stiff against his. God, please don't let him be gentle. She didn't know what she might do if he became gentle. She was not herself when he took her in his arms, when his mouth touched hers so sweetly.

"I will," he promised, "but first, God, first I have to . . ." His mouth met hers, interrupting his words. Elizabeth felt a moan well up inside her as his lips tenderly brushed hers. Back and forth, back and forth, a dozen times until she knew nothing but the sweet tingling of flesh and the aching need for more.

"You taste so sweet. God, I love the way you feel in my arms," he said against her mouth. He kissed her again and again, light nibbling kisses that asked for nothing more than to feel her mouth against his. Tanner heard her soft groan as her lips parted. He felt her knees give out just as he lifted her into his arms.

His first impulse was to carry her to her bed, but instantly he knew the error of his thoughts. He had no doubt that a few more kisses would see to the end of her already weakened resistance. The passion in her response made his mind reel. Their coupling promised to take him as close to heaven as he was ever likely to get. But what of tomorrow? Would she come to hate him when the passion eased and her senses returned? He couldn't chance it, for with every day that passed he grew more certain one night with her would never be enough. He'd want more. Much more.

Now Tanner groaned as his mouth left hers to nibble a burning path down her neck. It wasn't going to be easy, this seduction. He'd have to be careful. Elizabeth was a lady. It would take special coaxing to convince her to give up what he ached to possess.

Tanner, almost crazed with need for her, felt a moment's surprise as he suddenly realized he wanted her to need him. She had to come to him, wanting him as badly as he wanted her. His pride demanded at least that much. And until she did, he wouldn't know true satisfaction. "So soft," he murmured. "God, I love the taste of your mouth."

Elizabeth couldn't think. Still she was aware that he wasn't using force to hold her to him. She could break away and dash to the safety of her room. Why, then, didn't she move? Why did she sigh with pleasure as he sat her upon his lap? Why did she lean into him as he cuddled her gently against him?

Why didn't she stop him when he began to nuzzle her cheek, her jaw, her throat?

"Tell me you're not angry," he said, as he brushed his mustache over her jaw. "Tell me."

"I'm not angry," she breathed out obediently.

His tongue slid down the length of her throat, and Elizabeth sighed her pleasure as his mustache dried the damp inflamed skin. "You know I wouldn't hurt you, don't you?"

"I know," she whispered as her head, suddenly too heavy for her neck to support, fell back over his arm.

"Kiss me. I'll believe you mean it if you kiss me."

Elizabeth's eyes widened at his request. Her lips turned up at the corners. "A rogue," she said, laughing softly huskily. "I'm afraid I make it a habit never to kiss a rogue, Marshal Maddox."

Tanner's grin was devilishly persuasive. "Not even when he asks politely?"

Her lips came together primly as she lowered her gaze to the hollow of his throat. "If he were truly polite, he wouldn't ask."

"You mean he'd simply do the kissing?"

Her gaze raised to his again. Elizabeth would never know the sharp pang that tightened his chest at that innocent look. "I mean kissing wouldn't enter his mind."

Tanner chuckled. "It's clear to see you know little of the workings of a man's mind. I'm never with you that I don't think of kissing—and more."

"Never?" she asked in disbelief.

"Never," he swore, so solemnly she had no choice but to believe.

"Does this happen often?"

Tanner chuckled wickedly, his mouth continuing its tantalizing exploration of her neck and shoulder. Elizabeth hadn't noticed the unbuttoning of her bodice. Even now she gave no thought to how he managed to kiss her where she had moments before been demurely covered. "I haven't had it happen before," he said as his mouth brushed over a particularly sensitive spot. He heard her low moan of delight. "You like that?"

"Mmmmm," she breathed, his words hardly registering over the delicious sensations flooding her being.

"Tell me where else."

"We shouldn't be doing this. There," she said on a breathless sigh.

God, she was so warm and soft. Her response was almost more than he could resist. He trembled, hardly able to bear the strain of holding his need in check. A soft gasp left her parted lips as his mouth slid to her shoulder. "Oh yes," she groaned, unconsciously arching her throat toward his lips, "and there."

"We have to stop," she murmured, between kisses that threatened the last of her sanity. "I should go in," she whispered dreamily as his mouth stole the last of her breath.

Another button opened and she was exposed to his gaze. Elizabeth heard a muttered groan that bordered on despair as he pulled back. His breathing grew harsher, more labored. Her eyes opened to find his gaze upon her near nakedness. No man had ever seen her like this. Even in the heat of passion, Elizabeth's cheeks grew red as he luxuriated in the sight of her chemise and the sweet rounded curves of breasts swelling above the white material.

His gaze moved to lock with hers. Purposely, daringly, his finger grazed the tips of her breasts covered only by the thin cotton of the chemise. He smiled as they instantly hardened and gasped. "I'm going to kiss you there," he promised. "And when I do, you'll feel like you're melting." He felt her stiffen, even as her heart threatened to break through the wall of her chest. "Not now," he crooned, easing away her sudden alarm. "But soon. I'm going to touch you there with my tongue."

"No!" She struggled to free herself from his arms and almost sprang to her feet. For a second she seemed unable to stand, but with the help of the porch railing and iron determination she forced her legs to bear her weight. Her cheeks blazed with anger that he should speak so daringly. Trembling fingers worked obstinate buttons into place. "You shouldn't say such things."

Tanner had allowed her to come to her feet. She stood before him now, her head thrown back proudly, her hair in appealing disarray, her eyes glittering in resentment. She had to clear her throat twice before the words would come. "Never! Never speak to me like that again."

Tanner smiled. God, but she was lovely. It took every bit of his control for him to sit there and pretend that these intimate moments were less than earth-shattering. He leaned back comfortably and brought his right ankle to rest on his left knee. His eyes never left hers as he began to roll another cigarette. "I'm telling you so you'll think on it. So you'll be ready, eager for it the next time."

"There'll be no next time. And I won't think of it. No decent woman would."

His eyes glowed like black fire in the shadows as he promised, "You will. You'll think about it. You'll dream about it. And when you do, I'll know."

Chapter Five

He couldn't, of course. The man was arrogant beyond belief to declare that he could. Despite his announcement, it was impossible for anyone to know another's thoughts. Elizabeth berated her own doubts. His whispered tauntings don't matter, nor does his staring into your eyes, she told herself. He can see only what you allow. She shook herself to get rid of her disturbing thoughts. Lord, she couldn't let him do this to her. She couldn't let her fascination with him destroy what she'd worked so hard to accomplish.

Barefoot, Elizabeth moved through the dark, daring to light no candle at this late hour. At any rate, light was unnecessary, for she knew where everything was. She'd done this a dozen times and had not even needed the glow of the moon to aid her in dressing.

She made not a sound as she continued about her preparations. Her arms slid into a black shirt. Tight matching trousers were easily pulled up over naked legs and then belted at her waist. Seconds later a gun belt was secured about slender hips, and the heavy weapon was strapped to her thigh. Her long hair was pushed under a wide-brimmed black hat. Despite her diminutive size and the obvious shapeliness of her form, Elizabeth knew the disguise went far toward concealing the fact that she was a woman.

With boots in hand to guard against unnecessary sound, she slipped onto the window ledge and jumped to the ground. The soft thud of bare feet upon soft earth did not carry in the night. She leaned against the wall of the house, waiting for her heart to return to its normal rhythm. Close to his open window, she listened for any stirring within.

Nothing.

Crouched by the whitewashed picket fence, she stopped to slip on her boots. Then, bent almost in half, she ran the length of the fence and entered the small barn by its back door. Raven snickered in welcome at hearing her footsteps, and Elizabeth smiled as she reached out to give his neck a soothing caress. "You heard me, did you, boy?" she asked as she tried to control the pounding of her heart and the harshness of her breathing.

Elizabeth knew it was less the fear of being discovered by her new boarders than the excitement that always filled her during these moments. It never failed to amaze her that she found the nerve. Never in her life had she done anything so daring. Never had she thought of stealing another's belonging. She smiled as she saddled her horse. But she didn't steal his belongings, did she?

By rights, Stacey couldn't lay claim to any of the booty. The truth of the matter was, he'd stolen from the Army, put the blame on her father, destroyed her family's good name, and after the scandal had died down he'd left the service and bought himself a silver mine. Elizabeth had known the hatred and curses she'd bestowed upon him amounted to less than nothing, and because the law had not brought Stacey to justice, doing so became the one purpose in her life. She was determined to see to it that he did not enjoy his larcenous proceeds.

The horse was soon saddled, and she left the barn the way she'd entered. One hand on Raven's bridle, she led him along the shore of the gently flowing river, far from the house. The dwelling on the outskirts of town was long since cloaked in darkness when she finally mounted the stallion and raced over the countryside, coming to a stop about three miles away.

The dirt road had been marked by heavy wagon wheels and horses' hooves. She sat back in her saddle, willing her hands to stop shaking, her breathing to become even. She began her wait.

Alone in the dark, Elizabeth was besieged by thoughts of capture. She wasn't afraid, nor did she have any illusions about the penalty being less stringent because of her sex. She had no doubt that Marshal Maddox would one day find her out. It was highly unlikely he could live under her roof and never suspect the truth. Even though he might be taken with her, he was a man of no little intelligence and he had sworn to uphold the law. He'd never shy away from what that entailed.

Elizabeth sighed. Despite her lack of experience, she knew she hadn't the strength to resist him indefinitely. Each day they grew closer, nearer to the point where she'd gladly see him in her bed. She almost longed for it now.

She gave a slight shake of her head. No matter how enticing the thought, involvement with him was out of the question. She'd have to ask him to leave soon. It would be bad enough when he found out the truth. It would be worse if he was her lover.

Never! He could never become her lover. He'd know then. He'd know she wasn't the widow she pretended to be.

She was only asking for trouble by indulging in these sinful thoughts. Her mind was made up. She'd ask him to leave at the first opportunity. A wry half-smile lifted one corner of her mouth as she fingered the gun at her hip. Perhaps she'd be killed before she got the chance. Elizabeth accepted the knowledge that these nightly excursions could end in tragedy. The thought of death should have chilled her. It did not. She'd leave no one behind. Thanks to Stacey, she'd already lost all who would care about her passing. What remained to her was to see to this man's destruction. And she'd do just that for as long as her wits and her luck held out.

Elizabeth stiffened as she heard a carriage approaching. It had to be, for it was pulled by only two horses. Evidently the stage wasn't making a special run. Was this simply some unsuspecting traveler? She shook her head at the thought. No one would be so foolhardy as to brave the dangers of this land at night unless the mission be a grave one. Had Stacey hired his own transportation? Elizabeth felt a shiver of apprehension. Was this a trap?

Tanner Maddox silently cursed the unyielding wooden seat and useless springs of the old wagon as his backside became intimately acquainted with every rock, pebble, and rut in the road. His jaw clamped tight against the jarring, his long fingers curved around the edge of the seat lest he be thrown free, he wondered if the wheels were indeed as round as they had appeared.

"Are you sure we're on the road?" he asked after a particularly shattering jolt that seemed to have rattled his insides loose.

Amos nodded. "It's the wagon. The springs are gone."

Tanner grunted in response, while silently praying the night's mission was worth such torture. If not, another plan would have to be set into action. He wasn't about to subject himself to a ride like this again.

* * *

Some distance from the road, Elizabeth slid off her horse and tied the reins to a nearby bush. On silent feet, she crossed the road and lay flat upon the ground, near the cover of a large rock. The wagon was coming closer. She heard a man curse, his voice heavy with suffering, while another yelled louder than the curse for him to be quiet.

A smile curved her lips. Yes, she had hit upon the right vehicle. Surely no other traveled in secrecy. From the sound of it, they'd be upon her within seconds. Elizabeth reached for her gun and squeezed off a shot, aiming toward the sky. The night suddenly exploded with curses and answering shots. "Stupid bastard! Why did you stop like that?" Tanner yelled, holding on for dear life as the rickety wagon came to a sudden jarring stop.

Elizabeth frowned. She'd heard that voice somewhere before, but it was unrecognizable now, so tight with anger it was.

"What was I supposed to do? Someone shot at us."

"Move this goddamned wagon before I finish the job." Tanner grunted as he righted himself.

"Where is he?" a man yelled from the back of the wagon.

"Do you see anything?" cried another. Elizabeth gasped. Was that Dave? Was this a trap after all? Was there, in fact, no gold to be taken?

Another two shots were fired.

"Jesus! Don't go shooting at shadows. You're going to kill one of us. Spread out and wait. He'll have to make a move sooner or later."

Elizabeth listened to the sounds of booted feet hitting the ground as the men jumped from the wagon and ran in three directions. And then the night was still. Her heart pounded with terror. She had to get away, but she'd left her horse across the road. She would have to go around these men to get to Raven. She breathed a woeful sigh. She didn't have a chance. How was she to outwit four men? What was she going to do?

"Didn't I tell you to move this wagon?" the familiar voice bellowed. "Wait for us up a ways."

Elizabeth whispered a silent prayer of thanks that the night was blacker than pitch. True, she couldn't see a foot in front of her. But if she couldn't see, neither could they. The three men remaining vanished as the fourth drove the wagon on.

She felt a moment's panic—she'd never known such fear—and almost came to her feet to run blindly for her horse. By degrees, though, she managed to calm that wild impulse. Desperate, she tried to think. She had to get to her horse. But how? Three men lay in wait, ready to fire at the slightest movement or sound. Elizabeth took a deep calming breath, forcing aside the terror that threatened to overcome rational thought. She had to keep her wits about her. One mistake could be her last. If she circled behind the men and got to her horse before they noticed the animal, she just might have a chance. They had no horses. They'd never find her once she mounted Raven.

She eased herself up into a sitting position, praying the sounds made by shifting pebbles and dirt weren't as loud as they seemed to her. In the shadow of the rock, ·she removed her boots. Leaving them behind, she hobbled off, bent as close to the ground as possible. Over sand and pebbles, she worked her way along, biting her lips to keep back grunts when her toes struck rocks. Once she judged the road to be a good distance behind her, she moved in a half-circle in the opposite direction from the one the wagon had taken, and crossed the road, hoping she was far enough behind the men to silently retrieve her horse and be on her way.

She almost fell over him, so well did he blend into the shadows. She dared not retrace her steps. A loose pebble, a broken twig—anything—could give her away. Elizabeth's heart was pounding so hard she could hardly breathe. She couldn't imagine why he didn't hear it. Slowly, silently, she pulled her gun from the holster and firmly pressed it to the man's back. In a voice that shook with terror, she whispered, "Real easy, lay your gun down and slide back from it."

The man muttered an obscene curse and then stiffened, every muscle in his body readied to turn and pounce upon the villain above him, but the pressure of the gun on his back quickly dissuaded him from that notion.

Elizabeth waited as he complied with her orders,

waited, in fact, until he had moved an arm's length away from his weapon before she picked it up and threw it across the road. One of the men fired his gun at the noise the pistol made upon landing.

The man lying at her feet cursed again, the venom in his voice sending a chill up Elizabeth's spine. "Call your friend over here," she said, remembering — she didn't know how — to keep her voice low and whispery.

"Dave, get over here," he said.

A moment later a man came running through the dark, crouched down. "What?" he asked, and when there was no answer he inquired, "Maddox, where the hell are you?"

Elizabeth almost laughed as she realized it was Tanner who lay at her feet. "He's on the ground to your left. I wouldn't," she warned as she pressed her pistol into Dave's back. "Drop the gun and lie down next to him."

This is getting easier by the minute, she thought, almost enjoying herself. She had to force herself to remember she was in a very serious position. She didn't dare let her guard down for a second. Things might appear simple at the moment, but everything could change in a heartbeat.

One more to go. The problem was, how was she going to prevent these men from chasing her down before she reached her horse? She had to tie them up, at least for a few minutes, or they'd be on her like a pack of wolves.

The last man was the deputy sheriff. Luke Brown wasn't much of a deputy, being drunk most of the time, but in a town as crime-free as Willowbrook, with the exception of these latest happenings, of course, there wasn't much law enforcement needed. Luke gave her less trouble than the first two. When called, he came immediately and he threw down his gun before she even ordered him to do it.

"Take off your boots," Elizabeth ordered. Then she watched as all three men rolled onto their backs and sat up. Most especially she watched Tanner. She knew he meant to throw a boot at her. Even in the blackness she could make out the slight tensing of his shoulders. "Don't even think it, Marshal," she warned in a loud whisper. "Someone's sure to get hurt if this gun goes off." She relaxed just a bit as he and the other two men threw their boots behind them.

"Each of you pull your holster thong free and tie your ankle to the ankle of the man next to you."

"You're not going to get away with this," Maddox warned. "I'll get you one of these days."

"I know," she said in a harsh whisper, for she had no doubt that these nocturnal escapades would be brought to an end. Her luck couldn't hold out indefinitely. "But not tonight." A moment later she was gone.

Amid vicious curses, as the men struggled to untie the rawhide string, they heard a horse galloping over the countryside.

Careless of the danger involved, Elizabeth rode like the devil himself was in pursuit. Within minutes she was at her barn, both rider and steed straining for breath by the time she dismounted. Never in her life had she worked so fast. Raven was brushed down and in his stall within minutes.

She entered the house as she had left it. Her clothing was instantly discarded and shoved beneath her bed. She'd just managed to pull a nightdress over her head and slide beneath the covers when she heard a wagon rattle by her house and into town.

She sighed with relief, trying to ignore the niggling fear that made her uneasy, as the night's events came to mind. She knew, of course, it had been a trap. But what did that mean? Did Jonathan suspect her? Was that why he had left his appointment book lying open? Had he expected her to look?

Elizabeth shivered as fear spread through her. Was it all over? Would Marshal Maddox come now to take her away? No. She shook her head, trying to clear her thoughts. He didn't know. He would have said something if he had. Lord, he'd been angry enough to have called down all manner of curses upon her. Surely, had he known, he would have mentioned her by name.

Elizabeth sighed as she rolled onto her back and stared into the pitch darkness. She'd come as close to being caught as she cared to, and yet she knew she wouldn't quit until she had brought about Stacey's ruin. She would honor her pledge, no matter the cost. The suffering she was sure to know couldn't compare to what she'd already gone through. Jonathan Stacey couldn't be allowed to live in peace after what he'd done.

Tanner breathed a sigh of sheer exhaustion as he dismounted. He would have asked Jason to see to his horse, but the man was polishing off a bottle as he attempted to whitewash the barn. Tanner shook his head. He wasn't going to trust a drunk with the care of Chester. The animal meant too much to him.

Tanner sighed again and stiffly went about the chore of seeing to his horse. God, he was tired. He hadn't slept three hours in more than forty-eight. Idly he wondered if his landlady supplied her boarders with tubs of water. His heart began to pound with anticipation at the thought of seeing her again. He'd only been gone two days, and he was amazed at how badly he'd missed her. He needed to bathe, to eat and sleep, but most of all, he needed to see Elizabeth.

"You wouldn't have any coffee left, would you, ma'am?" he asked as he moved silently into her kitchen.

With a soft cry of alarm, Elizabeth spun away from the sink, a wet hand coming to rest against her breast as if by pressing it she could prevent her heart from crashing through the walls of her chest.

"I didn't hear you."

Tanner nodded, his gaze filled with hunger. How had it come almost as a shock to see her? Why hadn't he remembered how beautiful she was? "Sorry. I took off my spurs."

Elizabeth's gaze automatically went to his booted feet. She nodded. "You were gone so long, I thought—"

"You thought I'd left? Without seeing you?" he asked, his tone clearly telling her that the notion was impossible. His tongue came out to lick at parched lips, and his voice suddenly became husky and deep as they stared, across the width of the kitchen, into one another's eyes. "I've been in the saddle for two days straight . . . on nothing but a wild-goose chase." He shrugged, his disgust evident. "We set a trap, but got caught in it ourselves."

"What happened?"

"Damned if I know. Is Belle around?"

Elizabeth shook her head. "She's at the bank."

Tanner nodded, knowing if there was anything unusual in the bank's books, Belle would find it, no matter how deep she had to dig. "I know it's too late for breakfast, but do you think you could rustle me up somethin'?"

Elizabeth smiled. The marshal looked ready to fall asleep on his feet. "Sit down."

He shook his head. "I'd better not. I want to clean up. If I sit . . ." He sighed as he rubbed a hand over his face, leaving the rest of the sentence unfinished.

"You got a tub around here?"

"On the back porch. Pull it in, and I'll set water to boiling."

Elizabeth had a plate of ham and eggs, along with a half-dozen biscuits and fresh butter sitting in front of him by the time he'd downed half his coffee. Tanner's hungry gaze took in the tempting food even as he wondered if he had the energy to eat.

"Tell me what happened," she said as she emptied the first pot of water into the tub.

"We set a trap for the thief, two nights ago. He's a wily little thing. Got clean away."

"That's too bad," Elizabeth commiserated, while praying she was hiding her own knowledge of the situation. "Was anyone hurt?"

"No. If you don't count wounded pride."

Elizabeth smiled. "I'm sure you did the best you could. That's nothing to be ashamed of."

Tanner shook his head, his eyes starting to close as he downed the last of his coffee. "If you knew how small he is. God, I get mad every time I think I was outsmarted by such a little fella."

"You don't believe intelligence is necessarily in proportion to a person's size?"

"No, but it's so . . ."

Elizabeth silently laughed at his obvious frustration. "Why don't you forget about it for now. Maybe after you've had some sleep you'll be able to think more clearly."

"There was something familiar about the little

runt." Tanner's brow furrowed. "About his voice. I know him. I know that voice. If I could just remember where I heard it before."

"Your bath is ready," she said quickly, hoping to take his mind from such dangerous thoughts. She was suddenly breathless with fear. How long could she go on like this? How long would it be before he knew the "little fella" was in truth a woman?

"Do you know what you're doing?" he said, suddenly standing directly behind her, his hands holding tightly to her shoulders.

Here it comes. Terror gripped Elizabeth. In her life she'd never known such dread, yet she was determined to take whatever punishment the law saw fit to mete out. "What?" she murmured huskily.

Tanner turned her to face him. "You're making yourself indispensable."

Elizabeth couldn't think for a moment. She had expected condemnation, not pretty words, and his smooth teasing tone left her momentarily confused. She stared stupidly into his smiling face and forced wobbly knees to hold her up. She gave her head a slight shake. Lord, how was she going to live through this kind of terror? If she was this afraid now, how was she going to make it through her actual capture? Elizabeth pushed aside the horror that thought provoked. There was no sense thinking on it now. What would come to pass, would come to pass. "You're tired," she finally responded. "The next time you need to bathe, you'll have to prepare your own bath."

Tanner grinned, his eyes taking on a hopeful gleam. "Do you mean to bathe me?"

Elizabeth's eyes widened, and her cheeks grew pink as she took in the obvious invitation. "I think you can manage on your own."

"You don't know how tired I am," his eyes were dark, definitely slumberous, but filled with something she couldn't define. Something that set her pulse to pounding.

"I'll be sitting outside," she said, as she moved out of his reach. "Call when you've finished. I have to get back to preparing supper."

Elizabeth sat on the porch for a time. Then she paced. Finally she sat again. After consulting the timepiece pinned to her blouse, she walked around the house, took the broom that leaned against the wall near the back door, and swept off the front porch and steps. Again she looked at her watch. He'd been in the tub for more than half an hour. Perhaps he had already taken himself off to bed and had forgotten to call out to her.

Filled with trepidation, Elizabeth forced herself to enter the house. All was quiet. He must be sleeping, she thought. Please let him be sleeping. She felt a wave of relief as a soft snore broke the silence, and she smiled. But her smile became a parody when she realized the snoring sounds were coming from her kitchen. Elizabeth groaned as she entered that room and found him sound asleep in her tub.

Good Lord! What was she supposed to do? She couldn't leave him there. Miss Dunlap would have an attack of apoplexy if she came in and found him thus. Actually, Elizabeth wasn't taking the situation in stride either.

For a moment she thought of calling for help. Perhaps Dave would assist the man into bed. Instantly she thought better of that notion. The story of a naked man in her kitchen would be all over town within minutes. Elizabeth had gone out of her way to ensure her reputation. She wasn't about to become the subject of the town's gossipmongers, just because this man was so tired he'd fallen asleep.

"Marshal," she called from behind him. "Marshal, wake up. You fell asleep in the tub."

Nothing. If one didn't take into account the fact that his snores were growing in volume.

"Marshal," she said again, her voice decidedly louder. "You can not sleep here. Wake up!"

Still no reaction.

Elizabeth murmured a most unladylike word as she moved farther into the room, took the towel that lay ready for him, and held it before her to prevent seeing something she'd rather not be exposed to. She nudged his shoulder gently with her knee, and then again. "Will you please wake up?"

Tanner murmured something unintelligible.

"Marshal," she said, bending low so she spoke directly into his ear. "Get up. You have to go to bed."

"Mmmm," he muttered, one arm reaching lazily

around her waist and suddenly pulling her into the tub with him.

Elizabeth let out a shriek as the now-cool water penetrated her skirt, petticoats, and drawers. "What do you think you're doing?"

"What?" he asked sleepily.

She tried to get a grip on something, to get leverage, without touching his naked chest, so she might pull herself out; but even when she grasped the edge of the tub, he refused to relinquish his hold on her. "Let go of me this instant!" Elizabeth demanded.

"What?" he said again, still partly asleep. Then his eyes blinked open and he noticed that she was sitting on his lap in a tub—with all her clothes on. "What are you doing?"

"What am *I* doing?" she asked, clearly outraged. "I'm trying to get out of this tub. Let me go!"

"Why did you get in in the first place?"

"I didn't get in. You pulled me in."

Tanner helped her from the tub and then came to his feet. A tender smile curved his lips as he watched her dry herself with his towel. "Do you have another one?"

"Another what?" she asked as she raised her head. Since he was standing in the tub, and she had bent slightly at the waist, her eyes came even with the tops of his thighs. She blinked, not believing the sight before her. A moment later she heard some-one—had she done it?—utter a low groan; her eyes grew round and her cheeks burned.

"Another towel," he said easily as if he usually stood before a woman stark naked.

Elizabeth spun from the sight of him, but the water that had dripped from her clothing to puddle on the floor caused her to slip. As her heels slid out from beneath her, she fell back. Strong hands held her against what she knew was bare skin, and a low laugh came from deep in his throat. "Are you sure you ain't lookin' to join me in my bath?"

"I slipped. The floor's wet," she said, her explanation as stiff as her body felt.

"Are you goin' to get me a towel?" Tanner asked as his lips brushed against her temple.

"Here," she said slapping him in the face as she swung the sodden material.

"A dry one?" he said as he dropped the towel to the floor.

Elizabeth simply nodded her head. Already embarrassed beyond belief, she dared not trust herself to answer.

She was in her room gathering an armload of towels when she heard Belle's laughter. "You waiting for a train or somethin'?"

There was a sharp curse, followed by the splashing water. "What the hell are you doin' back?"

"Didn't expect company, I take it."

"Are you finished for the day?"

Belle laughed again. "Depends on what you've got in mind."

"Cut it out, Belle," Tanner snapped, annoyed to

112

feel his cheeks growing red. "You're not the least bit amusing."

"Damn! I never thought I'd live to see the day when Tanner Maddox blushed."

Elizabeth entered the kitchen to find Tanner protectively holding his dirty trousers against his naked front. Belle's gaze shifted to her obviously embarrassed landlady. "Damn," she muttered. "Did I interrupt something again?"

"Maybe you should think about getting a room at the saloon," Tanner offered as he wrapped a towel around his hips and began to gather up his clothing from the floor.

"Maybe you both should," Elizabeth declared as she walked regally out of the room.

Chapter Six

They came at night, for darkness best befitted these monsters spawned of Satan.

From the shadow of an outbuilding, Jason watched the lone, darkly cloaked figure enter the cabin. The hinges made no sound as the door closed softly behind him. But had the door caught the swift breeze and slammed it couldn't have been heard over the pounding of his blood.

The night was peacefully quiet. A breeze, warm and sweet, soughed softly as it moved over the tall grass that surrounded the wooden shack. Jason might have moved closer to peer through a window, to convince himself of the evil he knew to be conducted within, but he dared not. Two men armed with rifles and handguns guarded the building. They paced in the darkness, smoking cigarettes and silently moving about as they waited for those inside to finish their evil task.

He wondered if the guards knew what went on in the shack. He wondered if they cared, then shook his head, knowing they did not. All these men cared about were the rewards they got for a job well done. It mattered little to them who got hurt in the process.

A bitter, silent laugh slid past his tight throat, and a sneer twisted his thin lips. He felt no measure of amazement that he dared to sit in judgment now. Once he had been a religious man. He'd had his own small congregation. He'd preached the word of God and had followed His teachings. Followed them until he was put to the ultimate test. Unlike Job, he'd failed it.

Now, his teachings forgotten, his life shattered, Jason believed those past years a farce. How could he have accepted as true the meaningless words written by old men who knew nothing of the real horrors life held for some.

"Turn the other cheek." He almost laughed aloud. "Forgive seventy times seven." He shook his head and chuckled bitterly. Oh, he'd forgive all right. The moment that monster lay dead at his feet.

But that wouldn't happen on this night. Jason hadn't a chance to get to him while he was guarded. The armed men would cut him down the moment he showed himself. He'd wait. He was a patient man. One day soon he'd find a way.

Elizabeth looked over the rim of her cup, directly into warm blue eyes. Eyes that sparkled with humor. Eyes that had haunted her sleep for more than two weeks. As from the first, they set her heart to pound-

115

ing. They brought warmth to her cheeks and stirred some unnamed emotion within her breast.

He'd shaved. His smooth, brown cheeks and jaw almost begged for the touch of a woman's hand . . . or lips. The creases that framed his mouth, like slashes of a dimple, deepened when he smiled. If she closed her eyes she could almost feel the brush of his silky mustache against her skin. Elizabeth forced back the indecent need that suddenly filled her, and she diverted her gaze from temptation to the cup in her hand.

Lord, but he is beautiful. She had tried all afternoon and evening to forget that fiasco in her kitchen. She had especially tried to forget how the sight of his glistening wet skin had nearly robbed her of the power to speak. Darkened by the sun, it covered bulging muscles, and his wide chest, narrow hips, and long legs were, in turn, covered by a smattering of dark curly hair that almost cried out to be touched. She trembled, first in shock and now in remembrance of the most beautiful sight she'd ever seen. His naked maleness was stamped forever on her mind. She was sure to burn in hell for her wicked thoughts, for the yearning that had yet to abate. Just the memory of him standing naked in the kitchen stirred her. It brought on an ache she hadn't the power to control or appease.

"Elizabeth," he began almost hesitantly, nervously biting his bottom lip as he tried to find the right words. "I know you're upset. I swear I didn't mean to fall asleep in the tub. I promise it won't happen—"

"Why are you still here?" She was fighting against

116

the need to go to him, to be held in his arms, to be pressed against a body she longed to touch. "I thought you would have taken your things and left hours ago."

"Founders Day is tomorrow," he answered quickly. "The rooms above the saloon are taken. Probably will be for the rest of the week."

Elizabeth nodded as she came to her feet. She should have known it wouldn't be easy to rid herself of this temptation. But she would do it. She only had to keep her distance for a few more days. Surely some soul would need to return to his home before the week-long festivities ended. And then? she asked herself. And then he'd be gone. She moved to the sink and pumped water into a small pan. With a deep breath, she sought to calm the wild ragings within her. A moment later she began washing the evening meal's dishes. "After the festivities then. Once there's room, I expect you to leave."

"Elizabeth, I . . ."

She spun around, soapy water dripping from her hands onto the clean floor. "Marshal Maddox, there's no need to discuss this further. I simply want you out of my house."

"Why?" he asked, as he moved toward her. "Why are you so desperate to see me gone?"

"It's my house. I don't owe you an explanation."

"Why, Elizabeth?" he demanded when she turned back to her chore. He was standing directly behind her now. She could feel him towering over her, surrounding her. His clean breath disturbed the hairs

117

that had escaped their pins to lie against her cheek. "What are you afraid of?"

"Not you surely," she said, her voice barely above a whisper as she tried to ignore the scent of horse, leather, tobacco, and, worst of all, clean man. He wasn't touching her, but he might just as well have been. Surely touching would wreak no less havoc upon her senses.

"I didn't think so," he agreed. "Then it must be you you're afraid of."

"Me?" She laughed with false bravado. "Shall I ask myself to leave then?"

Tanner ignored her sarcasm. He knew she was afraid of what she felt for him. He could see the fear and the desire in her eyes. What he had to do was get her to admit to it. It was ridiculous that two adults couldn't give in to the pull between them and enjoy what each had to offer. His voice was low and sultry as he breathed the words close to her ear. "It matters little where I go. We both know the strength of what we feel for each other will not ease with space."

Elizabeth found herself biting her lip to keep a groan at bay. It took her a moment, but she finally got herself under control. Her back stiffened with resolve. She couldn't let this happen. His presence put all her plans in jeopardy. And when he found out the truth, as he most surely would, he'd only hate her for her deception. "You are talking in riddles. We feel nothing for each other."

"Truly?" he asked. "Then why can't you face me?"

"But I can face you, Marshal Maddox," she retorted, while giving silent thanks that her voice sounded cool and aloof. She pumped clean water into the pan. "I simply choose not to."

"Because you're afraid."

Elizabeth spun around. His taunting words seemed to unleash all her pent-up emotions. Her control had snapped. Angry that he dared to insist, she almost snarled as she allowed her rage to spill out, "Lord, you are insufferable. How dare you come to my house and accost—"

"Accost?" Without moving his feet, he leaned back a bit so he might better see her expression. Suddenly he laughed down at her. "Is that what I'm doing?" His eyes darkened with a mysterious gleam. "Or is it what you want me to do?"

"What I want you to do is to get out."

"Liar."

"Why, you . . ."

Tanner grabbed her flying hand, catching it at the wrist just inches from his face. He forced it behind her back. "Don't try that again, Elizabeth. I can't promise to be pleasant if I'm slapped again."

Elizabeth silently cursed her unthinking action. She knew she'd made a serious error. And because of that she was now pinned against him, held captive, her two hands clasped behind her back and held by one of his. "I've yet to see you pleasant, Marshal," she taunted bravely.

"Haven't you?" he asked. His hips pressed hers

119

against the sink, his free hand moving to dislodge the pins in her hair. Dark and lustrous and smooth, it fell down her back. Tanner had touched it before, twice before. Now he knew he'd never get enough of touching it. He couldn't keep back the groan that came to his lips as the silken strands slid between his fingers.

He pulled at them, just enough so that her mouth was raised to his. His lips hovered over hers as she muttered, trying for a sarcasm she could not achieve, "What should I do now? Go all aflutter over your supposed charm?"

Tanner grinned, knowing, despite her denial, she was suffering much the same yearnings as he. Yearnings that threatened their very sanity if they couldn't soon find appeasement. "Do what you feel like doing."

"I feel like hitting you over the head with my frying pan."

"Do you?" he asked, choking back a laugh. He released her, but his hands moved to the edge of the sink and he leaned forward, forcing Elizabeth to lean back in order to keep any distance between them. She wasn't unaware that her hips were trapped between his hands. The knowledge that he only had to raise his thumbs a fraction to caress her caused the pulse in her throat to beat wildly. His eyes were alight with taunting humor. "Then by all means, do it."

They stared at each other for a long moment. The house was silent but for the sounds of their breathing. Her lips trembled at the corners as she tried to keep a smile at bay. "Beast," she said as cool, wet, soapy hands came up to push at his chest.

Tanner laughed as he suddenly grabbed her waist and lifted her high above his head. "God, but you are adorable," he said, swinging her in a dizzying circle.

"Much too adorable to resist," he murmured as he suddenly stood very still and allowed her body to slide down the length of his.

"You shouldn't do this," she said, and then gulped as she watched her breasts come ever closer to his mouth.

"Do what?" he asked as his gaze threatened to incinerate her neatly buttoned blouse.

"Hold me this close," she said, but she didn't recognize her own voice. "Put me down."

"I am."

"Not like this," she moaned as his mouth closed over the tip of her breast. Her body jerked with the shock of his touch. She could feel heat blazing through her clothing. God, what would it be like if . . . She couldn't allow the thought.

She buried her fingers in his hair. It felt silky and cool. "Tanner," she whispered, unconsciously arching her back so she was forced closer to his delicious heat. In another minute she wasn't going to be able to stop him. Her body trembled as he held her tightly against him.

"Don't be afraid, sweetheart," he said taking her shivering for fear. "I only want to kiss you. Nothing else will happen."

And then he did just that, and Elizabeth couldn't hold back low whimpers of pleasure. She knew her feet had touched the floor, but she couldn't have stood on her own if not doing so would have cost her life. His lips gently brushed hers. His mustache, silky and smooth, nearly drove her out of her mind. Back and forth, his lips dragging at her flesh as if testing its softness, its pliability. And when she at last parted her lips, his tongue took every advantage. Deep, deep into her mouth it moved to rediscover the wonder of her texture and taste.

"I should call the sheriff," she said when he released her lips to send tingling chills down her back by kissing her ear and neck.

"Why? Do you think he wants to see this?" Tanner teased.

Elizabeth heard a girlish giggle and realized, with no little surprise, it had come from her. Lord, it had been so long since she had felt free to laugh like that. "I meant call the sheriff so he could—"

"Kiss you?" he inquired, his lips so close they touched hers when he spoke. "Not a chance."

"David is married," she said disapprovingly, and so simply that Tanner felt a strange tightening in the vicinity of his heart. Was she so innocent in the ways of men that she assumed married men did not lust for any but their wives?

"Why don't we?"

"What?"

"Get married," he said. The words just seemed to slip out. He hadn't meant to say them, but once he had done so, the idea took hold and he couldn't think of a lovelier notion. He hadn't thought he'd ever marry again. Not for ten years had he wanted a woman like this. Not since the night he had believed his life had ended, when Sarah and their child had died.

Elizabeth's eyes widened as she took in his words. A moment later she smiled at seeing his look of surprise. It was obvious he hadn't meant to ask her to marry him. He looked as shocked as she felt.

"You're not serious?"

Tanner realized he might have been thinking on other matters, like the warm wetness of her mouth and the smooth silkiness of her skin, when he'd muttered the words, but he had meant them. "I am. I want you."

"Do you ask all the ladies you want to marry you?"

Tanner laughed as his lips nuzzled the warmth of her throat. "It's not a habit of mine."

"How many have you asked?"

"Just one. I was married ten years ago. She died." His words were almost muffled by her skin. "How often have you been asked?"

Forgetting completely her former beaus and Stacey's recent proposals, Elizabeth dreamily entertained the impossible notion for a moment before she answered, "I'm afraid this is the first time for me."

Tanner pulled back. His eyes narrowed as he looked into dark, slightly dazed eyes. "The first? What about Stacey and your husband?"

Elizabeth blinked. Oh Lord, what had she said? In

123

her bemused state had she given herself away? She tried to explain away her words, but her tongue wouldn't move as it should. "Oh, yes, Mr. Stacey. I forgot about him."

"And your husband? Did you forget him as well?"

"My . . . my . . . husband . . ."

Tanner grinned at her obvious confusion. "What happened? Was it you who did the asking?"

"Of course not," she said, feeling a moment's annoyance at the laughter in his eyes. How was it he was able to keep his wits about him, when all he had to do was look her way and her legs felt about as strong as hot wax? And when he touched her she hadn't even that consistency. Elizabeth put some distance between them. He was watching her closely, studying her every expression. His eyes narrowed, and she felt blood rush to her cheeks. Was her guilt obvious to him? She turned away unable to withstand his searching gaze and moved awkwardly toward the stove.

"Then what?"

Elizabeth knew she had no choice but to follow her deception through to the end. There was no telling what he might come to suspect if he knew she'd lied about her marital status. "We sort of," she hesitated and gave a slight shrug, "just got married."

Tanner grinned as he leaned against the sink and watched her check the bread in the oven. "Did you?" Something wasn't right here. He hadn't been a lawman all these years not to know when someone was lying. "And how did you know what day to meet at the church?"

"Don't be silly," she said, her back to him.

"Elizabeth, look at me," he commanded, his voice low and husky. It was a moment before he heard her sigh as if in resignation. Then her shoulders stiffened as if she were undertaking a particularly unpleasant task. She turned to face him. "You were never married, were you?"

"Of course I was married," she insisted, guilt making her cheeks bright.

"Were you? What was his name?"

"John."

"His middle name," he shot at her.

He nodded in satisfaction at seeing her slight hesitation.

"Joseph."

"When were you married? And for how long were you married?"

Elizabeth hadn't expected anyone to question her so closely. She hadn't concocted a story. Rather than think up answers she might soon forget, she took the offensive. "Am I a prisoner? Why are you asking me all these questions?"

"You don't act as though you've ever been married."

"Really? And just how does one act when one has been married?"

"For one thing, a woman doesn't blush scarlet when a man talks about taking her to bed."

"Well, she does when that man is not her husband."

"And she knows how to kiss."

125

"And I don't?" Elizabeth asked, annoyed by his persistence.

"You do now, but the first time I could have sworn you'd never been kissed before."

"For your information, I've been kissed many times." And she had, but only by family members.

"But not by a man who knew how."

Elizabeth rolled her eyes toward the ceiling, and her hands curved into fists that came to rest on her hips. "Your ego is something to behold. Just because I didn't immediately respond, you think—"

"I could give you something more interesting than an ego to hold."

Elizabeth's brow furrowed as she tried to make sense of his words. She didn't understand them, but she hadn't a doubt, judging by his tone of voice and that dangerous gleam in his eyes, that he was hinting at something decidedly wicked. "What would that be?"

"Come over here and I'll show you."

"Really, Marshal," she said as if speaking to a wayward child, "do you take me for a complete fool?" Elizabeth never realized the innocence that shone clearly in both expression and words.

Tanner smiled at her daring. "Madam, I'd be the first to admit you are far from a fool." He watched her closely and then finally shook his head. "In fact, you're really quite good, but not good enough. You bluffed your way out of a sticky situation, even though you hadn't an inkling as to what I was talking about. If you'd once been married, you most definitely would

126

have known."

Elizabeth lifted her chin and shrugged her denial of his accusation. She then turned on her heel and began to sweep the already spotless floor before speaking again. "It matters little what you believe, Marshal. It's obvious you've associated with an entirely different class of widows, that is all."

Tanner chuckled. "You might be right," he said, knowing he'd wager an entire year's salary against the possibility of finding another widow quite so innocent. "But at the moment there's only one widow that interests me."

He grinned as she looked up from her sweeping. "You never answered my question, Elizabeth. Will you marry me?"

Elizabeth closed her eyes and shook her head.

"Why?"

"We hardly know each other. I can't marry a man I've just met."

"Shall I court you then?" His eyes twinkled with some secret laughter. "I imagine we could get to know each other quite well after a spell."

She shook her head again. "You'll be gone after you've finished your work here." She didn't bother to add that once he finished his job she'd be in prison, but she couldn't hide the emptiness that suddenly engulfed her as she imagined what she might have had with this man.

Tanner misunderstood the look in her eyes, imagining it to be reluctance to leave her home. "And you wouldn't consider coming with me?"

"My home is here. My friends. I'd have to give up everything and start over again," she insisted, knowing even as she said the words that her few meager belongings meant nothing. She would have given them up in a moment if that would have changed things. But nothing could change what she'd already done. No matter what she might feel for this man, it was far too late.

He shook his head. "Minor details, Elizabeth. Details that could easily be worked out." He decided it would be best to change the subject. This woman was much too set in her ways. What she needed was a little shaking up. "Come with me to the Founders Day celebration."

At the sudden change in subject, Elizabeth flashed him a delectable smile that just about curled his toes. She knew what he was about. He wasn't a man who took no in stride. No doubt he planned to pursue this subject at some later date. She'd just have to make sure he had no opportunity.

When she smiled, Tanner had the most powerful urge to take her in his arms, crush her against him, and keep her there for the rest of his life. "I want to kiss you again," he said, his voice low with need. "If you don't say yes, I might be forced to do just that in order to convince you."

"Well." She laughed, raising one hand and taking a step back as he advanced toward her. "If it will save me from suffering through another of your kisses, then yes, of course I'll go with you." She laughed again at his look of disappointment.

Then Tanner's pretended scowl slowly turned into the most wickedly delicious grin Elizabeth had ever seen. His mustache tipped as one corner of his mouth curled up, the deep groove in his cheek becoming deeper and more tempting. "I can't rightly remember a time when I've been so beautifully insulted."

"Oh, you're welcome," she said sweetly, as if he'd just given her a compliment. "I have many more barbs where that came from," she stated proudly.

Tanner was torn between a need to turn her over his knee and a desire to kiss her till that smart mouth of hers forgot how to give him sass. He took the broom from her and leaned it against the wall. "Fix your hair," he said gruffly. "I think it's best if we sit outside for a spell." He took her hand, barely allowing her the time to secure her hair in a twist at the nape of her neck. A moment later, he was guiding her to the front porch. "If insulting me makes your eyes sparkle like that, I can't wait to hear more."

Elizabeth laughed as he deposited her on a chair and then settled himself on one close by. He leaned back and watched her, bracing his right ankle on his left knee. "You may begin."

She giggled at seeing the gentle humor in his gaze, feeling uncommonly gay and daring. "Marshal, I can't rain insults upon your head at the snap of a finger. You'll have to give me reason."

She watched as he prepared to come to his feet, his

intent obvious, his eyes sparkling wickedly. Quickly she added, "On second thought, perhaps I could."

They were still laughing as Belle came trudging up the steps.

"Hard day?" Tanner asked.

Belle sighed and then leaned against one of the porch's supporting posts. "If I have to go over one more column of figures, I might just vomit."

Elizabeth shook her head as she bit back the laughter that threatened. Her eyes sparkled as they met Tanner's, but she quickly looked away lest she laugh aloud.

She liked Belle. She admired her courage even if her form of dress was a bit outrageous. She even liked her use of coarse language, and she wondered about the freedom the woman must enjoy since she did not adhere to society's dictates but spoke her mind as she pleased. Belle was rough and more than a bit bawdy. Her bawdiness probably should have repulsed Elizabeth, but instead it drew her closer. She wished she and Belle could be friends. But that could never be. "Would you like something cool to drink?" she asked.

Belle shot Tanner a dirty look as he lounged comfortably in one of the porch chairs. Then she remarked sweetly, "Oh, please. Don't go getting yourself in a tizzy. I'm exhausted, but that's no reason for you to be concerned." She seated herself and reached into her bag for a smoke and matches. She was puffing away, trying to light a cigar when she spoke again, her gaze directed at Elizabeth, "That would be wonderful, honey. Maybe a shot or two of whiskey on the side?" Again to Tanner. "You can get me a pot of hot water for my feet."

Tanner laughed as he watched a cloud of dark gray smoke circle Belle's head. "It's not your feet you sit on all day, Belle. Maybe the hot water would be put to better use if I could find a pan big enough for your—"

"Marshal!" Elizabeth was clearly aghast that this man, that any man, would mention a lady's derrière in casual conversation.

"Oh, don't pay him no nevermind, honey. He's just a big, ugly bully." Belle grinned as she shot Tanner a look promising retaliation. "I'll get him later for that."

Elizabeth couldn't really agree with Belle's nonchalant description of the marshal. He was anything but ugly. As a matter of fact she couldn't remember seeing a man half so appealing. Still, looks didn't grant him the right to speak so familiarly to a woman. Elizabeth had realized from the first that these two were old friends. Now she wondered just how friendly were they. She wasn't happy to admit that the obvious answer to that question brought her no measure of satisfaction. "As will I," Elizabeth stated, her dark gaze promising dire consequences for Tanner's breach in etiquette. The two women laughed as he groaned in anticipation of the future suffering he was sure to endure.

"How did it go today?" Tanner asked once Elizabeth was out of hearing.

Belle made a face. "He's not happy to have me underfoot all day."

"Tough." Tanner grunted. "Have you been able to find anything?"

"If the man is doing something illegal, I can't find it."

"Well, somebody hates his guts enough to try to ruin him."

"It has to be something from his past. Right now he's squeaky clean."

"Has any news come from Eureka?"

Belle shook her head in disgust. "It's obvious he's not well liked, but our operatives can't find anyone willing to talk."

"Afraid?"

"It looks that way. He owns half the town. I imagine that would stop a few tongues."

"What exactly are they saying?"

"Only that his silver mine has made him rich. No one seems to know anything else." She shrugged. "Whoever does is not talking."

"Maybe it's something that happened before Eureka."

"You mean when he was in the Army?"

Tanner nodded.

"The record shows he got an honorable discharge."

Tanner nodded. "Let's look into it anyway. There might be something there."

Elizabeth trembled so violently she almost dropped the tray of glasses along with the pitcher of lemonade. She was thankful she'd been near enough to the wall to find support, for her legs had threatened to buckle under her weight. A moment or two passed before she dared try to walk again. Her time was coming to a close. Once they checked out Stacey's doings in the Army, someone would surely remember the scandal and comment on it. These two were too smart not to relate the purchase of the mine with the disappearance of the Army payroll. When they investigated that, her father's name was sure to come up. Then she'd be found out.

With a sense of approaching doom, Elizabeth returned to the porch. It took some effort, but she managed to keep up a cheerful guise. Neither of her guests realized the fear she suffered. Neither of them knew that she wished her venture was all over.

Chapter Seven

Tanner's smile at spotting Elizabeth disappeared, and he seemed stunned. No other word could describe the look on his face. The glazed eyes, the slackened jaw, the sudden stiffening of his stance could all be attributed to the sight before him.

Of course a man of Tanner's thirty-six years couldn't be expected to have remained ignorant of what lay beneath a woman's skirt. He'd simply never seen what lay beneath Elizabeth's. And he hadn't, even in his most erotic imaginings, suspected she would wear black silk stockings held in place by a red lacy garter.

Tanner felt a wave of anger, the strength of which easily equaled his astonishment. Damn it! He was going to wring her neck. What the hell had come over her to make her raise her skirt in public? Who besides himself had had the pleasure of seeing white, creamy thighs, naked above black stockings, and the deliciously intriguing frills that lay beneath her demure skirt?

Tanner took a step forward and then came to an

abrupt stop as the explosive sound of a gun discharging split the peaceful afternoon. His gaze was concentrated solely on the woman and the boy. Still, he sensed the distant festivities had come to a halt.

He couldn't believe his eyes as he watched Johnny Blake fall amid a cloud of dust onto the dirt. For a split second Tanner couldn't fathom what he had seen. Lord! She'd shot a kid!

He covered the distance in a blur of movement. Had he not already been upset, due to what he took to be her apparent lack of modesty, he might have handled everything differently. As it was he came damn close to losing all control. Without thinking, he knocked the gun from her hand, sending it spinning through the air to fall some ten feet away and leaving her hand throbbing from the blow. He grabbed her slender shoulders in a viselike grip, and his fingers dug deep into tender flesh as he shook her until her straw hat lay at Johnny's feet. Her hair whipped free of its pins and flew in wild disarray around her face. "What the hell do you think you're doing? Why did you shoot him?"

Elizabeth, trembling still from the shock of the last few minute's happenings, never realized his fury. She couldn't understand what was causing her head to snap back and forth upon her neck. But soon enough his bellowing words penetrated the fog of terror that engulfed her mind. "I had to," she stammered, the words little more than a whispery gasp as she withstood his continuing punishment.

Tanner uttered a vile curse and gave her a mighty

shove that sent her spinning to the ground. The movement caused her skirt to rise almost to her knees. This time the sight of her black-clad legs barely registered.

Elizabeth felt the world spin by as she tried to shake away her dizziness. What in the world was the matter with this brute? Why, when she most needed his quick, confident control did he act like a madman?

"You had to?" he asked, his eyes filled with contempt. "You shot a little kid 'cause you had to?" he was horrified, unable to believe what he'd just seen. Unable as well to comprehend the reason behind so brutal an act.

"What?" she asked, slowly coming to realize what he believed. "You think I—"

"Shut up," he ordered. "I don't want to hear another word out of your lying mouth."

Shut up? Had this beast dared say those words to her? Elizabeth lost every semblance of composure. In the space of a heartbeat, she was so angry she was almost thankful she no longer held her gun. If she had she'd be mightily tempted to use it again, and on a much larger critter.

Without his help, help she would have refused had it been offered, she slowly came to her feet, her hands balling into fists as she fought to contain her rage. Her body trembled with the righteous indignation as she pushed hair back from her eyes. "Johnny wasn't shot." Her lips twisted into a snarl. "He fainted when the snake bit him. Instead of ranting on like some fool, do something!"

Tanner's head snapped toward the pale little boy. Johnny's face was pinched with pain. Obviously the boy suffered even though unconscious. Tanner scanned the still form, noting no obvious wound. Then his eyes widened with shock when he spied fangs still penetrating a trouser leg, the head of a rattler. Its lifeless body lay within inches of the unconscious boy.

"Jesus," Tanner muttered as he flung aside the head, and tore away the leg of the boy's trousers. A second later Elizabeth watched him cut into the double punctures. Without hesitation he began to suck at the wound. Almost immediately he spit a mouthful of blood and venom to the ground. Again and again his mouth returned to the boy's leg until blood ran freely from the cut and dripped in ghoulish fashion from Tanner's lips.

The sound of Elizabeth's gun had alerted the townsfolk to trouble. Many were now advancing upon them, and at some speed. Elizabeth could see them moving en masse away from the tables of food and drink.

Johnny had awakened while Tanner worked over him. He was crying. Elizabeth knelt beside the boy and put his head on her lap. "Don't cry, Johnny. I know it hurts some, but you'll be all right."

Johnny's dog returned from joyously chasing a squirrel to whine beside his master's prone body.

"See," Elizabeth remarked as she sought to take the lad's mind off his suffering, "I told you Rags would come back."

A moment later Dr. Thompson was there, issuing orders for the boy's father to carry him gently to his office. The crowd moved away, heading back to the festivities, but not before someone called out, "Good shooting, Marshal."

Tanner opened his mouth to set matters right, but he noticed Elizabeth's sudden look of panic and just muttered, "Thanks."

It was only then that Elizabeth realized what she'd done. Tanner had obviously seen her shoot. Now he was aware of her expert handling of a gun. How was she going to explain away the highly unusual fact that a lady not only possessed a gun, but she could separate the head of a striking rattler from its body faster and with more accuracy than most hired guns.

Would Tanner believe luck alone was responsible for that shot? There was no help for it. Elizabeth had no alternative but to bluff her way through this. She could only pray her excuses satisfied.

Tanner could have sworn he heard Elizabeth sigh. He wondered why and turned to gaze back at the woman still kneeling at his side. "Why don't you want anyone to know you did it?" he asked.

"Did I say that?" She came to her feet, ignoring his proffered hand.

"Your look did."

Elizabeth shook her head. "You misunderstood," she said without so much as glancing his way. She retrieved her hat and began dusting off the brown silt that covered every boot and dress hem in these parts.

"I was upset. I'm still upset."

In truth Elizabeth hadn't been half so afraid that the town would find out about her ability to shoot as she was that the marshal knew of it. He would question her now that they were alone. She could only pray he'd accept her answers.

"I don't think so," he said as a suspicious gleam entered his eyes.

Elizabeth allowed a long moment to pass before she returned, "You don't think what? That I'm upset? I can promise you I am."

"I don't think that's all it is," he said, his blue eyes narrowed as they studied her guileless expression.

Elizabeth felt her heart pound in her throat, nearly cutting off her ability to breathe. Fear. Was there any emotion half so intense? She took a deep breath and forced aside a wild impulse to throw herself in his arms and confess the whole of it. Instinctively she knew she'd find no quarter there. This man's whole life was centered around the law. He wouldn't hesitate to do what had to be done. Elizabeth brought her full concentration to the task of keeping her hands from trembling.

"How did you become so expert a shot? And why are you trying to hide the fact?"

"Expert? Me?" Elizabeth smiled. "I thank you for the compliment, Marshal, but you couldn't be more wrong. I never expected to hit the snake."

"Are you telling me your shooting was nothing more than luck?"

"What else? How many women do you know who

can shoot with any accuracy?"

"Only Belle," he said softly, his eyes still on her flushed face.

Elizabeth couldn't imagine what was going on in his mind. She dared not look into his eyes while proclaiming her innocence. He was experienced in the ways of criminals. He'd know she was lying.

While Elizabeth dusted her skirt, Tanner retrieved her gun and, placing it on his palm, held it out to her. "Do you always wear a gun?"

"Not when I'm at home," she responded as she took the small weapon from his outstretched hand and placed it in her pocket.

"I don't know of many women who carry them, at home or not."

"I've no doubt many do. One never knows when a weapon could prove necessary."

"But how many keep them in their garters?"

Elizabeth's brown eyes lifted to his hard gaze. So he'd seen that as well. "Are you accusing me of something?"

"No," he shrugged. "I think I was just surprised to see you lift your skirt in public."

"It was done before I thought about it."

Tanner nodded. "Much as a hired gun reaches for his weapon."

Elizabeth smiled. "A hired gun?" she asked, praying her voice held a note of innocence. "Is that what you think I am?"

Tanner said nothing, but he continued to stare into her eyes as if trying to understand some intricate puzzle.

"If so, why do you suppose I'm taking in boarders? Surely I could hire out my gun and better my standard of living by far." She grinned at the nonsensical notion.

Tanner sighed, knowing the idea was unreasonable. Still there was something about this woman. Something different. Something that didn't quite ring true.

Tanner felt a wave of confusion. He'd never known a woman like her before. He'd never felt the things he was feeling before. No doubt those feelings lay at the root of his confusion.

He had a time of it bringing his gaze from the tip of his boots. A moment later he cleared his throat. "Elizabeth, I want to apologize."

"For what?" she asked, her voice cool, her demeanor apparently unconcerned as she took a deep breath, relieved. She turned her back to him, arranged her hair, and replaced her hat.

"For shaking you like I did. From where I was standing, I thought . . ."

Her head tipped slightly. Dark eyes shot him a contemptuous glare from beneath the straw brim as she remembered his rough treatment. "You should have known better."

Tanner felt his cheeks darken uncomfortably. When was the last time a woman had made him feel such a fool? Not since Mrs. Rose, the teacher he'd had when only seven or eight, had caught him writing curse words on his slate. "It looked like you shot him," he said in self-defense.

"Marshal, surely you're old enough not to trust everything you see."

"Actually, that's about the only thing I can trust."

Elizabeth frowned. "Then I feel sorry for you."

"No need," he said, his voice growing hard with annoyance at her obvious refusal to meet his eyes. "I'm content with the way things are."

"How nice for you," she murmured. "Now, if you'll excuse me . . ." Elizabeth turned away and headed off.

Tanner instinctively reached out and caught her arm. He had become separated from her some time ago, when a few of the men had insisted he join them at the ale barrel, and it had been difficult to find her again. Now, after his outrageous treatment of her, she obviously wanted nothing more to do with him. Damn, he'd made a mess of things.

"You aimin' to give me the silent treatment 'cause of what happened?"

Elizabeth looked pointedly at the hand still holding her arm. "Certainly not. But I can't very well speak to you if you're not with me, can I?"

"What the hell does that mean? I'll be with you."

"I don't think so," she said as she shook herself free of his hand.

"Elizabeth, wait," he said as he watched her hurry away from him. A moment later he was again at her side. She shot him an enraged look as his wide hand reached for and swallowed hers. When she tried to pull away, he only tightened his hold. "You promised you'd be with me today."

She shook her head. "That was—"

"I know," he interrupted, "that was before I made an ass out of myself." He sighed as he stopped and turned her to face him. "What can I do to get you to forgive me?"

Elizabeth's anger began to slip as his blue eyes boyishly appealed for forgiveness. By rights she should never speak to him again. How could he think she'd heartlessly, cold-bloodedly kill a child? She might be nothing like the lady he supposed her to be, but a coldhearted murderer?

"I swear it was only the shock of hearing the gun go off and seeing the boy fall. Even when I saw it, I somehow couldn't believe you'd do such a thing."

"Really? Is that why you were so gentle and considerate?" she asked softly, unable to give in just yet. "I'm not mistaken, am I? It was you who threw me to the ground, wasn't it?"

Tanner could only groan in response. What in God's name had come over him? He had a temper, to be sure, but he'd never in his life raised a hand to a woman.

Elizabeth's resolve to see him suffer disintegrated as pain entered his eyes. Her heart began to pound. In another minute she was going to throw herself into his arms and beg him not to look so stricken.

In order to save herself that embarrassment, she smiled and suggested, "If you promise you'll go slow in the three-legged race, I'd forgive you anything."

Tanner grinned at the sparkle in her eyes. "Why?

143

Don't you want to win?"

"Not as much as I want to retain my dignity."

"I could hold you at my side and run without your help. We'd be sure to win then."

Elizabeth giggled at the thought. "We'd be sure to be disqualified."

"They wouldn't dare," he said, swaggering before her. He released her hand and hooked his thumbs into the belt he wore low on hips that were leaning toward her. "I'm the marshal around these parts."

The movement was so male, so blatantly enticing, Elizabeth felt color invade her cheeks and a warmth seep deep into her belly. Her words were softer than either expected when she finally remarked, "Then, as marshal, don't you think you should set an example of sportsmanship?"

Only the knowledge that most of the townsfolk were in clear sight saved the beautiful, tiny woman from being drawn into his arms.

Half the town was screaming encouragement at their awkward progress. They were in the lead, by far. No one doubted their victory.

Elizabeth let go of his waist and braced herself as the ground suddenly came up to meet them. She gasped as his body fell hard against hers. A moment later she laughed at the look of wicked enjoyment that flashed in his eyes. It had been no accident, this tumble. He had deliberately used the excuse that their legs were tied together to stumble and bring her down against him.

Every eye moved from their prone forms to the couple in second place, as Tanner rolled her over. His hand smoothed her skirt into place, lest one or two pairs of eyes linger and gain a knowledge of what he alone knew to lie beneath. In one movement, he twisted them and brought her to lie upon the length of him.

"That was an evil trick," she accused, as she slapped at his shoulder. She held herself as far above him as her stiff arms allowed. The position brought their hips into direct contact and Tanner enjoyed the moment to the fullest. "And just as we were about to win."

"What?" he asked, only half trying for innocence. "Our falling?"

"Tell me it was an accident," she dared as she rolled off him and sat at his side, her fingers untying the rope that held her left leg to his right.

"It was an accident," he repeated, without the slightest inference of truth.

"You could have waited until we crossed the finish line."

"Mmmm," Tanner agreed. "I probably could have, but it looked better this way." His gaze was anything but innocent. "I'd say it was well worth the loss."

Laughter bubbled from Elizabeth's throat. "You beast."

Tanner grinned at her laughter. "Come on, I've worked up a powerful thirst."

Elizabeth nodded. "A glass of lemonade would be

145

wonderful right now."

"Lemonade?" Tanner grimaced. "Actually, I was thinking along the line of a foaming glass of ale."

Elizabeth looked all prim and proper as she stood and dusted her skirt. "Perhaps, but it's obvious the marshal has sampled the brew to excess. What other excuse could there be for his fall?"

"It could be he took the only chance he was likely to get to hold his lady beneath him."

Elizabeth shook her head, her cheeks growing pink at the implication in his softly whispered words. "Our marshal is a man of integrity. He'd never stoop so low." Her smile ruined completely the stiff rebuff.

Tanner's mood swung from crushing despair to delight in her brilliant smile. "Are you teasing me, ma'am?"

"Certainly not." Unconsciously she dusted his shoulder. The movement was decidedly intimate, almost wifely. Elizabeth never noticed. Tanner did. "Our marshal *is* a man of integrity."

"What about your marshal?" he asked hopefully.

"Isn't he one and the same?" She met his eyes. Her look held such tenderness, Tanner had a time keeping his hands at his sides.

He shrugged. "I don't know. You keep referring to his as our, not yours."

"Oh? Is he mi—?" Elizabeth's cheeks flamed as she cut off the word. She hadn't realized how relaxed she'd become in his presence. She hadn't realized just how close they were standing, how intimate his look.

"He could be. It would only take a word from

you."

Elizabeth saw the crowd on her right move and found the exact thing she needed to change the subject. "The race is about to start." Her voice was low, slightly breathless, filled with emotion, not the least being confusion.

"Maybe he won't run. Maybe he'd rather his lady's company than the thrill of victory."

Elizabeth laughed. "We are confident, aren't we?"

Tanner's blue eyes twinkled.

"Maybe she'll have a glass of ale waiting for him at the finish line," Elizabeth offered as temptation.

"And a kiss?"

"Surely not. A kiss would only bring scandal upon her."

"You mean because he lives in her house?"

"I do."

"He would settle for a hug of congratulations."

"I'm sure he'll get that and more." Elizabeth's dark eyes flashed with annoyance. "Harriet has been watching him most of the day."

Tanner ignored her reference to the other woman. "If he can count on at least that, he's bound to come in first."

"If he doesn't hurry, he won't be racing at all," she said as she shoved him toward the starting line.

Tanner was gasping for breath. Damn, there had been a moment or two when he hadn't been sure he'd make it. But he had. He'd crossed the finish line a mere second before the runner behind him.

Elizabeth moved to stand before him. His hair was stuck to his forehead; his shirt was stuck to his back and coated with grime. He'd never looked more appealing.

"I believe I promised you this," she said as she offered him a cool glass of foaming ale.

Tanner ignored the glass and brought her hard against him. "You promised me more than that," he said as his mouth claimed hers in a quick fiery kiss.

The kiss was hard and hungry, but over so fast, Elizabeth would have doubted her senses had not her lips felt bruised and her skin sensitive to the abrasion of his beard and the silkiness of his mustache. He had kissed her! Here! In front of anyone who cared to look.

Her mouth tightened. "Marshal," she began, determined to let him know her opinion of his outrageous daring.

"Don't be angry, Elizabeth," he said, still gasping from his exertion. "I couldn't resist." A wicked smile touched the corners of his mouth, tipping his mustache off center. "You looked more delicious than a river of ale."

She shoved the glass into his belly. Not at all unhappy to see more than half of it splash onto his shirt. She was furious. "Your drink."

"You promised me a hug."

"Oh yes. Now that you mention it, I do remember we discussed something of the sort." Elizabeth spun on her heel and called out loudly, "Harriet."

148

Tanner groaned as the woman came dashing toward them. "Our marshal is in need of congratulations, wouldn't you say?"

Tanner hadn't the chance to utter a word, for Harriet threw herself in his arms and bestowed upon him a decidedly hungry kiss.

As she was doing so, Elizabeth walked away.

She was angry enough at the moment not to care how the marshal managed his escape or whether he escaped at all.

Tanner, his mouth pressed against Harriet's, followed the angry Elizabeth's departure with sparking eyes. He was going to wring her damn neck. All right, so he had kissed her. For God's sake, it was only a kiss. What the hell did she expect? What man in his right mind could resist? Especially when she smiled up at him as she had with such tenderness and pride.

If she didn't want to be kissed, she should have said so. Tanner completely ignored the fact that Elizabeth had done just that a number of times.

He tried unsuccessfully to break Harriet's hold. Damn, the woman was stronger than she appeared, and bold as they came. No decent woman would act like this. No decent woman would let a man . . . Oh, damn. He almost groaned aloud. He'd really done it this time.

No wonder Elizabeth was furious. If anyone had seen them kiss, people would no doubt accuse her of doing the very same things he was beginning to suspect Harriet of doing.

Tanner forced Harriet's arms from around his neck and tried to smile. "Thank you, ma'am."

"You were wonderful, Marshal. May I call you Tanner?"

"Don't see why not," Tanner responded, only half hearing her question as he searched the crowd for Elizabeth.

Harriet's hands were all over his chest as she went on, "I never saw a man run like that. You must be so strong."

"Where did she go?" he murmured, never realizing he'd spoken aloud.

"Who? Oh, Elizabeth?" Harriet shrugged while pressing her breasts against his arm. "It doesn't matter, does it?" She smiled prettily. "Why don't we go to the ale barrel? You look parched."

He might have been parched, but drinking was the last thing on his mind. "If you'll excuse me, ma'am, I've got to ask Miss Elizabeth something."

Tanner tried to get away from the woman, but Harriet wasn't about to let this prize go. Elizabeth had hogged him the entire day. It was time some other woman had a chance to gain his attention. She clung to Tanner's arm and coaxed, "Why don't you ask me instead?" Harriet made her gaze as alluring as she could, and she leaned closer to him. But those gestures were wasted on this man as was her soft, seductive promise, "You won't be sorry about my answer."

Tanner glanced down at Harriet, amazed to feel a flicker of revulsion. The woman was pretty enough and had he not had Elizabeth on his mind, he might have been tempted. Tempted, hell. There wasn't a doubt about it. If he hadn't wanted Elizabeth, he'd probably be hiking up this woman's skirt behind one of the town's buildings right now.

But he did want Elizabeth, damn it! He wanted her and only her. How the hell had she snuck up on him like that? When had it become so important to have her? To feel her body close to his, to breathe her clean scent, to hear her laughter, to kiss those sweet, sweet lips?

What made her different from this woman, from a hundred women? He didn't know, but he sure as hell was going to find out.

Tanner grinned down at the female clinging to his arm. "Actually, ma'am, what I wanted to ask her might be a bit of a shock to delicate ears."

"Oh, I doubt I'll be shocked, Tanner." Harriet laughed and then blinked flirtatiously. "You can tell me."

"All right then. I wanted to ask her to forgive me for embarrassing her like I did. We all know no decent lady would stand for being kissed in public."

Tanner ignored Harriet's gasp. He knew he'd just insulted her; he also knew she didn't deserve any better, considering the way she was hanging all over him and not caring in the least who might be watching.

"And since I have every intention of marrying the lady, I should have treated her with the respect due my future wife, don't you think?"

Tanner almost laughed at Harriet's reaction. Her

body stiffened, her lips grew thin, and her face turned bright red. "Marry . . ." She silently mouthed the word, her shock apparent. A minute later she cleared her throat and straightened her shoulders. In an effort to save what was left of her tattered dignity, she smiled, "Well, yes. I imagine you're right about that."

"Now, if you'll excuse me, I'm going to find her."

"Of course, of course," Harriet muttered, suddenly more than happy to see him go.

Tanner thought he saw Elizabeth. He made a dash for the table holding pies, cakes, and cookies, but by the time he got there she'd disappeared. When next he caught sight of her, she was talking to Stacey. Tanner's lip curled with dislike. She'd told him earlier that Stacey wouldn't be at the celebration, that he'd be working. Tanner couldn't be sure, but it looked like she was being helped into Stacey's carriage.

Again he hurried through the dense crowd, only to curse in frustration as the carriage drove off.

Tanner tipped the glass of ale and took yet another long swallow. Had she been inside? Had she gone off with the bastard? Was that why he couldn't see a sign of her anywhere? She might be headed for Stacey's white mansion, where that cold-eyed bastard would sprawl on top of her warm body.

Tanner bit back a curse, emptied his glass, and immediately refilled it. His lips were set in a tight line. He was going to kill her. The moment he found her, he was going to put his hands around her neck and strangle her. She'd been too prissy for a kiss, but

152

she hadn't hesitated to go off with that lizard.

Tanner leaned against the ale barrel, ignoring the usual dirty talk of the men who surrounded him, studying his glass and its contents. He'd needed a drink. Bull, he needed a hundred drinks. But most of all, he needed to stop thinking about that woman. If he didn't he was going to go crazy.

The dancing had been going on for some time. Elizabeth was laughing at one of Belle's bawdy comments as they stood amid the crowd circling the dancers when she felt a presence behind her.

Elizabeth stiffened at hearing the low, slightly slurred voice. "I don't know how I'm going to do it, but I'll get you for that."

Elizabeth turned an inquiring eye on Tanner's towering form. It was obvious the man was deep in his cups. His body swayed dangerously close to hers before he somehow righted himself. The scent of ale permeated the air, no doubt partially because she had spilled half a glass on him.

Elizabeth shot him a look of disgust. There was no denying the fact that he was drunk; yet his eyes were clear and filled with menace. That he should dare approach her in this state was infuriating enough, but the condemning look in his eyes raised her hackles. In an instant she was ready to fight. "Is something wrong?"

"Where the hell did you go?"

"When?"

"Do you know what it was like trying to get rid of her?"

Elizabeth lifted her chin in a deliberate show of indifference. "No, why don't you tell me? What was it like?"

How the hell did she manage to do that? She was a good two heads shorter than he was, yet she somehow managed to look down her nose at him. A nose that was pinched as if it smelled some particularly obnoxious odor.

"The damn woman has more arms than an octopus."

"I'm sure that must have been quite a hardship."

Tanner was getting madder by the minute as he remembered the clinging Harriet and the delightfully entertaining afternoon her smile had promised. He had refused to indulge himself because of this nasty female, and what did he get for going without? He got steely eyes, snide comments, and a knot in his stomach. "I asked you a question, lady. Where did you go?"

"Not that it's any of your business, but I went over to Dr. Thompson's to check on Johnny."

That sobered him a bit. In his search for Elizabeth, he'd completely forgotten the boy. "How is he?"

"He'll be fine." She nodded toward a wagon leaving town. "His father's going to fetch the things he'll need. Johnny will be staying with Dr. Thompson for a day or so, just to be sure. It seems you got most of the poison out."

"Why did you sic her on me?"

"Did I do that?" she asked, all innocence. "It just seemed you were so anxious for a kiss. I thought you'd be happy to find a woman willing." Elizabeth shot him a humorless inquisitive smile. "Did it matter what woman?"

"Ah," Belle murmured almost nervously as Tanner's cheeks colored. She knew the man well enough to recognize that he was about as close as she'd ever seen him to committing murder. She moved back a step. "If you two don't mind"—she nodded toward a man across the circle of dancers—"I'm going to ask that handsome gentleman to dance . . . before the fireworks start."

Elizabeth looked a bit confused. "The fireworks aren't until tomorrow night."

Belle glanced back and forth between the two combatants. She didn't want to stick around and witness this battle. She'd bet a year's wages it wasn't going to be a pretty sight. "I wouldn't put any money on it, honey."

Elizabeth's confusion grew as Belle almost raced toward her prospective dancing partner. "What is she talking about?"

"Who the hell cares?" Tanner snapped as he took her arm and nearly dragged her away from the crowd.

Chapter Eight

"Do you mind telling me just what you think you're doing?" Elizabeth dug her heels into the ground, only to find herself jerked forward again. Tanner never even noticed her resistance as he tugged on her arm. "Where are you taking me?"

Tanner had been going crazy for close to an hour, imagining the most explicit goings-on between Elizabeth and Stacey. He was in no mood to answer her questions. "If you give me a hard time, I'll just carry you."

"Let me go this instant," she said, first trying to draw her hand away and, when that proved useless, trying to pry his steely fingers from it. "I said, let me go!"

"We have to talk."

Tanner crossed the street and headed into the alley that separated the general store from the sheriff's office. He swung her hard against the wall and then pressed the lower portion of his body against hers to keep her in place.

Elizabeth's hands were between their bodies,

pressed against his chest. She tried to push her way free. "Do you m-i-i-nd?" she asked amid grunts of exertion.

"Yes. God damn it, I mind. I mind you siccing that little floozy on me. I mind you disappearing. And most of all I mind that lizard Stacey pawing you," Tanner retorted harshly.

"Mr. Stacey did not paw me." Elizabeth grunted again as she strained to push him away. "The only man guilty of pawing me is you."

Tanner ignored her last comment. "Don't try to deny it, damn it! I saw you with him. And before I could get to you, the two of you disappeared." He gave her shoulders a quick, hard shake, but Elizabeth was so filled with anger that she barely noticed. "Where'd you go?"

Outraged, Elizabeth glared at him, and her lips twisted into a snarl. "How is that your concern?"

"What were you doing while I was searching every corner of this town?"

Elizabeth's eyes narrowed. Tanner had unmitigated gall. "Are you insane? You have no hold on me. I'm not answerable to you."

"You'd better believe you are, lady."

"I'd better . . ." Elizabeth almost sputtered. She was unable to go on, for rage had tied her tongue in knots. She took a deep breath and finally managed to say sarcastically, "What gives you any right to tell me what to do?"

Had she been of a saner mind, she might have

realized the man was hardly himself, she might have spoken more carefully, at least until she was in a less dangerous, less isolated position. But Elizabeth's anger was so great she couldn't think beyond lashing back at this brute. "You cannot question my behavior."

"I sure can. You belong to me, and the next time you let that sonofabitch touch you, I'm going to kill him."

"I belong to you!" Elizabeth would have laughed at that ridiculous statement if she hadn't been beside herself with rage. Since that was the case, it was nothing short of a miracle that she managed to keep her tone for his ears alone. "Get your hands off me before I scream."

Tanner laughed. "I'll bet you didn't tell him that," he said just before his mouth claimed hers in a kiss that bordered on a violent assault.

"Tanner," she cried, the name muffled by his lips and almost unintelligible. "Stop it!"

Elizabeth was not about to stand for this kind of abuse. She hit his chest and when that brought about no response, she slapped his face.

A moment later her hands were securely held behind her back.

Despite his superior strength, Elizabeth felt not a flicker of fear or panic. Her determination never wavered. Never, never would she succumb to force. She cried out. "No!" Again the word was muffled by his mouth.

Despite the scent of his clothes, Tanner wasn't nearly as far into drink as Elizabeth imagined. He was enraged by passion, jealousy, and anger, not drunkenness.

It took a few minutes, but Tanner finally realized things were getting out of hand. Damn her to hell! He'd only wanted to shut her nasty mouth. He wanted her to admit the way things were between them. He tore his mouth from hers and was breathing heavily as he leaned forward, his arms braced against the wall, her body pinned against his. "I didn't mean to frighten you," he said. "I was angry and wanted to shut you up. I never thought it would get out of hand."

"You didn't frighten me. I'm not afraid of you."

Tanner grinned down into eyes glaring with rage. "So I see," he drawled lazily.

"Is this what you mean by talking?"

"What?" he asked, the word becoming a groan as she moved against him. She was trying to create some space between their bodies, but Tanner was so hungry to claim her it didn't take much to bring about a painful response. "I wasn't talking; I was kissing you."

"You said you wanted privacy so we might talk."

"I lied," he said, so openly that Elizabeth's anger suddenly vanished. He looked like a small boy caught in some mischievous deed. She couldn't hold back a giggle.

Tanner grinned at hearing the sound and pressed

his mouth against her warm neck. He breathed in the warm sweet scent he found there. "You're driving me crazy," he groaned, accentuating his words by pressing his hips tightly to hers. "God, I love the way you smell. What the hell is that scent?"

"Vanilla. And I wish I could say the same about you."

"What?" Tanner pulled his head back, and his brow creased until he remembered the cause of the scent that still emanated from his clothing.

"You smell as if you've washed your clothes in an ale barrel."

His sudden smile was as brilliant as it was devastating. It caused Elizabeth's stomach to do a somersault. Tanner chuckled softly, his lips inches from her own, tempting her to close the distance between them. "Yes. Well, it seems some fiery little witch spilled half a glass of ale on me this afternoon."

Elizabeth managed to duck beneath his arm. She dared not remain in place. Not when he smiled at her like that. Not when his voice deepened to that particular husky pitch. His manhandling didn't frighten her half as badly as his tenderness. "Did she?" her voice trembled just a bit. "I wonder why."

Tanner leaned a shoulder against the wall. Then, thumbs hooked into his gun belt, legs crossed at the ankles, he faced her. His first instinct was to reach for her and draw her carefully back into his arms. He forced aside the need, knowing by her nervous glances she was leery of him. Fear wasn't the emotion he wanted to instill. "She was a mite upset."

"No doubt more than a mite."

Tanner nodded. "Probably. But she set this she-wolf on me before I had a chance to explain."

"What was there to explain? You embarrassed her."

"I know, but it happened before I could think."

"Do you often kiss a lady before you consider the consequences, Marshal?"

"Actually I can't remember a time when I acted so rashly."

"What was different about today, then?"

"The woman."

"Oh." Elizabeth's heart was pounding furiously. She clasped and unclasped her hands. She wasn't sure she wanted to hear this.

"She was looking at me with such pride, such admiration, such—"

"No!" Elizabeth sounded shaken as she unthinkingly reached out and placed a hand on his chest. Had she really looked at him like that? Could it be her feelings were so blatantly obvious? If so, could she put all the fault on him? "Why don't we forget about it? I'm not angry."

Tanner still held her hand pressed to him. "Are you sure?"

"Positive."

He wasn't of a mind to release her just yet. He wasn't in any hurry to return to the festivities, not unless he could dance with her, and right then he couldn't imagine swinging her around in circles. He'd drunk at least one glass of ale too many.

A wicked light entered his eyes. Had it not been so dark in the alley, Elizabeth would surely have seen. Tanner was grateful she had not. "I hate to ask this, but do you think you could give me a hand?"

Elizabeth grinned. "If I'm not mistaken, you already have it."

Tanner laughed as he brought her hand up from his chest. He looked at it for a long moment before he bent his head and kissed it. "I do, don't I?" he whispered against her palm, and Elizabeth ran a dry tongue over dryer lips.

"Do you think I could use it to make me a cup of coffee?"

Elizabeth laughed and then shook her head at the confusing way he'd gone about asking. "There's coffee at the—"

He shook his head. "I've had enough partying."

She smiled her understanding and nodded. "Let's go."

She shot Tanner more than one puzzled look as he stumbled along the wooden sidewalk. Oddly enough, the closer they came to her house the more intoxicated he appeared. No doubt the ale he'd consumed was finally making itself known.

Once they left the sidewalk behind and he no longer had buildings to use as supports, he staggered wildly. Elizabeth put an arm about his waist. She never realized his arm had come around her shoulder, until she nearly staggered beneath his weight.

"Don't fall," she gasped as she felt her knees buckle. It took some effort, but she managed to keep them both from landing in the street. "God, you're heavy."

Tanner bit back a curse and eased up on the pressure. He hadn't realized how hard he was leaning on her. But it was essential she believe him drunk enough to need her help.

They were at the steps leading to the boardinghouse's porch before he spoke again. He didn't want to go inside. Not just yet. Once they did, he knew she'd guide him to the kitchen, and what he wanted, what he needed most, hadn't a damn thing to do with coffee.

He staggered and pulled her with him as he fell against the wall of the house. She was standing between his spread thighs, allowing him to hold her against him. His head dipped and he breathed in her delicious scent as his mouth and mustache brushed her cheek. "You smell good enough to eat," he said, his voice seductively low and filled with promise.

Elizabeth swallowed. In her innocence, she couldn't be positive, but she was almost sure he'd just made an indecent remark. It would be like Tanner to speak so boldly, she knew. Her eyes flashed warily as she raised her head. "Marshal, I—"

"My name is Tanner."

"Tanner," she began and then licked her lips ner-

163

vously. "I think we should—"

"I think," he interrupted with devastating persuasion as he brought his lips to hers, "that you've got the most beautiful, kissable mouth I've ever seen."

Elizabeth's usual common sense dissolved like a spoonful of sugar in hot tea. All she heard, all she knew, was the depth of emotion in his voice. His mouth merely brushed against hers. Not so startling a fact, considering she'd been kissed by this man before. Surely a kiss was nothing so drastic as to cause the thunderous pounding of blood that echoed in her ears. Surely the touch of his lips wasn't at the root of the tingling in her breasts that caused her nipples to tighten even as an ache began to grow within her.

But it was. His kiss might be gentle and sweet. His mouth might seem to demand nothing. Yet Elizabeth knew that beneath his tenderness raged a hunger that set her heart to pounding.

She moaned, delighting in his taste and scent. She never realized that it was his very lack of insistence that had awakened such a hunger in her. She wondered if it could ever be appeased. Gone forever was the notion that this man had to be denied. Elizabeth now fought a battle with her own needs. Could she find the strength to deny them?

Her lips parted as she boldly sought to deepen the kiss, anxious to experience more of this delicious pleasure.

Tanner felt her hunger and held steadfast to his resolve. He wouldn't push her. He wanted Elizabeth more than he wanted life, and he could have had her any number of times had he but pressed his cause. But he wanted more than acquiescence. He wanted her hungry for his touch. He wanted her lost in the throes of a desire so powerful neither of them could deny its existence.

Tanner felt her body soften against his. He fit her curves to his own unyielding contours and groaned his approval even as his blood began a pagan, lustful pounding.

Her arms came up to encircle his neck and draw his mouth more firmly to hers. Delicately her tongue met his.

Tanner thought his heart might stop at her sweet probing. He couldn't bear the pain, the beauty of it.

He bent and slipped an arm behind her legs. Without relinquishing his claim on her mouth, he lifted her up and carried her into the house. Moments later they were sprawled upon her horsehair sofa.

Elizabeth now grew reckless and bold. Her lips parted further as her tongue slid into the moist hot cavern of his mouth. Spurred on by his moans of approval, she found delicious pleasure in the meshing of lips, teeth, and tongues, until the world seemed to fade away and only hungry bodies, restless hands, and devouring mouths became reality.

Their mouths opened wider still to sample texture and taste. It wasn't enough. Elizabeth groaned and arched her back, silently pleading for his touch.

Greedy, so terribly greedy she couldn't think but to have more. She breathed in his hot panting breath, delighted in his sighs. She trembled to his growls.

Her hands moved wildly over his face, his hair, his neck and back. She couldn't touch him enough.

Her body ached with a need only he could ease. She no longer cared what the future might hold. She wanted this man and all the delight only he could give.

A low groan of satisfaction escaped her when his hands slipped around from her back to slide over the softness of her breasts. Her back arched instinctively. She ached for more of this ecstasy.

"My God, I'm so hungry for you," he said between the random kisses that grazed her eyes, her cheeks, her jaw. "I love your mouth. I can't stop kissing you."

"Do you want to?" she asked dreamily.

"What?"

"Stop kissing."

Tanner laughed, the sound lost in her mouth. "Hardly."

"Then don't. Don't," she pleaded as her tongue forged a burning path down his throat.

Tanner groaned. Why had he brought her to her couch? Once she was in his arms, why hadn't he taken her directly to her bedroom? Because he'd been afraid of frightening her off. Now he cursed his lack of insistence. Elizabeth was obviously as shaken as he. Her need was every bit as great as his. She moved restlessly beneath him, silently begging for more. He had to touch her. He had to get them into the bedroom before . . .

He heard a footstep and muttered a savage curse. An instant later he switched positions, almost throwing Elizabeth to the floor as he did so. Then he pulled her up so that she appeared to be on her knees, leaning over his prone form.

Dizzy from the abrupt movement, Elizabeth merely blinked in surprise. Then she blushed beet red as she realized someone was entering her house. She settled her backside upon her heels as she turned toward the opening door.

"Oh, dear me," Miss Dunlap said, her hand pressed flat against her thin breast as if to ease her shock at finding a man, apparently only partially conscious, sprawled upon the sofa and her landlady leaning over his body.

Elizabeth's mind raced ahead as she sought a solution to this dilemma. She cleared her throat before speaking. "Would you get me a damp cloth? It seems our marshal has been taken ill."

Tanner grinned at seeing Elizabeth's warning glare. "Good thinking," he said once Miss Dunlap's retreating footsteps had assured them of privacy. "Have you any plans on how you're going to get me to bed?"

Elizabeth realized for the first time that Tanner was as sober as she was. She should have been furious at him for so cleverly executing his hoax, but she couldn't seem to get angry. Instead, unexplainable joy filled her heart. Forcing aside her need to laugh, she predicted, "Oh, I'd venture to say you're about to have a miraculous recovery, Marshal. No doubt you'll then find the strength to get to bed on your own."

"I don't think so," he said, a decidedly wicked twinkle in his eye. "At least not alone." And then he added, ever so weakly, "I'm sure I can make it, ma'am. There's no need to bother yourself."

Elizabeth watched with nothing less than amazement as his wicked grin turned into a grimace of suffering. How had he known Miss Dunlap had returned with the cloth? Elizabeth shook her head and bit her lip to keep back a grin. He was good. So good in fact, had she not known better, she would have been taken in by his act.

"Should I go for the doctor?"

A definite yes and no were spoken in unison.

Elizabeth smiled at Gloria Dunlap's confusion. "He'll be fine. This isn't the first time Marshal Maddox has been taken with one of these spells."

"You mean the man is prone to fits?" Gloria Dunlap asked, her voice rising in alarm.

"I'm afraid he's particularly susceptible at certain times of the night," Elizabeth said, only half under her breath, while the marshal chose that moment to have a choking fit.

Miss Dunlap couldn't know he was struggling

against laughing out loud. "Are you sure he's all right?"

"He tends to get a bit overheated," Elizabeth said, as she tried to stuff the cloth in his mouth. "Once I've finished cooling him off, he'll be fine."

"Today's activities were probably too much for him," Gloria Dunlap commented while leaning over the couch and watching Elizabeth minister to the sickly marshal.

"Some men just don't know their limits," Elizabeth agreed.

Tanner wasn't at all sure he liked being talked about as if he weren't present. But what he liked even less was the way Elizabeth was using that damned cloth. She'd almost scraped the skin off his face with her less than gentle handling of it.

"Are you sure I shouldn't call for the doctor?"

"I'm sure. I've no doubt the marshal is feeling much more himself, aren't you, Marshal?"

"Oh, yes. I'm feeling much better, thank you."

Elizabeth raised his head and rubbed the cool cloth on the back of his neck. Suddenly she let it fall to the wooden arm of the sofa with a hard thud.

"Ow!"

"Oh dear me," Miss Dunlap said almost in a whine.

"You don't care for the coldness of the cloth? Is that it, Marshal?" Elizabeth asked as she tried to rise to her feet. She pretended to stumble. A moment later she fell forward and landed, elbow first, exactly upon Tanner's unsuspecting belly. No doubt the hundred pounds of pressure behind her fall had something to do with the fact that he instantly bolted into a sitting position. "I'll get you another. One that's a bit warmer."

"Don't," he said, finding it took no effort now to sound breathless and weak. "I'm sure I'll be fine."

"It's no bother, really."

"Thank you, ma'am, but I think I'll just take myself off to bed."

Elizabeth bit the inside of her lip to hold back the smile that threatened. "Good night then, Marshal. I hope you're feeling better in the morning."

"Think you're very clever, don't you?"

Elizabeth spun around at the sound of his voice, and her eyes went wide with shock at finding him standing inside her bedroom. "Get out!" she said in a loud whisper.

Tanner tried to ignore the fact that this woman, his woman, was clothed only in a light shift. It extended from neck to toe, but the material was so thin it barely concealed her charms. With a little more light, he'd be able to see clear through the damned thing. "I will, but I couldn't sleep knowing you had had the last word."

Elizabeth grinned and shook her head. What was she going to do with this man? He was big enough to dwarf her, and he was so strong, she suspected he'd easily best more than one man in a fight. He was respected, though not feared, by everyone in this town, yet when he looked at her like this, as if he were committing some boyish prank, it just about wrenched her heart. Something twisted in her chest, and Elizabeth could think only of pressing his face to her breast.

Dark curls hung over her shoulders and reached almost to her waist. They moved with her gentle breathing. Tanner felt the constant ache he was learning to live with grow in intensity. His fingers itched to feel the soft silky mass. "I will get even for what you did to me," he said.

Elizabeth's eyes sparkled. "I don't think so," she retorted, her voice husky with restrained laughter and the attempt to keep it low so her boarders wouldn't overhear.

"Oh, I will, lady." He swaggered up to where she stood in the center of the room. "And when I do, you'll be sorry."

"Will I?" she asked, her eyes glowing in the softly lit room. Tanner couldn't put a name to the emotion he read in them. All he knew was the sight of that tender expression brought an ache to his groin, an ache he wasn't likely to see end until he held her beneath him in bed. "Are you threatening me with physical harm?"

"Well, maybe not sorry exactly," he amended.

"What then?"

"I don't know," he said, frustrated. "All I know is I

171

can't sleep. You're driving me crazy."

Elizabeth looked surprised. "But I haven't done anything!"

"Haven't you?" he whispered, his lips so near hers she felt puffs of breath warm her skin. "I think you know better than that."

Tanner kissed her lightly, quickly, not daring to give in to the temptation she posed. He was at her door before he spoke again, "Damn it!" he said, obviously unhappy about leaving her. "Belle's waiting to talk to me, but the minute I get a chance, I'm going to show you exactly what you've done."

Elizabeth slowly eased herself down, as if a sudden movement might break something. She sat quietly upon her bed, her gaze still on the door through which he had exited. She breathed out a long morose sigh. She loved him. A searing pain clutched at her chest. She did not doubt that she would love him forever, and she knew that because of that love she was destined to suffer.

Chapter Nine

"What the hell do you mean, no one's heard of her?" Tanner snapped, keeping his voice as soft as anger permitted as he yanked the telegram from Belle's fingers.

"I mean exactly what I said," Belle responded. She took a sip of her whiskey.

They were sitting at the kitchen table, and the house was quiet but for their low conversation.

"That's impossible!" The lines at the corners of Tanner's mouth deepened as he fought down a surge of emotion that came perilously close to fear.

"It's not impossible and you know it."

"There's been a mistake," he announced, almost desperate for that to be so. "Check again."

Belle shot him a look filled with disgust. He had no business questioning her thoroughness at this late date. "Done." She nodded toward the paper in his hand. "That's the third time I told Frank to check it out. There's no mistake."

"She told me she came from—"

"She lied." Belle shrugged. "Either that or she's changed her name."

Tanner's brow creased as he sought to digest the ramifications of this new information. Why would Elizabeth lie? What was she hiding? He felt his stomach tighten as his whole body tingled with fear. What was going on?

The chair scraped against the floor as Belle came to her feet. "Look, it doesn't have to mean anything," she said, trying to ease his concern. "Talk to her in the morning. Perhaps you got the name of the town wrong."

Tanner shook his head. He hadn't been wrong. Elizabeth had lied to him. He wanted to know why she would lie about where she'd come from . . . if she wasn't hiding anything. He felt ill as suspicions tormented him.

Elizabeth checked her timepiece and frowned. It was very late; yet Belle and Tanner showed no sign of ending their conference at the kitchen table. Behind her bedroom door, Elizabeth had begun to wonder if they'd ever get to bed and allow her the opportunity to get on with this night's chore.

Finally, after what seemed like hours, the house grew quiet. Still Elizabeth waited, allowing them time to fall into a deep sleep before she silently completed the task of readying herself.

Almost an hour later she sat upon her horse, patiently waiting. The night wasn't nearly as dark as she'd have liked. The moon cast a bright silver light over the mostly flat sandy desert, creating shadows where it fell upon a spattering of cactus, tumbleweed, sagebrush, and rock. Elizabeth shrugged aside a chill of foreboding. This was far from being her first criminal excursion. She should now be able to take these escapades in stride; yet tonight her surroundings appeared unusually ghostlike, the dense silence almost eerie.

Until she'd come west, Elizabeth had never known this degree of intense quiet. Not a breath of air stirred. Nothing moved. She was engulfed in a silence so thick nothing could be heard but her own breathing and the pulsing of her blood.

Elizabeth shivered against the cold. Her hands were icy. Belatedly she realized she should have worn gloves and heavier clothing, for the summer was waning and though the days remained blistering hot, the desert nights, usually cool, were well on their way to becoming bitter cold.

Raven stirred restlessly beneath her. The last fiasco had shown her the folly of leaving him and approaching the stage on foot. She wouldn't repeat that mistake.

Both rider and horse blended into the shadowy protection of a huge boulder. Elizabeth had no fear of being seen until it was too late.

The horse stirred again, whinnying softly. No doubt his ears had picked up the sound of the approaching stage. A few minutes later, Elizabeth heard the rattle of wheels herself. Then the night came alive with sound. Unoiled springs screeched against the weight they were forced to bear. A whip cracked, probably striking the tough hide of a horse. A continual stream of curses flowed from the driver as he strained to keep the horses in line while the six huge beasts thundered down the dusty road, pulling the heavy stagecoach over the hard, rutted ground.

Elizabeth, stiff from the cold, was more than ready to see this night to a fruitful completion. She eased her gun from its holster and waited. It wasn't until the lead horse was just even with her position that she aimed her gun toward the sky and squeezed the trigger.

Elizabeth smiled as she heard the driver shout out in surprise and fear. An instant later a stream of vicious curses filled the night as he abruptly pulled up on the reins. The stage rolled thirty feet or more beyond her before it was finally brought to a stop.

Elizabeth breathed a sigh of relief. The next step would be to call out and have the driver drop the steel box to the ground.

She never got the chance.

The instant the stage stopped two men jumped from inside and rolled over onto the hard-packed road. Low to the ground, they became no more than moving blurs in the near darkness. Guns drawn, they fired simultaneously in Elizabeth's direction, again and again.

Without thinking, she returned the fire. In truth, she had no choice. Upon her horse, out in the open, she proved to be an excellent target. She couldn't take the time to turn her mount. Her only chance was to send her attackers in search of cover and then flee. She needed a little time to make good her escape.

One of the men cried out. Elizabeth knew one of her bullets had found its mark. She didn't consider the seriousness of her act, nor did she think the man might die. She knew only that she had to get away. The hand holding her gun seemed to work of its own accord.

No more than fifteen seconds had passed since the

stage had been brought to a stop, and the night had become an explosion of sound.

Elizabeth was calm — the trembling wouldn't come till later — as she backed her horse into the shadows. She was almost behind the boulder, relatively safe, about ready to turn and flee when she felt the blow. The force of it nearly knocked her from the saddle. She gave a soft, reflexive cry and tightened the grip of her legs around Raven.

Elizabeth didn't take the time to think. She moved with the instinct of any animal bent on saving itself. She'd been hit. A minor wound to the fleshy part of her arm, but already it bled profusely. She had to get back, take care of Raven, and look to this injury. And she had to hurry.

She bent low over her horse and raced like the wind to the safety of her home. Raven's galloping soon brought them to the lane that ran behind her house. Both woman and beast were straining for every breath by the time she walked her mount into the barn.

Waves of dizziness washed over her at the very thought of being shot. Determinedly she brushed them aside, gritted her teeth, and set about the task of seeing to her horse. Her left arm was pretty near useless, but she couldn't let that stop her. Raven needed to be unsaddled, wiped down, and covered for the night. He couldn't be left wet with sweat, lest he take a chill.

Elizabeth worked as fast as she could. She shivered as her straining caused the wound to begin to bleed again. Blood further dampened the sleeve of her shirt, and its wetness brought on a teeth-chattering chill. Her chore finished at last, Elizabeth headed toward the house.

It was dark. All appeared quiet. She disregarded the idea of taking the easier route and going in the front door. She couldn't chance being seen dressed as she was. Fortunately her window was close to the ground. Elizabeth knew she couldn't have managed any sort of climb with one arm hanging useless at her side.

The night's happenings had definitely taken their toll. She was trembling so she was almost unable to stand. Her body was slick with sweat when she finally managed to pull herself over the window ledge. Her arm ached like the devil; yet she had no choice but to rest for a moment, leaning against her bedroom wall. Knowing she had to see to her wound, she soon staggered toward the lamp that sat upon her mantel. With trembling fingers, she was reaching for the matches when a low voice caused her to jump and spin around.

"I wouldn't. The stage is sure to pass this way at any minute. Someone might wonder what the Widow Garner is doing up this late."

Elizabeth stood silent and still, her mind racing as she tried to come up with a plausible excuse for being out this late. She could tell him she'd been with Jonathan, but dressed like this? And why would she creep into her home through a bedroom window? Lord, why hadn't she thought to hide her clothes in the barn? Why hadn't she changed there?

Elizabeth sighed deeply. The time she had dreaded most was at hand.

Tanner rose from the chair. She could see his outline in the dark room, and she could gauge his fury by the tone of his voice. "What? No excuses? No sweet pleading for mercy?" he asked sharply. "Have you nothing to say?"

Elizabeth knew neither excuses nor pleading would suffice. She'd been caught red-handed, as they say. She had known from the first this day would come. There was nothing for her to do but take the punishment meted out for her crimes. "What would you like me to say?"

"You might start with telling me the truth. What were you doing tonight?"

Elizabeth wasn't at all sure she had the strength to withstand the coming confrontation. She let out another long sigh as she released the buckle of her hip-hugging gun belt with her uninjured hand, allowing the heavy leather and the gun to fall to the floor with a thud. Only then did she realize Tanner had held a gun, pointed in her direction, since she'd entered the room. She watched now as he placed it on a table just before he moved toward her. "I believe that's obvious."

"Do you?" His voice was hard; she imagined his eyes were filled with rage. "Why don't you tell me anyway?"

Elizabeth had no heart for this cat-and-mouse game he seemed bent on playing. She certainly wasn't happy about being found out, and yet a part of her was glad it was over. He'd arrest her now. There wasn't any sense in prolonging the outcome. "I was robbing the stage, of course," she retorted impatiently as she flung her hat toward the chair he'd vacated. "Are you satisfied?"

Tanner watched her hair fall from beneath her hat in a mass of tangled curls that cascaded down her back. Di-

179

sheveled, the raven mass glistened in the faint light of the moon. Elizabeth's soft clear skin looked startlingly white in comparison, and her dark eyes were huge, filled with fear. He could see that she was trembling despite her careless tone and attitude. She'd never looked more appealing. His fingers ached to reach out and bury themselves in warm silky hair. His lips grew fuller with the need to taste her. All he could think of was to bury his face in her scent, his body in hers.

He cursed his weakness and then shrugged. There was no longer a need to hold back this endless aching desire. This was no lady to be coddled and pampered. This woman was nothing but a thief and God only knew what else. She deserved no better than what she was going to get.

His mouth spread into a hard, evil smile. "Lady, I'm a long way from being satisfied." She heard a boot hit the floor, and her heart began to race as he stepped into the thin stream of moonlight coming from the window. He was taking off his shirt. "But I intend to be, real soon."

"Marshal," she murmured as his other boot was flung aside and the buttons of his trousers were opened one by one.

Elizabeth turned to flee. She knew no amount of pleading would sway him from his intent, but she wasn't about to stand there and take his abuse. And judging from the fury in his voice, the stiffness of his stance, she did not doubt that Tanner had every intention of abusing her. The moonlight shone from behind him, casting his face into shadow, but Elizabeth didn't have to see it to sense his fury. No doubt he believed she'd played him for a fool. He wouldn't be gentle.

She was almost at the door when his arms came about her waist and lifted her from the floor. A second later she was flung onto the bed. "You conniving little bitch!" he grunted as he stood over her. "And to think I asked you to marry me!" He knelt beside her, his knee and calf pressing against her legs, the pressure almost painful as he held them in place. His hands worked the buttons of her trousers free. "That must have given you a good laugh."

He slapped her hands away when she tried to stop him. "It's over, Elizabeth. You needn't bother to play the shy lady any longer."

When Elizabeth's hands again met his at the opening of her trousers, he flatly warned her, "If you're as smart as you'd like me to believe, you won't fight me. You're only going to end up hurt."

A shiver of dread went through Elizabeth, provoked by the lifeless, dull quality of his voice. He was going to take her by force, and there wasn't a thing she could do about it. But she wouldn't cower in fear and allow this man his way. "Then I'll end up hurt," she grunted, fighting him in earnest. Her hands balled into fists, and she swung her uninjured arm, grunting with some satisfaction when it contacted, with no little force, his cheek. She got in yet another blow, this one not quite as hard, before he managed to subdue her.

Elizabeth cried out in pain as he wrenched her arms above her head and locked them in place with one tight fist. Warm sticky blood seeped down her arm, but she would have died before she begged for quarter. Both

181

panting for breath, they stared at one another for long minutes before Tanner spat out, "You want it rough?" He shrugged as she simply grunted for an answer. "That's fine with me."

"I'll scream," she warned, knowing she'd do nothing of the kind. She'd die before she allowed anyone to learn of her shame.

"Go ahead. I don't care who knows about this."

"Marshal," she panted as she strained for calmness, still fighting against superior strength, "stop! Don't do this."

"Or what?" His jeering laugh was cruel. "Will I catch something? Are you diseased?"

Teeth clamped together, cheeks burning at his insult, she glared her hatred. "I wish I were," she said shakily. "It would be just reward for this abuse."

"It wouldn't matter," he said, his voice oddly hollow, almost without hope. "I can't let you go with this unfinished between us." He leaned closer, his face even with hers. Soft light from the window cast all but his eyes in dim shadows. From their dark depths they gleamed with hatred and need, and Elizabeth shivered with terror as he laughed at some secret joke.

I wonder if I can ever let you go, Tanner thought to himself. Something had died in him the moment he'd found her out. He had almost felt his heart shrivel with the agonizing pain.

He'd known. He couldn't say how exactly, but he'd known something was wrong almost from the moment they'd first met. Now, of course, it all fit. Her size, her ease at handling a gun, her friendship with Stacey, the telegram they'd gotten today. God, he'd been such a fool. He'd fallen in love with the very culprit he'd been sent to find and arrest.

What he couldn't figure out was why she had done it. How had a woman like her gotten mixed up in something like this? Why? Could it be he'd been wrong about her from the first? Was she merely playing the role of an innocent? He laughed softly, ridiculing himself. Of course! He'd grant her an excellent performance, but she'd been no more an innocent than he. Damn her soul to hell for the suffering he was sure to endure.

His mouth twisted into a grimace of hate as he settled himself down for a long wait. No doubt she gained her information from Stacey himself. Did she wait for the man to fall asleep after she'd bedded him before she looked through his papers?

Tanner groaned at the thought, and a rage the likes of which he'd never known seized him. He'd treated her like a lady, demanding nothing but what she was ready to give. He'd asked her to marry him. He was in love for the first time in ten long years. Why, in God's name, had he picked this particular woman?

Sitting alone in the dark, he almost wished she'd never return. If this night's escapade proved fatal, he'd suffer to be sure, but that suffering wouldn't compare to what he was sure to know if she came back. How was he going to bear the ordeal that lay ahead? How was he going to put the woman he loved in prison?

He leaned over her and watched her mouth draw up into a tight line. That sweet, delicious mouth. How many nights had he dreamed of kissing it, of having her kiss him in return? He watched her glare at him. It didn't matter. Nothing mattered now but finishing the game that started the moment they met.

Tanner wrenched her open trousers down her legs. They bunched at her ankles. With one hand he tore her shirt apart. She lay exposed, but proudly so. Elizabeth wouldn't cower for the likes of this brute. She sneered, then said, "I haven't the strength to win out against you, but you'll find little enjoyment in this act."

Tanner laughed softly at her threat. Little enjoyment? God, if she only knew. He had done little more than look and already his mind swam with an almost crazed need, knowing the pleasure that lay in store.

Her body was perfection. Soft, white, warm and inviting. Taking this woman would bring pleasure beyond compare. But his greatest pleasure wasn't in the taking. That would have been too easy. He wanted a complete victory over her. Before he was finished, he was going to see again that passion once glimpsed. His greatest delight would be watching her writhe beneath him. She was going to beg for his touch and love every minute of it.

Tanner's mouth slashed into a hard, cold grin as he lay full-length upon her. "You don't think so?" His free hand brushed aside her torn shirt and cupped a breast. His eyes never left hers as his thumb moved over the tip bringing it to a hard bud. "I can tell you right now,

184

you're wrong." He laughed at the soft sound of denial she made in her throat. "Not only will I enjoy this, so will you."

Elizabeth gritted her teeth against the dual need to curse him and to beg for mercy. Neither would serve a purpose. "I'll see you in hell first."

Tanner only laughed at her pledge. Ignoring her struggles, he dipped his head to her exposed breast. His lips tugged at the rosy tip, and he smiled in satisfaction as it grew harder and more sharply defined.

Elizabeth shivered at the touch of his mouth and wondered at the odd sensation. It was ridiculous to imagine his words might hold some semblance of truth. She'd never enjoy this. She hated this man. Hated his touch. Hated everything about him. "I despise you!" she swore. "If I had my gun, I'd put a bullet between your eyes." She bucked her hips trying to throw him off.

Tanner chuckled and leaned more heavily against her. His hand slid between their bodies as he released himself. Determinedly he ignored the feel of her, soft and warm against the backs of his fingers. Silently he promised himself the luxury of making long delicious love to her later. Right now his need was just too strong. "Bloodthirsty little bitch. I'll just bet you would."

"Arrest me," she begged. "Take me to prison. I'm guilty of all you suspect. Don't do this."

"Honey, it ain't goin' to matter all that much," he drawled against her skin. "What's one lover more or less?"

Chilled by fear, she almost blurted out the truth, but bit back the words. He'd never believe her an innocent.

Not after what he'd discovered tonight.

He was forcing her knees apart, no easy task since her trousers held her ankles together. She fought him with all her might, and still he won out easily against her considerably lesser strength. Her body stiffened. Her eyes closed. She clenched her teeth as she awaited the pain. She wouldn't beg. She wouldn't cry. She was strong enough to take the worst he could offer. She'd show him nothing he could do would have any effect. And yet, despite her brave thoughts she couldn't keep her body from trembling.

Desperately, she held to one thought. She couldn't win out against his superior strength, but when he was finished, she'd find her own pleasure. She was going to kill him. "Tanner, don't do this," she gasped breathlessly, shaking from terror and loss of blood even as she continued her useless efforts to throw him off.

He laughed aloud. "It doesn't matter anymore. Nothing matters but this," he said as he tilted his hips and drove deep, hard, and viciously into her tight dry body.

Elizabeth bit back the scream that tore through her. Her teeth ground into her lips until she tasted blood. Nothing she had ever imagined came close to that blinding pain. She'd thought she could take his worst, but she knew now she couldn't.

Elizabeth's anguished cry hardly registered against Tanner's absolute shock. His body stiffened, a sharp gutter word escaped his lips, and he instantly lost every erotic thought. A dozen questions ran through his mind. How could it be? She'd been a virgin. Why had she pretended otherwise? What the hell was a young innocent woman doing living by herself? Robbing stages? Stealing from the very man she professed to love? What game was she playing? Why?

Tears blurred Elizabeth's vision. She'd sworn she wouldn't cry, wouldn't give him the satisfaction of seeing her pain, but they came involuntarily to her eyes.

"My God," Tanner groaned. "Why didn't you tell me?"

She sniffed and swallowed, tears running down her cheeks. She tried desperately to keep her voice steady. "Would you have believed me?"

Her voice was lower now, filled less with pain than rage. "I'm going to kill you," she promised in a low whisper that projected hate.

Tanner cursed as he released her hands, knowing he would have responded with no more than a jeering laugh to any claim of innocence. His upper body was propped up on his elbows as he looked down into her beautiful face. With his thumbs, he wiped the tears from the corners of her eyes. "Why?" He shook her gently, desperate to find the answer. "Why did you pretend to be widowed?"

"Go to hell," she raged, and then she sighed disgustedly. "What's done is done." Her voice grew hard. Her distaste was obvious. "If you're finished, I'd like to get up now."

Tanner smiled. "Finished?"

Alarm rounded her eyes as she met his gentle gaze. "You don't want to do it again, do you?"

Tanner's heart was constricted by tender emotion. If nothing else, those words proved what her body had told him to be true. "Sweetheart, we haven't done anything yet."

"We haven't?"

Tanner groaned and buried his face in the warmth of her neck. He forgot his anger, his disillusionment, his insane jealousy. There was no way he was going to let this woman go. He heard her sniff again and murmured gently, "Don't cry, Liz. I'm sorry I hurt you. It'll never hurt like that again."

"I'm not crying. I never cry."

Tanner smiled as he listened to her watery reply.

He felt her stiffen as he eased himself off her and began removing her boots and trousers. "Easy," he breathed into her silky hair. "I'm just going to hold you. I promise I won't do anything more."

Elizabeth was almost lethargic as he lifted her to a sitting position and eased off her shirt. He imagined her soft groan of pain to be caused by the roughness he'd previously shown her. He wouldn't know till later of her wound.

Shrugging out of his own pants, he lay down beside her. Gently he held her against him, soothing her tremors, pressing her teary face into his chest. He rubbed her back until he felt her trembling ease. Slowly her body began to relax. Soon it grew soft and pliant against his.

Now it was he who trembled. It was killing him, this holding back. Tanner couldn't remember knowing greater pain. He couldn't hold her like this much longer and retain his sanity. His heart was pounding with the need to touch her, to kiss her, to love her until her tears flowed again, but in joy, her cries those born of ecstasy.

His fingers threaded through her hair as his hands

188

cupped the sides of her face and tilted it within easy reach of his mouth. When her eyes widened Tanner was struck by her look of fear. "Easy, sweetheart. I'm only going to kiss you. You like kissing don't you?"

Elizabeth felt her cheeks grow warm. It was so hard to admit to certain things; yet she knew she must. She nodded and watched in fascination as his mustache tipped crookedly in a smile.

Gently his lips brushed hers. Back and forth, back and forth, until she murmured a soft sound of pleasure and allowed them to part.

"I want to make love to you, Elizabeth," he whispered against her mouth.

"No!" She stiffened again, and her voice grew rigid from fear. "I can't. I don't want that again," she said, shuddering at the memory of the painful invasion, not caring about the despair that shone in his eyes. Elizabeth knew now why most women hated the more intimate part of marriage. What she couldn't understand was why any women liked it. Some did. She knew from the teasing comments, the secret smiles and giggles her friends shared that some liked it very much indeed. But as far as she was concerned it was an ugly act, shameful and filled with pain. She'd never do it again.

"It won't be that way again, darlin'. I swear it won't."

"Why not?"

Tanner let out a long sigh and silently cursed his earlier act. He had only himself to blame. This woman had never once shown him anything but sweet innocence. Why had he allowed his anger and jealousy to overcome his common sense? "I wasn't gentle before. It was all my

189

fault."

Elizabeth shook her head as he drew her closer, his hand on her hip, his fingertips kneading her derrière. "I don't think—"

"Let me show you," he interrupted. "If you don't like it, I'll stop. I'll stop anytime you say."

"Will you?" she asked doubtfully.

Tanner groaned. "It'll probably kill me, but I swear it."

He kissed her again, gently, sweetly, holding himself in rigid control. It wasn't until he felt her begin to relax again that he grew bolder. His lips widened; his tongue gently traced her lips. In fleeting feathery strokes it fluttered teasingly over them, only to penetrate the edge of her mouth and instantly retreat. Tanner smiled as she finally sighed softly, a sound of pleasure, and her lips opened wider beneath his in an invitation to deepen the kiss.

His tongue flicked over them, darting inside, bathing the sensitive inner flesh of her mouth with his taste, but still he refused to linger.

"Tanner," she breathed against his mouth, as an ache began to form in her. His teasing mouth and tongue were setting her heart to pounding, her body to trembling. His lips, burning hot, slid to her throat. His tongue danced along her skin, playing at the hollow beneath her ear. Chills ran down her back. She forgot her vow of hatred. She wanted this man to kiss her, really kiss her. "Tanner, please," she whispered anxiously as she sought to bring their mouths together.

He laughed softly as he watched the need come to life

in her eyes. "What, sweetheart? Tell me what you want."

"I want you to kiss me," she said boldly, no longer caring about the daring admission, filled with but one need. She had to feel his lips on hers.

"Like this?" he asked, as he continued on with the tender tastings, the almost painful torment.

"Like this," she said as her uninjured arm came around his neck and pulled his face down. Mutual groans of satisfaction mingled as opened mouths delighted in sweet rediscovery. Tongues explored with rapid enthusiasm, delving deep, drawing forth flavor, delighting in texture, while mouths sucked and lips tugged with growing impatience.

Pulling apart for the moment it took to fill their lungs, their mouths came together again, and Tanner groaned out his pleasure as lessons learned were shyly put to use. When she sucked at his tongue Tanner thought he might explode or die or both. He growled into her mouth and crushed her against him.

Elizabeth had never known pleasure to this degree. She felt as if she were floating, her mind dizzy with this overwhelming sensation, this growing need. She never realized how deeply her nails dug into his shoulder, nor was she aware that her hips arched hungrily, mindlessly into his.

Tanner groaned at the wild response he felt in her. It was too soon. She wouldn't find release, much less enjoyment, if he took what she offered now. She needed more before she was ready, no matter what she might feel at the moment.

"So beautiful," he murmured, his words muffled

against her cheek, his breath hot against her neck, her ear.

She sighed in disappointment as his mouth left hers, but the sigh became a low aching groan of anticipation as his mouth made a hot wet path to her breast. Elizabeth cried out softly as he took the tip deep, deep into burning flame.

Gentle at first, he suckled the tender tip. Kissing it, rolling his tongue over it, until she showed him with anxious movements and impatient tuggings with her hands that she wanted more. She groaned as he used his teeth and then sucked harder. Her back arched against him. The sensation was almost more than she could bear.

His hands lifted the heavy globes of flesh and pressed them together as he nuzzled first one and then the other.

Glorious. Elizabeth moaned in delight. It was almost too much. And yet, she found herself aching for something, something she couldn't name. Something she wanted desperately. "Tanner," she murmured almost drunkenly as her fingers slid through his dark hair and down his back. "Tanner."

He was rubbing his mustache over her flesh, sensitizing it all the more. She couldn't stand it.

Elizabeth squirmed, moving restlessly against him. In some far-off corner of her brain she realized the scratchy hairs of his legs and chest felt wonderful against her skin.

His mouth was lowering to her waist. He kissed, nibbled, and then soothed with exquisite dartings of his tongue. "Oh, God," she moaned, her mind sinking deeper into a fog of crazed desire. "I can't bear much more," she murmured.

His mustache grazed her hips and stomach as his mouth deposited biting, thrilling kisses everywhere it went. Elizabeth couldn't breathe as he got closer, closer to the core of her, closer to her most private parts. She bit back a moan as his mouth brushed over and then returned to linger for long wild moments at the juncture of her thighs.

She might have pulled back, but she was already too far gone in passion. She wanted his mouth there. She wanted it everywhere.

He was kissing her, licking her, sucking her, where no man had ever dared to touch her before, and Elizabeth thought she might die from the pleasure. Her legs parted, her hips lifted toward the burning, liquid heat of his mouth.

Tanner closed his eyes against exquisite pleasure. Had a woman ever felt so good, responded so sweetly? He breathed in her scent and found himself almost drunk on her taste. God, she was delicious. But he'd known it would be like this. The more he touched, the more he wanted, until he was lost in her scent, her feel, her taste.

Elizabeth was burning up, her body slick with sweat. Surely she wouldn't survive this sweet torture. Her hips rose higher, searching for an elusive something. She thought she found it, but it evaded her grasp and left her aching, aching until she thought she'd die from wanting.

A tight knot was forming across her abdomen. It spread and intensified, then became tighter, unbearably tight. Surely it couldn't go on without causing damage. "Tanner, please, my God, please."

Tanner knew she was close to finding release. He could hear it in her voice, in the shallowness of her breathing. He could feel it in the tightness of her body. "Let it happen, darlin'," he said against hot, moist, pulsing flesh. "Let it come."

She was burning for him. A wild and beautiful sight. He'd never known greater delight than just watching her, feeling her response. Tanner knew at that moment this woman had ruined him for any other.

Her head arched back. Her lips parted. Her fingers clutched at the bed sheets. Her body tightened to the breaking point. "Oh, God," she breathed out as she was caught up in the agonizing throes of explosive ecstasy.

"Oh, God," she murmured again as the pleasure came in harsh, aching, desperate waves that were tearing her to pieces. She couldn't bear it and she never wanted it to stop. "My God," she whispered moments later as her pleasures subsided.

He couldn't wait any longer. He entered her then, knowing she was at her most relaxed. "I know it's too soon," he panted against her lips. "You won't be able to . . . I can't wait any longer." And then his mouth was clinging to hers, devouring in his relentless hunger for her.

"Liz . . . oh, God . . . Liz," he breathed into her mouth. She was so tight, so unbearably tight, he thought he might lose the last of his reason. His hands went to her hips and gently guided her movements. He moved slowly at first, but soon his thrusts became hurried and then wild. "I can't hold back."

"Don't," she gasped as he drove into her. "I want to feel it all," she urged as her hips rose to meet his. "Don't hold anything back."

Deep, deeper in her softness, into her heat. He was drowning in her fire. Dying in her tightness. He'd never known a sensation, a moment, a woman to compare. Nothing could compare.

Tanner arched his body into hers. His face was a mask of agony as shudders wracked him and overcame all else but the woman he held so tightly in his arms.

Chapter Ten

Tanner's arms trembled as he held himself above her. He couldn't seem to get his breath, to find the strength to simply roll onto his side.

He managed at last to do both. Eyes closed, arms weighted, he reached for her and drew her to him. He couldn't remember a time when he'd felt so good, or so exhausted. "Are you all right?"

Elizabeth snuggled against his warmth and murmured that she was.

It was a long time before Tanner realized the arm beneath her was wet. He stiffened. "Are you crying?" he asked, peering down, unable to make out her expression in the dark. "Did I hurt you?"

Elizabeth muttered something indistinguishable. By now she was so content and so comfortable, she easily dismissed the slight ache in her arm.

"I did hurt you," Tanner said as it became more and more obvious that his arm was wet. "Damn!" He rolled her onto her back. "Why didn't you say something?"

Moving from her side, he reached for the candle on the night stand. A moment later a match flared to life and the taper cast a soft glow upon the room.

"God damn!" Tanner's eyes went wide with horror at the sight of blood. It covered his arm. He turned quickly toward the bed and spied the huge red stain. Dumbfounded, he could only stare. She was bleeding! What could he have done to cause her to bleed?

He turned and leaned over her. His face was gray and strained. "What happened? Why are you bleeding? Show me where you're hurt."

Elizabeth had been lying on her injured arm. At the time she had felt comfortable enough. Now that Tanner no longer held her, now that her mind was not centered on other matters, her injury began to ache in earnest. "It's my arm," she said as she shifted slightly and exposed the wound.

"How the hell. . . ?" Astonished, he stared at the small injury. It had crusted over with blood, but had since begun to bleed again. Tanner knew nothing he had done could have resulted in the wound. Obviously she had been hurt before returning to the house.

He moved closer, his eyes examining the bloody gash. "What happened? Did you get caught up on a tree branch?"

She shook her head and lowered her eyes.

Tanner gave her a short but sharp shake and then cursed as pain made her wince. "Tell me!"

"A bullet," she said, so matter-of-factly that once Tanner grasped her meaning, he had a time of it keeping his hands from her throat.

"Oh, a bullet," he repeated with exaggerated calmness. The deadly softness of his tone sent a chill of fear up Elizabeth's spine. "And how did you manage that?" Tanner knew without asking that she had been in a gunfight. She was too good with a pistol to have accidentally shot herself.

Elizabeth raised her eyes to his and sighed. Quiet rage had turned his features to stone; he showed not a flicker of compassion. "Tanner, I don't want to argue with you."

"I have no intention of arguing. I merely asked you a question," he said, so civilly he almost convinced her. Would have, in fact, if she hadn't seen his hands tremble as they released her.

She sighed again and brushed a black curl from her face. "I was robbing the stage."

He muttered a vile curse. "If you only knew how ridiculous you sound." He mimicked her, " 'I was robbing the stage.' You say it as if you're talking about baking a loaf of bread."

Anger flashed in Elizabeth's eyes as she yanked the sheet up with her good hand and covered her nakedness. "Do you want to hear about it or not?"

"Go on," he said with almost icy contempt; his gaze was murderous as he strove to contain his fury.

"There were men on the stage. Gunfighters, I imagine."

Tanner spit out a stream of unspeakably vulgar curse words, and he jumped off the bed, afraid of what he might do if he remained at her side. He then began to pace. Spying his shirt, he retrieved it from the floor. Within minutes he rolled a cigarette, using the paper and tobacco taken from one pocket, and lit it with the candle's flame. "Go on," he said as he exhaled a stream of blue smoke toward the ceiling, totally unconscious of the fact that he stood before her stark naked.

"Must you parade about like that?" she asked, unable to bring her gaze from the sheet. Her cheeks reddened as she became aware that his hips were almost level with her eyes.

"Like what?" he asked, momentarily confused by her change of subject.

"If you insist on having this conversation, I'd appreciate it if you'd put some clothes on."

Tanner uttered a hard, sharp, humorless laugh. "Little hypocrite. It's all right for you to rob a stage and have a gunfight, but a naked man upsets your sensibilities." He did not comply with her wishes. "Finish your story," he said.

Elizabeth ignored his jeering, contemptuous comment. Obviously this arrogant beast was going to do exactly as he pleased, despite her objections. She forced her gaze to remain on the sheet as she nervously creased its fabric. "After the stage stopped, two men jumped from inside. They started shooting before I could do anything."

"And then?"

"I shot back."

Tanner moaned as he ran a hand over his face. He was pacing again. "Why? Why didn't you just ride away?"

"I was too close. With their guns firing, I didn't dare turn away."

It was a moment before Tanner managed to control his anger at her. His voice was remarkably steady, considering the near hysteria that gripped him at the thought of Elizabeth being in a gunfight. "What happened next?"

"I shot one of them." She ignored his curse. "At least I think I did. I heard someone cry out." He cursed again, and she sighed wearily, "Is it necessary for you to respond to my every sentence with yet another gutter word?"

Tanner's lips barely moved. His blue eyes glared. "It is, if you expect me to keep my hands from your throat," he retorted, his tone low and threatening.

He released a deep calming sigh. "Let's hear it all."

Elizabeth, having no fear of this man, merely shrugged with her good arm. "That's all. I was almost behind the rock when I felt the bullet graze my arm."

Tanner threw his cigarette into the fireplace, closely examined her arm, and then went to the wash stand, all without saying another word. A minute later he returned to the bed, carrying a bowl of water, a cloth, and a towel.

His fingers shook as he worked at cleaning the wound. He kept thinking that the bullet, had it been a few inches to the left, could have entered her chest, perhaps even her heart. Sweat broke out over his forehead and lip as he imagined the damage one bullet could have done. He wanted to wring her neck. How dare she risk her life? Didn't she know what it would do to him if anything happened to her?

"Are you going to arrest me now?" Elizabeth asked, her eyes searching his tight, unreadable features. She was unable to stand another minute of his silence. She had to know what was on his mind. She had to ready herself for what lay in store.

Tanner shot her a quick hard look. "No. I'm not going to arrest you." It was a moment before he released a long despairing sigh. "I'm afraid I have no choice but to marry you."

Elizabeth hadn't realized she'd been holding her breath, awaiting his reply. The problem was, she'd never expected to hear those particular words and she was shocked. "Tanner!" He couldn't be serious, of course. He was a lawman. A United States Marshal. He wouldn't, couldn't take a criminal for a wife.

"What?" he asked almost wearily as he looked up from his ministrations.

Her eyes clearly told him of her confusion. "You shouldn't make light of this."

Tanner's smile was tight, hardly a smile at all. It was apparent that he wasn't the least bit delighted about his stated intention. "I've never been more serious in my life. It seems I've been stupid enough to have fallen in love with you."

Elizabeth's mouth dropped open in amazement. How could this man declare his feelings with no more emotion than he would show when imparting the time of day? Even if it were possible, she would never marry a man so cold. She shook her head, knowing the error of her thoughts. Tanner lacked nothing in the way of emotion. He was a man whose passions ran deep. He wanted her, lusted for her, but it wasn't love he felt. She breathed a small, remarkably sad sigh as she realized her disappointment. Did she want his love? Was that why she felt this sudden crushing sadness? She couldn't honestly say.

Tanner refused to look at her. He was tearing a small towel to thin strips as he waited for her to make some comment. No doubt it was too much to hope that she might reciprocate his feelings. His sigh almost bordered on despair when he realized, by her lengthening silence, she did not. He shrugged mentally, knowing she had no more choice in the matter than he did. Her feelings wouldn't be taken into consideration. He'd known almost from the first that this woman, no matter what she was, no matter what she'd done, was destined to be his. Gently he wrapped the toweling around her cleaned wound.

When he finished the chore, he put the bowl and toweling back on her dry sink. His back was to her when he spoke again. "If you get up, I'll change the sheets."

During their conversation, Elizabeth had determinedly averted her gaze from his nakedness. But now that he had his back to her, she looked up from the sheet and greedily absorbed his long tan form, noting the muscular thickness of his thighs, the narrowness of his hips. He was outstanding. A beautifully shaped male. Idly she wondered if all men were as wonderful to look upon.

"I can't marry you," she said, her voice oddly shaken and whispery soft, for the sight of him was greatly affecting her.

Tanner laughed at that comment. "I'm afraid neither of us has much of a choice."

"I do. I won't marry a man I hardly know."

Tanner laughed again and, as he turned and leaned

202

his hip against the dry sink, smugly retorted, "You've been to bed with me. I imagine you know me well enough."

"You know what I mean," she responded, her face growing red as she was reminded of the things they had done. She muttered a near-silent curse. His casual stance didn't help matters any. How was she supposed to carry on a civilized conversation with a man standing across from her, naked as the day he was born? "I can't."

"Oh, I think you will," Tanner remarked confidently. "You see, the law states that a wife cannot testify against her husband."

Elizabeth shrugged. "So?"

"So it works in the reverse as well."

"And if I refuse?"

"If you refuse, I'll have no alternative but to take you back to Virginia City and see you hang."

"Hang!" Her voice rose slightly, "Are you mad? I only robbed the stage. Surely that doesn't warrant a death sentence. I didn't—"

"Shoot a man tonight?" he finished for her. "And if that man should die? What then?"

He didn't seem to want or need an answer. He shrugged. "It matters little. The intent was to do bodily harm. Our laws don't look kindly upon attempted murderers.

"Where do you keep your nightdresses and sheets?"

"In the second and fourth drawer," Elizabeth said as she nodded toward her dresser while offering a silent prayer for the man she'd shot. Till this minute, she'd been preoccupied with her own need to escape and her confrontation with Tanner that had ended in lovemaking. She hadn't once thought about that poor man.

A moment later Tanner stood before her, gown in hand. Gently he helped her from the bed. But when he tried to pull the sheet from her, Elizabeth held on to it tightly. She wouldn't stand here naked before him. What they'd done together, in the dark, was one thing, but to be fully exposed to his gaze was too much to ask of her.

"If you give me a minute" — she nodded toward her door — "I can manage."

Tanner smiled and suddenly, unexpectantly yanked the sheet from her grasp.

Elizabeth gave a short startled cry, and her hands flew to protect herself from his gaze.

"There's no need for you to be embarrassed. Not around me," Tanner said as he drew her to him. Feeling her stiffness, he let his hands run down the length of her back as he lowered his head and breathed in the clean sweetness of her hair.

"Better?" he asked after a time.

Elizabeth shook her head. It would never be better. She couldn't imagine a day when she'd be at ease in this man's company, never mind standing naked in his arms. She shivered and realized for the first time that the room was decidedly cool.

"Here, let me help you," Tanner murmured as he created some space between their bodies. He slid her gown up over her head and slipped it over her injured arm. "I don't want you to get cold." That took some doing since Tanner's hands seemed particularly reluctant to allow the material to fall into place. Elizabeth could only gasp as he touched her in the most outrageously possessive manner. Finally he managed to smooth the garment down the length of her.

His eyes glazed with rekindled passion, Tanner thought he had never seen a more beautiful sight. Elizabeth's lips were swollen from hungry kisses. Her breasts were heavy and full, their pink crests tight as she unconsciously arched against the movement of his fingers. Her waist was slender, her hips smooth and full. His body trembled with the need to take her again, but he wouldn't. Tomorrow would be soon enough. He took a deep calming breath and held her against him. In doing so, he inadvertently nudged her arm. "Does it hurt much?" he asked when she groaned softly.

"No," she managed to say, though she wondered if her cheeks would ever again reclaim their normal color. Her breathing, light and shallow from his erotic touchings, grew more so as she met his warm gaze. "It's just a bit sore."

The white gown, settled in place, contrasted sharply with the dark hair that swirled deliciously around her face, over her shoulders, and down her back. Tanner was tempted, greatly tempted, to put aside his resolve and take her again.

His lips were inches from her own. She could feel soft, warm puffs of breath against her mouth as he asked, "Why didn't you say something when you first came in?"

Elizabeth lowered her gaze as she suddenly realized the mortifying direction of her thoughts. She didn't want him to kiss her, she silently insisted. A woman didn't crave a man's kiss; she endured kissing for the man's pleasure. That was the way of decent women. But was she decent? Would a decent woman grow wild, almost crazed with need in a man's arms? Would she have permitted the disgraceful things they'd done together? She didn't know anymore. She'd never known she was wicked enough to enjoy a man's touch, and that knowledge terrified her. Elizabeth sighed and wished she had someone she could talk to, someone who could tell her the way of things. Her voice shook as confusion and fear settled in the pit of her stomach. "I was so surprised to find you here, I forgot all about it."

He pulled off the soiled bedding and flipped over her feather mattress. The clean bedclothes billowed as he shook them out over the mattress. A moment later the corners were tucked neatly beneath it. Elizabeth watched in silence as he went about the chore. When he finished, he crawled into the bed and held up the covers in silent invitation.

"You can't mean to sleep here?" she asked, her eyes round with surprise at his actions. There was no way she was going to share her bed with this man. This naked man. Not after the things they had done, the very same things she suddenly realized she wanted to do again.

"You didn't seem to mind much just a while back. You were a-cuddlin' up against me, already half asleep when I noticed the bed was wet."

Elizabeth's cheeks grew darker than ever, and her eyes sparkled with embarrassment over his constant references to what had taken place between them. It was bad enough, what they'd done. Did he have to talk about it? Why, the man practically gloated. Practically? No, he was gloating. She'd have to be blind to miss that gleam of laughter in his eyes. How could he take this so lightly?

Tanner shrugged aside the annoyance that flared in her eyes. "We're getting married in the morning. It makes little difference if we spend tonight together."

"It does make a difference. Go back to your own room."

"And leave you alone?" Tanner's teeth flashed in a broad grin. "I think not." He shot her a hard, knowing look. "The night's still young. There's no telling who else you might shoot."

Elizabeth's dark eyes narrowed with menace, as she spoke through stiff lips. "As a matter of fact, you would be my only consideration."

Tanner laughed at her threat. "If you don't come over here, I'll just come and get you."

"You're not much of a lawman," she said, her voice dripping disgust as she realized acquiescence was imminent. She was moving toward the bed, about to obey him. What was the matter with her? Had she no backbone? Why was she giving in to his demands? Because it's what you want, a soft voice within her said.

"You don't think so?" he asked, his lips twisting into a grin. "Why?"

"I was under the impression that lawmen are honorable." Elizabeth grumbled as she slid into the bed and lay stiffly beside him. "They don't force ladies into their beds."

"Ladies who rob stages are probably an exception," he said lightly, his eyes sparkling with laughter. "And this isn't my bed."

207

"Your attempt at humor is pathetic."

Tanner sighed as he laid on his back and gazed up at the ceiling, feeling oddly content though she was not very happy. His mouth curved into a smile as he remarked, "Let's see. I'm not much of a lawman, nor do I possess a devastating sense of humor. Dare I ask your opinion of me?"

"I wouldn't," she warned almost flippantly.

Tanner chuckled as he pinched out the candle, rolled over and pulled her into the warm, hard curve of his body. "Then maybe I'd better not."

"No." The husky, sleepy sound came from behind and above her as she tried to slip from under Tanner's arm. "It's not even light out. You're not getting up."

"I have to start the fire," she murmured with a sleepy yawn. "There's breakfast to make."

"Let them make their own," he grunted near her ear as he hugged her tighter and cuddled his hips closer to hers. Tanner made a soft sound of pleasure when he realized her gown had slipped up during the night and her bare backside was now pressed snugly against his lower body. "God, this feels good."

"I have to get up," Elizabeth said, sounding slightly shaken as she realized he spoke the truth and his growing hardness pressed against her bottom.

Tanner reached beneath the covers, his fingers running over her bottom and slipping between her legs. "No, you don't."

"What will Belle and Miss Dunlap think?" she said.

Then she gasped softly as she helplessly allowed the delicious caress.

"I'll tell them you're indisposed."

Elizabeth knew that was impossible. "Marshal," she said stiffly, fighting the need his touch had instantly brought about, "this is ridiculous. Let me up!"

Tanner laughed as he rolled her onto her back and leaned over her. His legs kept her securely in place as his hand had its leisurely way with her body. "I think you can call me Tanner. You'll be my wife in a few hours."

"I won't be," she declared. Then he touched a particularly sensitive part of her and she bit her lip and closed her eyes as she silently fought seduction. "I'm not going to marry you."

Tanner ignored her last statement. His grin was wicked as he gazed down at her. "You like that?"

Elizabeth would have wrestled with the devil before she'd admit to liking what he was doing. "Like what?" she asked as she pushed his hand away.

It immediately returned to what it had been about, slyly drifting back to what Tanner seemed most happy to investigate. In the predawn dimness, his teasing gaze gleamed with laughter when she scowled.

"Let me up."

"Aw honey, you know you don't mean it."

"I most certainly do." Elizabeth's voice sounded whispery soft and breathless, when it should have sounded firm.

His hand moved just a fraction lower. She was moist and hot, her body ready and wanting, no matter how she might deny it. He slid his finger deep into her heat

209

and watched with fascination as her eyes rolled back just before they closed, her soft indrawn gasp seeming to lift her breasts closer to his mouth.

Tanner never thought to deny himself the pleasure. With what felt like one lightning-fast movement, her gown was pulled over her head and flung aside. Immediately his mouth lowered, his tongue a hungry burning flame licking at her straining breasts even as his hand returned to rediscover and relish her moist heat.

Elizabeth gave out a soft sound as his hand nearly drove her mad with its movement.

"Marry me, Elizabeth," he said as he settled his hips in the sweet soft hollow of hers. "Tell me you will," he insisted as he entered her with a swift hard thrust. Tanner almost laughed with joy at hearing her low groan of pleasure. She loved everything he was doing to her. She could not deny him what he wanted most.

"It doesn't matter what I say," she whispered breathlessly as he moved within her. "I'll deny it later."

Tanner's laughter bubbled from deep within his chest. When had a woman so intrigued him? When had he last been so dazzled? "Witch!" he grunted as he pulled back and then thrust forward again. "So I can't convince you?"

"You might as well stop trying," she gasped, straining for a boredom she found impossible to maintain.

"I suppose I should stop this as well then," Tanner taunted wickedly, attempting to pull away.

"Don't!" she commanded, her voice insistent, her hands suddenly holding his hips to hers.

Their eyes held for long minutes, each staring into the

dark hungry depths of the other. "Say you will," he demanded, allowing her no quarter as he moved into her again, deep, deeper, with desperate thrusts that sought to conquer and claim her.

"I will, I will," she cried as both her body and mouth opened, accepting, delighting in his delicious loving.

Tanner couldn't believe it. It was better than the first, and he'd thought that time the best imaginable. Gasping for breath, he finally lay exhausted, his face cushioned upon her soft breast.

It took superhuman effort, but he finally managed to turn onto his side and bring her limp body with him. Elizabeth snuggled against his chest, an arm and leg thrown familiarly over him.

"I lied," she breathed out the words on a long sigh of exhaustion.

A long moment passed before the low sounds of laughter filled the silent room. He squeezed her tightly to him and rocked her lovingly in his arms. "We're goin' to have one damned exciting life together."

"Maybe," she grunted unhappily. It was apparent Elizabeth Garner wasn't one to give in gracefully. "But if you keep squeezing me like this, I expect it will be fairly short."

He laughed again and slapped her bottom. In retaliation she pinched two hairs from his chest. Instantly her hand closed over his mouth to quiet his startled yelp of pain. "Shush. You'll wake up the entire house."

Tanner kissed her palm. A moment later his lips parted and his tongue moved in lazy circles against her smooth skin. He smiled as she drew her hand away, grumbling in a decidedly unladylike way. "Do I say that while you're . . ."

"What?" she asked when he hesitated, her eyes full of laughter.

"To put it gently, while you're beneath me, crying out for more."

Elizabeth shook her head, a soft smile touching her lips. "God, you are a beast. Am I destined to be forever tormented by you?"

"You're destined to be forever loved by me." He snuggled against her before he asked, "Why? Tell me why you did it."

She shook her head. It wasn't necessary to ask. She knew full well what he meant. She'd waited since last night for him to bring the subject up. "It doesn't matter. What's done is done."

"It was important enough for you to chance your life. Tell me!"

"Stacey killed my father and ruined my family. For that I've sworn revenge."

Tanner cursed as he held her tighter in his protective embrace. "Why didn't the authorities take care of it? Why have you made his destruction your personal crusade?"

"There was no proof. Besides," she shrugged as if the idea held little importance, "he didn't actually pull the trigger. But he might as well have.

"It was years ago. I was little more than a child. He was a captain in charge of the Army payroll. My father worked directly under his command." Elizabeth took a deep breath as if searching for some inner strength.

"Guards were murdered, the payroll was stolen, and my father was accused.

"They say he couldn't live down the scandal. They say he committed suicide."

"They say?"

"I don't believe it. I'll never believe it."

"You suspect Stacey to be the culprit?"

"I don't suspect it, I know it!"

"Are you sure you're not looking for—"

"A scapegoat?" Elizabeth uttered a sound that barely resembled a laugh. "Hardly." She moved slightly, her gaze upon the ceiling as she spoke. "If you'd known my father . . ." She shook her head. "He was as incapable of killing himself as he was of stealing."

"Someone killed him?"

Elizabeth only nodded for an answer. "And made it look like suicide."

"But why pick on Stacey? Surely another could have been responsible."

"You're right, another probably could have, but it was him." She turned to glare at Tanner. "Where did the money to buy his silver mine come from?"

Tanner shrugged. "Maybe he won it at cards?"

Elizabeth smiled. "Have you ever seen him play?"

"Does that mean he doesn't?"

Elizabeth sighed. "You've done some investigating, Marshal. Does he strike you as the sort of man who takes chances?"

Tanner took and then released a long deep breath. "So you contend that Stacey stole the Army's payroll and bought a silver mine, leaving your father to take the blame."

"Exactly."

"And he never imagined anyone might grow suspicious of his sudden wealth?"

"Why should they? Who would think to ask where the money came from? He was hundreds of miles from Washington, months away from the scandal."

"Why would he have your father killed? I presume you believe that he's a murderer as well as a thief."

"There was a chance my father could have proven himself innocent. If so, suspicion would then have fallen on Stacey. Only the two of them knew the exact time and route of the shipment."

"Still there is no real proof."

"It doesn't matter," Elizabeth tossed her head. "I don't need any real proof. I know —"

Tanner interrupted her. "I'm taking you away from here."

She glanced his way. "Unless you're willing to arrest me, I don't see how."

"Meaning?"

"Meaning, I'm far from finished with this man."

"Damn it! Elizabeth, you can't think I'd allow you to further jeopardize yourself. Now that I know, I'll —"

"What? You'll arrest him? On what charge?"

"I'll find something."

Elizabeth shook her head. "Not good enough. That monster is going to suffer for what he did."

"And you think you're the one to deliver justice?"

"The law can't do it," she taunted.

"Am I supposed to sit by and watch?"

Elizabeth shrugged. "Not exactly."

"What exactly?"

"Now that you know, you could help."

"Help you rob stages?"

She shook her head. "Help me ruin him. It doesn't matter how."

Tanner let out a round of curses as he nearly jumped from the bed. He pulled on his pants and cursed again as he stubbed his toe against the bedpost. He was so goddamned besotted he'd almost gone along with her plea. Lord! What kind of power did this woman possess? Just thinking of how easily he could slip under her control scared the shit out of him. "You're out of your mind. If you think I'm going to spend the next ten years or more behind bars because of you, think again."

Tanner glared at her. "Get out of that bed, and do it now. I'm going to tell the preacher we're getting married today." His eyes narrowed as he took in her look of defiance. "If you know what's good for you, you'll be ready when I get back."

Chapter Eleven

Apparently she didn't, because she wasn't.

Tanner knew he'd have a time of it. He hadn't been under any delusion that she'd meekly obey him. He'd figured he was in for a good fight. What he hadn't counted on was that when he returned, she'd be gone.

She probably had an hour on him. He muttered a low vicious curse as he hurriedly saddled his horse. He'd needed to know the status of the injured man, or he'd never have stopped by Doc Thompson's. The doc could talk till tomorrow without hardly taking a breath. The time Tanner had spent with him had afforded Elizabeth the chance to run.

The man she'd shot had suffered no more deadly a wound than Elizabeth herself. At least Tanner didn't have to worry about protecting her from being charged with murder. Although how he'd have managed that, he hadn't a clue.

He grinned as he mounted up. He could almost taste the satisfaction he'd know upon finding her. It would definitely be to her benefit if he didn't find her too soon, though, for his fingers itched to wring her neck. He needed to calm down a bit, and a long ride would be just the ticket. One thing for sure, before this day was done, she was going to have a problem sitting in a saddle.

The sun beat down upon the flat, almost barren landscape, creating relentless, breathless heat. Tanner's hat was tipped low over his eyes, but the wide brim offered little protection against the glare. No doubt the sun's rays would one day leave him with a permanent squint. The lower half of his face was covered by a cotton neckerchief, but dust managed to filter through the material and enter his nose and mouth. Sweat poured down from under the rim of his hat. It ran down his back, but it dried almost as quickly as it formed. He raced on.

Her damned horse could just about fly. How the hell did she manage to maintain such a speed? Horse or woman would have to tire. Was she so desperate to get away? Tanner's lips twisted into a sneer. A stupid question.

The sun was low in the sky when a stream of curses and a few desperate prayers broke from his stiff lips. His body suddenly relaxed, letting him feel the aches caused by hours of tension. It was growing darker by the minute. He'd known he'd lose her trail in the darkness, and soon. But he'd spotted her fire. It was miles away, yet easily visible in the flat desert. Her first mistake. Her second would be to give him any lip.

She sat before her campfire, apparently unaware that she was no longer alone. Tanner was amazed at the sudden calm that filled him upon finding her.

He'd expected to rant, to rave, to threaten her with bodily harm if she dared do anything so foolish again, but his anger seemed to have evaporated. What he did was silently relish the sight of Elizabeth's slim back, the smooth length of her creamy neck, the gentle curve of her deliciously full breasts. She befuddled his mind, and his craving for her knew no relief.

His mouth twisted into a grin at seeing her dark shirt and trousers. No matter how she might try to disguise herself, a man would have to be blind not to know that slender, shapely form was a woman's. "I reckon you figured I'd given up a way's back," he said as he went to stand directly behind her.

Elizabeth didn't move a muscle. She'd heard the approaching horse. For a time she'd cradled her revolver as she waited for her uninvited guest to make himself known. But upon hearing him dismount and approach her camp, she'd put the gun aside and reached for her coffee. "Actually I was hoping you wouldn't bother," she said, her gaze fixed on the small campfire.

"You figured wrong."

"So I see," she said, never looking his way as he settled himself upon her blanket. She sipped the hot coffee.

"Do you realize just how dangerous it is for a woman out here alone?"

Elizabeth smiled. From the moment she'd realized who had come upon her, she'd known he'd rant on about that very subject. "I can protect myself," she said with an indifferent shrug.

"Can you? Is that why I was able to come up upon

you without your knowing?"

Elizabeth laughed. "Did you?"

"Did I what?"

"Come upon me without my knowledge."

"If you knew someone was out there, why didn't you do something?"

"I did," she said, lifting her leg no more than an inch to show him how close her gun was to her hand.

"So? Why didn't you use it?"

Elizabeth raised a slender shoulder in a shrug. "I knew it was you. I know your step." She never realized just how telling that statement was, nor did she see the sudden flash of his smile or the light of victory in his eyes.

The fire crackled. For some moments that was the only sound at the campsite. "It'll never work, you know," she said with a weary sigh as he returned with his saddlebags and helped himself to a cup of her coffee.

Tanner sat at her side again, legs apart, knees raised and elbows balanced upon them. He moved only his head as he asked, "What?"

"Our getting married."

"Why not?"

"Because people can't marry under duress and live happily ever after."

"Few live happily ever after in any case. And I'm not under duress."

"But I am."

Tanner breathed a deep sigh. "Would it be so bad? Surely you plan to marry at some point. Would marrying me be such a horror?"

"No," she answered honestly. "Except for the fact that I hardly know you."

He glanced at her profile and then back to the fire. "I think you know me well enough. I think you love me."

"Marshal, I'm not even sure I like you very much."

"You like the things we do in bed," he declared with unbearable male arrogance. "That counts for something."

Elizabeth had a powerful urge to dump her coffee on his obstinate head. She couldn't stand his unbearable insistence that she had no choice but to go along with his suggestion. Just because he wanted to marry her, he assumed she would agree. And if the beast didn't stop gloating over what they'd done in bed, she wasn't going to be responsible for her actions. It took some effort, but miraculously she held her temper in check. "Maybe," she admitted, although her tone suggested she was less than happy to do so. "But I've heard tell, husbands and wives come out of their bedrooms now and then."

Tanner chuckled. "For food and water?"

Elizabeth couldn't hold back a smile. Still, her eyes never left the fire. "It won't stop me, you know. You might be able to force me into this marriage, but every chance I get I'm going to—"

"We won't be staying on. I think it's best to remove you from temptation."

"Won't people become suspicious? The robberies will stop after we leave."

Tanner realized she might be right. In any case he wasn't about to chance her becoming a suspect. "We'll leave after a reasonable amount of time. By then people will believe the thief has moved on to greener pastures. During that time I'll keep you closely guarded."

Elizabeth tried another argument. "You won't be happy. No man would be happy with an unwilling wife."

But Tanner had an answer for that as well. "My eyes aren't filled with stars, Elizabeth. I know what I want. I'll be satisfied."

Before she had a chance to open her mouth and present further arguments, he continued, "And once I have you in bed, you'll be satisfied as well."

"You think that's all there is to it? After a night spent in bed, I'll be happy?"

"I reckon once I fill your belly a time or two, you'll be happy enough."

Elizabeth shot him a look that told him silently and yet more clearly than words the error of his thinking.

"All right," he conceded. "Tell me what will make you happy, and I swear you'll have it."

"I want the world to know the truth about Stacey. I can't think about my happiness until that happens."

Tanner thought for a moment. "Suppose I begin an investigation. Suppose I find something, some piece of evidence that might eventually bring him to trial. Would that satisfy your lust for revenge?"

She shrugged. "If he's found guilty."

"Damn you, Elizabeth! You know I can't guarantee something like that." Tanner flung his hat to the ground and ran his fingers through his hair. "Hasn't he taken enough from you? Do you want to give him your life as well?"

"I made a pledge to my mother that I'd clear my father's name."

"God!" Tanner snapped, obviously shaken. "What kind of a mother would send her daughter on such a mission?"

Elizabeth looked at him coldly. "I made the pledge after she died. My mother was a gentle soul. Too gentle to live down the loss of my father and the horror of scandal." Her voice wavered slightly as she stated, "I think she welcomed death."

"Meaning what?" he asked in a less than gentle tone. "Meaning you weren't enough for a mother to live for? That's bull and you know it." Tanner hadn't a doubt that anyone who knew this woman would find her reason enough to live. Especially her mother.

"I never said she didn't love me. What I meant was, she was a lady of delicate health. The circumstances surrounding my father's death were too much for her to handle, that's all."

Tanner's tone softened measurably. "You've done the man some damage, honey. Isn't that enough?"

Elizabeth answered his question with a silent look of disbelief.

"I know you love me, Elizabeth."

"I don't," she lied. She couldn't tell him the truth. He had enough power over her as it was.

"You do," he countered. "I can see it in your eyes every time you look at me. Are you willing to throw it all away? Everything the future holds for us?"

Elizabeth refused to even consider the possibility that he spoke the truth. She loved him, but she didn't want to. She didn't want to love anybody. As far as she could see, loving only led to pain, and she'd had enough pain to last her a lifetime. Finally she chose to ignore his question entirely. "I believe in keeping promises," she said.

"Even when keeping such a promise guarantees your own destruction?"

"Even then," she answered with a smile that lacked its usual warmth. Not for the first time, she wondered what her life might have been if she hadn't vowed to clear her father's name.

"It's lucky for you, then, that I came along."

Elizabeth's smile brightened at his cockiness. "Do you think so?"

Tanner nodded, while sending her a teasing grin. "You need someone to save you from yourself."

"And you're just the one to do it?"

"Damned right."

Elizabeth gave a soft chuckle. She'd never met a man so sure of his abilities, so confident of himself as Tanner. Her words were censorious, but they were spoken with such obvious pleasure they set his heart to pounding. "I don't think I've ever met a man quite so full of himself as you, Tanner."

Laughing chocolate eyes met blue ones in the dancing light of the fire. But the laughter in their eyes slowly faded, leaving raw hunger in its place. Elizabeth licked suddenly dry lips while a pulse beat wildly in her throat. She hadn't missed the sudden flash of yearning in his gaze and didn't keep her response at bay.

"Take down your hair," he said thickly, suddenly

223

breathless with sexual hunger as he watched the fire-light dance across her beautiful features.

Elizabeth smiled, filled with confidence in her hold over this man. And she was woman enough to want to put this knowledge to the test.

He had proven his determination. That he wanted her was obvious. This man wasn't about to let her go, no matter how she might insist or how often she might run. The thought that she had little to say in the matter might have, only moments ago, filled her with fury, but right now it only brought on a rush of excitement. Her thoughts became suddenly clear, even as desire blurred the edges of reason. She wouldn't refuse him. She was going to marry him, and she realized for the first time that it wouldn't be against her will.

She came to her knees, facing him as her fingers moved to do his bidding. "I don't want a husband who'll be gone for weeks at a time."

"I won't be." Tanner had already given this matter some thought. He was never going to leave this woman. Not ever. Not even for a short period of time.

"Will you stop marshaling then?"

He shook his head. "There's enough to do in Virginia City to keep me busy. I can send off those who won't mind the traveling.

"You have beautiful hair." He reached up to play with a thick dark tendril that had fallen over her breast, then watched with some awe as the silky curl curved around his finger, holding him to her as surely as if they were bound by chains. He smiled at that thought, knowing no chains could be stronger than his own desire. He'd never, never needed a woman more. "I wanted to touch it since the first day we met."

Elizabeth smiled in response to this softly spoken confession. "Why didn't you?"

Tanner laughed. "Had I given in to my wants, I've no doubt you would have done me bodily harm."

Elizabeth grinned. "So it wasn't honor alone that made you act the gentleman?"

"Honor . . . no." He grinned as one of her brows rose wryly. "It was terror, pure and simple. I could hardly see straight for wanting you, but if I touched you I knew you'd kick me out, probably with a black eye."

Elizabeth grinned. "Probably," she agreed. "Actually I did kick you out, for all the good that did."

"Open your shirt."

"Here?" Her eyes registered surprise, though a daring smile lifted the corners of her mouth. "I don't—"

"There's no one to see but me. Open it."

Elizabeth swallowed. Her fingers shook just a bit as they moved to the black shirt she wore. "I'll be cold."

It was Tanner's turn to show disbelief.

The harsh, almost desperate sound of his breathing as the last button was disposed of only added to her confidence. "Now pull it from your trousers."

Elizabeth complied with his softly spoken plea. In doing so, the material parted, for an instant exposing a flash of cherry tipped white flesh.

"Lady"—Tanner found the effort to talk almost beyond him—"I'm going to love you until you can't think, never mind find the energy to get up. But you're likely to run into trouble if you tease me any further."

"Am I teasing you?" she asked with exaggerated innocence, knowing the torment she was subjecting him to. Tanner could only groan and willingly bear the delightful pain.

"I promised myself I was going to warm your backside for running away this morning."

Without showing the slightest flicker of fear, Elizabeth smiled. "Do you always keep your promises, Marshal?" she asked as she reached beneath his leather vest for the buttons of his shirt.

"Eventually." His breathing was labored and shallow by the time she opened the last button. Her hands never actually touched his flesh and for that he was almost thankful. There was no telling what it might do to his control if he felt her warm hands on him. She parted the shirt, holding the material away from his skin. Her gaze was warm with pleasure as she surveyed what she'd uncovered. "Right now I have in mind other places to warm you."

Elizabeth smiled. Her eyes sought his and then returned to the strong column of his throat and the width of his muscular chest. "You're a beautiful man, Marshal."

"Have you seen so many you know that to be a fact?"

Elizabeth grinned as she raised her gaze to his. "I can honestly say I've seen none to compare."

Tanner laughed at her wickedly sly look. "And my mastery as a lover? How would you compare that?"

"I've never had a lover who was so"—she took a deep breath and slowly released it as she forced the smile from her lips—"greedy for compliments."

"Witch!" he growled as he lunged for her and spun her to the ground. On stiff arms he held himself above her. "You've never had a lover, period!"

Elizabeth was laughing at his narrowed-eyed expression. "Is that so?"

"It is."

"Then why ask?"

"God! You're driving me crazy."

"Am I? How?"

"Just by being you. Just by making me want you more than I've ever wanted a woman in my life."

"Do I do that? Make you want me?"

"Open your shirt," he responded, his voice low and gravelly.

"It's already open," she said.

"Open it," he growled out the demand.

Elizabeth slowly moved aside the material that covered her breasts. Her smile was the gentle smile of a woman who knows the power she holds over her man.

Tanner lowered himself so that his chest grazed the tips of her breasts, abrading her with his scratchy hair. With a groan Tanner gave up the teasing motion and lowered his mouth to a warm, tempting crest. Gently he sipped at her flesh, his lips and tongue soothing the slight injuries caused first by his teeth and then by the stubble on his cheeks and jaw. "I can't decide if you're an angel or the devil himself. Your eyes, your smile, your body promise me heaven, but I know only pain."

227

Elizabeth laughed, feeling her confidence grow by leaps and bounds. "That's not true. It doesn't hurt when I do this," she said as her hand moved to his chest. Deliberately provocative, she spread the fingers of both hands through the dark hair there, gently glided them to his underarms and down to his waist and then back up again over thick smooth muscles.

"Touch me. Oh, God, touch me before I die," he choked out. His body, held above hers, trembled in anticipation as he watched her hands move lower over his chest to his belt and then bravely cup the hardness of him in a palm.

His gaze met hers as she cradled him, moving her palm up and down his hard length. "I love you, Elizabeth."

Elizabeth swallowed against the intensity of his words, against the depth of feeling she read in his eyes. She couldn't form the words. She didn't want to believe that she ever would. For so long she'd known only fear and the need for revenge. She couldn't easily put aside what had now become a part of her.

She lowered her gaze, looking distinctly uncomfortable.

Tanner's smile was gentle and loving. "You don't have to say it. The words will come when you're ready."

He lowered himself to his elbows, his gaze never leaving hers, his mouth a breath from her lips. "Promise me only that you won't run again."

Elizabeth shook her head. "I can't."

Tanner smiled. "Then I'll just have to keep watch over you until you can."

His hand cupped her jaw and then moved down the length of her, to linger between her breasts and then at her waist. Her trousers fell open. A moment later they were pulled down her legs. "Although I'm beginning to enjoy the sight of you, particularly the sight of your backside, in trousers, I believe I prefer you in a skirt."

Elizabeth giggled. "Do you? I wonder why?"

"Because it's going to be simpler to reach some very important parts." His fingers found her luscious heat and entered her with a hard thrust. He smiled as a soft cry escaped her and her hips instantly rose to meet his hand. A moment later he smiled again as he listened to her low groan. "You like that?"

"A bit," she croaked.

Tanner chuckled at the wicked look in her eyes. "Just a bit?"

"Marshal!" she gasped as his hands picked up speed and moved in the most intimate fashion imaginable. "I . . . I'm sure you know, no de — decent woman would admit to the things you seem to want to hear."

"Wouldn't she? Not even to the man she loves?"

"I . . . I don't know." Elizabeth gasped, her voice becoming strained and breathless, her eyes clouding over with desire as she tried to remember what she was about to say. "Do" — she was breathing rapidly, desperately — "do you . . . think that's proper?"

"Anything is proper if a man and woman love each other."

Her hips strained toward the quickening movement of his hands, rising from the ground in urgent need, while an arm slid around his neck and tugged his mouth toward hers.

Tanner teased her lips with light airy kisses until he heard her moaning plea. "Kiss me . . . please, kiss me."

Elizabeth cried out her joy as the searing heat of his mouth closed hungrily over hers. Greedily she accepted the invasion of his tongue, almost savage in her taking of all he could give.

Her mind grew dizzy, her body so light she seemed to be floating as she was willingly enveloped in a passion so great it threatened to shatter her soul.

Tanner felt her tighten and pulsate around his fingers and smiled at the choking sounds that were escaping her. Her nails pressed into his shoulders as she held on while the world spun away. A moment later she collapsed beneath him, weak from the delicious torment he'd inflicted.

"Lord," she breathed on a shaken sigh as she buried her face in the warmth of his neck. "It's shameful the things you do."

Tanner laughed as he worked himself free of his own clothing and then rolled them over so that she was laying upon him. "Do you think so?"

"I think you're terribly wicked," she murmured against his chest as her mouth gently sipped at his skin, tasting the texture and scent that was his alone. "One can only wonder if you learned such vile things in the bowels of hell."

Tanner grinned and said nothing as her mouth made its leisurely way across his chest. Her eyes met his, a devilish gleam in them. "What? Nothing to say? No excuses for your debauchery?"

"Only that I'm thrilled beyond compare that I can use these skills to make you happy."

"Happy! Ha! You're greatly mistaken there, sir. I'm not the least bit happy." Her smile belied her words. A moment later her mouth found one of his nipples in her wanderings. By his sudden gasp she knew the spot to be sensitive, so she followed his earlier example by paying delicious attention to it. "Actually, I've hated every minute I've been forced to spend in your arms."

"Have you?" he chuckled at the outrageous lie. "That's too bad, since you're apt to be spending quite a bit of time there."

"I hope you're properly penitent for the torment you've so far inflicted."

"Oh, indeed," he said as his hips moved seductively against hers. "Shall I promise never to be so forward again?"

With her arms, Elizabeth supported herself above him. She gazed down at his tender expression. She shrugged and then grinned when he moaned low as her breasts swayed and rubbed across his chest. "I suppose you could try, but one wonders if you might have a bit of trouble keeping your word." She laughed softly as his mouth tried to capture a swaying breast. "I think you like too well the female anatomy."

Tanner grinned. "And I think you are a witch and already too well learned in the art of teasing a man."

Elizabeth laughed and snuggled her face to his chest. Was it only last night when she'd thought she'd never be at ease with this man? How had she suddenly grown so brave, so daring? She couldn't imagine what had come over her. She only knew that she was enjoying every minute in this man's arms. "You can't take back what has been learned," she said with a great deal of arrogance as she sat up.

Both were conscious of the fact that their bodies were bare where they touched. They didn't move for some moments, each lost to this luscious sensation.

Then Elizabeth felt him stir beneath her. A moment later she was rubbing herself upon the hardness of him, her head thrown back as she fully enjoyed the delicious movement. "Marshal," she said softly as she leaned down to bathe his tempting mouth with moist, hot kisses. "You'll have to tell me what you want. I haven't the experience you might expect from your everyday merry widow."

Tanner smiled. "You're doing fine so far."

"I know," she said, admitting to her own pleasure with a wicked smile, "but I've never exactly sat like this before. Are you sure there isn't something in particular I should do?"

"Take me inside you, Elizabeth," he groaned against her lips. "Sitting up, take me, now."

It wasn't the easiest thing he might have asked of her. It took some doing, especially since Tanner offered no help and she was inexperienced enough not to know quite how to go about this chore. But once she accomplished what she'd set out to do, her eyes squeezed tightly shut as she lowered herself fully upon him and allowed the unbearably sweet sensation to invade every nuance of her being.

"Ohhh," she whispered, sighing as he began to rock his hips.

His hands moved to her then, guiding her movements and then reaching inside her open shirt to gently cup her breasts. His thumbs ran over the tips, then thumb and finger swirled the tips into tight aching buds until she uttered a soft wanton cry and allowed her head to fall back on her shoulders.

Bliss, perfect bliss. Nothing could ever feel as good, as right, as wonderful.

A low hum of pleasure slipped from her lips as his hand reached for the juncture of her thighs. His thumb pressed forward and gently worried her tiny pearl of passion. He felt her harden, then soften, then harden again.

"Tanner," she said, her voice low as she felt the strength of the approaching release. Its promised unendurable depth sent a wave of fear through her, and she wondered if she'd survive such pleasure. "I can't."

"You can," he insisted as he rolled them over, holding her in place with the weight of his body when she might have fled.

"Too much, too much. I can't," she drew in shallow, labored breaths, her eyes wide, filled with the beginnings of an ache that threatened to tear her in two.

"Let it come," he panted, his thumb still rotating even as he moved above her. "You won't be sorry."

"Tanner, it's killing me," she groaned, her body breaking out in a sheen of sweat while the almost painful sensation centered solely and with desperate urgency near her female core.

He kept up the pace, moving quick and hard as she turned from trying to escape to answering his every thrust with soul-shattering groans of anguish.

Her throat arched, her head rolled back and forth. Crazed with need, she strained toward him, demanding more, more. Her strength was of no little consequence. She held him tightly between her thighs. Her arms clung to his shoulders, her nails bit deep into his flesh. She wanted him and all he could give.

She felt the tension straining at her insides, tearing. How much more could she take before she broke? More! More! She couldn't breathe. She couldn't think. She could only feel this unbearable savage need.

Her legs released his hips. Her heels now pressed into the blanket beneath them as she lifted her hips high, desperately straining, hungry for his every vicious thrust. "Ohhhh . . ." It was a low guttural aching sound soon absorbed by his warm mouth.

Tanner felt her close tightly around him. Her body shuddered and then the sweet waves of pulsating pleasure spread through her.

It was only then that he allowed his own release. Eyes closed, head flung back, teeth gritted, he opened himself to the pleasure and the pain. His body shuddered and slumped upon hers as it pumped its life-giving fluid deep into his mate.

Chapter Twelve

Tanner groaned, caught still in the throes of an almost diabolical pleasure that only seemed to grow in strength as she stirred beneath him. He nuzzled the softness of her neck. "If you know what's good for you, you'll stop that," he breathed against her ear.

"It's because I know what's good for me that I can't," she said in a slightly strained voice.

Tanner raised his head, his brow creased as he waited for her to make herself clear. "Meaning?"

"I hesitate to mention it," she said between gasping breaths, "but I'm having a bit of trouble breathing."

He heaved a great sigh of satisfaction as a smile twisted at his lips. "That's because it was so damn good. I still haven't caught my breath."

Elizabeth might have chuckled at this unbelievably arrogant male declaration, but she could only manage a smile. "I was referring to the fact that you're squashing me to death."

Tanner grinned as he lifted himself to his elbows. "Is that better?"

She shrugged. The movement caused her breast to quiver. He watched, fascinated by the delicious movement, and had a time of it bringing his gaze from that soft, enticing flesh. "Are you planning on staying like this for the remainder of the night?" she asked.

He grinned down at her, his brows rising and then lowering rapidly. "The idea holds some merit."

Elizabeth grinned, her eyes twinkling with deviltry. "Not if it should turn any colder. I can't imagine what Dr. Thompson would say if you suddenly developed a case of frostbite on uh . . . to put it delicately, certain extremities."

Tanner laughed. "Would that be a particularly important extremity you have in mind?"

"Aren't all extremities important?" she asked as she batted her lashes in an outrageous fashion, while a teasing smile curved her lips.

"Some more than others. You'd agree, if you were honest."

"Very well then, I'd say it's very important."

"Good," he grunted with satisfaction. "Now you're starting to think like a wife." He rolled her over so she lay upon him, meanwhile wrapping them both in the blanket.

"Am not!"

Tanner laughed. "Now that sounded just like a neighbor's daughter who used to fight with her brother."

Elizabeth laughed and slapped at his shoulder. "Make up your mind."

"I have. You've got a dirty mouth."

"Have I?" She laughed softly, obviously taken

aback. No one had ever accused her of such a thing. Up till now no one had ever had cause. "Just because I mentioned a certain extremity?"

"Yup."

Elizabeth shrugged. It was useless to argue the point, especially since she couldn't help but agree with him. "No doubt it's the company I keep," she said, her dark eyes alive with laughter.

"So now it's my fault?"

"Of course it's your fault," she retorted, in a tone that implied he should have known without asking. "Did you ever hear me talk like that before?"

"Before what?"

"Before . . ." She hesitated. "Before you know what."

"Before this?" he asked as he moved his hips up, rubbing them suggestively against hers.

Elizabeth raised her head and sighed as she saw his victorious expression. "Oh, Tanner"—she might have said darling, so gentle was her tone—"you're bad, you're very, very bad."

Tanner slid his hands beneath his head. The stars that dotted the velvet sky above them glittered. Had she proclaimed him King of the United States, he couldn't have looked more smug. "Granted." He nodded in agreement. "Still, that doesn't excuse you."

"I imagine you will eventually tell me what you're hinting at," she said as her head tried to find a comfortable spot on a hard chest and her body snuggled against his heat.

"Madam, we're talking about the fact that you have a dirty mouth, and exactly what I'm going to do about it."

Elizabeth laughed and said offhandedly, "Will you wash it out with soap?"

"It's better, I think, to wash it out with my tongue."

"Oh?" Elizabeth's whisper was slightly breathless, as the ramifications of the act proposed were instantly brought to mind. She inched herself up until they were face-to-face, and then leaned her elbow on his chest and supported her head with her raised hand. "I should have known you were working up to something here." His chest was rising and falling unevenly, making it difficult if not downright impossible for her hand to hold her head as he tried to restrain his laughter. "Fell right into that one, didn't I?"

She grinned as he finally gave up and laughed aloud. "It took a while."

"Still, I have to admit it does sound interesting."

"Shall we give it a try?"

"I don't know." She shrugged. "I wouldn't want to put you to any trouble."

"I promise you, it's no trouble."

"Why do I believe that?"

He laughed as he rolled her beneath him. "Could be because it's true."

"This is your last chance," she whispered, her eyes darting from him to the entrance of the church and then back again as if she expected him to make a mad dash for freedom.

"I know." Tanner grinned.

"All you have to do is turn around and walk out.

I promise, you won't hurt my feelings."

Tanner laughed and then turned to the puzzled preacher. "You can start anytime you're ready."

"Are you sure?" the man asked. He hadn't heard a conversation quite so startling between a bride and groom in his thirty years as a minister.

Yes and No were said in unison.

Mrs. McAndrews, who was acting as their witness, gave a soft gasp of surprise.

Elizabeth shot her a gentle look. "Don't mind us, we're always like this."

"Get on with it," Tanner insisted, dragging out the words with slow emphasis from between clenched teeth.

"I think the lady is having second thoughts," the reverend offered.

"She's not," Tanner's arm came around Elizabeth, his fingers digging deep into her side. She gasped at the strength of his obvious warning to her to behave. "Are you, my dear?"

"Of course not, sweetums," Elizabeth said through gritted teeth, as she wrenched herself from his hold.

"Maybe at some future date—" Reverend McAndrews began, but Tanner cut him off with a definite and none too softly spoken, "Now!"

Elizabeth wasn't your everyday kind of woman. She'd never longed for a romantic courtship and a wedding with all the trimmings. Actually she'd thought little on the subject, having, over the last few years, other matters to occupy her time and thoughts. But now that she was standing in a church, about to embark on the holy state of matrimony, Elizabeth felt saddened by the fact that she hadn't even managed to be wearing a pretty new dress for the occasion. Tanner was so anxious he'd refused to wait even for that.

Wearing her best dress, a long-sleeved blue silk that was drawn together at the back to form a bustle, she shot Tanner an aggravated look. He hadn't even thought to get her flowers. And the ring he was about to place on her finger was at least two sizes too big. Elizabeth could only pray this wasn't an omen of things to come.

"Well, now you've done it. Don't say I didn't warn you." Elizabeth said as she allowed Tanner to escort her from the small wooden church.

"I won't. Let's go to bed."

"Spoken like a true husband," Elizabeth said despairingly. "No matter how you deny it, I know that's the reason you married me."

He was about to help her into the waiting buggy when he grinned and then muttered cockily, "I've already had you in bed. I didn't have to marry you to get you there again."

"Oh, my God." The soft moaning sound came from behind them.

Both Tanner and Elizabeth spun around to find Miss Dunlap, apparently about to congratulate the newly wed couple, her face turning every shade of red. There was no doubt in their minds that the woman had heard at least the last part of their conversation.

"Gloria! I'm so glad you came," Elizabeth said as she glared at her husband and then elbowed him out of the way before poor Miss Dunlap fainted at their feet. With her arm around the older woman's thin waist, Elizabeth asked, "Won't you join us? We were about to return to the house."

Tanner scowled at hearing the easily offered invitation. He wished he had the nerve to tell the woman to get lost for a few hours. Damn! Elizabeth would just about skin him alive if he said what was really on his mind, but he wanted his wife to himself. Was that so unusual a request? If Jason had remained sober long enough to do what Tanner had asked, a bottle of wine and flowers were already waiting in her bedroom. He couldn't wait to get back so Elizabeth might show her appreciation of his thoughtfulness.

The church was situated at the opposite end of the small town. It wasn't necessary for Tanner to hire a buggy since Elizabeth walked to church every Sunday, but he felt the occasion warranted the small expense. Elizabeth motioned Tanner to aid Miss Dunlap into the carriage, and Tanner sighed with defeat as he silently did her bidding.

They were almost at Elizabeth's door when Miss Dunlap managed at last to overcome her mortification. Her voice was soft and terribly shy when she said, "Mabel and Harriet sent me. They're already at the house. If you had only given us more time, we could have had a larger celebration."

Tanner's growl at the thought of company awaiting their arrival resembled that of a wounded bear, and caused Miss Dunlap to shiver with fear. He had purposely not let a soul know of his intentions. He didn't want to face a crowd of people just now, having a much more private celebration of his own in mind.

It had taken him three days to overcome her flimsy excuses. Three days to manage to drag—almost literally—Elizabeth to the church. Three days and nights of suffering from his need to bed her again. And now he'd have to wait untold hours before his plans could be put into action.

"Why, that's a lovely gesture," Elizabeth said, casting a wicked glance at her husband and knowing well his intent. "How many are there?"

"Oh, quite a few," Miss Dunlap responded. "It was lucky for us that Mabel met Mrs. McAndrews at the apothecary."

"That was lucky, wasn't it, Tanner?"

"Very," he murmured, although anyone over the age of three might have noticed his lack of enthusiasm.

"I came to pay my respects and wish you every happiness, my dear," Stacey said as he took her hand and brought it to his mouth for a light brushing of cold lips. His eyes were hard; his mind filled with rage. The little bitch had strung him along, pretending to be in mourning, while she was obviously bedding the marshal all along. Well, she wasn't going to get away with that. No one played Jonathan Stacey for a fool.

His lips twisted into a grimace of disgust as he closely studied what he had once believed to be somewhat agreeable features. She looked awful. Softer than usual, more womanly, more confident.

Almost as though she'd just come from a good tumble in bed. Odd, he had never thought of her as a sexual being. She was always so cool, so ladylike. That was what had drawn him to her in the first place. Now there was something about her that almost reeked of carnality. Only it was the wrong kind. Jonathan shuddered with disgust and wondered how a man could find pleasure with a woman, most especially a woman like her.

"Thank you, Jonathan," Elizabeth murmured. Then she was momentarily startled as a possessive arm swiftly encircled her waist to pull her back against an unyielding form.

"You didn't tell me we had another guest, darling," Tanner admonished gently. "Would you care for something to drink, Stacey?" he asked as he shook the man's hand.

Stacey shook his head. "I'm afraid I can't stay. Pressing business," he offered as an excuse, in a hurry, now that he'd formed a plan of revenge, to make good his escape.

Tanner held Elizabeth at his side as Stacey's carriage slipped into the cover of darkness. "Is he expecting another shipment tonight?"

Tanner's arm tightened at her question. A question he had no intention of answering. "I wondered, from the first, what you saw in him. If he doesn't resemble a lizard, no one does."

"You thought it was his money," she retorted with a wicked smile, as she realized he was trying to change the subject. "He is, isn't he?"

"And I was right."

Elizabeth laughed, her eyes widening in surprise

as she realized the truth of his words. "I suppose you were, only I didn't want his money for myself. What time?"

"He had plans for you."

"How do you know that? You're not going to answer me, are you?"

"I can see it in his eyes. Stay away from him. Right now he's furious."

Elizabeth remembered the icy look of cold hatred she thought she saw in Stacey's eyes, and she shivered. How could it be that Stacey and Tanner both had blue eyes. While Jonathan's always appeared so cold, Tanner's almost burned with heat.

Feeling the involuntary movement, Tanner teased, "Was that for me . . . or him?" He turned their bodies toward each other. His arms circled her waist as he pressed the lower half of his body against hers and leaned back so he might see her face.

"He gives me the shivers. I could probably get the information, if I nagged you long enough."

"Probably, but it won't do you any good. You're going to be busy tonight." He breathed a long sigh as he realized he'd just admitted exactly what she wanted to hear. "I could wring your neck when I think you risked a relationship with a man like that."

"Was there another way?"

"Of course there was. You could have put aside your ridiculous plan."

Elizabeth's lips tightened as she glared into eyes that had grown hard at the thought of her being in danger. "It wasn't at all ridiculous. As a matter of fact things were going along famously, till you came to spoil it all."

"Till I came to save you from yourself, you mean."

"Actually I mean no such thing. A few more months and I would have ruined him."

He gave her a quick hard shake. "Cocky little brat. More than likely you would have been dead." He sighed and slowly shook his head. "I can only thank God I found you before it was too late."

Elizabeth glared up at him, her hands on his chest, her arms stiff as she tried to create some distance between their bodies. "And if I hadn't done it? How do you suppose we would have met?"

"A happening that has brought you many hours of pleasure, I'm sure."

"Oh, indeed it has," she said, her lips curving in a sarcastic grimace.

Tanner laughed as he put aside her hands and snuggled his cheek against the silky softness of her hair. His whisper was low, intimate and filled with longing. "I think we were destined to meet."

"So you believe it's all written down in some big book, long before we're born? You don't think we all have choices?"

"I believe we are all offered choices. Whether we take them or not is probably inconsequential. I would have met you no matter what."

"And just how do you suppose we would have met if I hadn't come west?"

"I would have come east, of course."

"Oh, of course," she concurred, with no small amount of sarcasm. "With the express purpose of finding me, no doubt."

"If I'd have known I would find you, I would have done it years ago." He groaned as he held her more closely against him. "When the hell are they going home?" he asked, referring to the guests that had settled in her parlor and kitchen. Settled, he began to believe, for the night.

Jonathan sat before his luxurious desk in his finely appointed library and worked late into the night. He wanted to have the papers ready for delivery first thing in the morning. As a wedding gift, of sorts. He chuckled at his own black humor.

Close to midnight, he threw down his pen and blotted the document dry. A smile curved his thin lips as he surveyed his night's work. The document called in her note. He'd be the owner of her little shack by the first of the month. When she and her husband were out in the street, perhaps she might realize what she had thrown away.

He'd wanted her for his wife. Had chosen her out of the hundreds he might have had. Dressed correctly, she could have had a place among his finest possessions. As someone who would be hostess for his affairs as he paved the way toward gaining the office of governor. He needed the respectability only a wife could provide. He needed heirs as well, to the vast empire he was building.

He hadn't imagined the needed act to be enjoyed by either of them, of course. It was simply a necessary part of marriage. To enjoy a woman, any woman, was beyond his comprehension.

Stacey consulted his timepiece and came to his feet. He pulled a cloak over his shoulders and reached for his cane. Hanner would have set up the

246

meeting by now. He was going to be late. No matter, the boy would wait. He was paid well enough for both his body and time.

Stacey smelled the smoke, but attributed the scent to the fires that were never extinguished because he couldn't tolerate the cold, not since Washington in January of sixty-three.

He wouldn't hear the alarm when he was miles out of town, and for a very short time, while he was with the boy at the abandoned shack, he wouldn't even care what was happening.

"Looks like Stacey's place is on fire! The flames are shooting higher than the Rockies," a man called out as he rushed to Elizabeth's open front door and then dashed on to the next house.

Within moments Elizabeth's house was emptied, leaving only her and Tanner. Even Belle and Miss Dunlap had gone to see the flames.

"Aren't you going to help?"

"Help how? I'm sure the flames will do just fine without my blowing on them."

Elizabeth grinned. "I meant help put *out* the fire, not add to it."

Tanner leaned against the doorjamb and watched her move about her kitchen. He raised his glass to his lips and took a final sip. "Now why should I do a damn-fool thing like that? If the fire went out, everyone would more than likely come back here."

"You don't like my friends, I take it?"

"Elizabeth, I love your friends, but not nearly as much as I love you."

Elizabeth smiled as he put his glass on the table and purposely blocked her path to the sink.

"Put the glasses down."

She ignored his order. "If I help, do you think we could bring the extra table back to the barn?"

Tanner grinned as he took the glasses out of her hand and put them in the sink. He held her about the waist when she would have walked off again. "If you help, I think we could have ourselves a wedding night, after all."

"But this place is a mess."

"Tomorrow will be soon enough to straighten it out."

She shook her head. "I'll never sleep, thinking about all I've got to do."

"You won't sleep anyway," he promised. "And I can guarantee you won't be thinking about cleaning your house."

Elizabeth laughed as he took the step that brought their bodies into contact. "Pretty sure of yourself, wouldn't you say?"

"Maybe," he said as he reached down and slid an arm behind her knees. He grunted dramatically as he swung her up against him. "You'd better watch what you're eating, wife. I'm not sure I can hold you if you gain any more weight."

"You beast," she said on a soft laugh, knowing he could, and probably would, hold her if she were twice her weight.

With Elizabeth in his arms, Tanner bent and extinguished every lamp in both the parlor and kitchen. "Now that should give them a hint, if they're thinking about coming back."

Elizabeth giggled. "Maybe you should lock the doors and bar the windows."

He shook his head. "Then I'd have to get up and answer Belle's banging. You don't think she'd be discreet enough to find somewhere else to sleep tonight, do you?" He didn't bother to mention the fact that Miss Dunlap had gone along to see the fire as well. Both of them knew Gloria would sleep outside before she'd find the courage to disturb them with her knocking.

Elizabeth's arm went around his neck, while her free hand played with a lock of dark hair that insisted on falling over his forehead. "Have you known her a long time?"

"A very long time."

She worried the corner of her lower lip. "You seem close."

"We are."

It was on the tip of Elizabeth's tongue to ask how close when Tanner grinned and asked almost hopefully, "Are you jealous?"

"Have I reason to be?"

"Not a one," he said as he swung open her bedroom door. Gently he lowered her to her feet. Elizabeth had expected that he'd carry her to the bed. Her expression showed her surprise.

Tanner didn't say a word, but slowly turned her so her back leaned against his chest. His arms encircled her waist and held her against him.

Elizabeth's gaze took in the candlelit table set for two. More candles had been lit at each side of her bed, a bouquet of slightly wilted flowers lay on her pillow, a bottle of wine sat in a bucket of what was

249

probably warm water. She shot him a look of amazement. "When did you manage this?"

"I had Jason set it up while we were at the church. When everyone was running out the door to look at the fire, I came in here and lit the candles."

Elizabeth smiled as she moved to the table. "We were having chicken?"

"And cheese, bread, and fruit," he held up two pears.

Elizabeth's hand came to lie flat upon her breast. Her voice was fluttery and so soft as to barely be heard. "I don't know what to say. I'm so surprised."

"You thought you were marrying some unfeeling brute, didn't you?" he asked as he opened the bottle of wine and filled two stemmed glasses with ruby colored liquid.

Elizabeth grinned as she took in his knowing look. "The thought did cross my mind."

"When?"

"When I didn't get flowers at the church and then the ring was too big."

Tanner examined the ring she could only keep on by bending her finger and grinned at its size. Gently he took it from her and dropped it into his pocket. "The smithy offered to work on it, but I think we'll have it made smaller in Virginia City. Or I can just buy you another one, a better one."

"No!" she said, never realizing the feeling behind the words. "I want that one."

Tanner had a time of it holding his arms at his sides. He wanted to crush her against him. This woman might not admit in words that she loved him, but she told him in a thousand other ways. "I have something for you."

Her eyes widened. "Something else?"

He took a box from his pocket and handed it to her.

She shot him a teasing look. "Nothing is going to jump out at me when I open it, is it?"

Tanner simply smiled. "Open it."

Elizabeth did as he asked and then gasped upon finding a thin pink gold chain. On the chain was a delicately painted porcelain heart, its edges trimmed in filigreed gold. She opened the heart and frowned at finding it empty.

Oddly misted brown eyes lifted to his warm gaze. "I can't tell you how much I love this. It's so beautiful."

"You're not going to cry, are you?"

"I never cry. Don't be silly."

"We'll have to have miniatures done, for the inside."

She nodded and then asked, "Will you put it on?"

"Do you want to wear it now?"

Elizabeth smiled at his surprise. "Of course I want to wear it now. I told you I loved it, didn't I?"

He wished she would tell him she loved him most of all, but he wouldn't push her. Tanner knew she'd tell him when she was ready.

"I have one more thing to give you."

"Tanner, you shouldn't." She shook her head. "This is enough. More than enough."

"No it's not," he said as he took a box from under her bed and handed it to her.

Elizabeth's jaw dropped as she opened the package. Inside was a red silk robe, the fabric so thin as

251

to almost be transparent. Hemmed and belted with a thick band of silver rope, it was the most spectacularly luxurious and no doubt the most expensive thing she'd ever owned. "Where did you get this? No shops in town carry this kind of thing."

"I went to Mrs. Walton's. She made it."

"Mrs. Walton made this?"

Tanner nodded. "She made a nightdress to match, but you can't have that."

Elizabeth laughed. "I can't? Why not?"

Tanner ignored her question, and his eyes darkened, growing hot with need. "Go put it on. Then we'll have our wine."

Tanner kicked off his boots, removed his waistcoat and tie, opened a few buttons of his shirt, and then sat at the small table. His back was to her, allowing her the privacy she needed to change.

"Tanner," she said from the other side of the small room.

"Hmmm?"

"I don't think this is very modest. Maybe you should give me the nightdress as well."

Tanner first turned only his head and then, as if in a daze, his body. Elizabeth looked terrified. But she needn't have worried. He couldn't have moved if it meant saving his life. She'd taken the breath from his lungs and the strength from his limbs. All he could do was stare.

The robe covered her from neck to toes. In an effort to cover what was needed, she had pulled it tightly against her and belted it at her waist. She was right. It wasn't the least bit modest. He had to clear his throat twice before he could get out the words. "Come over here, Elizabeth."

"Tanner, didn't you hear me?"

"The chicken's cold and probably none too good after sitting out all afternoon and evening. But I think you should have a little cheese and bread. I didn't see you eat a thing tonight."

"I was too busy."

"That's usually the way of things at these gatherings," he remarked conversationally.

"Are you going to ignore the fact that I've asked you for the nightdress?"

Tanner smiled and gave a short nod of his head. "I'm going to ignore your asking, but I'd have to be dead to ignore the fact that you haven't got it on." His gaze moved over the entire length of her. "This is exactly how a bride should dress on her wedding night."

Elizabeth felt her belly tighten, and the tips of her breasts stood out shamelessly as if begging for his touch. She knew he could see through the fabric, and that knowledge only caused her to long for cover. It flashed into her mind that she might successfully dash for the bed, thereby finding cover, but Tanner would either believe her all too anxious, and burst out laughing, or he would drag her back to the table. Either happening would be less than dignified.

Elizabeth had never felt so exposed. Even naked she hadn't felt so . . . naked. She glanced longingly at the spread. She needed to drape it around her shoulders. But judging by the way Tanner was watching her, she'd have about as much chance of catching a rainbow as she would of hiding her body from him on this night.

It wasn't that she didn't want to go to bed with him or do the delicious things she knew they'd indulge in. She was just naturally modest and unused to being so blatantly on display.

Abruptly she dropped into her chair. "Is it?" she asked slightly breathless. She could almost feel the heat in his eyes. With a shaky hand, she reached for her glass. "I think I will have a little wine."

Tanner grinned as she downed the entire glass. Obediently he refilled it as she held the empty glass out to him. "Take it easy this time."

Elizabeth laughed at his concern. "Wouldn't want your wife drunk on her wedding night, I take it?"

His eyes twinkled with laughter. "I don't know. Should we give it a try? It might be fun at that."

Elizabeth laughed. "Take my word for it, it's not a pretty sight. Especially in the morning."

"Have you been drunk before?"

She nodded as she bit into a pear. The juice slid over her chin, and she hastily wiped her mouth with a cloth napkin. Tanner's body shook with the desire to have licked the juice away himself.

"When?" he asked, more than a little startled at the degree of need that crashed into him. This wasn't the first time for them. His ardor should have cooled some by now. But it hadn't. If anything, it had only grown in strength.

"When I was sixteen." She smiled at the memory. "I was finally old enough to attend one of my father's parties. I was so excited. Our house was a young girl's dream. It was just about filled with men. Officers under my father's command," she added in explanation.

Tanner felt his chest tighten with discomfort. He knew he was jealous. He also knew the emotion to be ridiculous. It didn't help much.

"Anyway, because I was so excited, I didn't eat all day. And then I had two glasses of wine." She shot him a helpless look and explained, "I was thirsty from the dancing.

"As the story goes, I got a bit carried away." She laughed. "Actually, I had to be carried away."

Tanner chuckled at her clever wording. "So? Have you learned your lesson?"

"After I recuperated." She groaned at the thought. "It took a few days. Lord, was I sick. My father taught me how to drink."

Tanner's brows rose with surprise. "Did he? Why?"

Elizabeth shrugged. "I think he must have noticed the look in the eyes of the men at the party. Beasts, one and all. With a pig among them."

Tanner grinned.

"I imagine he wanted me able to hold my liquor, lest one of them, at some future date, have his way with me."

She laughed again. "Eventually, though they never realized the fact, I could drink any one of them under the table."

Tanner's gaze glittered with suppressed laughter.

Elizabeth shrugged. "So goes the story of my saved virginity."

"Thank you."

"For what?"

"For saving it for me."

Elizabeth laughed. "Tanner, you're hardly better than those men. You've got the same look in your eyes."

"I'd kill anyone who dared look at you like that."

Elizabeth grinned, between bites of bread and cheese. "Would you? Why?"

"Because you belong to me."

She gave a slow nod. "I guess I do, now that we're married."

"The thought doesn't seem to bring you unending joy." Tanner cursed himself for being every kind of fool. He knew better than to bring the subject up, but he was so damned jealous he wasn't thinking straight. What the hell had he expected? He'd forced her to marry him and now—damn it!—was he stupid enough to expect her to be happy about it?

Elizabeth smiled at his frown. "You're quite wrong, you know," she said, reading his thoughts correctly.

"Am I? How?"

"I'm not unhappy."

"You're not?" he looked amazed.

"Of course not." She smiled at his dazed look. "I can guarantee you this, Tanner. You'll know when I'm not happy."

Tanner came to his feet and took her hand. Slowly she rose from her chair. They stood for a long moment, neither saying a word, each staring into the depths of the other's eyes. He couldn't begin to tell her the extent of his relief, while she felt her heart swell, expand, and fill with a love she knew would last till the end of time. "And you don't hate me for forcing you to marry me?"

Elizabeth grinned. He wasn't going to get off so easily. Without thinking, and in a decidedly wifely

256

fashion, she smoothed down the collar of his shirt. Then her fingers toyed with the long, dark hair that brushed against its snowy stiffness. A wicked smile curved her lips. "Well, maybe just a little."

Tanner closed his eyes and groaned, knowing all hope for reason was forever lost. She hated him, "just a little," and for that he could have conquered the world.

His arm trembled even as he reached behind her knees, to hold her high against his chest. "I love you, love you," he murmured as he buried his face in the sweet fragrance of her hair.

Elizabeth's hands framed his face and brought it to her waiting lips. Her mouth opened to blend sweetly, wildly with his. It was a long time before either of them managed a reasonable thought again.

"Where are you going?"

"Shush. Go back to sleep."

"Forget it." His arm went around her waist and pulled her back upon the bed. Tanner considered it a miracle that he had managed to sleep at all. With her hot naked body pressed close to his, oblivion had been the farthest thing from his mind. And the chances of a few hours of rest were suddenly out of the question.

"Lord, are you suspicious," Elizabeth grumbled as she allowed him to pull her back.

Tanner laughed and crushed her tightly against him. "Judging by your past actions, I'd say I have every right to be suspicious. Besides, you're wasting your time. I heard the stage roll by at least an hour ago."

Elizabeth giggled. "No doubt you believe me to be of superior strength. Even if I were of a mind, I'm far too tired to rob a stage tonight."

"Wore you out, did I?" he asked, his gloating tone most annoying.

Elizabeth turned her head as far as she could to glare at his shadowy form. "No more than I did you."

Tanner murmured contentedly as he tucked the lower half of his body against her rear. The fact that they were both naked only added to his pleasure. "Where were you going?"

"To get a glass of water."

"Thirsty?" he asked, his voice growing thick and heavy as he again felt stirrings of desire.

"No. I wanted to take a bath." His smile widened as the sarcastic words penetrated his otherwise preoccupied mind.

He chuckled softly as he pushed himself from their shared warmth and stumbled toward the table holding a pitcher of water. Upon his return, Tanner cursed as he tripped over one of his boots and fell upon the bed. Elizabeth heard the muttered curse, but never got a chance to ask what was wrong.

An instant later, sputtering with shock, she wiped away the water that had drenched her face and hair with the edge of her sheet. "I'm relieved you didn't bring the whole pitcher." She laughed softly as he struck a match. "It seems I got my bath after all."

"Why did I put out the candle?" Tanner asked.

"I believe we were sleeping. People usually sleep in the dark," she answered with reasonable logic.

"I know, but look at what I've been missing."

His gaze was hungrily absorbing the delicious sight of her rose-tipped naked breasts. Heavy, they filled a man's hands to overflowing. Her hair, mussed from sleep and as black as midnight, fell over her shoulders, almost covered the enticing flesh. Her lips, swollen from the hundreds of kisses they'd shared, looked dewy soft and sweet. Her skin was pink and warm from the hours spent cuddled in his arms. She was the most desirable woman he'd ever known.

Elizabeth smiled and wantonly allowed the sheet to fall to her hips. She sat facing him, the upper half of her body exposed to his warm gaze, while she fully enjoyed the effect her nakedness was having on him. "If I'm not mistaken, you didn't miss a thing."

Tanner grinned, knowing the truth of those words. There wasn't a part of her he hadn't touched, caressed, licked, and kissed. There wasn't a part of her he didn't want to touch again.

"I would have thought you to be well satisfied by now."

Tanner came to his knees, showing her clear proof of her error. He laughed as he watched her eyes widen. "Did you?" He moved closer and whipped the sheet to the floor. His eyes darkened as they took in the erotic sight of her nakedness. "It appears I only have to see you to want you again."

Elizabeth reached a boldly hungry hand toward him. As it gently explored the rigid muscles of his chest and stomach, the other hand unashamedly moved down to his hardened shaft. "How long do you expect this phenomena will last?"

Tanner tried to concentrate on what she was saying, but the ecstasy of her touch momentarily disallowed conversation. "Mmmm," was the best he could do at the moment.

He fell back against the headboard, half reclining, his legs separated, his hands clasped together under his head so he might fully enjoy her exploration. His eyes appeared dazed, his hips arched into her moving hand. "That's it. Oh God, yes. Touch me."

His obvious delight only stirred her on. She grew bolder. Her mouth found his nipple. Tanner jumped at the contact

"You don't like that?" Elizabeth asked, while a wicked smile curved her lips.

Tanner never answered her question. In truth he seemed incapable of saying anything more than, "Oh, God." And as her mouth went even lower, her tongue creating a burning path until it joined her gentle hands, the words grew into a soft chant of pleasure.

Tanner, even with all his years of experience, had never known ecstasy to equal this. Yes, he had taken a woman to his bed when there was need. He'd held his share in his arms. He had kissed willing mouths and touched eager flesh, but never had a woman's touch, a woman's body, brought him to this level of exquisite agony.

He moaned when she kissed his pulsating shaft, and he thought the pleasure surely too much for his heart to handle. But when her mouth opened and her tongue licked at his burning flesh, Tanner cried out in delight. And when she slowly lowered her mouth over his burning sex, it nearly robbed him of his sanity.

Elizabeth felt the room sway dizzily as she suddenly found herself lying on her back, Tanner's weight crushing her into the soft feather mattress.

"Where did you learn that?"

Her eyes widened at taking in the dark emotion in his eyes. She giggled. Did he believe her suddenly experienced? Even knowing he was the first, was he suddenly jealous? "Where do you think?" she answered noncommittally.

"I don't want to think," he said tightly as his narrowed gaze watched her open expression. "What I want is more. But not now."

"Why not?"

"Because it's too good. Because I'll never find the strength to pleasure you if you go on."

"You could always pleasure me later," she offered as a solution.

Tanner's large hands cupped the sides of her face. "I expect I will. Again and again. You don't mind, do you?"

Elizabeth smiled in response to the tender look in his eyes. He hadn't bothered to ask before. He'd taken and given time and again, until they'd fallen asleep from sheer exhaustion, content in each other's arms. The softness in her eyes brought a groan from his chest.

"I imagine I can bear this wifely chore."

"Your hair tickles," she said as she lay sprawled over him.

"Where?"

"Everywhere."

"I'll shave it off."

Elizabeth giggled. "All of it?"

"If you want."

"My, my, aren't we agreeable today? I'll have to remember what I did. Maybe, with enough practice, I could convince you to join me in my adventures."

Tanner's arm tightened at the mere mention of her nightly escapades. "I'll join you in any adventure but the one you're thinking of."

Elizabeth laughed at his expression. If he was trying to look fierce, he was failing miserably. "How do you know what I'm thinking?"

"That's simple enough. You're always thinking about Stacey."

"Where does it bother you?" he asked, abruptly changing the subject.

"What?"

"My hair."

"It doesn't. It tickles, and I think I like it very much."

"Then I'll grow more."

Elizabeth laughed into the warmth of his neck. "Just like that?"

"Mmmm," he sighed as he cupped her rear and pressed her more firmly against him.

"You're not getting frisky again, are you, Marshal?"

Tanner chuckled as he adjusted her legs so that she lay fully upon him. "Frisky? Why I wouldn't think of it, Miss Elizabeth.

"Actually, I dare you to find a frisky bone in my

body."

"Oh, no you don't. I know where that game ends." He laughed.

"I should get up." His hold tightened. "It's almost time to start breakfast." He rubbed his hands down her back, cupping the roundness of her backside. "Maybe I'll just rest for a minute."

"My thoughts exactly, ma'am."

Chapter Thirteen

His dark clothes blended into the shadows. No one, not even the guard that occasionally paced along this side of the house noticed his presence. Physically, he was a weak man, but it hadn't taken much strength to lift himself over the wall. Especially the back wall where thick vines grew.

The dogs were caged for now. He could hear them barking in the distance. It was Sunday, and Stacey was due to go out again.

Jason worked as fast as he could. He had to hurry before the gates were locked and the dogs were allowed to roam free again.

His knee hit the small can of kerosene, splashing a goodly amount of the liquid down his leg and into his boot as he poured the fluid along the length of the back wall. He couldn't think why he hadn't done this sooner. What right did that man have to live in luxury while his Jed no longer lived at all?

Jason's mouth twisted into a sneer as the past came again to haunt him. He never felt the kerosene run again into his boot. He was aware only of the agony of seeing his son's body hanging from a rafter in the attic. He saw it as clearly as if it had just happened.

Jason's only solace had been that Letty hadn't lived to see that day.

For months after the funeral he'd lived in a drunken stupor. He'd been so confused. He couldn't understand, couldn't begin to fathom what had driven the boy to such lengths. It wasn't till months later, when he was going through Jed's personal belongings, that he found the reason behind his son's death.

It was all written down. Jed had kept a journal. Jason had it still. He'd kept it, along with the few trinkets that marked the birth and death of his only child. Jason remembered how he'd felt the day he'd found the journals. His body had turned cold, never to grow warm again, as he had read of the pain, the guilt, the torture his son had suffered at Stacey's hands. Yet Jason had never known, never guessed, never imagined that his son had been repeatedly raped by that monster.

It had taken the better part of a year to find Stacey. Then Jason had watched; disguised as the town drunk, he knew Stacey's every movement. Wednesdays and Sundays, Stacey met the boy at the abandoned shack. Saturdays he saw Miss Garner for a few hours.

Jason couldn't understand her involvement with the man. He knew she was the one behind the robberies. He'd watched her leave the boardinghouse, dressed in black trousers and shirt. Why would a nice lady like that involve herself with such a demon? Why would she then rob the man?

Jason shrugged. It wasn't important. The only thing that was truly important was that he kill Stacey.

Escorted to and from work by armed guards, the man spent the rest of his time behind the walls of his mansion. Jason had no chance to get at him without being cut down.

It wasn't that Jason was afraid. You had to want to live in order to feel that emotion. And he hadn't cared if he lived or died since finding his son's body. He just wanted to make sure he got Stacey before the man's guards got him.

One day he would. One day the guards would grow lax, and he'd take the opportunity offered.

Jason struck a match. He hadn't thought about the spill his clothes had absorbed, when he threw the match toward the wall of the house. The kerosene went up with a loud whooshing sound. But it wasn't the house alone that burned. Jason realized too late that he'd spilled some of the fuel. He watched in confusion as smaller flames danced around his feet and then suddenly ran up his leg and side to lick at his face. When his hair caught fire, his horrified screams were lost in the roar of the larger blaze.

He hit at the flames with his hands, only to find the liquid kerosene sticking to them and burning them as well. The pain was enormous, worse than he could have imagined. Hot blue-red flames licked at his leg and fanned all the brighter as he began to run. He threw himself over the wall. Upon landing on the ground he writhed in agony, unknowingly putting out the flame. Crumpled and broken, he lay gasping, weak with shock. The worst of the pain had yet to come. It didn't take but a few minutes.

Jason had never known that degree of agony. His suffering, combined with the stench of burned flesh, emptied his stomach of the little he had taken in for supper. He lay there hurting like he'd never hurt before, too weak to move.

Stacey was, as predicted, miles away by the time flames licked at the roof of his mansion. He hadn't undressed. He never did during these diversions. He looked around the stark bare room as the boy knelt before him. He might have invested in some furnishings. At least a bed and a comfortable chair, but he'd known from the first that this boy wasn't worth the expense.

The boy's father was paid well to send him to the shack twice a week, but it was obvious from the bruises that often spotted the small body, the boy's heart just wasn't in what he had to do.

This boy wasn't as good as Brian. Stacey smiled. Most people thought Brian was about sixteen. Actually the lad was close to his twenty-second birthday. Stacey had been mildly surprised upon learning that. As a rule, he didn't enjoy men. Usually they were too big and too strong. No, he liked his partners small and young.

Even though Brian was more experienced and much better at performing the acts Stacey enjoyed, he knew he'd soon let him go. Yes, Brian loved him and showed it in every way possible, but the young man was a bit too possessive. Stacey enjoyed variety, and he wasn't about to take Brian's sulking whenever his eyes roamed. Stacey shrugged. He never could keep a relationship monogamous, no matter how good it was.

Stacey gestured for the boy to come closer. As usual, he did what Stacey commanded. Stacey enjoyed the feeling of power that gave him. And knowing the boy disliked what he was forced to do added to Stacey's enjoyment.

No doubt it was this that Stacey missed in sexual contacts with adults. He needed the seediness, the perversity of doing something wrong. It made everything so much better for him.

Belle watched Tanner's face as he read the telegram the next morning. "Tell Frank to forget it. Elizabeth is no longer a suspect," he said as he folded the paper and slipped it into his shirt pocket.

"You knew."

Tanner nodded. "She told me."

"So?"

"So what?"

"So why did she lie?" Belle nodded at the telegram Tanner held. "She wasn't a widow."

"She was afraid to travel as a single woman. No one bothers a widow lady. So she invented a dead husband."

Belle nodded. "What are you going to do?"

"Do about what?" he snapped. Then he smiled a bit stiffly. "It's no crime for a woman to pretend to be married."

"No but it is a crime to rob a stage."

268

"I hope you don't think she did it."

"She had the best motive we've come up with so far."

Silence was Tanner's only answer.

Belle smiled. "Damn! Who would have thought a little thing like her could pull off something this big?"

"I told you she didn't do it."

"So you did." Belle dismissed his words with a shrug. "But it all adds up. You married her. Now you can't testify against her. Am I right?"

"Did you ever think I married her because I love her?"

"I'm sure you do. But that doesn't make her innocent."

"Belle, for God's sake, be serious. Would I take a thief for a wife?"

"Don't try to con a con, Maddox. I've seen enough women try to hogtie you. This is the first one you went after. You wouldn't give her a minute's peace till she went along with you to the church."

"The second."

Belle smiled at the correction and repeated, "The second. I didn't know Sarah. Are they at all alike?"

"Like night and day."

"I suppose Sarah would never have robbed a stage."

Belle only laughed at his menacing look.

"Was she as shy?"

Tanner burst out laughing. Shy? He might have thought Elizabeth shy at first. Actually she was, but he'd never associate the word with her again. Not after last night. After last night he had a time of it

269

remembering she was a lady. In bed, she became as wanton as the highest paid courtesan and fortunately, never thought she shouldn't. "Belle, I can't compare the two."

"I suppose the robberies will just suddenly stop now."

Tanner glared in her direction. They'd better, if his wife ever wanted to sit again. He gave a slight shrug. "I don't know why they should.

"Where's Stacey staying?" he asked hoping Belle wouldn't notice that he had changed the subject.

She did, but she only laughed at his obvious attempt. "At the bank. He's got an office as big as a house."

Tanner nodded, remembering the first time he'd visited the man there.

"Is there a need for me to hang around?"

"Why? Is someone waiting for you back in Denver?"

Belle was as smart as they came. She knew Elizabeth was guilty. She knew as well that Tanner wasn't about to give up any information. It didn't matter. The man was head over heels in love. If she was ever lucky enough to know that kind of emotion, she'd probably do much the same.

"What would it hurt?" she asked as they walked hand in hand across her back yard. "If you loved me you would do it."

"It's because I love you that I won't."

"You're going to protect me from myself, is that it?"

"Exactly."

"Suppose I don't want or need your protection?"

"You might not want it, but you're getting it anyway."

Elizabeth tipped her head to the side and sent him a teasing look. She hesitated for a moment as she regrouped her thoughts. "All right. We'll leave love out of it. Let's think about this logically. With the two of us working together, there'd be half the danger. We could watch each other's back."

"If you were thinking logically, we wouldn't be having this discussion."

Elizabeth let that comment go unanswered, but Tanner was soon to discover the conversation was far from over. "Let's see," she said as if to herself. "How would a wife go about convincing her husband to do her bidding?" Elizabeth decided at that moment that, despite her previous objections, she liked being a wife and that she liked even more having Tanner as her husband. Yes, she liked that very much indeed. "What exactly would she do?" she asked as a wicked light danced in her eyes.

Tanner only groaned.

"What do you think?" she asked, as if he would actually tell her the truth.

"I think you're wasting your time. There's no way you're going to refuse me in bed," he said knowingly. "You want our lovemaking as much as I do."

"Bed?" Elizabeth giggled, her eyes widening in feigned surprise. "Did I say anything about bed?" She shrugged. "Besides, you don't know anything for a fact. I could have been acting out a role."

Tanner decided he wouldn't push her on this

point. He knew the truth, but there was no telling what she might do if pressed. Wisely, he changed the subject. "Elizabeth, I'm a lawman. I can't involve myself in something like this. I've already gone against everything I believe in just to protect you."

"So how could it hurt if you did a little more?"

Elizabeth received only a menacing glare as an answer. But she wasn't the least bit afraid of Tanner. "I'll do it with or without your help," she said stubbornly.

Tanner knew she'd do no such thing. Not with the watch he had set on her. "I'm going to put you over my knee if you keep up this kind of talk."

"Really?" Elizabeth giggled as she turned to face him, walking ahead of him but backward. A wicked light of anticipation danced in her dark eyes. "Will you bite me there again?"

Tanner grinned at seeing her eager expression. "You liked that, did you?"

Elizabeth pursed her lips much like Miss Dunlap did when encountering a disobedient child, but Tanner wasn't fooled. She couldn't deny the laughter in her eyes. "I'm afraid I haven't the slightest idea as to what you're talking about." An instant later she picked up her skirt. Knowing no one could see but him, she purposely brought it higher than what could be considered decent and then ran like a little hellion across the back yard, straight into the barn.

Elizabeth held a hand over her mouth, trying to control the laugher that threatened to bubble out of control. In her entire life, she'd never acted so wild, so childlike, so uninhibited. Despite the fact that this man wouldn't see things her way, she'd never felt this happy.

Standing atop a bale of hay, she watched Tanner walk into the barn. With a cry that much resembled an attacking Indian, she launched herself from the hay and landed upon her husband's back. Her arms encircled his neck, her legs his waist, as she hung on.

Both of them were laughing as he pulled her over his shoulder. A moment later, while holding her in his arms, he fell into a mound of soft hay. "You little . . ."

Elizabeth waved her finger, her mouth suddenly prim. "Now be careful what you say, Marshal. You are, after all, talking to your wife."

"Am I?" He chuckled, then stared down into warm brown eyes. A smile teased the corners of his mouth. "Name one wife that would jump on her husband's back like some damned wild Indian."

"Me," she said simply.

Tanner groaned as he adjusted himself to lie full length upon her. His hands held hers even with her shoulders. "Since we're already positioned, I take it you'd have no objection to a roll in the hay?"

Elizabeth laughed at noting the devilish gleam in his eyes. Pretending ignorance she asked innocently, "I've heard the expression before. Was I wrong to imagine it meant something quite naughty?"

"It does."

"Really?" Her eyes widened as she grew more obviously interested. "Tell me, what?"

"Well, it might be better if I showed you."

She smiled. Her eyes grew soft, her mouth became sweetly beckoning, her voice was now slightly breathless. "Then what are you waiting for?"

Tanner thought himself the luckiest man alive. How many wives were this eager for the joy of loving? How many abandoned every restraint and willingly participated in it?

He watched her for a long moment, and just before he lowered his mouth to hers, he heard her whisper, soft almost pleading. "Tanner?"

He groaned, unable to get enough of the taste of her. Every time he kissed her it was as if he'd never kissed before. She was the sparkle of a bubbling stream, sunshine on a summer day, the innocent laughter of a child, a cozy fire on a cool night. She was everything good, with perhaps more than a little of the devil thrown in. She made him feel new, alive, strong and anxious to hold on to and treasure every minute God allowed them together.

Elizabeth heard the moan again. Although she had every reason to utter the sound, considering what Tanner was doing with his mouth and tongue against her breast, she was positive it hadn't come from her this time.

"Tanner," she murmured, but the sound was almost instantly swallowed up in a passionate kiss. She said his name again.

"What?" he asked, obviously farther along in his passion than she. He broke away only to return before she had a chance to say another word.

Elizabeth's hands cupped the sides of his face and forced his mouth from hers.

"Tanner," she whispered, as he went about the joyful task of furthering his passion. His mouth was depositing short, delicious kisses along the length of her neck when he managed an answer.

"Someone is moaning."

"I know," he breathed out. "I can't help it. I want you so damn—"

"No. I mean, someone *else* is moaning."

"What?" he asked. His mouth abruptly left her warmth; his eyes grew wide as her words finally penetrated the fog of desire that had held him in its grip.

Elizabeth's gaze moved toward the sound. "There, I think," she said, so softly he couldn't have heard unless he'd been positioned only inches from her mouth.

Tanner lifted himself from her and moved on silent feet toward the sound.

She was right. Someone was definitely moaning. At first he imagined it was one of the many children that were forever underfoot, perhaps imitating the sounds they'd heard, but no. Whoever was making this sound was obviously in some degree of pain.

Tanner brushed aside the cover of hay. His eyes widened in shock at taking in Jason lying barely conscious, curled on his side.

Tanner shot Elizabeth a look that clearly showed his confusion. What the hell was Jason doing there? Elizabeth kept a room for him in the house. Perhaps he'd fallen into a drunken stupor.

"Who is it?" Elizabeth made a small sound as she came to Tanner's side and saw for herself. "What happened? Why is he out here?"

"Maybe he's sick." Tanner watched as she knelt beside the man. He saw her reach for his head. "Don't! Don't touch him. He might be—

"Damn it!" he snapped, as she did exactly what he'd warned her against doing. "Is this a sample of the obedience I can expect from you?"

Elizabeth shot him a nasty look. "If you expect obedience from me, Tanner, you're sure to be disappointed."

"Well, at least I know where I stand, don't I?"

Elizabeth dismissed his pouting words with a shake of her head. "We can argue later. Help me get him into the house. He's burning up with fever."

"Wonderful! And you touched him."

"Are you going to help me? Or will I do this myself?"

Tanner snarled a complaint as he awkwardly brought the man up against his chest, but he came to a sudden stop as a most ungodly stench filled the air. "What the hell is that smell?"

Elizabeth gasped as she noticed the condition of Jason's clothes. "My God! His clothes are burned. Half his hair is gone! He's been in a fire!"

Jason was small and weighed next to nothing. It was no effort for Tanner to bring him to his room.

Elizabeth hovered nearby, issuing orders as she pulled the covers from his bed. "Be careful. Watch his leg." Tanner gritted his teeth and said nothing in response to what he considered to be unnecessary commands. But when she reached for the man and began to dispose of his clothing instead of acting like the refined lady she was supposed to be, Tanner shoved her out of the room.

She cried out his name in annoyance as she was pushed into the hallway, but Tanner took no notice. No wife of his was going to look at another man.

He didn't care how old and wrinkled, or sick that man might be.

"I'll undress him. Once I have him ready, you can come back in." Unceremoniously he slammed the door in her face.

Elizabeth shook her head and paced the floor outside Jason's room. She couldn't believe her husband was jealous of an old man. But he was. How ridiculous could the man be? Lord, what had she gotten herself into? Exactly how possessive and jealous was this man she'd married? And why was she wasting time in pacing when she needed to collect salves and bandages?

By the time Elizabeth returned with a pan of warm water and the needed medical supplies, Jason's door was ajar. Tanner ignored her entrance as he leaned over the bed, holding a bottle of whiskey to the man's lips.

"I sent for Dr. Thompson," she said, "but he's at Sally's again. I wonder if it's another false alarm. There's no telling how long he'll be there." Elizabeth received only a grunt for an answer.

Apparently Tanner was sulking. Well, she had no time to think about his childish reactions now. Jason needed all of her attention. She brought the sheet that draped Jason's lower body from his feet to his knees, revealing the grotesque sight of badly burned flesh. With warm water, she gently began the tedious task of removing the grime and the pieces of blackened matter that clung to his leg.

Jason was obviously in agony. Even though he gulped down the brew Tanner offered, he couldn't get enough whiskey in him to dull the pain.

Elizabeth soon gave up her chore. She was only adding to the man's misery. Gently she placed a wet cloth over the entire leg and up his side, hoping it would loosen some of the material. She'd work on it later, hopefully when he'd drunk enough to feel no pain.

The fire appeared to have raced up his leg, causing the most damage there. But the skin on his face and his head were burned as well. Actually one side of his body was terribly damaged. Gently, she smoothed a salve over the left side of his torso, and then she wrapped him in clean cloths.

"Let the whiskey get to work before you start again."

Elizabeth nodded.

"I want to talk to you," Tanner nodded toward the door. "Outside."

Elizabeth looked up into eyes filled with anger. Her first impulse was to defy Tanner, but she didn't feel up to adding to his wrath. She allowed him to escort her from the room.

He led her directly across the hall. The moment he had closed the door to her room behind them, she turned and asked, "What?"

"How many men have you nursed?"

Elizabeth looked at Tanner, her mouth dropping open in amazement. She'd never expected his mind to be running along this route. "What are you talking about?"

"I want to know."

"None."

"You expect me to believe that? You've never seen a man before, and yet you were about to take off

278

Jason's trousers? You touched his body as if you did that every day."

"The man is hurt. You're being ridiculous."

"Am I? I don't think so."

"Tanner," she strained to achieve a calmness she was far from feeling, "Jason is an old man."

"So?"

"What do you mean, 'so'? He's old and he's hurt. Someone has to help him."

"Do you know how he got burned?"

"Of course not. How would I?"

"Is he in on it? He's more to you than a handyman, isn't he? Have you two been working together?" He wanted to ask if they had done more than work together, but he was suddenly terrified of hearing her answer.

"Working together? What are you talking about?"

Tanner reached for her shoulders and gave her a hard shake. "If I find out you're lying, I'll —"

Tanner grunted and bent in half on receiving the sudden blow to his midsection. Wisely Elizabeth stepped out of his reach. Still, she wouldn't run. She wasn't afraid of him. "Don't think because we're married you have the right to bully me. I'll never take abuse from you. You might as well know that right now."

Elizabeth watched as Tanner turned and sat on the edge of her bed. He said nothing as he positioned his elbows on spread knees and held his head in his hands.

He knew he'd given her a scare. Damn his soul to hell! What had come over him? How could he have imagined Elizabeth with that old man? Whatever possessed him to think there might have been something between them? He knew he'd been the first. Some things there was no denying.

It was just the way she went about opening another man's trousers. Tanner had stared in amazement as she'd reached for the buttons, unable to believe his wife was about to take off Jason's clothes. And the way she smoothed the salve over the man's chest and stomach. And then there was the smell. . . .

"I'm sorry."

"What's gotten into you? What in the world are you thinking?"

"Jason set the fire last night."

Elizabeth gasped. "How do you know?"

"His clothes still smell of kerosene."

"But that doesn't mean . . . Why? Why would he do such a thing?"

"I don't know. Yet," he added as he stood up, his gaze boring into the depths of her as if searching for an answer she didn't possess. Without another word, he walked out of the room.

"How is he?"

Elizabeth had no need to turn and face him. As always, she knew by the sound of his footsteps, that this particular man had entered her kitchen. She shrugged, keeping her attention on the chore before her. She was cutting a large, fragrant roast into thick slices and laying the slabs in the center of a platter edged with buttered potatoes. "He's sleeping. Dr. Thompson came, but there was little he could do. He left some laudanum for the pain, but . . ." Elizabeth shrugged again as her words faltered. "Are you hungry?"

"Starved."

Elizabeth gave him a weak smile. She'd never in her life wanted to feel his arms around her more. That afternoon had been a horror. She needed to smell his clean scent — would she forever smell burned flesh? — to lean against his hardness, to regain her strength in his arms. But now wasn't the time. "Would you knock on Gloria's door and tell her supper is ready?"

"Elizabeth" — he groaned — "the woman hates me. It's bad enough that we have to sit at the same table every night. Don't make me talk to her."

She grinned, put down her knife, wiped her hands on her apron, and moved to stand before him. How was it this man could appear fearless and of immeasurable strength while retaining a vulnerability that brought an ache to her chest? Small hands came up to encircle his neck as she leaned into him. "She does not. She's just shy. Where's Belle?"

"She'll be along in a minute."

Elizabeth felt measurably stronger just standing in his arms. "I want to tell you how sorry I am for what I did."

"For not obeying me?"

She leaned back as far as their loosely clasped arms allowed. "Tanner, you have to understand. I'm not used to having a man take control of anything I do." She smiled. "I'll try, but I can't promise I'll always do as I'm told."

"Well, I reckon that's somethin'."

281

"But that wasn't what I was talking about."

"Oh, you mean you're sorry for hitting me."

Elizabeth nodded.

"Let me get this straight. You're allowed to hit, but I'm not. Is that it?"

"That's about right," she said, and then she let out a short startled shriek as he growled, grabbed her waist, and spun her around in dizzying circles.

"What am I going to do with you?"

Elizabeth's laughter was as gay as a young girl's as she fell against him. "Smother me with kisses?" she offered as an answer, while a devilish twinkle entered her eyes.

Tanner groaned and again thanked his maker that this woman knew nothing of her former shyness once she was in his arms. She was boldly aggressive, an answer to any man's most secret fantasy, and he loved her. "If I do supper will get cold," he teased in return, wanting nothing more than to hold her and kiss her for the rest of his life.

"One day. Married just one day and already you're thinking more about food than . . ."

Elizabeth and Tanner, although their embrace was less than passionate, broke apart almost guiltily at Belle's untimely interruption. "Didn't anyone ever tell you it's impolite to eavesdrop?" Tanner asked.

Belle's wide skirts swished as she moved past the couple and settled herself at the kitchen table. As always, she helped herself to a glass of the whiskey Elizabeth kept there for her. "I wasn't eavesdropping. If I wanted to do that, I'd listen at your door." She nodded in the general direction of the bedrooms. "The sounds that come from there—"

"Belle!" he said. Then he cursed in exasperation as Elizabeth's eyes widened with shock and her complexion turned decidedly gray. He put an arm around her waist and drew her to his side. "She didn't mean it, sweetheart." Directing a fierce look at his partner, he added, "Did you, Belle?"

Elizabeth's complexion had run the gamut from deathly white to the color of Belle's prettiest red petticoat. To put it mildly, she was pained, and Belle knew she had finally gone too far. Used to saying exactly what she pleased, she sometimes forgot she should watch her tongue in the company of ladies. And Elizabeth, no matter what Belle might suspect her of having done, was most definitely a lady. "Don't mind me, honey," Belle said, trying to make amends. "I just know how to get him where it hurts." She silently cursed her wayward tongue as the small woman paled again. "Sometimes my tongue runs away with itself," she added.

Elizabeth was quieter than usual throughout dinner. Tanner carefully watched her every expression as she listened to Miss Dunlap tell of the day's happenings. What should have been a mildly amusing story barely sparked a smile from his lady's lips.

It seemed one of the boys, no doubt that troublesome Tommy Harrington although Miss Dunlap had no real proof, had set a small pile of rags to smoldering in the back corner of the schoolhouse. When Miss Dunlap noticed the smoke, she had immediately run to extinguish the more smokey than dangerous blaze. What she hadn't realized at the time was that the rags had covered a goodly amount of manure. Apparently she hadn't realized what she

283

was stepping on until it was far too late.

It had taken more than an hour to clean the mess from the floor, her high button boots, and the hem of her skirt. She wondered if the scent would ever completely disappear from the schoolhouse.

Tanner gave a near-silent but definitely morose sigh, as he reached for the bottle of whiskey. He couldn't believe that a few carelessly spoken words had jeopardized the most beautiful relationship he'd ever known in his life. He shot Belle a menacing glare, wishing he could, for just a minute, get his hands around her neck. There was no telling the damage her big mouth had done.

He couldn't wait for the meal to end so he could speak with Elizabeth and find out.

"We need to talk," he said as she slowly ascended the steps of her front porch. The damned woman had literally disappeared the moment the kitchen was put to rights. Lord, he'd searched for her for almost an hour before deciding he'd simply have to wait her out. Her horse was in the barn. On foot, she couldn't have gone far. He knew she'd have to return eventually. At least he hoped so. For the last three hours he'd sat upon her rocker, smoking an endless stream of cigarettes as he waited.

Elizabeth almost managed to hide her surprise. It was obvious she hadn't expected him to still be up. One hand went to her pounding heart as she turned swiftly to face the empty street. Her voice was very soft when, after a moment's pause, she began. "Tanner, I don't think . . ."

Instantly he was on his feet, his arms around her, pulling her tense body to his. "That's right," he said gently as he brought his mouth near her ear. "Don't think. Don't listen to people and their stupid remarks. Just—"

Elizabeth abruptly turned to face him. Her eyes were wide, filled with horror, but her words were soft as she cut him off. "She heard us. My God, I've never been so embarrassed. I never thought, never realized anyone might hear. What must they think?"

"No one heard a damned thing. Belle's always spouting some ridiculous nonsense. She only said that because—"

"Because she heard."

"Elizabeth, please. Don't do this to yourself."

She shook her head, refusing to meet his eyes. "I was thinking tonight. About how easily I've put aside my morals since you came into my life."

"What the hell are you talking about?"

Even in the dark, Tanner could see her flush with embarrassment. "I've been acting like one of those loose women who live over the saloon."

"Damn!" Tanner groaned. "How the hell can you compare yourself to one of them?"

"You must think I'm awful," she said, her eyes fastened on the middle button on his shirt. "I have no explanation." She gave a slight shrug. "I don't understand what came over me. I only know I'm sorry."

"Come with me," Tanner said none too gently as he nearly dragged her down the steps and away from the house. He was some distance away from possibly being overheard before he spoke again. Holding her close in his arms, he prayed to God to find the right

285

words. "First of all, you've nothing to be sorry about. If I didn't like . . . if I didn't love everything you've done so far, I would have told you." He took a deep steadying breath. "You're wonderful. Everything you do is wonderful. It takes my breath away just to think about the things we do together. The little sounds you make when I love you"—he heard her groan and pressed her face tighter against his chest—"are heaven. You can't know how it adds to my enjoyment to hear them. It drives me crazy with wanting you."

Tanner gently slid his finger beneath her chin and tipped her face up. It was well after midnight, but the moon gave off enough light to clearly read her expression. "I'd never lie to you, Elizabeth. Do you believe that?"

Elizabeth nodded, her eyes filling with unexplained tears.

"Then believe this. If both parties are willing, there's nothing, absolutely nothing that a husband and his wife do together that's shameful."

Elizabeth said nothing. She lowered her eyes to his shirt button again.

"Do you believe me?"

"You're not sorry I acted like a loose woman?"

Tanner groaned and then smiled. "I'm not sorry. I could never be sorry. But only with me, you understand."

Elizabeth's lips curved into a soft, hesitant smile. "Are you sure?" She bit her bottom lip. "I haven't disgusted or embarrassed you?"

"God." He groaned softly as he drew her closer and rubbed his face against her hair. "I'm going to wring Belle's neck." He released a long sigh before he spoke again. "You're a lady, Elizabeth. Everything you do, from your speech and your walk to the gentle way you treat people, proves just how much a lady you are. You could never do anything that would embarrass me."

She took a deep breath. "I . . . I feel a bit self-conscious. I don't know how to act."

"Act the way you always do."

Elizabeth giggled, still not daring to look at him. "Like a loose woman?" she teased.

"The looser the better," he declared. "Especially when we're alone."

They stood locked together for a moment. It wasn't until he felt her shiver that he realized how cold it had grown. Elizabeth smiled as she allowed him to lead her back to the house. "Ah, Tanner." She shot him a nervous glance. "I don't think I can, ummm . . . I don't think . . ."

"We don't have to do anything, Elizabeth. I'm only going to hold you tonight. If you're afraid that sounds will carry, we'll go somewhere else when we make love."

She smiled as she glanced his way. "You wouldn't mind?"

"Not if you promise to make it up to me," he teased. Elizabeth's smile was so sweetly innocent, Tanner felt his heart contract.

"And how could I do that?"

Tanner whispered near her ear, "By being wild and hungry for my kisses. By begging me to touch you, to kiss you, to rub my mouth and tongue all over you. And most of all, by crying out with pleasure when I love you." He chuckled softly when her shocked expression slowly became an eager one as she gave his suggestion some thought.

They began to walk again. After a few steps, she asked, "Are you very tired?"

"Not terribly. Why?"

"I just remembered there was something in the barn I wanted to show you."

"Is there? What?"

She recalled the things he'd just told her. His softly spoken words had made things right between them again, still it took every bit of nerve she had for Elizabeth to finally manage a breathless, "Me."

Chapter Fourteen

"But why can't I stay here?"

Stacey frowned. He detested whining. Why did it always have to come to this? Why didn't the boy know he couldn't always have his way? Stacey's lips twisted in an expression of disgust. Brian would sulk now, perhaps for days. He really disliked these kinds of confrontations. Actually he disliked confrontations of any kind. Clearly it was time for Brian and him to part company. Stacey had seen it coming. The fire was excuse enough. "There isn't enough room, for one thing. For another, I've a reputation to keep up. What would the people in these parts think?"

"I lived at your house and no one said anything."

Stacey's eyes hardened at being reminded of his recent loss. "The house was large. Many people lived there, including the servants and the guards." Not that it seemed to have helped, Stacey thought. He paid them enough. At the very least they should have seen to his property.

"I'm going to miss you. I don't like sleeping alone."

"Yes, of course," Stacey responded. "And I shall miss you, as well. But until the house is repaired, we'll have to keep things as they are."

"I hate living over the saloon. The women there are disgusting. They smell."

"Why don't you rent a room from Mrs. Garner—I mean Mrs. Maddox. Now that she's married, I'm sure she has at least one room empty."

"And live in the same house as that man?" Brian shuddered. "He's worse than the woman."

"Mmmm," Stacey murmured, not really concerned. He looked through his papers. "I'm afraid we all have our crosses to bear.

"Have you seen the file I left on my desk this morning?"

Brian nodded toward the row of cabinets behind the desk. "I put it away."

Stacey sighed as he came to his feet. It was useless to go through this again. The boy had been told over and over not to straighten Stacey's desk until the end of the day. At any rate, he'd be gone soon enough. Stacey made a mental note to see that the lad who took Brian's place would be a bit less compulsively neat.

"How's he doin'?" Tanner asked softly as he stepped into the room.

Elizabeth shook her head and bit down on her bottom lip, her eyes clearly revealing the hopelessness of the situation. So far, Jason had lasted a week. That he'd lived that long was a miracle. "Not good. He's in terrible pain."

Tanner nodded as he came up behind her. "You're tired," he said as he put his arms around her waist and pulled her back against his chest. "Why don't you lie down for a while? I'll watch over him."

She shook her head. "I have supper to start."

"Go to bed, Elizabeth. You've hardly had four hours' sleep in two days."

"What about—"

"Belle or Miss Dunlap or I will put something together for supper. I want you to rest."

"How are Sally and the baby doing?"

Tanner chuckled as he remembered Dave's obvious delight. "If I'm not mistaken, Sally had little to do with the actual birthing process. There's no other explanation for the way the man struts around town, boasting of his accomplishment."

Elizabeth laughed and leaned comfortably against him. "Are all new fathers similarly impressed?"

"I reckon I've traveled too much. Haven't had a chance to notice things like that."

"And you have no firsthand experience?"

"Is that a sneaky way of asking if I've got any offspring stashed away?"

Elizabeth giggled. "You said you were married once before."

His arms tightened around her. "My first wife died in childbirth, the baby with her. The idea of your having a baby scares the hell out of me. I don't know how happy I'd be about it."

"Every woman doesn't die in childbirth, Tanner. Look at Sally."

"Your hips aren't as wide as hers."

Elizabeth's head snapped up. Her eyes glared into

his. "And you're an expert on woman's hips, I take it. How do you know hers are wide?"

"I can tell when she walks. How else would I know?"

"What are you doing looking at another woman's hips? What else have you been measuring?"

Tanner grinned, aware of her jealousy. He felt a jolt of happiness. "Loving you doesn't make be blind, sweetheart."

"I don't think I like the idea of you looking at other women."

"I swear, I only do it so I can silently boast I've got the best."

Elizabeth shot him a look of utter disbelief. It didn't add to his credibility that she found him hard pressed not to laugh. "No doubt." She laughed herself as she turned in his arms. "I suppose that leaves me with only one option."

"That being?"

"I'll have to do my share of looking."

"Don't let me catch you at it," he warned.

"Then don't let me catch you," she retorted as she poked his chest, her eyes hard with determination.

Tanner laughed and hugged her. "I love you.

"What have you got there?" he asked at hearing the rustling of paper.

Elizabeth held out the sheets she had tucked into the waistband of her skirt and handed them to him. "This came while you were at Dave's office."

Tanner's gaze studied the official-looking documents. A moment later he glanced up at her. "I told you to be careful. I knew the man was a snake from the first moment I laid eyes on him."

Elizabeth smiled. "Actually, if I remember correctly, what you said was, 'He reminds me of a lizard.'"

Tanner grinned. "You don't seem particularly upset for a lady who's about to lose her home."

She shrugged. "I'm not."

"Would you mind telling me why?"

Elizabeth's scrunched-up expression clearly told of her reluctance to face a particularly unpleasant task. "Actually, I was hoping you wouldn't ask."

"Elizabeth"—his voice lowered in warning—"you're not planning on doing anything I wouldn't approve of, are you?"

"I hope not." She shrugged as his eyes narrowed dangerously. "I'm only planning on paying off the loan, Tanner. You needn't give me any of your evil looks."

"Why don't you just sell the house? We won't be here much longer."

"Because that takes time and because it's a matter of principle. I'm not going to let Stacey get his hands on the place. He's just doing this for spite."

"How are you going to pay it off?"

She shrugged and answered evasively, "I only owe three hundred dollars."

Tanner whistled softly between his teeth. "You've been able to save that much running this place, and in only a year?"

"Well," she dragged out the word as if it contained two syllables, "not exactly." She was obviously uncomfortable over being questioned.

"What exactly?"

"I have a little set aside."

It all became clear to him. "From the money you stole? I thought you gave it all away."

"I did. At least most of it."

"How much didn't you give away, Elizabeth?" he asked, dreading her answer.

Elizabeth mumbled a few indistinguishable words.

"How much?" he insisted.

"Seven thousand."

Tanner moaned. One hand went to his head, the other sought the foot of the bed in case his legs gave out.

"I wasn't going to keep it," she said, twisting her hands nervously. "I swear I wasn't."

"Of course you weren't." He was dazed. "Then why did you?"

"I didn't know who to give it to." She bit her lip and chanced a glance in his direction. Everything looked all right so far. Tanner's complexion was slightly gray, not the fiery red she'd half expected. "Usually there is some needy family, but . . ." Her voice trailed off.

"How much have you given away?"

She took a deep breath and narrowed her eyes in concentration as she calculated, "Well let's see, I gave the Harrisons four thousand." Elizabeth ignored another of Tanner's pain-filled moans. "And then Mr. and Mrs. Berkly. I think they got six."

"Oh, my God."

"And there were the Samples. I gave them nine, five, if I'm not mistaken."

"We are talking in terms of thousands here. Am I right?"

Elizabeth nodded.

"Is there a particular reason why you picked these people, and those amounts?"

Elizabeth looked with unseeing eyes at her twisting fingers. She shrugged. "I gave whatever I took. And they were the ones who—"

"Stacey foreclosed on their homes!" Tanner said, remembering the Harrisons being mentioned when he'd first come into town. Tanner simultaneously felt so damned proud of her and so horrified that she had jeopardized her safety, he didn't trust himself to go near her. Right now, there was no telling whether he'd give in to the urge to hug her or to strangle her. Wisely, he kept his distance.

"Well, they needed help," she said righteously, as if that was reason enough to rob a stage. "What was I supposed to do?"

In frustration, Tanner ran a hand over his face. "How the hell am I supposed to answer a question like that?"

"Don't get upset. I'll find someone deserving. I promise. Just give me a little time."

Tanner's voice was low, his eyes were glazed as if he were in shock. He couldn't believe the words that were tumbling from his mouth. He couldn't believe he was actually becoming a party to this fiasco. "There's an orphanage in Virginia City that—"

"Oh!" she flung herself against him, her arms circling his neck. "That's a wonderful idea." Then she became aware of his stiff stance and of the fact that he hadn't brought his arms around her. She leaned back and took in his tight expression. "You're not angry, are you?"

"I don't know what I am. Stunned probably." He

sighed as he gave in to at least one of his urges and wrapped his arms around her waist. "I've been so upset since finding out you were behind it all, I hadn't thought till now about the money."

"I didn't take it for myself."

"I know. How did you manage the actual disposal? You didn't tell those people . . ."

She shook her head. "They never knew who left it on their doorstep. I just dropped the package, knocked, slipped into the shadows, and waited for someone to open the door."

Tanner shook his head and tried for a threatening tone. "If I ever find out that you're even thinking of doing something like this again, I'll—"

Elizabeth laughed. "Of course I'm thinking about it, silly." Her laughing eyes met his suffering gaze. "Haven't I tried to talk you into joining me?"

"It's best, I think, for us to drop that particular subject. I want you to get some rest. And I mean now!" he said as he escorted her from the room to her own bed.

Jason died that night. It was very late. Tanner had just left their bedroom. She could hear him in the kitchen making a fresh pot of coffee. It was his turn to sit by the man, and he needed the brew to stay awake the five-odd hours till dawn.

Elizabeth had been sitting quietly at Jason's side, when the suffering man had suddenly come wide awake. Pain and feverishness showed clearly in his eyes, but his voice was steady and unusually strong as he said, "I want to thank you, ma'am."

Elizabeth supposed he meant to thank her for her care. She didn't know that Jason had been half-awake during the conversation she and Tanner had had earlier. He'd known all along she was behind the robberies. Now he knew she had been trying to ruin the monster. He didn't know why, but he guessed it wasn't so all-fired important that he should.

Elizabeth smiled and was about to reply when he continued speaking. "Look in the bottom drawer. Use it." He took a long, shuddering breath. "Get him," he said just before that last breath slipped from weakened, fevered lungs.

Elizabeth gave a soft cry as she watched his eyes slowly grow blank. It was another few seconds before she realized he'd stopped blinking. Tanner was suddenly at her side. She leaned into him as his arm came around her. "It's all right, sweetheart," Tanner said. He'd seen enough of death to know the man was gone. "He's better off. He was in horrible pain."

To Elizabeth it was unbearably sad that anyone could be better off dead. "I know," she whispered.

Tanner reached out, closed Jason's eyes, and brought the sheet up to cover the man's face. "Come to bed now. You're exhausted. Morning will be soon enough to send for the doctor."

Elizabeth nodded as Tanner extinguished the lone lantern by the side of the bed. Then she allowed her husband to guide her from the room.

Tanner took her robe from her and helped her into bed. He left her for a moment to put out the lamp he'd left burning in the kitchen. When he returned he found her curled into a tight ball, shivering. Gently he drew her into the warmth of his arms. "I'm so cold," she got out through jaws clamped together to prevent her teeth from chattering.

"Because you're upset," Tanner reasoned. "I'll warm you." His arms encircled her and pressed her closer to his body's heat. Gently he ran one hand up and down her back.

"Do you realize there's not one person who'll cry?"

"Most people die the way they lived, Elizabeth. Maybe he liked being alone."

"No one likes being alone," she countered. "I feel so sorry for him."

"I know. I figured that's why you let him stay here."

"He helped around the place, Tanner. He might not have had any money, but he did his share."

Tanner knew well enough the man had not. Almost every job Jason started remained unfinished. The barn was painted on only one side. Perhaps a dozen or so bricks were laid at its entrance, while a shallow ditch awaited more. Two shutters hung loose at the back of the house, and all the windows needed a coat of paint. Yes, Jason had been far too content with a bottle to have worked overly hard for his keep. Still, Tanner wasn't going to argue about that. "I know." He snuggled closer to her, trying to think of words that would ease her sadness. "You go to church every Sunday, sweetheart. Don't you believe something better awaits us all?"

"You know I do."

"So you don't have any real reason to feel sad."

"Except that he was alone."

"He's not alone now."

Elizabeth sighed, knowing the truth of his words. Knowing as well that he was trying to make her feel better. God, how she loved him for that. She'd loved him for a long time. It wasn't till this moment that she could admit it aloud. She draped an arm over his chest and said simply, "I love you, Tanner," feeling somewhat amazed at how easily the words came.

"I know, sweetheart." He was glad that she'd said it for the first time in this moment rather than in the grip of passion. Somehow it held more meaning this way.

"Do you?" she asked. He could hear the smile in her voice. "I suppose you know; you're very cocky."

"As a matter of fact, I am." He grinned. "And that's probably one of the things you love most."

Elizabeth laughed, but she didn't dispute his claim. "And arrogant. Usually I can't abide arrogance, you know."

"But you like it in me."

Elizabeth came up on an elbow. The glowing embers in the grate lent more than enough light for him to see her smile. She gave him a light kiss and then said, "It annoys the hell out of me, but I love you anyway."

Tanner chuckled. He'd never heard her use profanity before. Somehow it only added to her allure.

"Don't curse. It makes me hot. And I'm too tired for a trip to the barn."

Elizabeth smothered her laughter against his chest. "Everything makes you hot."

"And you love that as well."

Elizabeth looked down at her husband. Her eyes twinkled with warm laughter. "I love everything about you."

It was close to three weeks after they buried Jason before Elizabeth could bring herself to go through the man's belongings. She hated this chore and had thought more than once that she should have someone else do it. In the end, however, she realized the poor man had no one but her. She couldn't let a total stranger handle his things.

She took the packet from the lower drawer and put it on the bed alongside the pitifully small pile of clothes. Most of his things were so worn and old, they were no better than rags. She could hardly give them away, for she knew no one in this small town that would have them.

With a sad sigh, Elizabeth gathered the few garments together, along with his minimal toiletries, and she took them out to the rubbish pile. A moment later she returned to strip and air out the bed.

It was then that she picked up the packet.

Feeling more than ever that she was invading the man's privacy, Elizabeth was hesitant to open the rag-covered parcel. Finally, she put aside her discomfort. There was always the chance she might learn of a distant relative, someone who should be notified of the man's demise. Gently she opened the packet and took what turned out to be a thick journal into her parlor. Her healthy coloring turned gray, and her eyes glazed over with shock by the time she finished reading the last page.

Jason had had a family. A wife and a son, both deceased. Apparently his wife had died years ago, while his son had killed himself because Jonathan Stacey had used him sexually. Elizabeth stared in amazement at the words she saw before her. How had the man gotten away with that? Elizabeth gave a short humorless laugh. Money. How else? A man, no matter how evil, could get away with almost anything if he knew the right people and had enough money.

Elizabeth remembered Jason's last words. *Use it. Get him.* She'd thought at the time that he was rambling, that his wits had deserted him. Now she knew what he'd meant.

Her eyes glittered with the fire of revenge. Jason had given her the perfect weapon to destroy the man whose evil ways had brought devastation to everyone he'd ever touched. She knew why Jason wouldn't use the information himself. He couldn't bring disgrace on his son's name. But she wasn't about to hesitate. The innocent parties were dead. Nothing could hurt them now.

The only question that ran through her mind was, how was she going to go about using this information? To hand it over to the law would result in an investigation. But that might not result in his being punished. Stacey might somehow manage to get himself off the hook.

A deliciously dangerous smile curved Elizabeth's lips as an idea began to take shape. He wasn't going to get out of it this time. If it was the last thing she did in this life, she was going to make sure that Jonathan Stacey answered for his crimes.

* * *

Elizabeth carefully composed her letter, making sure to separate emotion from fact. Then she signed the missive, adding to it the last page of the journal—the actual suicide note.

Tanner was at Dave's office. No doubt, if Dave had recuperated from the birth of his son, the two men were finishing up the investigation of the fire. Tanner was positive that Jason had been responsible. Elizabeth only prayed he was right. The poor man deserved at least that much satisfaction.

Elizabeth gathered up the things she needed and walked to the newspaper office. Mr. Carlton was sitting at his desk, his feet resting on its surface, his bearded face tilted toward his shoulder as he slept. The bell attached to his door notified him of her entrance and startled him awake.

Elizabeth smiled as an embarrassed flush darkened that part of the newspaperman's face that wasn't covered by his beard. He didn't like to be caught dozing. "Afternoon, Mr. Carlton," Elizabeth said.

"Afternoon, Mrs. Maddox. I've just finished placing the news of your wedding." He nodded over his shoulder toward the back room, where a bulky printing press stood unattended. "It's ready for the next edition."

"Ah, Mr. Carlton," she began, while praying the man would go along with her idea, "how much would it cost to have a few pages put into print?"

Mr. Carlton quoted her a price.

"Would you do me a favor?" At the man's nod, she went on, "I need a hundred copies of this." Elizabeth extended the papers in question.

Mr. Carlton's complexion grew redder than ever

as his eyes took in the suicide note and Mrs. Maddox's letter. "Maybe you didn't know, ma'am, but Mr. Stacey owns this newspaper. You're asking me to risk everything. My wife and kids—"

Elizabeth smiled, shook her head, and interrupted him. "If I'm not mistaken, Mr. Stacey owns just about everything in this town." She shook her head again. "But no. I'm not asking you to print this in the paper. I'm just asking you to make me a hundred copies." She gave him an encouraging smile. "No one need ever know where they came from."

"Well"—he shrugged—"seein' as there ain't no love lost between the two of us. Meaning Mr. Stacey and myself, of course," he added and then turned beet red.

Elizabeth began to wonder just how red the man could get without bursting into flame. "Of course," she said, having a time keeping the smile from her lips.

"I know you ain't gonna tell anyone, right?" he asked hopefully.

Elizabeth laughed. "Absolutely right, Mr. Carlton. You have my word on it." She sighed with relief. "Besides, after the folks around here read this, I'm positive where and how it was printed will be the last thing on anyone's mind.

"And once the law hears about it, I think it will be Mr. Stacey who'll be worried, nobody else."

"Are you sure you want to do this? You got your name all over this here page."

"I'm positive, Mr. Carlton. Thank you."

Elizabeth took a few bills from her purse and laid them on the counter. "Can I come back in a few hours, or perhaps tomorrow to retrieve the originals? I'll be needing them to give to the authorities."

Mr. Carlton nodded. "It'll take me some time to set up the print. I should be finished at five o'clock. Will that be all right?"

Elizabeth knew it wouldn't. What excuse could she give Tanner for going out alone at the supper hour? "I'll pick them up tomorrow, if that's convenient."

Mr. Carlton nodded, and Elizabeth soon left his office, her heart lighter than it had been in years.

Elizabeth smiled down at the baby in its cradle. "Everybody always makes those silly cooing noises, but I can't seem to do that without feeling ridiculous," she said to the infant's mother. "What should I say? Hello, Joseph?"

Sally laughed. "You could. It won't matter much what you say. Just say it in a soft tone."

"How do you know . . . ?" Elizabeth's gaze went to her friend. Then she shrugged. "You know . . . how do you know if . . . ?"

"If you're having a baby?"

Elizabeth nodded, feeling her face grow hot.

"Well, for one thing your monthly time stops, and some women feel a bit ill in the mornings."

"You mean as though they won't be able to keep anything down?"

"Yes." Sally regarded her friend for a moment and then shook her head. "But it's a bit too soon for you. You've only been married a month. You probably wouldn't feel anything that fast."

You might if you slept with your husband almost

a week before you were married, Elizabeth added silently.

"Did it hurt?"

Sally smiled at the little boy sleeping so peacefully. Already her memory of the pain had dimmed. "A bit," she admitted. "But I'd do it again in a second."

"Would you?"

"Once you have a baby," she said with all the confidence of a new mother, "you'll know what I mean."

Tanner smiled as he watched Elizabeth go about the business of emptying the basket. "As far as I can remember, picnics give you headaches."

Elizabeth looked up into his smiling face and frowned. "When did I say that?"

"You told me you were going to have a headache, so you couldn't go on a picnic with me."

"Oh," she laughed softly. "You mean when you first came?" She shook her head. "It wasn't a picnic. You asked me to go riding with you."

"Actually," he said, purposely picking up on her innocent comment while a wicked light danced in his eyes, "I hadn't come yet, but I certainly wanted to with you."

It took her a second. "Tanner!" she gasped as comprehension dawned. She was suddenly on her knees and pushing him to lie flat upon the blanket. Leaning over him, she ignored his laughter. "Is that the way a man talks to his wife?"

"I have no idea how other men talk to their wives. It's the way I talk to you. You might as well get used to it."

She shook her head, though trying to control the smile that teased the corners of her lips. "Disgraceful."

"I know how we can be even more disgraceful." His voice was suddenly low and silky, filled with sensual promise.

Elizabeth laughed when she tried to get up and found his arms like bands of steel, around her back. "It's broad daylight. I'm not taking my clothes off out here."

"Tsk tsk, Mrs. Maddox." He shook his head in reproach, while a slow dangerous smile curved his lips. "What a deliciously lascivious mind you have. Actually, I wasn't about to suggest anything quite so decadent."

Elizabeth shot him a look of suspicion. "What were you going to suggest?"

"I was simply going to mention that we would have more privacy if we had this picnic in the loft of your barn."

Elizabeth frowned and then used a word no lady should even know, never mind repeat. Suddenly she was up and repacking the half-empty basket.

Tanner watched in amazement as she hurriedly went about the chore. "What are you doing?"

"Nothing."

"It certainly looks like something to me. As a matter of fact, it looks as though you're repacking our food."

"I am."

"Why?" he asked curiously.

"Because this isn't the place where I want to picnic."

Tanner's brow creased in confusion. "Isn't it? Weren't you the lady who was cooing over how wonderful this river water was going to feel on her feet? Didn't I hear you say you love this spot and these shady dogwoods?" Elizabeth hadn't answered him as yet. She pulled on the blanket, forcing him to get up. "It was you who said all those things, wasn't it?"

"Of course it was."

"So I thought you liked it here."

"I do."

"Then why are we about to go somewhere else?"

"Because, as I said, this isn't the place where I want to picnic."

"Then why did we come?"

"Mr. Maddox"—Elizabeth spoke so primly that Tanner hadn't a clue as to what she was about—"we haven't come as yet. But if we move these things to the barn, I fully expect we will."

It was his turn to take a moment before understanding. When he did, he simply closed his eyes and groaned. God, but he loved it when she talked that way. Like an obedient child, with a grin so silly it bordered on the ridiculous, he silently followed her to the buggy.

Neither spoke on the drive back to Elizabeth's home. Their mutual silence continued as they made their way into the barn and climbed the ladder to the loft. It was almost as if both were afraid to utter a sound, lest it bring to an abrupt end to what little civilized controls they possessed.

They were breathing hard by the time the blanket

was thrown over a padding of hay, but suddenly their movements stilled and they simply stood staring at one another, positioned on opposite edges of the blanket.

"You've got me so I can't wait another minute," he gasped, trying desperately to control his need. "Take off your clothes."

Elizabeth tried to smile, but her thickened blood seemed to disallow the movement. Her lips just wouldn't respond. She'd known, of course, that he'd react to her last daring remark. She'd said it for just that purpose. But she hadn't dreamed that she, too, would be caught up in this primitive need. She couldn't think of nothing, but what she was about to experience. She wanted him to touch her so badly that she could barely speak. Hadn't been able to, in fact, during the entire trip back. Even then she'd felt the tension mounting. Now it was stealing her very breath away.

As if on cue they began undressing at the same moment. His clothes were nearly torn away as strong, impatient fingers struggled to undo stubborn buttons and ties.

Elizabeth's trembling had nothing to do with the barn's cool interior. It was the look in his eyes that set her heart to pounding, her fingers to shaking, as she tried to rid herself of unwanted garments.

They were gasping as if they'd run miles by the time they stood naked, their clothes carelessly dropped around their feet.

"Say it," he said as he saw her begin to speak and then hesitate.

Elizabeth's warm dark gaze moved hungrily over

his body, resting for a long moment on his most masculine part before it moved to his eyes. "I want you so badly I'm afraid I'll die if you don't touch me," she said, never thinking to deny her own need.

He closed the distance between them and pressed their burning bodies together. "I'm afraid this won't be as gentle as you might like."

"I don't care. Oh, God, I don't—" Her words were cut off by the wild pressure of his mouth.

Elizabeth's groan was a mingling of hunger and delight as his tongue slid easily beyond the barrier of her lips and teeth. She felt her knees buckle as his wet heat swirled deliciously with her own.

He took from her and gave back all that was in him. Neither held back, but thrilled to the joy of their mutual need.

His features were drawn and flushed when he finally managed to tear his mouth from hers. "I love you," he said. Gasping for breath, he forced more words past the ache that nearly obliterated all but his desire for this woman. "I've never felt like this before."

"Then love me, Tanner. Love me until I die of the things you do to me."

Tanner groaned as his hands moved to each side of her waist. He brought her up and then down, sharply impaling her on his blood-thickened arousal. He heard her cry out, but knew it wasn't pain that caused the sound.

Her eyes closed as his pulsating organ filled an emptiness that hadn't before existed. Her head was thrown back as she inhaled deep into her lungs the sensual scent of their mating. Her legs hugged his hips, locking behind them, while her arms did the same to his neck.

"This feels so . . . so," She was unable to find a word that would convey the shattering ecstasy she knew.

"Fantastic?" he offered.

She shook her head, barely able to speak. "Better."

Tanner's heart was beating almost out of control. He tried to bring a moment's rationality to this coupling but couldn't. He wanted too much. She felt too good in his arms. She held him too tight.

"Hold on to me, this is going to be rough," he said as he knelt on the blanket.

Holding her tightly against him, he began to move with almost vicious thrusts. His mind engulfed in a shimmering haze of passion, he heard only the guttural sounds of her pleasure as he dove deep, deeper into the tightness of her.

He felt her pulsating waves of relief surround and squeeze at his sex, and he listened to her cries as he surged deeper, harder, harder, growing with each movement more wild, more desperate to claim this woman as his forever.

It was beyond his power to hold back. His body shuddered with exquisite pain and she was there again, their mouths joining and absorbing his cries, his and hers, mingling as he poured his love into her.

They lay perfectly still. The only sounds in the barn were deep breathless gasps and soft groans.

"Thank you for remembering to bring wine," Tanner said as he finished what was left in his glass and poured more.

He eyed his wife with no little appreciation as she lay brazenly, comfortably, and deliciously naked beside him. Leaning back against a bale of hay, she sipped from her own glass. She raised one leg as she concentrated on balancing the glass on her stomach. Her skin was pink and abraded, especially around the tips of her breasts, where his beard had brushed a bit harder than it should have.

Tanner rubbed his face, silently promising to shave closer the next time she thought to picnic. He smiled and watched as she tried to even her breathing in order to keep the glass straight. Never had he seen a woman more exotic, more beautiful, more relaxed in her nakedness; yet he knew she hadn't a clue as to how tempting she was. It was at times like these that he simply couldn't believe she was his wife. He must have done something awfully good to deserve this kind of luck.

"We could have chilled it," she offered with a deliciously innocent look, "if we'd stayed at the river."

"The river didn't have a view like this." Tanner said as he reached out to run a teasing finger around the red tip of her breast. He watched her glance his way and smiled. "Besides, if we'd chilled it, it wouldn't have felt half so good when I did this." Tanner tipped his full glass and poured a goodly amount of the red wine over Elizabeth's naked breasts, watching in delight as the liquid spilled to her belly and lower.

"What in the world are you doing?" she asked, more surprised than anything else.

"Mmmm," he murmured. "I seemed to have made a mess." He glanced around and then looked back at her shimmering, red-tipped breasts. "You wouldn't know where I could find a towel, would you?"

Elizabeth grinned. "In the house."

Tanner shook his head. "Too far. Besides, Miss Dunlap is apt to grow a mite upset if she sees me run through the house like this."

Elizabeth laughed. "No doubt."

"Well"—he shrugged—"since we don't seem to have a towel anywhere nearby, I guess I'll just have to find another means of cleaning it up." His head lowered as he immediately set about the delicious task.

Elizabeth laughed when he lowered his mouth and licked away the wine. "You wicked, wicked man," she said softly, her voice filled with delight.

"I've always loved warm wine. It goes so well with a hot woman," he said as he used tongue, lips and mustache to absorb the liquid.

"With any hot woman?"

"With this hot woman."

Elizabeth nodded in satisfaction. She stretched and purred like a kitten as she adjusted her derrière on the hay padded blanket. "I just wanted to be clear on that particular subject."

It was a long time before either of them thought of any other subject.

"Are you hungry?"

"I was hungry before. Now I'm starving."

"Well?" he asked, coming to a sitting position. "When are we going to eat?"

Elizabeth laughed. "Since the picnic was my idea and I made all the food, I think you should serve me."

"But the barn was my idea."

"Mmmm, and a very good idea it was," she said apparently having no intention of moving. "But I think you've been justly rewarded."

Tanner bit her stomach as she reached for her blouse. "I'll feed you—but on one condition."

"What?"

"We eat naked."

Elizabeth laughed as she threw her blouse onto the pile of clothing. "Is there another way?"

"You dropped another crumb," Tanner said, hovering above her, his grin clearly telling her of the pleasure he'd get from licking it off her breast.

"Remind me to always bring cold fried chicken on our picnics," Elizabeth murmured as she purposely slid her foot between his thighs. "You do a wonderful job as a napkin."

She shot him a wicked grin. That, combined with the luscious teasing of her foot, brought renewed desire to beat with maddening precision in his groin. "If you should ever tire of your present vocation . . ." She giggled as he growled and then nibbled on deliciously sensitive flesh.

"Would you hire me out?"

Elizabeth shot him a dark, menacing look. "No doubt you could make us a fortune, but I don't think so." Her eyes held a clear warning as she continued, "I suggest, if you know what's good for you,

you'll work solely for me."

"And who will pay my salary? How will we eat?"

"I've got it." She snapped her finger and grinned as if struck by a brilliant idea. "I'll rob stages. Surely we could live—"

He flipped her over so fast she might have weighed no more than a feather. Elizabeth was helpless and weak with laughter by the time he stopped biting her backside.

He turned her back again to face him. "Don't ever let me hear you say that again."

"Darling," she said, coming to a sitting position and then running her hands over his warm chest, his shoulders, his neck, while deliberately brushing the tips of her breasts against his hairy chest and belly, "your punishment would be a bit more effective, if you made sure I hated what you're doing."

"The next time," he promised, "I'll bite you harder."

Elizabeth only raised her brows. Her grin was delightfully wicked. Tanner hadn't a doubt the idea held some real merit. "Will you?"

"What am I going to do with you?" he groaned as he turned her so she sat between his legs and leaned comfortably against him. She sighed with delight as he reached around her to play with her breast.

"Where do you live?"

"In Virginia City."

Elizabeth turned her head and shot him a warning look. "I know that. If you don't want me to get dressed, answer the question. Where in Virginia City? In a room? A house? A farm?"

Tanner laughed. "Bossy little thing, aren't you?"

Elizabeth finished the wine in her glass and turned to him. A smile curved her lips as she came to her knees. She swayed and caught herself. "Am I? Bossy, I mean?"

Tanner eyed her curiously, for he hadn't missed the sudden problem she was having retaining her balance. "Don't you know?"

She shook her head and grinned. "All I know is that I can't seem to stop laughing."

"That's because you're happy."

"No, darling," she said as she suddenly fell against him, "that's because I'm drunk."

Tanner watched her for a minute and then grinned as he realized the truth of her words. She was drunk. No wonder she'd rocked to one side and back again. This woman, who had bragged about her ability to hold her liquor, was tipsy on three glasses of wine. "I thought you said you could drink any man under the table."

"I could, but I'm a bit out of practice." She watched his lips curve into a smile and wondered what she'd said to cause that. "You have to keep in practice, you know."

He chuckled and gathered her more comfortably against him. She was sitting on his lap, when he said, "Now is the perfect time to get you to tell me your deepest, darkest secrets."

"How come?" she blinked in confusion, her childish tone and expression oddly out of place considering the fact that she was sitting naked on her husband's lap.

"Because you're drunk and unable to keep them to yourself," he offered as an explanation.

"Ohhhh," she said, while nodding her understanding. Only the nod brought a groan as a wave of dizziness caused the loft to sway crazily. "Then it's too bad I don't have any, isn't it?"

"Oh, there must be something," he teased. "The look in your eyes is far too wicked. I suspect you're a bit less saintly than you'd like people to believe."

Elizabeth giggled. "Oh I'm far from saintly." A moment later she smiled again. Her eyes were wide, and they sparkled with smug satisfaction as she whispered conspiratorially, "As a matter of fact, I do have a secret. Want to hear it?"

Tanner smiled at her mischievous expression, his heart twisting with joy, knowing it wasn't possible to love this woman more. "What?"

"I'm not positive, mind you, it being a little early and all, but the chances are good, at least it looks like it might be—"

Tanner's laughter interrupted her nonsensical dialogue. "I take it you're about to make a point of some kind?"

"Was I?" she blinked in confusion, forgetting her train of thought and then smiling again when she remembered. She snuggled into the warmth of his chest. She was already more than half-asleep before she murmured, "I was telling you we're going to have"—the long pause was filled with a gusty, sleepy yawn—"a baby."

Tanner smiled as he listened to the words trail off into a sleepy sigh, and he promised this would be the last time she'd drink more than two glasses of wine. Here they were, in the barn, with all the privacy they could have asked for. The afternoon stretched out before them, filled with delicious promise, and she was too drunk to stay awake.

Suddenly he stiffened as her last word registered. "Baby!" he exclaimed, tipping back her head and looking down into her sleeping face. "Did you say 'baby'?" he asked, but he might as well have been talking to a wall. All he received by way of response was a gentle snore.

Chapter Fifteen

"This is a nice surprise," Stacey said, with as false a smile as his lips could manage. "Please sit down. Make yourself comfortable." He nodded toward the chair opposite his desk as he slid onto the one behind it. A light of victorious anticipation gleamed in his eyes. "Now tell me, what can I do for you, my dear?"

"Well," Elizabeth began, purposely giving the impression that she was loath to bring up the subject, "it's about the note that's suddenly come due on my home."

Stacey had a hard time concealing how he was gloating. He shook his head, pretending a measure of compassion. "I was terribly sorry about that." His shrug was meant to convey helplessness, but the expression in his eyes easily belied that. "It was nothing personal, you understand. It's just that money is tight right now, what with all the losses the bank has taken recently."

"You mean, all the losses you've taken," she corrected, happy to see his expression grow grim.

"Yes, well . . ." Jonathan ended the sentence with a shrug. His eyes hardened again as he remembered his most recent loss. If it wasn't for this bitch, and the fact that the marshal couldn't bring himself from her bed, the villain behind the robberies might already be in prison. Most important of all, Stacey's home might have remained untouched. What Maddox saw in her, he couldn't imagine. Stacey had to cover a shiver of revulsion at imagining her softness, her womanly, musky scent. He shook himself from those disagreeable thoughts. "Is there something in particular I can do for you?"

Elizabeth would have loved to have told him exactly what he could do—she had heard Belle use that line—but she reminded herself that she was a lady and ladies simply didn't say such things. She kept her smile sweetly innocent as she remarked, "Actually that is the reason I've come."

Stacey shook his head. "If you're here to ask for an extension, I'm afraid there's nothing I can do."

"Jonathan, I thought we were friends."

"Of course we were friends. I like to think we still are. But this being business after all . . . I have investors to answer to. I'm afraid my hands are tied."

"I thought you might say that," Elizabeth smiled as she reached into her reticule and took out a small packet. "Actually I haven't come to ask for an extension. I've come to settle my account," she said pleasantly as she placed the small open packet of bills on his desk. Her eyes sparkled, but with a Herculean effort she held back the laughter about to bubble up in her throat. It was obvious he had agreed to see her, expecting her to beg for an extension on her loan. It was equally apparent he was shocked into silence to find that note suddenly paid.

There followed a long moment of silence during which Elizabeth watched Stacey stare at the bills. His face grew paler than usual and then became red with anger. He seemed unable to utter a word. "I think I should get a receipt, don't you?" She shrugged and then fed him his exact words, " 'This being business after all'?"

"Of course," Stacey managed to reply, his voice sounding amazingly like a croak. "I'll have Brian write one out immediately."

A few moments later, Brian exited the office and Elizabeth pocketed her receipt. Stacey cleared his throat as he rose and took her extended hand. "Not that it matters, but would you mind telling me how you managed to get ahold of this much cash?"

Elizabeth thought over her words carefully. It was dangerous, but she knew she was going to give in to temptation. She felt not the slightest flicker of fear. After all, what could the man do? Would he dare to publicly accuse the wife of a U.S. Marshal? Elizabeth almost laughed aloud at the thought, knowing no one would believe it of the sedate Widow Garner. She smiled pleasantly and admitted quite candidly, "Why from the robberies, of course. How did you think I got it?"

She wasn't the least bit sorry she'd said it. Seeing that look on Stacey's face was worth any danger she might be placing herself in. For if the man had appeared shocked before, it was nothing compared to the amazement that now immobilized him.

"You!" he gasped. "You! You!" For a moment, the

man seemed incapable of saying more than that one word. His eyes appeared to be ready to pop from a face turned scarlet with rage. "You were behind those robberies. It was you all along."

"I'm afraid so," she answered, giving forth a rich and confident laugh. "It's perfect, don't you think? I've just paid off my home with the money I stole from you."

"Do you realize what you've just admitted?"

"Certainly."

"You know, of course, I'll see you in prison for this."

Elizabeth chuckled softly. "I don't think so."

"Don't you?" His mouth twisted into an ugly sneer. "And pray tell, why not?"

"Because I'll deny it, of course. After all, it's your word against mine, isn't it?" Her voice grew sugary sweet. "Now, who would believe such an outrageous story? Imagine, the Widow Garner accused of robbing stages." She made a soft tsking sound. "Why the idea is ludicrous, to say the least." Elizabeth laughed happily as she moved toward the door. "Should the story come out, I'm afraid people will believe it the ramblings of a rejected suitor." Elizabeth turned to face him; having the length of the room between them added greatly to her confidence, for he looked ready to pounce upon her. "It was pleasant doing business with you Jonathan. More pleasant than you knew for a long time. And, oh yes"—she hesitated for just a second and then grinned—"do have a nice day."

Tanner slammed the front door so hard that the frosted half-circle of glass above it shattered and made tinkling sounds as small pieces fell unheeded onto the parlor's hard, buffed floor. He was going to wring her neck and nobody was going to stop him. "Elizabeth," he roared as he began to search through the empty rooms.

She was out back, soapy from fingertips to her elbows, scrubbing a week's worth of soiled clothes in a huge tub of hot water, when she heard his call. She breathed a deep sigh, knowing without a doubt the reason for the fury in his voice. Earlier that day, and with the exception of the newspaper office, the church, and of course the bank, Elizabeth had distributed her pamphlets, leaving small piles in every store in town, including the saloon. It was beyond the realm of possibility that Tanner had yet to come across one. Indeed, his roaring of her name and the fact that he'd returned hours earlier than expected were proof that he had found at least one. Elizabeth sighed almost wearily as she readied for the coming confrontation. No great fear froze her heart. Still, she didn't by any stretch of the imagination look forward to being subjected to her husband's anger. Slowly, as she wiped her hands on her apron, she walked toward the house.

Having searched each bedroom, he was in the kitchen and heading for the back yard by the time she stepped inside. "You bellowed?" she asked pleasantly, thanking God her voice showed no sign of her inner trembling.

Tanner glared at the petite, lovely, completely delectable woman standing before him. He'd seen grown men, hard, tough men who'd lived most of their lives within reach of their guns, quake at his fury, yet his wife showed not a flicker of apprehension. His hands twisted the offending sheets of paper until they ripped in half.

"Why did you do it?"

She knew better than to pretend she had no knowledge of the notices. Tanner was in no frame of mind to be treated lightly.

"I found the papers among Jason's things."

"I gathered as much." Tanner nodded, his mouth grim and tight beneath his mustache. "What I want to know is why?"

"Someone had to."

"And you took it upon yourself to do it?"

Elizabeth nodded.

"Do you realize what you've done? Do you know the weapon you've placed in his hands? The man can destroy you, and I haven't a doubt that he'll try."

"You won't let him," she said with such confidence that if his blood wasn't already boiling those words would have seen that it was.

Tanner took several deep breaths, straining for control. He was certain he was on the edge of madness, needing only the right word to send him forever into insanity. His voice was low, barely a whisper as he glared down at her. "I'm happy to see you have such confidence in me, but just for my own information," his voice suddenly rose to an ear-deafening shout, "how the hell do you suppose I can stop it?" Tanner ran a frustrated hand through his hair. "He's at the sheriff's office right now, screaming for Dave to send for the circuit judge in order to file charges against you."

"Me?" she asked, her eyes growing huge as she blinked with surprise. "For what?"

"Don't you realize it's against the law to spread these kinds of rumors? I believe it's called defamation of character."

Elizabeth shrugged. "Are you here to arrest me?"

Tanner almost laughed aloud, the idea being so ludicrous. God, he wanted to strangle her and there she stood, so damned calm she might have been asking if he liked some confection she'd just whipped up. "And if I were?"

Elizabeth shrugged again. "Then I'd have no choice but to go with you, would I?"

Tanner's huge hands reached for her shoulders. Her head was snapping back and forth as he was not gentle. "You little fool! Why didn't you just give the papers to me? I could have brought them to the governor. Justice would have been served."

With a grunt, Elizabeth shoved herself away from his punishing hands. She held on to one of the kitchen chairs till the dizziness he'd inflicted abated. "I've told you once before, I won't be abused."

Tanner's mouth twisted in a sneer. "I wonder if it wouldn't do you some good to take your punishment. Maybe a short stay in jail would lessen that superior streak of yours."

Elizabeth ignored his sarcasm and instead remarked upon his earlier question. "The people around here needed to know what kind of animal he is. Since when is it against the law to tell the truth?"

"The truth?" Tanner sneered. "Have you proof? Have you anything beyond your father's word that he was innocent?"

Elizabeth shook her head. "He was, Tanner."

"I don't doubt it for a minute, but it's still your word against Stacey's."

"How did he manage to buy the silver mine? He stole the Army payroll and let the blame fall on my father."

"He doesn't have to explain to anyone how he did it. Not right now, in any case." Tanner punched his leg as he began to pace her small kitchen. "If you'd given me the papers, we could have done something. Eventually an investigation would have uncovered those very facts. And your father's name would have been vindicated."

Elizabeth gave a disparaging laugh. "Eventually? Exactly how long is eventually, Tanner? How many other people will he destroy before eventually arrives?"

Tanner tried to gain control of his emotions. He needed a cool head or he'd never find a way out of this mess. "We're talking abut two separate happenings here. One is what he's done to your family. The other is the fact that he's responsible for a young boy's death."

"The money was stolen. All the Army has to do is look into the fact that within months after his retirement, Stacey purchased a silver mine. That in itself should be the proof they need to convict him."

"It'll never come to that. They only have your word. They won't begin an investigation without good reason."

"I believe I just gave them that."

Tanner sighed. "We have to have some time. I

have to think."

"What is there to think about? Isn't a suicide note as good as a death-bed confession?"

"Elizabeth"—he released a sigh of disgust—"there's no proof that Jason's son wrote that note. Just because you say he did, does not make it so. It's only one slip of paper. Anyone could have written it, including yourself."

Elizabeth waved away his reasoning with a fragile movement of her hand. "I have the rest of his journal. The handwriting is the same throughout."

Tanner's eyes widened. "You have it? All of it?" He felt his legs weaken with relief as she nodded.

"More than likely you were right." Elizabeth gave a small shrug. "Jason probably did set the fire. He had reason enough to hate the man. The boy's journal tells of years of abuse. He couldn't take any more."

Tanner took another few turns around the kitchen before he came to an abrupt stop. Standing directly before her, he said, "I want you to pack a few things. We're leaving for Virginia City the moment I straighten out this mess. Give me the journal."

"Why?" she eyed him suspiciously.

Tanner's voice became a low feral growl as he warned, "Don't push me, Elizabeth. I promise you, it wouldn't take much for me to forget that you're with child and to beat the tar out of you. I'm amazed that I didn't do it today—on sight."

Tanner watched as her dark eyes narrowed and then hardened. Her hands balled into fists and came to rest on her slender hips. He knew she was about to come back with some pithy remark, and he realized he was sure to lose control of the situation if she did. Quickly he seized her by the upper arms and lifted her off the floor. "Shut up and listen to me. Give me the journal. I'll show it to Dave, then tell him we're off to Virginia City to clear up this mess. Once he sees the evidence, he won't hold you. He'll know Stacey can't press charges."

Elizabeth was in her room throwing clothes into a carpet bag when the front door slammed again. Now what? she wondered. Had he changed his mind and come back to beat her as he'd threatened?

Let him try it, she silently mused. Just let him lay one finger on me and I'll tear him limb from limb. "I'm not afraid of him. I'm not afraid of any man," she muttered.

"You should be, my dear," Jonathan Stacey was standing at her bedroom door. "I promise you there are men to be feared. Like me."

Elizabeth gasped and spun around to face him. Her heart was pounding so hard it nearly choked her as she spoke. "Get out of my house, Jonathan. My husband will kill you if he finds you here."

Stacey's grin showed perfect white teeth. "Your husband just left. I think we have a few minutes."

"For what?"

"For you to tell me where you got that note and whether there's anything more I should know."

Elizabeth laughed. "So you can find a way out of this mess?"

Stacey answered with a negligent shrug.

"And you think I'll help you?" Elizabeth sneered.

"Mr. Stacey, I was the one who circulated those papers. Why would I help you after what you've done to my family?"

"You'll help me in order to save your life, of course."

"Meaning you have every intention of murdering me, as you did my father?"

Stacey laughed. "Your father, my dear Elizabeth, was much like his daughter, troublesome in the extreme. He refused to be quiet."

"So you murdered him."

"What would you have had me do?" Stacey shrugged. "If he had told his story in court, someone might have believed him.

"Now be a good girl and tell me what else you have in the way of evidence."

Even if Elizabeth had been so inclined, which she most definitely was not, she couldn't have given the man what he wanted. Tanner had the journal. But no matter. She'd never have given this man an advantage. No, he wasn't going to learn the extent of the evidence against him, not until it was too late. He wouldn't worm his way out of this. Not if Elizabeth could help it. She glared at him, relieved after months of pretending to show her true feelings at last. "Get out of my house."

Stacey shrugged again. "We're wasting time." He moved just enough to allow another entrance. "Take her, Brian," he said. "And you needn't be extra gentle," he added as he turned from the door and headed out the back way.

In truth, Brian wasn't gentle. Within an instant, by twisting Elizabeth's arms, he had brought an involuntary scream to her lips. But before she had a chance to utter the cry, he'd clamped a hand over her mouth, effectively sealing it off.

A moment later he had no need to muffle a scream, for her pain was so excruciating she'd fainted. Brian lifted her limp form over his shoulder, and careless of the bruising she endured as her body was banged against the doorway, he walked out the back door and dumped her into the waiting wagon. A large piece of canvas was then thrown over her and the metal boxes upon which she'd landed.

Stacey was on his way out of the country. He had no particular wish to live out his remaining days in Mexico. Actually he'd had his heart set on being the next governor of this state. But that little bitch had seen to the destruction of the plan.

Still, all was not lost. He had more money than he'd need in a lifetime, and more would be coming in on a daily basis. At least until the government, as he had no doubt it would, confiscated his holdings.

They were perhaps a good two days of hard riding from the border. With the wagon loaded down as it was with gold, it was bound to take closer to a week to make it, but, once there, no one could touch him.

Brian pulled himself up onto the driver's seat. A moment later he snapped the reins over the horses' backs and they were off. The two hired guns brought up the rear.

Stacey grinned. By the time Maddox found out she was missing, he'd be hours away. By the time the man realized exactly who had taken his wife, it would be too late.

Stacey only hoped the marshal would come after him. He wanted to kill Maddox, to kill them both. As the wagon bounced over the rutted road heading out of town, he toyed with the idea of exactly how he might go about it.

"Elizabeth!" Tanner called upon entering the deserted house. He walked into the bedroom, expecting to find her packing. To his surprise, he found the room empty.

A puzzled frown creased his brow. The carpet bag lay upon the floor, half its contents spilled out. What was going on? God damn the woman! Couldn't he leave her for a minute? Couldn't he, as her husband, expect her to obey a direct order? Where the hell had she gone off to now?

Tanner walked into the kitchen. He was at the table, nursing the bottle left there, when Belle walked in the front door. The chair fell to the floor as he came to his feet. A glass half-full of whiskey in his hand, he moved to the parlor door. "Where the hell have you been?"

"Actually, I was visiting someone," Belle said, the soft look in her eyes telling Tanner more clearly than words what that visit had entailed. "What business is it of yours?"

Tanner shot her a look. He'd thought she was Elizabeth returning. He'd forgotten Belle existed while he'd stewed about his wife's disappearance these last two hours.

He downed the whiskey remaining in his glass before saying to his long-time partner and friend, "You look like you've just had yourself a good toss."

Belle laughed. "Jealous?" she chuckled softly when he looked incredulous. "I didn't think so. I'd say you're getting your share. It is you and your wife I hear sneaking out to the barn every night, isn't it?" And at his shrug, she asked, "So what's your problem?"

"I have none. I don't give a damn where you were or who you were with. I thought you were Elizabeth."

Belle's blue eyes sparkled with laughter. "How nice to be missed," she said sarcastically. And then in a more serious tone, she asked, "What's she gotten herself into this time?"

"How the hell should I know? I told her to pack, and when I got back she was gone."

"I take it you saw her little news item?"

Tanner scowled. "I saw it."

"The lady has guts."

"You need more than guts, Belle. You need brains to get somebody like Stacey."

"And you think she doesn't have any?"

Tanner looked disgusted. "I know she does. It's fear she doesn't have. At least not enough of it to keep her safe."

"Is that what you want? A coward for a wife? Someone who'll jump at shadows and whimper, cling to you in terror during a storm?" Belle shook her head in amazement. "You knew what you were getting. If you didn't love her for what she was, why'd you marry her?"

"Don't be a fool. Because I love her doesn't mean I have to like everything she does."

"Where is she?"

"Good question. If you remember, that's what I asked when you came in."

"You mean she's missing?" Belle's voice was filled with real alarm.

"For the moment." He shrugged. "She probably went over to Sally's to say goodbye."

"She didn't."

"How do you know?"

"I saw Sally on the way home. She was just leaving the apothecary."

"Maybe Elizabeth is watching the baby while Sally went on some errands."

"Tanner, Sally had her baby with her."

He nodded, his blue eyes growing wide with fear, his lips stiffening. "Why am I getting the feeling I should be very worried?"

"Because Stacey drove out of town a few hours ago. I just stopped at the bank and found the safe empty."

Tanner turned white. He hadn't known till now that the man had taken the gold. "He said he had business out at the Worths' ranch. There was no reason to detain him. Not until Elizabeth showed me the journal. Dave and a couple of men went out after him." Tanner didn't need to be told Stacey wasn't anywhere near the Worths' ranch. The man was gone for good.

Belle was about to ask about the journal when the glass Tanner was holding fell to the floor and smashed into a thousand pieces. He seemed to be in shock. "Do you suppose he has her?"

"I don't know, but I'd say if anyone had a reason to take her—"

"He left before she turned up missing."

"Meaning he couldn't have circled back?" Belle didn't bother to add that they both knew Stacey was capable of anything. If Elizabeth was with him she was as safe as she'd be with a rattlesnake.

"Get dressed."

Belle was about to make some comment, but Tanner cut her off. "In riding clothes. I'll get the horses ready." He shot her wildly decorated hat a look of disgust. "And for Christ's sake, wear something normal."

"It's almost dark. We'll lose the trail soon."

The temperature was steadily cooling as night approached, but Tanner's body was drenched in nervous sweat. His heart pounded with dread as he helplessly watched the sun slip slowly over a distant mountain ridge. He cursed his uncharacteristically slow thinking. Why hadn't he thought from the first that Stacey might have taken her?

He certainly would have if she weren't his wife. It wasn't beyond his realm of understanding that a wanted man might take a hostage. Why hadn't he thought it might happen to the woman he loved?

Because it had been easier and considerably less terrifying to imagine Elizabeth had deliberately disobeyed him again, he had simply refused to accept the fact that she might be in danger.

Even now, he couldn't allow himself to dwell on it.

In fact he instantly pushed the thought from his mind when it came, for to do otherwise allowed visions of what could happen to Elizabeth to render him helpless. He had to maintain control. He had to keep his wits about him, or he'd prove useless when Elizabeth needed him to be cool.

It was getting harder to see. Night was about to fall, and the wagon's trail would soon be lost in darkness. Every second that passed brought them closer to darkness and the promise that continuing the search would be an exercise in futility.

Why hadn't they thought to bring lanterns? Granted following a trail at night would be slow going, but at least he would remain active. At least . . .

Belle brought Elizabeth's horse to a stop. "We'll have to stop. It's impossible to see."

"We can't."

"Tanner, if we go on and manage to pick up a trail, it might just be the wrong one. If that happens, we could wander this area for days and never find her."

"We know they're heading for Mexico."

"Right, but—"

"No buts, damn it. If you want to stop, then stop. I wouldn't get any rest knowing she's alone with that bastard."

Belle let out a weary sigh. She couldn't blame her partner. If it were her love, she'd be wild with the need to find him.

"If we come across them in the dark, Elizabeth could get hurt."

"We'll see their fire long before they hear us. We'll

figure out what to do once I have her in sight."

"He's not going to do anything, you know."

Tanner cursed. "What the hell do you know? He could be hurting her right now."

Belle shook her head, knowing the movement couldn't be seen in the dark even if Tanner had been looking her way. She was trying to calm her friend, only half believing what she was saying herself. "The man has no interest in women."

Tanner's features twisted into a look of disgust. "And to your way of thinking that will keep her safe?" He shook his head, wishing it was that easy. "It's not impossible that the man hates her guts, right?"

Belle nodded.

"Do you think it's likely he'll treat her kindly?"

She hated to admit it, but she knew Tanner was right. "Probably not. But that doesn't mean —"

"It means" — Tanner wiped his face with the sleeve of his shirt — "there's no better way for him to show his hatred, to vent his rage, than to abuse her. It doesn't matter that he prefers men to women. There's only one way to abuse her that counts. Believe me, he's not going to hesitate to use it."

Elizabeth moaned softly as the wagon hit its thousandth hole and bounced, jarring her entire body and banging her face against a metal box. That she was going to be terribly bruised was the last of her worries.

She had long since lost all feeling in her hands, for they were tied tightly behind her back. The rope was attached to her feet, pulling them up behind her and twisting her body into an unnatural position. Her back ached unbearably, and her shoulders felt as though needles had been plunged into them. She swore she was about to suffocate under the heavy canvas.

Were they never going to stop?

Her face was covered with sweat. The trickling rivulets of it just about drove her mad as they ran down her neck, sides, and back. She cursed the gag that covered her mouth. If she could only lick her own sweat, that would help. As it was, her tongue was swollen, her mouth dry as cotton.

Lord, but she had to get water—and soon.

Elizabeth dozed beneath the drugging heat of the sun. Soon even the jarring movement of the wagon did not keep her awake. She dreamed of water. Cool rippling streams of it, rivers that rushed by, loud and cold, slapping against her body. Rain falling from the sky, drenching her through and through as she frolicked with Tanner beneath a cloudburst.

Her dreams were disturbed by rough hands reaching for her. She shivered against the sudden cold, her mind foggy with sleep. For some reason she fought against clearing it. Vaguely she wondered why.

Someone slapped her face. The stinging blow brought her awake. "That's better, bitch." The voice came out of the darkness as her hands and feet were untied.

Elizabeth bit her lip to keep the scream inside, her pain worse than she could have imagined as life-giving fluid rushed to blood-starved limbs. She was thrown carelessly to the ground and left there.

Pain! Pain! She wanted to free herself from its clutches. She'd never known the likes of it.

She took long, slow breaths as she tried to will away the worst of the pain, but she could not move. She could only lie in the dirt and moan, her body shaking as agony seemed to rend her very core. And then finally, amazingly, it began to fade, until it was nothing more than a dull ache.

Tears of relief filled Elizabeth's eyes. They slid slowly down her cheeks. In desperation she tore the gag from her mouth, her swollen dry tongue greedily absorbing what it could.

Four men sat around a campfire not twenty feet away, ignoring her very existence. She watched with envy as they sipped coffee. And almost cried aloud as one of them emptied the last of his cup upon the ground.

At that moment, she would have sold her soul just to be allowed his leavings.

Elizabeth dared not make a sound. She knew she was better off being ignored, only too aware that the time would come when she'd relish these moments. She trembled with fear as she waited for the men to turn to her. She hadn't a doubt she'd be sorely abused, and she was certain they'd kill her when they finished tormenting her. Stacey, most of all, had reason to want her dead.

Why hadn't she kept her mouth shut? Why had she bragged about the robberies, taunted the man? Hadn't she known he was capable of anything, including murder? He had already killed to achieve his ends. Her own father was dead at Stacey's hand.

Lord, what a fool she'd been not to fear the man. She'd believed herself beyond his revenge, beyond his evil power. All because of Tanner's strength.

Tanner! Oh God, he'd be so worried. And it was all her own fault. Everything that had happened was caused by her own arrogance.

Elizabeth had no doubt that Tanner could save her — and would, if he only knew where to look. She groaned inwardly, knowing the impossibility of her situation. There'd be no saving her this time. Tanner wouldn't realize for hours that she'd disappeared. By then he wouldn't have any idea where to look.

One of the men who were forever at Stacey's side — she didn't know their names — knelt at her side and brought a battered cup to her lips. "Easy," he said as Elizabeth tried to down the liquid in one gulp.

She spoke not a word, but her eyes clearly told him of her gratitude. The man nodded and moved away.

Moments later, Stacey chuckled as he stood over her. With a hard tug, he took her by the hand and brought her to her feet. Elizabeth found it impossible to walk. Her legs simply wouldn't hold her weight, not after being tied and twisted behind her all day. She fell and received a kick for it. She was again wrenched to her feet. This time she managed to remain standing until she was shoved to the ground near the fire. Only by turning her body at the last second did she manage to miss the flames. "That's better," Stacey grunted, his face a mask of hatred as he watched her sprawl out before him. "Who wants to be first?"

The two men who worked as his bodyguards made grumbling, unintelligible comments.

"Haines, how about you? You want to be first?"

"No thank you, sir," the man said gruffly.

"Come on, Haines, no need to be shy. I know you like women. I've heard enough stories about you and the ladies above the saloon."

Haines shook his head. "You don't pay me enough for me to rape ladies. Besides, when her husband catches up with us—"

"He won't." Stacey shook his head. "He doesn't know we have her." He shrugged and then smiled. "As a matter of fact, I'm sorry now that I didn't leave him a note of some kind. I would have enjoyed putting a bullet between the bastard's eyes."

"What about you, Darnell? You interested in servicing the lady?"

"Sorry, Mr. Stacey, but no lady's worth my balls. I seen the way her husband looks at her."

Stacey laughed. "I'm afraid you've bestowed upon our illustrious marshal qualities he does not possess. Believe me, he can't read minds. He doesn't know where she is. And he's not about to find her."

"All right, Brian." Stacey looked toward the boy. "You do it."

Brian shivered with revulsion. "I couldn't."

Stacey laughed. "You think it's disgusting, do you? Well, it doesn't compare to some things, but it's not as bad as all that."

Stacey emitted what sounded like a mournful sigh, but his eyes showed he was gloating. "I'd hoped to see her plenty abused before I had my turn. Are you gentlemen positive you won't indulge?"

The bodyguards refused with nods. They weren't about to chance their lives for a few minutes with the lady. Still, their resolve didn't extend to the point where they wouldn't watch. Both men were avidly waiting to see what lay beneath their captive's clothing.

"Hold her down," Stacey commanded, but not a man moved to do his bidding. He sighed with disgust as he freed his soft member and knelt before Elizabeth.

"No!" The startled cry hadn't come from Elizabeth but Brian. "Don't touch her. I don't want you to touch her. She's disgusting."

Stacey chuckled. "You might be right, but this is something the bitch deserves."

Stacey leaned over her, only to catch a sharp blow to the jaw as Elizabeth fought him off and struggled to come to her feet.

"Bitch!" he screamed as he returned the blow and gave her a few to spare. But his landed with such force they momentarily rendered Elizabeth senseless. Instantly her skirt and petticoats were lifted almost over her head and her drawers were ripped away.

The two bodyguards groaned simultaneously. Like most men, good or bad, they appreciated the sight of a good-looking woman, and this one was a better sight than most. They couldn't take their eyes from the creamy whiteness of smooth thighs above black cotton stockings. And what they saw above that caused an instant hardness in their trousers. Idly they wondered if they hadn't been a bit too hasty in refusing Stacey's generous offer.

He, meanwhile, was working feverishly to bring

himself to a hardened state. He fondled his limp member and squeezed his genitals as he cursed Elizabeth's flying feet. She had come to her senses, but another blow to her jaw took care of that.

Brian was beside himself with jealousy. He couldn't stand the thought of his lover touching another, especially a woman. He shivered with revulsion. How could he bear to be touched by a man who would touch this creature. He couldn't allow it. Jonathan was his. No one else could have him, even if this act was but the punishment she deserved.

Brian never realized he had the gun in his hand. He only meant to warn Stacey to get away from her. He never meant to pull the trigger, but he had to stop his lover from committing this horrible deed. It was Brian Stacey should have been bending over, not that bitch.

The gunshot startled everyone, including Brian himself.

Elizabeth's body jerked as Stacey fell forward. She was being raped. Idly she wondered if she'd survive it. Even though she was dazed from the blows she'd taken, her brow creased as she experienced confusion. Odd, it felt as if he were simply lying on her. Ready for the pain, Elizabeth couldn't understand why she felt no penetration.

"Damn!" Neither man thought about what he did, but both bodyguards drew and shot. Bullets struck Brian's pristine shirt, and he fell to the ground, dead.

Only then did Darnell and Haines take in the destruction around them.

Chapter Sixteen

The sounds of gunfire traveled far in the cool desert night. Unbeknownst to the three people left alive, they alerted more than one group of riders.

Elizabeth finally took the opportunity offered and pushed Stacey off of her. She made a soft sound as she watched his limp body roll away.

Automatically her hand went to her skirt to cover her nakedness. Her arms didn't seem a part of her, and she had to concentrate to make them do her bidding. Her movements were jerky and uncoordinated as she pushed her hair away from her face and raised herself to a sitting position.

She watched the man who now lay at her feet, waiting for him to suddenly rise and grab her again. That he would she didn't doubt. What she couldn't understand was why he hadn't done so already, why, in fact, he hadn't finished what he'd set out to do. Desperate to create some space between them she edged backward. She was shaking so hard she knew she'd never manage to stand.

Stunned, she scanned the camp. It took her a moment to realize that Brian, too, lay upon the ground. His eyes were staring sightlessly toward the sky, while the two men standing over his body were smoothly holstering their guns.

What had happened? Obviously there'd been a shooting. Why hadn't she heard the gunfire? Could she have been so lost in panic, so dazed by the blows she'd taken that she had been oblivious to the shots?

No one spoke as she managed at last to stand on trembling legs. She watched the gunfighters warily. Would she be their next victim? Oddly enough, they never glanced her way. For the moment it seemed they had forgotten she existed.

"Now what?" Darnell asked.

"Damned if I know." Haines shrugged.

"Look like we're out of a job."

"Looks that way."

"So what do you reckon we should do?"

Haines shrugged again. "I figure it'd be a waste to leave all this gold and just ride off."

"I was thinkin' along the same lines." Darnell nodded in agreement. "Far as I know, Stacey ain't got no heirs. What about the woman?"

"What about her?"

"I say we let her go." Darnell gestured in Elizabeth's direction. "She's mighty good-lookin', but I have a yen to spend some of this money. Seems to me all the money in the world couldn't take us far enough if we took up where Stacey left off."

Haines agreed and then turned to Elizabeth. "You can go, Mrs. Maddox."

A moment went by before Elizabeth managed to

respond. "Go? Now? In the dark?" She was terrified of leaving but dreaded staying. She wanted to get away from these men. Although not openly aggressive, they offered her no safe haven; yet she was loath to part from them and face alone the dangers of the desert at night.

"You can take my horse and canteen," Haines offered. "You should be back home in a couple o' hours."

"I don't know which way to go," she said.

Haines recognized the fright in her eyes. "Nothin' ain't gonna happen to you," he said, imagining those words would ease her fears. "See that star up there? The bright one?"

Elizabeth looked in the direction he pointed and then nodded.

"Just stay east of it. It'll bring you back to the river. From there you'll find your way."

"East?" she asked stupidly. Unable to think, she began to tremble. She had suffered a great deal in these last few hours.

"To the right," Haines explained.

Elizabeth nodded again. "Thank you." She held back the tears that threatened. "Thank you both, very much."

She was backing slowly away. Though she was grateful that these men had not harmed her in any way, she did not feel at ease with them.

Suddenly the three of them heard a deep angry roar. It wasn't like anything they had ever heard before, and it sent gooseflesh up their backs. An instant later Tanner's horse was amongst them, its hooves kicking up sand. Only Tanner was no longer in the saddle. He was flying through the air and landing on Haines, because that man had been standing a bit too close to his wife.

The sound of flesh hitting against flesh was lost on Elizabeth as she cried at finding her husband suddenly, magically there.

As the two men rolled over the ground, each trying to strangle the other, Tanner's sharp gaze spotted Elizabeth's tattered drawers in the sand. Wild with renewed rage, he almost killed Haines before Elizabeth could jump on his back. With one arm encircling his neck, she pulled backward, all the while screaming for him to stop.

Tanner couldn't breathe, but he was determined to kill the bastard who had dared to touch his wife. Not realizing what he was doing, he suddenly flung Elizabeth over his head. Only the sight of her skirt flying before his eyes brought sanity to his crazed mind.

Leaning full-weight on the arm he had across Haines's throat, Tanner brought his gun from its holster. He then leaned back, substituted the pressure of a gun for his arm, and came to his feet. Motioning with his free hand, he indicated that Haines should get up. Darnell wasn't ignorant of the fact that Belle had him in her sights. Because of that, he hadn't dared to come to Haines's aid.

Both men stood perfectly still, hardly daring to breathe as they held their hands up in surrender. Tanner pointed his gun at one and then the other.

Elizabeth had landed hard a few feet from the two men, but she had no time to cater to her aching body. As quickly as possible she got to her feet. It took only one glance at the gunfighters' desperate expressions for her to know her help was needed. Instantly she defused the situation, and the two men were thankful that they had not given in to temptation. "They didn't do anything, Tanner. I'm all right."

Tanner's gaze took in Stacey's body. He walked over and kicked it with the tip of his boot, then grunted with satisfaction.

"Did he?"

"No."

"But he tried."

Elizabeth only shrugged for an answer.

"Who killed him?"

She couldn't say. She honestly didn't know.

"The boy," Darnell offered. "Stacey was about to rape your wife. We shot the boy. It happened so quick, we just pulled our guns and fired."

Tanner nodded as he glanced at Brian's bullet-ridden body. He raised an arm in invitation, silently beckoning his wife to join him. He heard her sigh softly as she burrowed into his side. Gently he held her there, pressing her firmly to his body. "Tell me what happened."

"They were letting me go, Tanner. As a matter of fact, I was just about to get on this nice man's horse."

Tanner gritted his teeth. "And which 'nice man' was that?"

"Me," Haines said.

"You were giving my wife a horse? Why?"

"So she could get back home. Look, Marshal, I ain't much, but I ain't one to abuse ladies."

346

"You're right about that, Haines," Tanner snapped. "You ain't much."

"Tanner," Elizabeth said reproachfully.

"We didn't do anything. There ain't no reason for you to—"

"Maybe you didn't," Tanner interrupted, the flash of his teeth holding not a glimmer of merriment, "but both you 'nice men' were going to allow somebody else to do something. Weren't you?"

The gunfighters shrugged, unable to deny the truth of that statement. What could they have done? Were they supposed to kill somebody, their own boss, because he was doing something they didn't really go along with? "I swear, we never touched her. We told Stacey you'll kill whoever did."

"You're right about that. But you forgot what I'd do to any man who sat by and watched."

A shot suddenly rang out, and Haines staggered forward, a puzzled look in his eyes. He'd thought he'd known better. Despite the man's rage, he'd never have believed the marshal could shoot him in cold blood.

Elizabeth stiffened and she screamed, "Tanner! My God, what are you doing?"

"God . . . oh, God." The soft moaning sound came from Darnell as he watched his partner fall to the ground. "We didn't do nothin'. Don't kill me, Marshal. Please. I swear, we didn't do nothin'."

Tanner looked with some confusion at the gun in his hand. He knew for a fact that he hadn't pulled the trigger; yet the man who had seconds ago been standing before him now lay dead at his feet.

Tanner caught Belle's movement from the corner

347

of his eye. Already she'd dropped to the ground, and she now rolled for cover behind the wagon. In one smooth motion, he swung Elizabeth up on his horse, almost wrenching her arm from its socket in the process. Without a word spoken, barely allowing her to gain her balance, he hit the animal's rump. "Get out of here!" he yelled just before he dove under the wagon and rolled to join his partner.

It took Tanner's shouting to snap Darnell out of his shock. Only now did he realize the marshal hadn't fired his gun. They were being bushwhacked. Someone was firing on them and—sonofabitch!—he made a perfect target standing in the light of the fire.

He might have made it if he'd run for cover, but Darnell figured the wagon was a few steps too far away. He didn't want to chance being out in the open that long. Instead he dropped to the ground, and as he descended, quite by accident, a bullet caught him right between the eyes.

The horse that carried Elizabeth raced like a demon through the black desert night. It took her some time to realize what was happening. It took her longer still to manage to bring the animal under control. She didn't fear her mount, for Tanner's horse was a gentle beast and obeyed a rider's commands. At least when Tanner rode him.

Finally, Elizabeth sat shivering upon the nervously prancing animal. She couldn't imagine simply obeying Tanner and returning home. She wasn't about to leave him in the midst of a gunfight and not come to his aid. There was no telling how many men were firing on those she'd left behind. Judging by the shooting that was going on, more than a few.

Elizabeth swung the horse around and headed back. She had no handgun, but Tanner had left his rifle on his horse.

Five men sat on horseback in a small circle. Inside that circle Belle stood alone. In her hand she held a pistol. Cold-bloodedly she aimed it and pulled the trigger, knowing as she did she was bound to meet the same end as her friend. She heard a click—empty chamber—and the men roared in appreciation of her bravery.

Tanner and Belle had managed to pick off three of the outlaw gang before the last five charged the camp. The desperados didn't give Tanner a chance to worry about being outnumbered. Quickly, mercifully, for they could have inflicted great suffering on him, he knew no more.

The men muttered amongst themselves as they watched the red-haired woman glare her defiance. It was obvious she knew her fate. The only problem they had was who was going to have her first? The leader of their gang had been killed. His death was no loss. Not a man left would mourn his passing, except for the fact that they'd probably kill each other for the first go at the woman.

Carlos had been with Navarro and his gang longer than any of the others. It was only right that he should now take command. "Ortiz," he said, "put the woman on your horse. Sanchez, see what's in the wagon."

The four men looked startled for just a moment,

but soon Ortiz and Sanchez obeyed the orders. It didn't matter to them who led. They all knew they'd only be at each other's throats if someone didn't take command.

Sanchez suddenly called out all manner of praise to the Blessed Mother. A moment later, all the men were beside themselves with glee. They screamed, they raced their horses in circles, they shot their guns into the air in celebration.

God had been good to them, they reasoned. Box after box had been filled to the brim with gold coin. Had anyone ever been luckier? It was enough to make all of them richer than they could ever hope to be. And on top of all that, they had this beautiful woman to share.

This *muchacha* was going to become their favorite. Yes, they had women back at camp. But none of the others were as brave, none of them looked like her.

While the outlaws were carrying on, Belle was wondering how the hell she was going to get out of this one. She'd been in tight fixes before, but never alone and never in one this bad. It wasn't that she had no fear of dying. She did, but she wouldn't show her fear. To do so would only give these men a greater edge.

From the looks in their eyes, she knew what was in store. Belle was far from an innocent. She'd had her share of men, and she refused to worry much over the fact that she'd soon have another. Perhaps more than one. She gave a mental shrug. One man was, after all, a lot like another. If she played it smart and attached herself to the leader, she might save herself some abuse. The man might even keep her for himself. Keep her, that is, until she managed to find a way out of this mess.

The horses of the dead men were gathered and tied to the back of the wagon. One of the desperados flicked the reins over the team and the happy outlaws moved off into the night.

Belle, her arms around the man before her, averted her gaze from Tanner's body. She couldn't think on the loss of her best friend right then. With any luck at all, there'd be time for that later.

Elizabeth galloped into the camp moments after the wagon pulled away. "Noooo!" she cried as she flung herself from the saddle and raced to his side. She knelt by Tanner's inert body, her heart beating furiously. A small puddle of blood had formed in the sandy soil beside his head. Elizabeth turned him and lifted the upper half of his body. She put her head to his chest and listened for a heartbeat, but her own was pounding so hard, she heard nothing.

"Damn you!" she cried as she held him tightly against her, not caring that his blood soaked the shoulder and bodice of her dress. She shifted, unable to see his face. His head fell back, his eyes were closed, his body was limp and silent. Tears rolled freely down her cheeks to mingle with the blood that covered one side of his face. "Damn you, Tanner, don't you dare die!' she sobbed, knowing in her heart, even as she said the words, it was too late. Pain pressed on her chest. She couldn't take in air without the agony of it slicing deep, deep into her soul. Silently she prayed to be allowed to join him.

How had she come to love him so desperately that life meant nothing without him? She rocked him back and forth and then shook him as anger mingled with sorrow. "Tanner, I'm going to kill you for doing this to me," she declared, lovingly smoothing his mussed hair. "I hate you! I hate you. You always were a mean bastard." Elizabeth's wild words were muffled by his warm skin. She shuddered as she wondered how much longer it would remain warm.

"What do you mean, I'm mean? When the hell have I ever been anything but kind to you?" he asked, so clearly he might not have been injured at all.

She screamed and shoved him away, causing his head to hit the ground hard. "Ow! Sonofabitch!" Tanner grunted as he managed with uncoordinated movements to lean on an elbow and hold his head. "What the hell are you pushing me around for? Can't you see I'm hurt?"

Elizabeth had scrambled at least four feet away in less than a blink of an eye. Now she watched in shock as he scowled and then came to a sitting position. He winced as he gingerly touched his still-bleeding wound.

"Hurt! Hurt?" She moved closer, her whole being filling with a mixture of relief, love, and anger. Anger being the most prevalent feeling, her hands balled into fists. "I'd like to show you real hurt, you . . . you . . ." She couldn't think of a word bad enough to call him. And then her face began to crumple as she suddenly realized he wasn't dead after all. He was talking to her, just as if she hadn't found him unconscious. Just as if she hadn't cradled

352

him in her arms while thinking him dead. She shuddered violently and her hands went up to cover her face. Then she rocked back and forth on her knees as if trying to hold back a pain that couldn't be borne. "I . . . I thought you were dead," she sobbed. "My God, I thought you were dead."

Tanner's annoyance evaporated. "I'm not dead, darlin'. Don't cry." Now their positions were reversed. He was holding her and rocking her in his arms. "I'm sorry you were scared."

He scanned the empty campsite. Empty but for four lifeless bodies. Suddenly he remembered. His body grew stiff with dread. "Where the hell is everybody? Where's Belle? What happened?"

He was coming to his feet, knowing the answer even as he asked the questions. "I don't know." Elizabeth sniffled. "I just got back."

"What the hell are you doing here?" Tanner asked, realizing at last that she was supposed to be on her way home. "Didn't I tell you to go?" He winced at the pain in his head.

"Don't yell, Tanner. It only makes your head hurt."

He cursed in frustration, knowing she was right, but loath to admit to it. "Don't tell me not to yell. I'll yell if I damn well please."

Elizabeth shrugged. She could see the pain in his eyes; yet this stubborn man refused to listen. "Fine," she said as she went to pick up her discarded drawers. She dabbed at his wound with them as she continued, "Go ahead and yell. It doesn't change the fact that I'm here and I'm not going anywhere without you."

Tanner sighed, took the cloth from her and wiped

at his bloodied face. "Will I be forever cursed with a disobedient wife?" He sighed. He knew he wouldn't want her any other way, and he also knew he would love her till his dying breath. He shook his head, trying to clear the last of the fogginess. He hadn't time now to worry about her obedience, or more to the point, the lack of it. He had to find Belle, and he had to do it fast. There was no telling what those men were already doing to her.

Actually Tanner hadn't a doubt as to what the outlaws were up to. He could only pray that Belle was strong enough to bear their abuse until he could find her and get her away from them.

"What are you doing?" Elizabeth asked as he moved among the bodies, turning them over and systematically searching pockets.

"I'm looking for a gun," he said over his shoulder. "I can't do much for Belle without one."

"Belle!" Elizabeth remembered for the first time that Belle had ridden into the camp with Tanner. She'd known, of course, when Tanner had put her on his horse that they were under attack. She'd simply forgotten everything when she'd thought him dead. Her eyes widened, her mind unable to fathom the puzzle of Belle's disappearance. Suddenly she gasped. "Tanner they've got her! My God! What are we going to do? How are we going to get her back?"

"We?" Tanner's lips tightened into a thin white line, and the lines that bracketed his mouth grew deeper.

Elizabeth began to calm down some as she forced Belle's predicament from her mind and concentrated on her husband's growing anger. "Of course 'we,' " she declared confidently. "You'll need help."

"And just what kind of help can I expect from a troublesome, disobedient wife?"

Elizabeth's eyes narrowed as her own anger came to life. "Do you plan to stand here and rave all night, or are you going to do something?"

She had never heard the particular curses this question provoked, but knew by his tone they were vile.

"And exactly what do you expect me to do without a gun?"

She ignored his ravings. "We have a rifle." She didn't bother mentioning that had she not returned he wouldn't have had a horse on which to go after Belle, nor would he have had the weapon he'd no doubt need once he found her.

Tanner shot her a look that had made many a man quake in his boots.

Elizabeth merely scowled. "Say what you must and be done with it. The longer we wait, the longer it's going to take us to find her."

He had never been so angry with a woman. He knew she spoke the truth when she included herself in Belle's rescue. But how the hell could he take her with him? If he did he would be putting her life at risk. Yet he could not leave her behind. Not alone, on foot, and unarmed in the middle of the desert. He'd never be able to concentrate on what he had to do while worrying about her safety. Tanner shook his head. No, it was better by far to take her with him. At least then he'd know she was safe. Well, he told himself, as safe as circumstances allow.

"We don't have much of a choice. We can't follow

tracks at night."

"But—"

"There's no need to nag, Elizabeth," he remarked, his tone hard and cold. He dabbed at his wound only to find it was hardly bleeding. He threw her undergarment to his feet. "If we can't see, we'll only wander aimlessly around the desert. Getting lost won't help her much."

Elizabeth nodded her agreement, knowing he was right. Still, it wasn't going to be easy. How in the world were they going to bear waiting till dawn? Worse yet, how was Belle going to bear these long hours?

Tanner grunted in satisfaction and then said a silent prayer of thanks as he turned Brian's body over and found a gun lying beneath him. Apparently the men who had attacked them had grown a bit careless once they'd realized the wagon was filled with gold. Besides the rifle, it was the only other weapon they had.

"What's our plan?" Elizabeth asked, her enthusiasm obvious as she gave up her pacing and came to sit at his side.

Tanner glared at her. "How would I know?"

Elizabeth ignored his anger and suggested, "We could ride back to town and get help."

Tanner shook his head, knowing by the time help arrived it would certainly be too late. "There's no time."

Elizabeth sighed. "How many men were there?"

"Far as I can remember, about five."

"Do you think they've already . . ." She couldn't bring herself to say the words aloud. What might be happening was too horrid to contemplate.

"I don't know," Tanner leaned back and pulled his wide-brimmed hat over his eyes. "We won't know till we find her."

"Do you think we will?"

"Find her?" he asked, and at her vigorous nod, he sighed and closed his eyes again. "We'll find her."

"How can you sleep at a time like this?"

"If I don't, I won't be much use to anyone." Besides, his head was killing him. The bullet had made a clean furrow along the side of his scalp. Tanner wasn't worried about that, but he had to find Belle. Without him, she didn't have a chance.

Chapter Seventeen

Tanner bit back the groan that threatened. The world swirled dizzily around him, and he felt weak as a new-born babe when the ground seemed about to come up to meet him. At the last moment he realized he was about to fall and clutched the horn of his saddle.

"What's the matter?"

"Nothing," he said, his voice raspy, his throat dry. They'd finished the last of their water some hours ago. That didn't help his fever any. He couldn't remember when he'd needed a drink more. "Just thirsty."

"Tanner, don't lie to me. You're sick. You're burning up with fever."

"I'm not," he lied, knowing it wouldn't help matters any for her to worry. There was nothing either of them could do except pray they'd reach water soon. "And I told you before, don't press me."

Elizabeth bit her lips to force back a smart retort. Why was it when she spoke openly of her concern for her husband, he resented it, but when Tanner voiced his worries, it was only right, only the duty of a caring husband?

Elizabeth sighed with frustration. She'd known something was wrong from the first moment she'd awakened. His eyes had had a glassy sheen, and when she'd reached for his forehead, he'd shaken her hand away. And he'd tossed and turned most of the night.

Darn the man! He was so thick, it was a miracle a bullet had managed to dent his skull. Elizabeth wondered if anything else ever could.

She knew Tanner was desperately ill. She wouldn't be surprised if the wound, although it had appeared to be clean, was now festering. She couldn't know for sure because he kept his hat pulled low over his eyes and refused to let her see the gash.

Elizabeth peered over Tanner's shoulder. She squinted against the glaring rays that bounced off the rock formations on each side of the deep gorge. She knew Tanner had to be suffering. She had no wound; yet she was developing an unbearable headache. Much to her relief they soon exited the narrow canyon and were greeted by a dry, warm breeze. It might not have been the most refreshing current of air she'd ever known, but Elizabeth welcomed it nonetheless, for inside that pass nothing had stirred.

Almost immediately she spotted the dark buildings whose outlines were blurred by shimmering waves of heat. Far off in the distance. "There's a town up ahead. Can we stop?"

"We don't have a choice. We need water."

Elizabeth nodded as she clung tightly to his back. She felt him sway again and knew he would have fallen more than once had she not been there to hold him in the saddle.

Every step the horse took increased his agony a hundredfold. He wanted to groan, felt the release would somehow help, but he held back, knowing every sound he uttered was scrutinized by his wife. They'd been in the saddle for six hours and during that time she hadn't once stopped pestering him about how he felt.

He'd only managed to shut her up by admitting that he had a headache and saying her voice was adding to his pain. He hadn't lied. He did have a headache; only it wasn't as simple as that. A few years back when he'd taken a bad fall from his horse, he'd felt the same way he did now: nauseous and dizzy. He hadn't been able to see clearly and he'd had the same god-awful pain in his head.

The buildings looked a lot closer than they actually were. It was almost dark by the time Tanner's horse trotted down a dry, dusty street lined on both sides with weathered, disreputable-looking buildings that could only be referred to as shacks. He pulled the horse to a stop before a large dead tree that served as a hitching post for the patrons of the local watering hole. Near the tree stood a wooden trough, filled with greenish water. Elizabeth's stomach felt a bit unsteady, but the horse didn't seem to mind the color a bit. He sank his muzzle deep into the cool trough, splashed, neighed, shook his head, and then happily drank again.

Tanner needed a cup of coffee and maybe two gallons of water to go with it. There had to be a cafe somewhere in this town. Besides the fact that he was near useless right now, and couldn't have helped Belle if he'd tripped over her, Elizabeth couldn't be expected to ride much farther. He hated to do it, but he knew they were going to take a room for the night. If he was lucky, maybe there'd be a hotel or roominghouse. He only hoped to find something clean. For himself, he couldn't have cared less, but he knew Elizabeth would be horrified to find tiny creatures in their bed.

He listened to her groan as she slid off the animal's back, wondering if he had the strength to do the same. He leaned low over the horse's head and managed to roll from its back. As gently as he could, so as not to jar his head any more than necessary, he actually slid to the ground.

Elizabeth secured the horse to the one of the metal hooks that had been set into a dead tree, as Tanner staggered toward the buildings. She took the saddlebags and rifle before she joined him on the sidewalk. With her help, he finally entered a building that smelled sickeningly of stale whiskey, unwashed bodies, and cheap perfume.

Tanner couldn't focus his eyes. He knew from the smell they had entered the saloon, but he couldn't see a damned thing. He blinked a few times and then gave up. More asleep than awake, he dozed where he stood.

Elizabeth sat him on a chair near the door and then sought out the bartender. "Would you have a room to rent?"

Manuel Silvaro's real name was James Wood. Years of running from the law had caused him to change it a dozen times. His hair and eyes were dark, his skin olive in hue and browned by many hours spent in the sun. He looked Mexican, and spoke the language as if he'd lived his entire life south of the border.

Three years ago he'd won this place in a game of cards. From that day on, he had become an innkeeper of sorts.

No one would accuse Silvaro of having a kind bone in his body, nor for that matter would any complain that he was particularly evil. His only real concern was making money. He didn't care where it came from; he only cared that it ended up in his pocket.

Right now he was observing with a clinical eye the beautiful young woman who had approached him. He knew with a face and body like hers, she could make him a lot of money. All she needed was a little cleaning up and she'd have the men in these parts waiting in line outside her door. Silvaro licked his lips at the thought. He always did that when he was thinking about money.

"Your man got something catchin'?" he asked suspiciously. "I don't want—"

"No. He was hurt in a fall." Elizabeth quickly responded. She'd expected the man to speak only Spanish and had been relieved to hear English. For a moment there, she hadn't been able to imagine how they were going to communicate. "I need a place where he can rest."

Silvaro nodded. "Upstairs." The man named a price, and Elizabeth shook her head. "How much is that in American money?"

"Three dollars a night. In advance."

"Three dollars!" Elizabeth gasped. "I could stay at the finest hotels in New Orleans for as much." She didn't know whether she could or not, but paying three dollars for a night in this decrepit building was ridiculous.

362

Silvaro shrugged. "But you ain't in New Orleans, lady." He turned his back on her and began to wipe the dust from the few bottles that lined the counter behind the bar. He should have told her five a night. There wasn't another place for fifty miles, unless she wanted to sleep out under the stars. There was a mirror behind the bar. He spoke to her reflection. "Take it or leave it, lady."

Elizabeth nodded. "Just a minute," she said.

She walked back to where Tanner sat, and shook him awake. "Give me some money," she said. "It's three dollars a night, in advance."

Tanner muttered a curse, not really understanding what she'd said. He was cursing because he'd been half-asleep, and when she'd wakened him his headache had started up again.

Elizabeth reached into his trouser pocket and took out a roll of bills. A moment later she counted out six dollars for the owner. "I'll need it for two nights. Is there someone who could help me get him up the stairs?" she asked.

Silvaro nodded. "It'll cost you another dollar."

Elizabeth shook her head, suddenly annoyed. Three dollars was more than enough for a week's stay in this hole, and now he wanted another dollar for an act of human kindness. "I'll do it myself."

It took some doing, especially since she carried both guns and the saddlebags while she tried to keep Tanner from crumpling to the floor, but she finally got him to the stairs. She thanked God the railing was strong, for with her arm wrapped around Tanner's waist, they banged into it a dozen times before they reached the upstairs landing. Once up there, Tanner staggered and almost fell backward, and Elizabeth used her last ounce of strength, to press him against the wall lest the two of them tumble headfirst down the length of stairs.

She was shaking almost as badly as he by the time she managed to steady him against the wall. She shot the grinning bartender an evil glare as she turned Tanner in the direction of their room.

Elizabeth's work for the night was far from over. Tanner had fallen into a deathlike sleep the moment she'd gotten him onto the bed, but she still had to get water, toweling, and clean sheets. They both needed a bath, but that would have to wait until she had the energy to tote buckets of water up the stairs, assuming there was a tub somewhere in this town. They had to have sheets, however. She was not going to sleep on bedding that was encrusted with dirt.

"I need water, clean towels, and sheets," she said, eyeing the bartender and expecting the worst.

"It'll cost you."

"I never expected it wouldn't."

"I'll have someone bring them to your room."

"I'll get them myself, thank you. How much and where?"

Moments later, Elizabeth struggled up the back stairs. In each hand she carried a bucket of cool water, and tucked under one arm she had coarse, but fairly clean, sheets and two scratchy towels, along with a precious bar of soap, the only one to be found in the place.

Downstairs a woman screamed and then laughed, and Elizabeth started, almost sloshing water over the edges of the buckets. A moment later a number of boisterous men came into the saloon, or the cantina, as she supposed it was rightfully called. God, she hoped they weren't going to be this loud all night. If so, she might lie awake until dawn.

Huffing and puffing, grunting and straining, Elizabeth managed at last to remove the dirty sheets and roll Tanner onto clean bedding. She was gasping for breath as she rid him of his boots, trousers, and long johns. Eyeing his shirt and vest, she shook her head. He was going to sleep in the rest of his clothing. She hadn't the strength to get anything else off him.

Elizabeth was cleaning his wound with cool water when he came awake. "Where are we?"

"In a room over a cantina."

"Lord, Elizabeth! What the hell are we doing here? Don't you know what people do in these rooms?"

Elizabeth had been listening half the night to the comings and goings of men visiting women in the rooms alongside theirs. She'd been embarrassed at first, but soon reasoned that what these women did was none of her concern.

"I'm afraid you're much too ill for any of that nonsense," she said, and her gaze narrowed. "How would you know what goes on in these rooms?"

As sick as he was, Tanner managed a grin. "Little wretch. When I get you out of here, I'm going to tan . . ." In midsentence, he fell asleep, as he'd been doing on and off for most of the night.

An hour later he stirred again as she changed the cool cloth that covered his brow. "What the hell is that noise?"

"It seems the men downstairs are enjoying themselves a bit too much."

"Where are the guns?"

"On the dresser." Elizabeth nodded toward them.

"Push the dresser in front of the door."

"The door's locked." The fact that the lock worked had amazed Elizabeth. Nothing else in this place did. The windows wouldn't stay open; the lanterns were out of fuel. The drawers in the dresser were stuck. Permanently, she imagined.

"Do it anyway. Now!"

"All right, all right," she mumbled as she left the side of the bed to do his bidding. He was sound asleep by the time she returned.

It was barely dawn and Elizabeth stood with her back against the door, her arms outstretched as if she were guarding the exit from the room. "You're not leaving. Get back in that bed before I knock you over the head and throw you back in it myself."

Tanner swayed. Determined to overcome his dizziness, he put a hand on the feather mattress and insisted, "Get my pants."

"Tanner, you've got to be the most stubborn man I've ever come across. How in the world do you expect to find Belle when you can't stand without my help?"

Suddenly there was a loud bang at the door, and a slurred, drunken male voice whispered for someone named Chichi. From the sound of it, his mouth was pressed against the wood.

"Next room," Elizabeth called out through the closed door.

Tanner's eyes narrowed as he watched his wife from across the small room. "How do you know she's in the next room?"

"I don't. I've been sending the men there all night." She shrugged and then went on, "Judging from the sounds that come through these paper-thin walls, no one's had reason to complain."

Tanner grinned. "And it doesn't embarrass you?"

Elizabeth's dark eyes twinkled. "Let's say I've had time to get used to it."

Tanner lifted imploring eyes to his wife. "Elizabeth, I've got to find her. She'd do nothing less for me."

"I understand that," she said soothingly as she pushed him down on the bed, "but you can hardly be of any help in your present condition."

"I'm better."

"You're not."

"We'll lose her trail."

"Maybe, but you'll find it again."

"What if it was you? What if you'd been taken by five men?" He seemed tormented by the thought. "Don't you see every minute counts?"

"Tomorrow, Tanner."

"I've lost a full day already." He punched the bed in frustration.

"No you haven't. We traveled all day yesterday, remember?"

"Then I'll lose today."

"I know, but it can't be helped." She watched him struggle to keep his eyes open. "Tomorrow."

Belle released a tiny sigh of relief as Carlos came

into the shack. He was carrying another bottle, only half-full. This was her first night at their camp, and he'd been the only man to touch her so far. If her luck held out, it would stay that way. Not that the others hadn't wanted her, but Carlos had insisted — she understood a little Spanish — that the woman was his.

There had been a fight, but apparently Carlos had won. And for that Belle was grateful.

The man might be a murderer and thief, but he was a damn sight cleaner than the others. Besides, he treated her no worse than some respectable, so-called gentlemen she'd known. He'd been gentle enough, though insistent that she perform certain acts she had no liking for.

Being an independent sort, and having had the privilege of choosing her partners for years, Belle couldn't stand the thought that she now had no choice. Still, it could have been worse. The man could have been one of those monsters who got their kicks out of hurting.

Carlos stripped off his trousers, and wearing nothing more than a grin came toward the bed. Belle eyed the man clinically. He was by no means unattractive. Small and wiry, he still had enough between his legs to pleasure a woman. And unlike most of his gang, he washed fairly regularly.

Belle smiled as he came closer. She hated his guts, but she'd do what she had to, of course. She'd do it till she got her hands on a gun. And then she was going to blow the bastard's balls off.

"Take it off," Carlos said in an odd mix of Spanish and heavily accented English, while nodding toward the shift she wore.

Belle complied, knowing defying him would only force him to get rough. She had had enough beatings as a child. She was not going to suffer that kind of treatment again, not if she had anything to say about it.

Carlos knelt on the bed and took a long swallow from the bottle. He offered Belle a drink and then shrugged when she refused. A few minutes later he'd finished the bottle off, and he threw it into a corner.

Since he had already consumed two full bottles of tequila, Belle hoped he'd drunk enough to fall asleep. But Carlos wasn't near his limit. He moved over her, placing his knees on either side of her hips. He smiled down as he reached for a heavy breast and began to play with the nipple.

His first taking had not stirred her in the least, so Belle doubted this man ever could. Still, knowing what was expected, she smiled and then moaned softly as if she enjoyed his touch.

Then she noticed the difference. He was not hurrying as he'd done before. She might have been a bit hasty in her judgment here. Maybe she could enjoy his touch, just a little. She didn't much like the thought of it, but there was no way she could stop her body from reacting.

It was a full hour before Carlos lay over her, panting and exhausted. Lord! he had the stamina of a bull. He said something she didn't understand, but from the glint in his eye she imagined he was boasting over how many times he'd brought her to climax.

Belle didn't care. As far as she was concerned, there was nothing shameful in what she'd done. Like eating, like sleeping, sex was a natural need of the human body. She didn't have to love the man to enjoy what he could do in bed. Apparently she didn't even have to like him.

She smiled in response to his smug grin. She was still going to shoot his balls off.

It had been quiet for hours. Elizabeth judged the time to be somewhere around noon. Tanner had been sleeping peacefully for quite a while. The skin around his wound looked a little less red and even though his fever had yet to break, he didn't feel as hot.

She dressed and slid the handgun into the pocket of her skirt. Whoever looked closely might see that the weight of it pulled at the fabric, but Elizabeth did not care. She couldn't go downstairs unprotected. And she had to go—or starve.

As quietly as possible, she pushed aside the dresser and left the room.

She was working in the small kitchen behind the bar when she jumped as a deep voice sounded behind her. "Food's extra."

Elizabeth shot a killing look at Silvaro, but it only brought a smile to his hard-featured face and a gleam of interest to his eyes. He grinned and went to stand next to the stove where she worked.

"I wasn't stealing it. There was no one around." Elizabeth took the bean mixture and filled six corn tortillas. A moment later she wrapped the entire lot in a towel. "Have you got something hot to drink?"

Silvaro grinned and took a step closer. "That depends. How hot you thinkin' on?"

It was obvious from his tone of voice and the leer in

his eyes that the man had something other than food in mind. Elizabeth ignored his question. "A bottle of tequila will be fine."

Silvaro nodded toward her makings. "You got a lot of food there. You looking to leave already?"

Elizabeth hadn't been thinking of leaving till that moment, but the look in the man's eye told her she wasn't safe. She grabbed another dozen tortillas and tried to walk around him.

"My husband's much better. He wants to leave earlier than planned."

"You paid for two nights. It would be a shame to waste the money."

"It doesn't matter."

The next thing Elizabeth knew she was trapped in his arms. He was nearly breaking her back as he bent her over, his mouth, disgustingly wet, slobbering over hers.

Elizabeth almost gagged at the scent of him. She struggled, desperately trying to free herself. It was no use. She couldn't begin to match this man's strength. He released her mouth at last and Elizabeth took huge gulping breaths as she tried to control her need to scream.

Tanner was too ill to help her, and no one else would answer her calls. No one else would care.

"You don't have to leave. Why don't you think about staying here for a while?" Silvaro produced what he hoped was an enticing grin. It wasn't. "I've been thinking about you all night."

"Let me go!"

"I've been thinking about how good we'd be together."

Elizabeth shot him an incredulous look. *The man can't possibly mean in bed! Can he?* She was married. Apparently a little thing like a wedding band made no difference to him. The man was no better than an animal. "Let me go this instant!"

Silvaro chuckled. This woman had fire. He liked them tough. Even though she spoke and acted like a lady, he could see the flames in her eyes. Especially when she was mad. Damn! He couldn't wait to get her in his bed. As a matter of fact he wasn't going to wait. The kitchen would do just fine.

"With your looks we could make ourselves a fortune. I know men who'd pay plenty for a go at you."

Silvaro was backing her up to the table. His mouth came down on hers, while one hand slid into her hair and held her head still.

Elizabeth's small towel-wrapped package fell to the floor, and she let out a muffled cry as he forced her back against the table. He was fussing with her skirt, trying to lift it, when she remembered the gun.

A moment later it was pressed hard to his belly, while at the same moment a deep voice came from behind him. "Move away from her."

Silvaro instantly raised his arms and backed away. There wasn't a woman on earth worth getting killed over. He didn't have to look to know that her husband was standing in the kitchen. He wasn't taking any chances. He'd seen the rifle they'd brought in yesterday. It was probably pointed at his back right now. "You all right?" Tanner asked as he watched a white-faced Elizabeth pocket the gun.

She nodded. Then, looking disgusted, she wiped her mouth with the sleeve of her shirt. A moment later she stiffened as she remembered the man's words. He'd wanted her to work for him, just like Chichi did. She shivered with revulsion. "Tanner, we've got to get out of here."

He grinned. "My thoughts exactly."

"Sit down while I get our things and put some food together."

Tanner nodded and did as she said, not for a moment taking his gaze from the man who stood in the middle of the small room.

"I'm thinkin' I'll put a bullet between your eyes. What do you say?" Tanner was amazed that he hadn't already done it. He'd never known rage more powerful than that inspired by a man touching his wife.

Silvaro gave him a shrewd look. "I didn't mean anything by it. She's a pretty lady. I wouldn't have hurt her."

Tanner nodded, knowing the man was lying. It didn't matter. He wasn't going to kill him anyway. He could just imagine Elizabeth's horror at having to step over a body to pack the food.

Besides, the sound of the gun might attract others, and Tanner barely had the strength to hold a gun, let alone engage in a gun fight.

She wasn't gone more than a minute. Upon returning, Elizabeth packed the saddlebags with food. She then ran to the bar and brought back two bottles of tequila, as well as the gun and the box of ammunition she'd found under the bar. She filled their canteen from the pump out back and returned to the kitchen.

"We can't leave him like this," her eyes darted wildly around the room, searching for something they might use to tie up the owner of the cantina. "He might shoot us when we leave."

Tanner nodded and then grinned when he spotted a door in the floor, under the table. It was a cellar of some sort. A good enough place to put the man for the time being. He motioned with his gun for Silvaro to move.

"What about all this food and the tequila?" Silvaro didn't mind so much the loss of the woman, although he could have made a fortune on her after he'd used her for a bit, but it literally made him sick to think she was taking all this food and not leaving him a cent. "Who's going to pay me for it?"

Elizabeth shrugged. "I paid for two, we used the room only one night." She nodded at the bulging saddlebags. "This will make us even."

"What about my gun?" the man almost whined as he entered the earth cellar.

Elizabeth left three more dollars on the table and then smiled as she pulled the heavy table over the trap door.

Her eyes were sparkling as she looked from the money to her husband.

"Leave it," he said.

A wicked smile curved her lips. "You're beginning to sound like my conscience."

"Since you don't appear to have one, I'd say you should be grateful."

"Whoever hears his calls will probably take it anyway," she reasoned.

"That's not our problem. Leave it."

Elizabeth gasped as she stepped outside. "Someone stole your horse!"

Tanner slowly shook his head, but before he could

respond, she said, "Let's go to the stable and steal one for each of us."

He shot her a look of disbelief. "You're getting carried away, Elizabeth."

"Besides, Chester won't let anyone ride him but me. He probably just got loose and wandered out back."

Tanner gave a shrill whistle and winced as pain shot clear through his brain. A moment later his horse meandered out of an alley and came to a stop directly before him.

Elizabeth grinned as they started out of town. Tanner heard her soft chuckle. "Enjoyed yourself back there, did you?"

"Some." She nodded, then kissed him on the back of his neck.

"I'm beginning to see I've got myself a problem that's a hell of a lot worse than I first thought. You really enjoy stealing."

Elizabeth laughed. "I only steal from the deserving."

"And you figured the Mex deserved it?"

"Of course he deserved it. He charges three dollars for a room, for goodness' sake. Have you ever heard of anything so shocking?"

Tanner grinned at her outrage. "Can't say that I have, darlin'."

Chapter Eighteen

They were traveling for hours before they came upon the wagon's trail again. It headed directly for the mountains up ahead. And Tanner knew there was no pass through them.

That had to mean their camp was somewhere in those mountains. He groaned out a curse. Things couldn't be worse. How the hell was he going to get into that camp when he probably had to climb hundreds of feet to do it? Impossible. He was having a time of it just staying in the saddle.

Tanner gave a slow shake of his head. There was no sense asking for trouble. He'd have to wait until they came across the wagon before he started worrying.

It was dark by the time he pulled his horse to a stop before an abandoned wagon. The heavy boxes were gone, as were their contents. He knew the outlaws couldn't be far. There was no way they could transport that much gold on horseback for any great distance.

"They're up there, aren't they?" Elizabeth asked as

she scanned the dark peaks of a shadowed mountain that consisted entirely of reddish brown rock, not a tree or blade of grass breaking its barren starkness.

Tanner nodded as he felt her slide from the horse. "We won't be makin' camp. No fire tonight."

Elizabeth groaned as her legs threatened to crumple beneath her. She forced herself to walk, knowing the movement would bring sensation back to her numb limbs. Riding any length of time always made her legs weak. Sitting in a saddle for hours was bad enough, but riding behind one left the insides of her thighs raw. She could hardly move without the most god-awful pain. Hobbling about, her lips thinned into a grimace, she asked, "We're not going to wait till light, are we?"

Feeling particularly frustrated, Tanner snapped, "Can you see a path?" Damn, when was the dizziness going to stop? Because of it they'd taken double the time necessary to reach this mountain. He knew he was taking his anger out on her, and that was wrong, still he couldn't seem to hold his tongue. Without waiting for an answer, he remarked nastily, "Then by all means, lead on."

Elizabeth didn't take offense as she might have. It was easy to see that he was upset. "If we wait till light they'll see us."

Tanner knew she was right, of course, but he found himself arguing anyway. "We could wander on the base of this mountain for hours before we find anything. Besides, you might get hurt stumbling around in the dark."

"I'll wait here."

Tanner shot her a disbelieving look. "Right. And

377

I'm the Queen of England."

"I will!" she insisted.

"For how long?"

Elizabeth only grinned. Tanner could just about make out her smile in the near-black night. "I figured as much."

Tanner breathed a long dispirited sigh. What the hell was he arguing about? He knew they'd have no chance without the cover of darkness. Suddenly he realized the problem. The thought of Elizabeth participating in a gunfight brought chills down his spine. How the hell could a man lead his wife into battle? There had to be another way. He couldn't chance her life. Tanner sighed again, knowing he had no choice. "Make sure your gun is loaded," he said unhappily.

Elizabeth's only answer was a smile. A moment later she said, "Wait! I have a better idea."

Tanner cursed. "I can't believe this. Who the hell is the marshal here?"

"You are, of course."

"Then for God's sake, listen to me!" he snapped, his voice rough and filled with annoyance.

"Tanner, I'll listen. Just let me say one thing."

"What?" His voice was heavy with disgust.

"We could wait till it's almost dawn before we do anything. They'll all be sleeping by then, don't you think?"

Tanner nodded. "No doubt that's exactly how things will work out. But first we have to find their camp."

Elizabeth responded to his plan with a nod of her own and a softly spoken, "Wait here."

Tanner watched in amazement as she started toward the mountain. A moment later he grabbed her arm and swung her around. "Where the hell do you think you're going?"

"To find a path. Your head is giving you some trouble. There's no sense in tiring yourself."

"Elizabeth, the only thing that's giving me trouble is you. Right now I'm greatly tempted to tie you to the wagon. If you say or do one more thing to aggravate me, I swear I'll do it."

Tanner moved ahead of her. "No matter what happens, you will stay behind me. Have I made myself clear?"

Elizabeth nodded. "Yes."

Tanner grunted suspiciously at hearing her meek tone of voice. Enough was enough. "Let's go."

He led the way. Only moments later Elizabeth realized they were on a narrow rocky path. It suddenly curved around a huge wall of stone and led into a deep canyon. Tanner instantly dropped to his knees and pulled Elizabeth down behind him. Only a wall about four feet high kept them from being seen by those below.

Elizabeth's eyes widened in surprise as she peered over the wall. Below them was a flat area surrounded by towering rock walls and lit by numerous campfires. Against the far wall sat a decrepit wooden shack. Inside it, Elizabeth thought she saw a flickering light.

To the left of the shack was a small rope-bound corral that held at least a dozen horses. A few women sat around one of the fires, but Belle wasn't among them. Two men sat on the ground, maybe twenty feet away, each leaning against one of the boxes from the wagon as they lazily brought dark bottles to their mouths.

Suddenly a man laughed and both Tanner and Elizabeth gasped with fright. The sound wasn't more than five feet away. No doubt the man's attention was centered on something else. Tanner almost groaned aloud. Thank God, their whispers hadn't been heard.

He motioned for Elizabeth to stay put as he moved silently around the next bend. She heard a muffled sound and a low groan, followed by a soft thud. Instantly she turned the corner and came face to face with her husband. There was a man lying at Tanner's feet. A dead man.

"Didn't I tell you to stay there?" he asked, so softly she almost had to read his lips. But his mood wasn't anywhere near being soft. It was easy to see by the scowl on his face, that Tanner was ready to strangle her.

Elizabeth might have mentioned that he didn't actually *tell* her anything. He had merely motioned for her to stay. Wisely she thought better of further antagonizing him. "You might have needed help."

"I need help all right," he retorted, his voice barely above a whisper. "As long as I have you for a wife, I'm always going to need help."

Elizabeth ignored his sarcasm. "There's a man standing on the ledge over there." Tanner ducked lower, his movement so fast Elizabeth could only watch in amazement. Suddenly she was yanked down next to him.

Tanner shot her a scathing look.

"How are we going to get down there without being seen?"

"How the hell should I know?" Tanner snapped as he inched his way up and peered over the short wall, taking in the entire canyon. Elizabeth was right. There was a man standing on the ledge, just opposite them, obviously another guard. Tanner cursed.

"Why do you always do that?" she whispered, suddenly level with him as they both looked over the short wall.

"Do what?"

"Say swear words."

"When the hell do I do that?"

"Whenever you're upset."

"Then I reckon you answered your own question."

"It's a nasty habit you've gotten yourself into, Tanner. It's not a good idea. When the baby comes, he'll be doing as much."

Tanner groaned. Leave it to Elizabeth to talk about something like that now. "We'll discuss that later. Now be quiet while I think."

She waited only a moment, before she ventured, "Any ideas yet?"

"Elizabeth," he said, his tone low and definitely threatening.

"Just asking," she quickly responded. "I have a plan."

Tanner shot her a look of annoyance. "Yeah? What?"

"I could walk down there. They'd be so surprised, you could get the drop on them."

"Where the hell did you learn to talk like that?" he asked as he turned to look into eyes alive with excitement. The damned woman sounded like a gunfighter.

"Get the drop on them? From the penny novels I read."

Tanner sighed his disgust. "Forget it. We'll wait till morning. He'll probably come down by then."

"What if someone else takes his place?"

Tanner shrugged. "He's drinking. Soon he'll have to . . ." Tanner cursed again as he watched the man calmly open his trousers and relieve himself against the canyon wall.

"I guess that takes care of that notion." Elizabeth's voice was filled with laughter. "You'll have to think of something else."

Tanner looked at the body at his feet. A moment later he was pulling the dead man's clothing off.

"What are you doing?"

"I'm going to wear his clothes and walk down there."

"Oh, really?" She was obviously annoyed. "And what happens when the guard sees you?"

"That's why I'm wearing these clothes," Tanner said as he struggled to pull the man's pants off. "If he sees me, he'll think I'm this fella."

"And when the shooting starts?"

"Just stay here and stay down."

"For goodness sake! You're going to get us both killed if you insist on treating me as if I'm made out of glass." He was just about to argue with her when she added, "You can't do this alone. You need my help."

Tanner was quiet for a long time. He did need her help. He needed someone's help, or they were

382

never going to get out of there alive. "Tell me the truth," he said as he pulled off his own trousers. "Did you mean to hit the rattler exactly where you did?"

"Well," she dragged out the word, "not exactly. I meant to hit its head. I missed, 'cause it was already moving."

Tanner's blue eyes widened. One leg in the outlaw's pants, he sat motionless. "You pulled your gun from your garter and hit a striking rattler?"

"I missed by about two inches," she said, her voice low, as if she were admitting a failing. "I was startled. I didn't hear him until it was too late," she explained.

Tanner grinned as he suddenly squeezed her tightly against him. Then he let go of her and continued dressing. "Stay here."

"Tanner!"

"Listen to me, damn it! Stay here! I'm going down. By the time they realize I'm not one of the guards, I'll be close enough to kill them. When the shooting starts, take care of our friend." Tanner nodded toward the guard across the canyon.

Elizabeth didn't much like the idea that he was putting himself in danger, but for the moment she couldn't think of a better plan. "Wait! Don't go. Maybe we can think of something else."

"I've already done a lot of thinking, and this is what we're doing." Tanner was putting the outlaw's large hat on as he spoke.

"Suppose there are men hiding in the shack?"

"There's one inside. At least one. No doubt he's the reason Belle isn't walking around down there."

Elizabeth bit her lip, her eyes darkening.

"Don't worry, darlin'. Everything will be all right."

Her eyes hardened as she silently swore nothing was going to happen to Tanner. Not while she lived. "Take care of the man in the shack. I'll worry about the rest."

He grinned. God, but she was a cocky little thing. Tanner had never wanted to kiss her more than at that moment, but he knew where it might lead and he needed a clear head for the next few minutes.

He backed away, lest he give in to the temptation. "Be good," he said as he turned, stood, and calmly walked down the path and into the canyon below.

Elizabeth's heart was pounding like it never had before. She had to concentrate to hear over the sound of it. She needed to listen closely. The slightest sound or change could mean death within seconds. And there was no way her man was going to die. Not that night. Not ever, if she had anything to say about it.

One of the men was seated on the ground, his back against a rock, two of the three women positioned on either side of him. The other man had sauntered away from the group with the third woman. That pair stopped near one of the campfires, and the man pulled the woman closer. Elizabeth groaned. She knew what was going to happen even before the woman reached into the man's trousers. She didn't want to see it.

Then, suddenly, she reasoned that this was most likely the best thing that could happen. If the outlaws were busy with their sinful doings, they might not notice Tanner. Elizabeth shook her head, knowing they were bound to notice him eventually. He couldn't just walk in and take Belle out without being seen.

All she could do was pray and shoot straighter than she'd ever shot in her life.

The man with the two women noticed him first. He called out a remark in Spanish. Tanner's answer was muffled as if he were slurring his words. The man said something else. Tanner only waved.

He was on the floor of the canyon now, but Elizabeth could see the man below had tensed. Why hadn't she thought of this? Why had she let him go? There was a password, and Tanner didn't know it!

The man who had spoken earlier suddenly pushed the two women aside and rolled flat to the ground. He was reaching for his gun when Elizabeth put a bullet into his skull. The resulting gore didn't register. She didn't have a second to think on what she'd done. She knew the guard had been alerted to her position. In an instant she fired again, and the man across from her gave a long mournful cry as he fell off the ledge to the canyon's floor.

Once again—and for the last time—she fired the rifle, and the final man, possibly the woman beneath him as well, found eternal reward.

Damn! thought Tanner. She's better than anything I've ever seen. Here he'd been thinking her softly spoken boast was so adorable, but she hadn't been bragging. He hadn't had the time to pull his gun free of leather and three men were already dead. Tanner didn't think there was a faster or more accurate gun in the West.

Elizabeth watched Tanner jump over a fire and

385

throw himself against the wall of the shack while the two women lay cowering, crying out in high-pitched, echoing voices to be spared.

They needn't have bothered. Now that she had the time to see the destruction she'd caused, Elizabeth couldn't bear the horror of it. It didn't matter that she'd had no choice. It didn't matter that these men got no better than they deserved. It didn't even matter that it was necessary to save her husband's life. Elizabeth simply wasn't near as tough as she'd thought. She couldn't become an executioner without something giving.

Suddenly she was shaking so badly she couldn't hold the rifle. It slid from her hands, hit against the canyon's sloping walls, and broke into several pieces as it landed on the stone floor below. She neither noticed nor cared.

Elizabeth turned and leaned back against the canyon wall. A second later she was on her knees, retching, her body wracked by painful heaves. She couldn't stop shaking. She couldn't stop crying. And most of all, she couldn't stop the horror of what she'd done from playing again and again in her mind's eye. Finally her mind decided it could no longer bear the agony and simply closed off. Without thinking, like a dying animal seeking its last comfort, she curled herself into a tight ball. She stayed like that, tears sliding over her dirt-smudged cheeks, staring at the rock opposite her, until she was found.

Carlos jumped from the bed while the first gunshot echoed through the canyon. His back was to Belle as he peered out the dirt-smeared window.

Careless of the fact that he was naked, he grabbed his gun and moved beyond the piece of canvas that served as a door. A shot rang out, and Belle heard a body drop.

She pulled her shift over her head and ran to the window. She couldn't see a damned thing, except for the fires and . . . Good God! The camp appeared to be littered with bodies, including Carlos's.

Belle pulled on her split skirt and tucked the short shift inside. Next came her blouse and vest. She had her boots in her hand when the next shots were heard. She'd never dressed faster in her life.

She was standing just inside the door, an empty bottle raised high over her head as she waited for the killer or killers to come inside. Her mind raced over the possibilities. They were obviously under attack, but who the hell was doing the attacking?

Another band of outlaws? Or had the law stumbled upon this maggoty lot? She wouldn't know till the shooting was over. In the meantime she wasn't taking any chances.

"Belle! Get your ass our here, right now!"

Tanner! Good God, it was Tanner! Belle grinned as she threw the bottle aside and swaggered out the doorway. Her hands were on her hips as she shot him an evil glare. "Should have known a bullet wouldn't do much damage to a head as thick as yours."

Tanner grinned and then the two of them were laughing as Belle made a flying leap into his arms. "Damn! I've never been so glad to see anyone," she said, her face crushed into his chest. She felt him stagger under her slight weight and knew the bullet

387

he'd taken had done more damage than he was likely to admit. "How the hell did you find me?"

"Followed the wagon's tracks."

Tanner laughed as Belle squeezed him tightly around the middle. "I don't know why I was worried. Should have known you'd land on your back," he said while eyeing the dead, naked man at their right.

"The saying is, 'Land on your feet,'" Belle corrected.

Tanner laughed as he nodded toward the man. "Maybe, but not in your case."

"Oh, that." Belle grinned. "Can I help it if men find me irresistible?"

Tanner grunted his disbelief. Then he released her and walked toward the corraled horses.

Belle was at his side, separating the two that had pulled the wagon from the rest. "You didn't do this alone," she said, as she looked around the canyon. "Who else is here?"

"Elizabeth."

Belle laughed at the ridiculous notion. "Who else?"

"I told you who else."

"But you sent her back when everything started. How did she. . . ?"

"She never left." Tanner's aggravation returned just from remembering how mad she could make him. "Damn woman doesn't listen to a word I say."

Belle laughed. "God, Tanner, I couldn't be happier to see this. If anyone deserves—"

"Shut up."

"Where is she?" Belle asked, ignoring the words just spoken.

"Up there." He lifted his head and nodded.

"Elizabeth!" Belle called.

Tanner put a hand to his head. "Oh, Lord! Don't yell. My head is splitting as it is. Every damn thing echoes a million times in there."

"Maybe we'd better plan on stayin' a day or so."

"Why?"

"You don't look so good. A little green—"

"Bull. I've just got a headache."

"Fine," Belle dismissed him with a wave of her hand. If the man was stupid enough not to know when he was hurting, who was she to insist? "I'm going to find your wife."

Belle wasn't happy when she finally came across Elizabeth. Tears were still flowing down her cheeks. Elizabeth rocked back and forth. No amount of talking on Belle's part could bring her attention from the rock she faced.

Belle placed a hand on Elizabeth's forehead. Her skin was clammy and cold. Something was wrong. "Tanner! Get the hell up here," she yelled, unconcerned about his headache.

In all the years he'd known her, no matter their numerous and sometimes desperate predicaments, Belle's voice had never held an edge of panic. Tanner was seized by terror. It rose up from his innards to squeeze at his chest. Something was terribly wrong.

It wasn't easy, but between the two of them they got Elizabeth down the narrow path and into the cabin. An hour passed and she still lay huddled beneath every blanket they could put their hands on. The sun was just coming over the horizon. A fire had been laid in the small stove. The heat was intense inside the cabin, a person could hardly breathe.

Tanner had seen enough to know if Elizabeth didn't come to her senses soon, she was apt to die. He couldn't believe God would give him this woman and then take her away almost before he had had a chance to love her. Dragging himself from beneath crushing waves of despair, he allowed himself a ray of hope. He wasn't mistaken. Her body was growing warmer.

Her breathing gentled and grew deeper and more even, while her heart seemed to ease its pounding.

Tanner sat beside her at first, rubbing her arms, her hands; and when that brought about no reaction, he stripped away his clothes and lay at her side. Holding her in his arms, he pressed her against his body and began to talk. He knew she wasn't aware that he was holding her. Actually she was in some kind of strange limbo where she wasn't aware of anything. But she would be. God damn it, together they were going to lick this thing.

Gently he ran his hands over her back, up and down in a soothing motion, and he began to talk. He talked for a long time. His voice grew dry, but still he went on. It wasn't long after he started that Elizabeth closed her eyes. Tanner could have sworn he heard a deep trembly sigh.

"I . . . we rode our butts off that day. It was a miracle the horses survived. As it was, not one of us could walk when we got there."

Elizabeth snuggled her head more comfortably against his chest. "And all along I thought you were the strong, silent type."

Tanner grew still as death. Was his mind playing tricks on him? Did she really speak? "Are you awake, Elizabeth?"

She rolled onto her side, flung an arm over his waist and murmured low, "No, I'm sleeping. Shhh. You don't want to wake me up."

God, this woman was unlike any he'd ever known. Even now, as traces of his terror lingered, when he could hardly believe the wonder of this moment, she could bring a smile to his lips. "Why?" he asked, feeling his heart begin to pound with almost unbearable joy.

Elizabeth chuckled softly. "Because I'm a monster when I don't get enough sleep."

"You're a monster anyway," he said, closing his eyes against the pleasure of the feel of her warm body.

Elizabeth laughed again. "Tanner, I really do love you, but you're going to have to ease up on these frisky moods of yours."

He wanted to laugh, to squeeze her till she begged for mercy, to shout out his joy. Instead he pressed his face into her hair. A sob broke from his throat and tears burned his eyes as he thanked God for this miraculous gift and silently swore to cherish Elizabeth for as long as he was allowed. His voice was husky with emotion when he asked, "Am I? Why?"

Elizabeth gave a lusty yawn. "Because I never get a chance to sleep anymore." She barely finished the sentence when Tanner realized she had drifted off.

* * *

Dressed again, he walked out of the cabin. Belle's gaze never left his face. She sighed with relief at seeing his smile. "She's sleeping."

"Good." Belle nodded. "What do you suppose happened?"

Tanner nodded toward the bodies scattered about the canyon floor. "She killed them."

Belle's eyes widened in surprise. She'd known Tanner couldn't have entered the hideout and remained alive without backup, but she hadn't imagined Elizabeth had done this much. "All of them?"

"Except for the naked bastard. I did the honors on that one," Tanner replied. "She's an excellent marksman. Still, it wouldn't surprise me if Elizabeth had never killed before. I think the shock of what she'd done was just too much for her to bear."

"You're probably right. I remember the first time I killed. Emptied my stomach right there on the spot."

Tanner nodded his agreement. He didn't know a lawman who took killing in his stride. No matter that it was sometimes necessary, it was hard to accept the fact.

"What are we going to do with them?"

Tanner followed the direction of Belle's nod. Two women sat against the rock wall, obviously terrified. "Give them each a horse and a handful of coins and let them go."

Belle grinned. "You know, of course, if we give them any of the gold, it's as good as stealing. Maybe you're picking up some of your wife's characteristics."

Tanner grinned. "I doubt anyone will miss a few coins."

Belle laughed and headed toward the horses, while Tanner gave each of the women gold. Neither spoke a word as they carefully listened to his instructions on how to find their way south. They were going home. It didn't matter the life they'd led, they were getting a second chance.

Tanner watched the two women lead their horses up the rocky path and out into the desert. "We could have taken them in, you know," he said quietly.

That didn't matter to him. The women had probably been held there against their will. Bringing them before the law would have accomplished nothing.

"How long are we planning on staying?"

"A few days. Elizabeth is going to need some rest before she starts the trip back."

Belle nodded and then grinned. Her eyes sparkled happily. "I'd say the woman's got you hog-tied, and you love every minute of it."

Tanner grinned at Belle's outrageous comment. Damned if she didn't talk like the raunchiest cowhand. Most of the time, she talked worse than a cowhand. Tanner chuckled, and his eyes glittered with happiness. "I'd say you're right."

Chapter Nineteen

"I can hardly believe we're finally in our bed-room."

Elizabeth laughed. Belle had left for Denver that morning. She had been sorry to see her go. She'd miss her, except at moments like these. "There's no reason to go to the barn anymore. No one can hear us. Gloria snores louder than you." She listened for a moment to the sounds coming from across the hall. "I doubt she'd wake up if I stood at the bottom of her bed and screamed."

"The sleep of the innocent," Tanner remarked, just before he stubbed his toe on the bedpost, let out a stream of curses, and then fell forward, almost crushing Elizabeth as he landed upon her. "God damn it!" he grunted. "Maybe we should have gone to the barn after all. At least the loft doesn't have a damned bed to trip over."

"Ummm," Elizabeth murmured as she wriggled beneath him, "Now those are love words if I ever heard them."

Tanner grinned as he settled himself more comfortably upon her. "Is it love words you want?"

"Actually anything would be better than your usual curses. You could talk about your job, or your horse. . . ." Elizabeth giggled as Tanner bit her shoulder.

"How about if I tell you how beautiful you are? Would you like that?"

"Mmmm. It couldn't hurt," she said, slightly breathless as his mouth lowered and his teeth grazed the tip of her breast.

Tanner raised his head and smiled as he watched passion come alive in her eyes. "And what would you say if I told you I love the taste of your mouth?"

"I'd say you're getting better," she returned, but the words were slightly muffled; his lips seemed to have gotten in the way. Gently his mouth touched hers, depositing sweet teasing kisses as it brushed the corners. He ran his tongue over her full lips and then chuckled softly at her warm eager response.

"But if I told you those things, you'd have to say much the same to me, you know."

"Would I?" Elizabeth was having a hard time concentrating on what he was saying. Not only did he seem reluctant to deepen his kisses, but his fingers were moving over her breasts, causing her to squirm as he circled their tips while never touching the aching centers.

"I'm afraid so. That's the way it works."

Elizabeth tried to pull his mouth to hers, but Tanner stubbornly held back. Her eyes narrowed with annoyance, and she silently promised to see the end of this game. Her hand ran over his chest and down his hard stomach. She watched with no little satisfaction as Tanner gasped and squeezed his eyes shut as it finally found what it was searching for. "Mmmm?" Elizabeth murmured. "What do you think I should say?"

Tanner moved his hips and breathed a shaky sigh as she tightened her hold. "You could remark on how handsome I am."

One of his hands, as insidious as his smile, had slid down the length of her and was now investigating in bone-melting detail what she wanted him most to explore. Tanner rolled onto his side, and Elizabeth threw her leg over his hip, allowing him further access. She sighed with the pleasure of his touch, but forced herself to concentrate on their conversation. Somehow talking only added to the deliciously wicked moment. Her smile was as sly as his. "Taking for granted, of course, that you are handsome."

"Of course," he said, his smile growing into soft laughter.

Her mouth moved over his chest and fastened upon a flat nipple. Alternately she sucked and then tickled it with her tongue. "And what else could I say?"

"That you love me madly."

"Oh, but I do."

"I know that, but you have to tell me more often," he said as he moved over her and slid his length deep into her welcoming heat.

Elizabeth groaned as she felt him fill her. A moment later his teeth and lips were tugging at her breasts. "Oh, God," she groaned and then forced herself to remember their conversation. "Yes," she said, "I'm beginning to see just what you mean. Shall I tell you now?"

"Any time you're ready, darlin'," he said as he pulled back almost to the point where his body separated from hers and then drove deep into her again.

Their bodies would be slick with sweat, their breathing no more than harsh desperate gasps, their hearts pounding as they found the pleasure only lovers can know, before she'd realize she'd forgotten to answer.

Elizabeth moaned as Tanner rolled away and cuddled her to his side. She snuggled close to his chest, smiling as the heavy dusting of hair on it tickled her nose. Elizabeth couldn't remember a happiness to equal this.

Relaxed and sleepy after more than an hour spent in his arms, she silently marveled at how well things had turned out. Tanner had petitioned the governor to reopen her father's case. With the evidence they now had, Elizabeth was confident that her father's name would soon be cleared.

Stacey was dead and suffering, she imagined, a just reward for all the evil he'd wrought.

Miss Dunlap was buying the boardinghouse, so Elizabeth and Tanner would be leaving for Virginia City by the end of the week.

And best of all, with Tanner's gentle coercion, Elizabeth had overcome the horror of what she'd done and was feeling her old self again. Except for a little nausea in the mornings, she'd never felt so healthy and strong.

"I think I'm going to like having babies," she murmured against the warmth of his throat. "I feel better than I've ever felt."

Tanner chuckled as he ran a hand over her hip and then squeezed her rump. "You certainly do."

Elizabeth swatted his hand away, but it only rose to cup and play with her breast. "And I suppose you'll soon be nagging at me to give you more, right?"

Elizabeth joined him in laughter at the thought. Then she forced the humor from her voice and remarked solemnly, "I think it's your husbandly duty, Tanner."

He grinned. "How many do you want?"

"I don't know. We'll start with this one and see what happens."

"And suppose I don't want more than one?"

Elizabeth shrugged. "I imagine I could convince you to see things my way," she murmured as she purposely brushed her hips against his.

Tanner happily closed his eyes as she moved against him. "Belle thinks you've got me hog-tied."

Elizabeth came up on an elbow. She looked down at her husband's grinning face. "Oh, she does?"

Tanner chuckled at taking in her less than happy expression. "Yep, I'm afraid she does, darlin'."

Elizabeth sighed as she lay down again. "What did you tell her?"

"I told her she was right."

Elizabeth turned only her head toward him. "Did you?"

Tanner shrugged. "She had herself a good laugh at my expense, but there's no sense denying the fact.

You got me hog-tied all right and by my ba—"

The movement of her hand rivaled the speed of sound. Tightly it pressed against his mouth, instantly cutting off the flow of words. "Don't say it!" Elizabeth came up on her knees. "Don't you dare say it!" She glared down at her husband's shaking form. He couldn't hold back his laughter.

A second later Elizabeth grunted upon impact as her body was suddenly sprawled over him. "God, I love you." He breathed out the words.

"Just because you love me, gives you no right to talk like a . . . like a . . . I don't know what." She tried to get up, but his hands were locked behind her back. "If you really loved me, you wouldn't say such things."

Tanner rolled them over. Their legs were intertwined, his hips pressed firmly against hers. He leaned on his elbows, holding his upper body above her. His fingers brushed aside the long black tendrils that had fallen over her face. His eyes had never shone so gently. "I love you all right," he said, his voice rough and insistent. "I love you more than I've ever loved another human being.

"Far as I can tell, nothing's ever going to change that."

"And after this baby, you won't be angry if I try to convince you to give me another?"

Tanner's eyes danced with deviltry. "You think you know how to do that?"

"Convince you?" she asked, and then, not waiting for his answer, declared with all confidence, "Of course."

"Just in case, why don't you start practicin' right

now?"

Elizabeth giggled at noting his all-too-obvious anticipation. "It's a thought, I suppose."

"That way you would probably get better and better at it."

"Do I need to get better?"

Tanner watched her for a long moment before he shook his head and grinned. "I ain't answerin' that. If I say yes, you'll probably get mad. If I say no, you won't try."

Elizabeth laughed. "I don't think I've ever known a man quite so careful. Maybe you should give some thought to public office."

"The only thing I can think about right now is how you're goin' to convince me."

"Would you like me to show you?"

Tanner nodded and then softly said, "Oh, God," as Elizabeth pushed him onto his back. It would be the last thing he'd have the strength to say for a long time.

As planned, they left town at the end of the week. The journey back to Virginia City was long, dusty, hot and dry. Tanner could have made it in three days, but because of Elizabeth, he took five. Still, she was exhausted when she reached his home. The dark circles under her eyes took weeks to fade.

As she grew more rounded with child, all Tanner could think about was Elizabeth and the baby she was to have. He prayed constantly for her safety. He couldn't overcome the terror that often gripped him in the dead of night.

His first wife had died in childbirth. He'd loved Sarah, but that love couldn't compare to his feelings for Elizabeth. Tanner knew he wouldn't survive if something should happen to her.

He grew afraid to touch her, terrified that he might somehow hurt her. It took no little amount of seduction on Elizabeth's part to get him to forget his fears and make love to her. From the first, she'd been exhausted by the time they were finished. Now, since she found herself doing most of the work, almost always she instantly fell asleep, but she didn't have the heart to tell Tanner he was making her work twice as hard.

Except for Tanner's constant nagging about her welfare, Elizabeth couldn't have been happier. Tanner's friends accepted her and proved to be delightfully friendly. His home was small and bare, obviously in need of a woman's touch, but Elizabeth had every intention of making it lovely and warm, the moment he allowed her to pick up anything heavier than a thimble.

"Sonofabitch! I knew I shouldn't have listened to you. We're miles from town. Suppose I can't get you back in time?"

Elizabeth shook her head in disgust. She never should have told him. It would have been better by far to let him think she'd had enough of buggy riding and wanted to rest. Now she'd have a hysterical male on her hands when she needed calmness most. But Tanner had seen her wince at the pain, and she had foolishly answered his question before she'd thought. "Tanner, you're sounding more like a husband every day."

Terrified, he shot her rounded belly a look. His mouth was grim, his eyes bleak. "And you a wife."

Elizabeth giggled. "Well, now that we've properly insulted each other, why don't you help me into the buggy?"

Tanner did as she asked, actually he did quite a bit more than that. He didn't help her, he carried her. "I can walk, you know. Having a baby hasn't made me an invalid."

He cursed.

"Tanner," she said, her tone a distinct warning.

"I know, I know. I won't say it again."

Her features tightened and she gripped her belly. Sweat broke out over his lip, something she couldn't see since he still sported a heavy mustache, but he couldn't hide the terror in his eyes. "Don't be afraid, darling," she said softly as she leaned comfortably— at least as comfortably as a woman in the midst of labor could—against him and wrapped his arm around her as he snapped the reins over the horse's back. "Women have been having babies for quite some time now. Everything will be fine."

Tanner groaned. His skin was sickly gray in color. Was he going to faint? Elizabeth held on to him lest he fall over the side of the buggy and break his neck. "Are you all right?"

"No." He groaned, and immediately she pushed his head as far as it could go between his legs. "I'm goin' to kill you if you die," he said nonsensically.

"I know, darling. I promise not to die—if you'll start this buggy and get us home."

"Do you, Elizabeth?" he asked a few minutes later as the buggy finally started its slow progress toward their home.

"What?" she asked, the word short and sharp as she was caught up in another back-wrenching pain.

His voice was strained as he watched her writhe in pain. "Promise not to die."

Oh . . . no! It wasn't supposed to be happening this fast. Especially not with the first. Dr. Tom said it would be hours, maybe a full day, possibly even more after the water broke before . . . "Uhhhhh," Elizabeth groaned, unable to hold the sound inside.

"What? Is it bad?" Tanner brought the buggy to a stop. His eyes were wild with fear. "Are you all right?"

"I'm fine." Elizabeth got the words out between clenched teeth. The pain eased a bit and she said more evenly. "I'm fine, really." It was then that she realized it had indeed been hours that she'd been in pain. Even last night she'd awakened in some degree of discomfort! Why hadn't she imagined it was her time? Why had she pleaded with Tanner to take her out? How foolish could she be to think that a ride in the country would ease the dull ache she'd felt in her back?

Tanner had every right to be furious with her. No doubt, after he'd gotten over the shock of what was sure to come, he would be.

"Uh, Tanner, I think you should forget about hurrying back."

"Why? Have the pains stopped?" he asked hopefully, but one look at her pinched expression told him otherwise. "Is the ride too rough? Should I carry you? It's only three miles."

Elizabeth laughed at the thought of being carried all the way back. "It's not that." She took a deep breath, several in fact as the pain eased and her body rested before the next assault. "I don't want you to panic, but I'm having the baby now!"

"God, God, oh my God." He pulled her into his arms. "Don't do it now, Elizabeth. I don't know what to do."

She would have laughed if she could, but she was caught up in another pain and could do nothing but grit her teeth till it eased. "I don't think you have to do much, Tanner, except maybe find me a place where I can lie down."

He moved like a wild man. Almost throwing her off his lap, he jumped from the wagon and then gathered her into his arms. For a second it looked as though he wasn't going to put her down. Finally he sat her in the shadow of a rock.

"I'm not goin' to make it."

"You are!" she answered instantly, and with a definite edge to her voice, she caught a fistful of his shirt and pulled him toward her. "I need your help. You can't leave me out here to do this alone."

Tanner swallowed deeply, and forced aside the lightheaded feeling that had held him in its clutches. Elizabeth was right. She knew. Women had been having babies almost since the beginning of time. There might never be a moment when she'd need him more. He had to be here for her.

Tanner nodded. "All right. Tell me what you want me to do."

Elizabeth watched as he hovered over her. "Help

me get my underthings off," she ordered. Then she gasped as another pain came, tight, hard, splitting her back in two as the baby fought to make its entrance into the world. "My petticoats too," she grunted out.

"Do we have any water left?"

Tanner nodded again.

"Use my drawers to clean the baby and wrap it in my petticoats. There's not much more you can do." She was shaking like a leaf, finding it impossible to stop her teeth from chattering as she spoke.

"Are you cold?" he asked, and without waiting for her reply, he ran to the buggy and pulled out the blanket they had been going to use at their picnic.

"No-no," she shivered, even as he gathered her tightly into its folds. "I don't know why I'm shaking." She shoved the blanket off. "I c-can't stop."

"But you're not cold?" he asked, obviously puzzled by this strange phenomena. "Are you sure?"

"I . . . I'm su-sure."

Elizabeth was already bearing down by the time Tanner returned with the water. He knew the pain had to be unbearable, for she held on to his hand, almost crushing the bones in his fingers, as she made guttural sounds of agony.

Tanner had faced down murderers, but he had never known terror such as he now felt. And it was awful to be helpless. She was having a baby, and there wasn't a damned thing he could do for her.

The pain came again, this time blotting out all else but the need to push. Her face grew red as she bore down. She gasped for breath and pushed again. "It's coming."

"Now?"

"Nooooow!" she screamed as she grabbed hold of his shirt and nearly tore it from his body. She grunted as she pushed again.

A half-hour passed and then another. Elizabeth's entire body was dripping with sweat. "Help me, help me," she begged. She didn't care that her loss of control increased Tanner's torment a thousandfold. Her body was breaking apart, splitting in half. It was as if it belonged to another, and she had no control over it. It would do what it must.

Again she pushed, having no power to hold back. And then she felt something odd. "Help me, Tanner. Look and see what's happennnnn . . ." She couldn't finish as the need to bear down came upon her again.

Tanner raised her skirt and knelt between her knees. He'd seen enough horses fold their young. He wasn't unaware that the baby's head would probably exit first. But the feelings that overcame him at the sight was almost too great to bear. The baby's head was already free of its mother.

"It has dark hair, Elizabeth."

She laughed upon hearing his amazement. "We both have dark hair, Tanner. It would be unlikely . . . Ohhhh."

"It looks stuck. Push again."

Elizabeth was gasping for air.

"Push!" Tanner insisted. "It can't stay like this."

Having been tutored well by her husband, Elizabeth uttered one of his favorite gutter words and then bore down with the last of her strength. She felt an almost euphoric sense of relief as the baby suddenly slipped quite easily from her.

"Oh, Elizabeth! My God! Look what you did," Tanner babbled in amazement as the tiny creature sprawled upon her skirt.

Her body might have been dead for all the strength that was left in it, but her heart filled with a surge of emotion that would never find its equal and her mind became as clear as the bright, sunny day.

"Let me see," she said softly, and she smiled as Tanner awkwardly held up a slippery, tiny baby boy. She'd never seen anything so wonderful. A moment later tears blurred her vision. She wiped them away with the back of her hand, but more only came to take their place. She couldn't tell what the baby looked like. "Is he all right?"

Tanner stood looking at the tiny bundle in his arms. "I don't know. He's not making any noise." Instinctively, Tanner gently cleared the infant's passage, and in the next moment he was laughing as his son let out an ear-shattering, no-nonsense scream, his rage obvious at being thrust into a world he had no reason to like. Tanner's mouth spread into a proud grin. "I'd say he's just fine."

"Sounds a bit like his father already, if you ask me," Elizabeth remarked amid tears of joy and soft laughter.

Tanner chuckled as he carefully placed the baby on her stomach and began to wipe him clean. Tears were streaming down his face. He never thought to wipe them away. All he could do was grin like a besotted fool.

Both Elizabeth and the baby were soon tended to.

It wasn't long after that she opened the buttons of her blouse and put the child, wrapped in her frilly petticoat, to her breast.

Tanner sat at her side and watched. His expression grew solemn as tiny lips parted and began to suck. His eyes clouded again with tears at the sight. He couldn't imagine anything more beautiful. "I love you, Elizabeth. I reckon I'll never love you more than at this minute."

Elizabeth smiled as she watched him lean down. Gently he kissed her lips and then the baby's head. A moment later he was lying at her side, his hand holding their child's head as the baby made gusty sucking sounds. "I'd appreciate one favor, though."

"What?"

Tanner rolled onto his back. His eyes closed as he remembered these last terrifying hours. "I know I promised you could have as many as you want, but please don't ever do this to me again."

Elizabeth's sudden chuckle didn't quite hold the sympathy he was aiming for. She forced aside her grin and commiserated with him. Poor dear, she thought. One might suppose that he was the one who had done the work, considering his exhausted state. Her voice quivering as she forced back laughter, she finally replied. "I'll do my best, darling." He was already snoring.